Reluctantly Royal

KELLE Z. RILEY

*To my sister and best friend, Kandy Zeiher Petrovic.
I am so grateful for you every day.*

*And to Thomas Patrick Riley, husband, lover,
soulmate, and light of my life.*

ACKNOWLEDGMENTS

Writing a novel is hard work. Publishing a novel is even harder work. Without my team of dedicated experts and tribe of writer friends, this work would not have been possible. Special thanks go to:

- Tina Winograd, editor extraordinaire. Your input always makes my work better!
- Connie Leap and Theresa Huber, proofreaders. Thank you for catching errors and providing feedback. Your comments challenged and inspired me.
- Katie Salidas, formatter. Thank you for taking on this task and turning my manuscript into a real book.
- Ron J. Rice, Novel Cover Designs by RJRice Photography, cover designer. Your clear eye and ability to turn my words into evocative images is second to none.
- Laurie White, PA. Thank you for helping me manage the social media aspects of the writer's life and countless other details. I'd be lost without you.
- Special thanks to my beta readers and writer friends, Susan Gibberman, Dyanne Davis, Denise Swanson, Frederica Meiners, and Cheryl Woodson. You are my writer tribe. You inspire, motivate, and help me find my way out of plot corners I've backed into. Thank you for the many helpful discussions and great plot twist ideas!
- Thanks to the rest of my writer tribe, members of CARA; Windy City RWA, GRW, TGN, CWG, KOD, and the Crazy Buffet Club Writers. You are a constant source of inspiration, prodding, and laughter.
- Thanks to my family, for standing by me and supporting me as I pursue my dreams.
- Finally, thanks again to Tom Riley, for knowing when to guard my writing time and energy, and knowing when to pull me away from the process. This one's for you.

All errors and omissions are mine alone.

TABLE OF CONTENTS

Chapter 1

June, the royal wedding of Constantine Phillippe Ramon D'Malia

Gracie tightened her fist around the locket as her gilded carriage wove its way through the streets of the island kingdom of Melesia. The familiar shape soothed her frazzled nerves and provided a tiny piece of home amid the foreign finery.

Today's fairy-tale regalia was nothing more than an illusion, broadcast via satellite to every cable channel in the world. She straightened her shoulders and ignored shouts from reporters, cameramen, and film crews along the parade route, focusing instead on the coach at the head of the parade where her sister and new brother-in-law rode in regal splendor.

Her sister, Jill, made a radiant bride. She would have anyway, even if it had been a regular wedding, rather than a royal wedding to Constantine D'Malia, king of an important Caribbean archipelago.

Thank goodness Gracie's official part in the festivities was over. She rubbed her thumb along the worn gold of the locket that she'd let her sister carry during the wedding ceremony. The chatter of the strangers in the coach beside her faded into insignificance. Their smiling faces and crowd-pleasing waves blurred before her eyes.

Twelve years rewound themselves in her memory, taking her back to the year she turned eight. To the week her father gave her the locket. When he was still alive. When she and Jill giggled and shared secrets.

Now, all she had of her father was a faded photo. And her sister was a distant stranger. Despite occasional strained words of affection, Gracie wasn't sure they even liked each other anymore.

The carriage bumped to a halt, bringing Gracie back to the present and landing her smack dab in the middle of reality. The bizarre reality of a royal wedding. A footman helped her down the single step and into the media frenzy below.

Her chest tightened, the beat of her pulse pounding the air from her lungs as they closed in, scraping away her defenses like piranhas peeling flesh from a victim. She forced her lips to curve, shielding her raw, private emotions from exposure. She'd never let someone record her vulnerability again. She breathed, relaxing the tightness as she sailed forward, head high.

The wedding party wound its way through the Grand Hall, past the Queen's Gallery, and toward the ballroom. Gracie's steps slowed. Royal cousins and Melesian nobility swept past her and up the stairs to the balcony, following the bride and groom.

Gracie clutched the locket and kept her smile in place. A few more seconds and she'd be out of media range. A minute after that, she'd be plain Gracie Bradley of Ohio again, not the royal bride's half-sister. An hour from now, she'd be immersed in a book and the morning would be an uncomfortable memory.

She eased toward an exit leading away from the ballroom. A few more seconds…

"Miss Bradley?"

Gracie turned. She cast a longing glance at her almost-escape route then braced herself as a reporter headed her way, cameraman in tow. The king's younger brother and presumptive heir, Crown Prince Stephan, intercepted them. Flicking her a dismissive glance, he edged between her and the reporters.

His assessment stung. Apparently not even professional makeup, hairstyling, and designer gowns made her acceptable. Gracie bristled at his high-handed treatment, but his words brought her to her senses.

"Ladies and Gentlemen, if you have a moment, I'd like to introduce you to the bride's sister." Gracie's younger sister, Amber, stood by his side, glowing with all the innocent enthusiasm of a seventeen-year-old charmer. The press, from the looks of it, loved her.

Gracie slipped out of sight until a masculine laugh drew her attention back to the ballroom. A handful of reporters converged on Prince Stephan as if drawn by his elegant gestures and easy smiles. *Like bees to honey.*

He laughed again, and Gracie took an unconscious step forward before she forced herself back into the shadows. *Intelligent women did not fall prey to dashing princes. She was immune. Curiosity caused her rapid heartbeat. Nothing else.*

She studied him, mentally cataloguing and analyzing each detail like a scientist observing a specimen.

His quick smile should have made him less imposing than the rest of the royal family, but instead, it accented the subtle authority that radiated from him. He demanded attention. He personified flawlessness. Polished shoes gleamed. A sharply pressed military uniform outlined his broad shoulders and lean torso. Not a single golden hair fell out of place.

As he chatted with the gathering crowd, expressions—humorous, interested, intrigued, concerned—flitted across his face, each fading away leaving his smooth honey-gold skin unmarked by emotion.

Until he turned in her direction.

A sharp, irritated frown puckered his brow, and his lips tightened. The full force of his disapproval hit Gracie in an instant, even as he turned away, his features resuming their normal composure.

A rush of heat, fueled by anger and embarrassment, washed down her body, leaving her lightheaded in its wake. How dare he judge her as unsuitable? His polished perfection embodied the royal image, but she was a woman of substance, not image.

In the world outside the glass bubble of the monarchy, her intelligence would trump his sophisticated smoothness every time.

Gracie turned and took two firm strides down the hallway and out of sight before kicking off her shoes and allowing her shoulders to slump in relief. The anger seeped from her body, leaving her disgusted with herself for staring at him like a starstruck teenager. She took a deep breath to calm her racing pulse and restore her analytical world view.

With luck, she could avoid any further encounters with the overbearing prince during her short stay on Melesia. And when she returned in the fall, she'd be nothing more than another transfer student, finishing her degree, awaiting graduate school, and best of all, living in the dorms far from the influence of the royal D'Malia family.

Stephan risked another glance toward the marble archway and breathed an internal sigh of relief when he saw it was empty. Gracie, Jill's painfully shy sister had—finally—made her escape. He'd spent every ounce of charm he could muster to keep the press focused on him while she lingered near the edges of the ballroom. A few more seconds and he wouldn't have been able to protect her from their zeal.

Having solved the problem of Gracie's privacy, he turned to other issues, smoothly directing the press to the outdoor gardens and returning Amber to her mother.

Those lingering in the ballroom consisted only of a few high-ranking Melesian citizens, the American family and friends of the new queen, and palace staff. He headed to the stairs to join the bride and groom, only to be cut off when Lady Ophelia de Lyons hurried forward and grabbed his arm. Her husband followed, an apologetic yet slightly weary look etched on his face.

Once the epitome of Melesian aristocracy, Ophelia barely resembled the beauty she'd been as a young woman. Bitterness, more than circumstance or age, had etched fine lines into the corners of her eyes and mouth.

"Prince Stephan." Ophelia gave him a cool smile. "What a pleasure to see our king happy with his love match! Just as my dear Gregor and I are. We couldn't be more pleased."

Stephan murmured in agreement, not challenging her obvious lie. Ophelia's ambitions outstripped any love she felt for the baron she'd married. "Always a pleasure to see you, as well."

"If I might have a moment of your time, Your Highness." Her vise-like grip contrasted with the forced deference in her tone.

"My time is always at your disposal." Stephan turned to them, carefully disengaging her hand and placing a polite kiss on her knuckles before guiding it to her husband's arm.

Her smile dimmed a bit. "Despite today's joy, my brother's disgraceful behavior toward our king distresses me. Treason. Murder plots." She shuddered. "The king was right to strip him of his title. However, Gregor and I fear for my niece Sophia."

She drew her husband closer to her side. "With her guardian imprisoned and her..." Ophelia paused meaningfully, "marriage prospects gone, we were hoping to petition the king for a favor."

"The royal family holds Sophia in the highest regard." Stephan waited, knowing Ophelia had more on her mind than the king's opinion of Sophia.

"That is a comfort. Now with the king married and soon—we hope—with an heir on the way, we wondered if he might consider something more substantial."

Stephan spared Gregor a sympathetic glance. Ophelia had a gleam in her eye that caused tension to grip his gut every bit as tightly as she'd gripped him earlier. He crossed his arms and raised an eyebrow, silently inviting her to finish her petition—quickly.

"As I was saying, Sophia's uncle is in jail. Her father—may he rest in peace—would have been next in line for the de Lyons title. With no male heirs remaining, might the king consider giving the title and lands to Sophia?"

Stephan hid his surprise, smiling blandly. A woman trained to the position could rule a duchy or even a country. But Sophia? Would she want the burden? Could she handle it?

"Your concern for Sophia is admirable, Lady Ophelia. I will convey your request to the king. At an appropriate time." He glanced pointedly at the hall, decorated in celebration of the royal wedding. "For now, please enjoy the festivities."

With that, Stephan turned and climbed the stairs, pondering the situation. Ophelia and her deposed brother were as alike as twins when it came to political machinations and lust for power. Sophia had never been more than a political pawn to either of them.

Before he counseled his brother on any moves in the game they were playing, he'd make damn sure he understood the role of every player on the chessboard. And he'd do everything in his power to protect the players—king, queen, and pawn alike—no matter what it took.

Chapter 2

Gracie crept down a deserted corridor, shoes still dangling from her fingers, and slipped into a reception room far from the cameras and microphones. The thick, luxurious carpet soothed her bare feet as effectively as the quiet room soothed her nerves.

"Someone else seeking refuge from the crowds."

Gracie's gaze flew to Lady Sophia de Lyons, who sat in a wing back chair, serene and thoughtful. Although they were similar in age, size and coloring, Lady Sophia radiated elegance and poise.

Caught by another royal. This time, Gracie couldn't summon her anger as a defense. Beside Sophia, she felt more like an awkward, gangly child playing dress-up than a twenty-year-old woman.

You're the smart sister. Her mother's voice echoed in her memory. Smart enough to know when it was time to leave. She turned to the door.

"I envy you." Lady Sophia's voice carried a hint of inbred authority and eloquence that Gracie envied, in spite of her own egalitarian principles.

Gracie hesitated. "Why? You belong here. I'm just the bride's sister, dressed up and trying not to embarrass her."

"Exactly. Soon the press will forget you. They'll hound me for weeks, prying to see if my wounded heart is mended." A faint edge of bitterness crept into her voice.

Gracie eased herself onto a sofa, arranging the unfamiliar layers of formal skirts around her. "Was your heart really broken? Were you in love with Constantine?" The uncensored words popped out and hung in the air, muffled by the thick carpet and brocaded wall hangings. The sound of the ocean, faint from beyond the windows, somehow magnified the silence in the room.

"Love was never part of the picture for us." Sophia rose and walked to the French doors, beckoning Gracie to follow. "I envy him too. He broke the rules and found love. Alex and Helena are also in love," she said, referring to the ailing King Emeritus who'd abdicated in favor of his half-brother. "I'm just the spare bride who's now out of a job."

"I don't understand."

"How could you?" Sophia stepped onto a shallow patio with a view of the balcony where Jill and Constantine stood surrounded by the royal family, smiling at the cheering crowds below.

"Look." Sophia pointed to them. "A royal wedding is a fairy tale come true. If I'd been on the balcony instead of your sister, the fairy tale would have unfolded in exactly the same way. Except the looks in their eyes are real. They love each other. He and I would have been pretending.

"I'm very good at pretending. From the moment I came to live with the Duke de Lyons, he's prepared me to be the spare bride. He fed the press with enough romantic nonsense to fuel the illusion. I played along."

Sophia's words stirred uncomfortable memories of a time when Gracie's life had been defined by a newspaper story and a lie too.

"What do you mean—the spare bride?" she asked, distracting herself from her own memories.

"Royal sons are *the heir and the spare.* Alex was the heir. Helena was raised to be his bride. Constantine was the spare. I was the spare bride. At least that's what the duke planned."

"It must have been awful." Gracie knew the Duke de Lyons—dubbed the Disgraced Duke by the press—had been involved in a plot to control the government. The plot, which implicated her sister for theft and treason, had nearly gotten Jill killed.

Sophia was another pawn in the duke's quest for power, locked in a role chosen for her at birth. No matter how beautiful the island paradise, Gracie could never be at home in a place where birth determined more than worth.

She prayed Sophia was right about Jill's marriage, but the emotional chasm between the sisters was too wide for her to know. The older sister she'd once adored had disappeared the night their father died. In her place was a stranger. The nine-year age difference between them might as well have been a generation. Gracie no longer knew if Jill was the kind of woman to marry for love—or something else.

"It makes a great story." Sophia's cultured voice lured Gracie back to the present. "'Lady Sophia, Foster Daughter of The Disgraced Duke, Jilted by the Prince Who Broke Her Heart.' The tabloids will adore it."

Damn. Sophia's words transported Gracie back to the days surrounding her father's funeral. *Such a beautiful child,* the mayor murmured, staring at the photo of Gracie and Daddy. *Too bad about her father.* He'd used her photo and story in the local newspapers to campaign for everything from new road construction to improved driver safety classes.

The articles twisted her memories until Gracie hated the beautiful, fatherless child they described. The papers soon forgot her, but Gracie never forgot their power over her.

She swallowed and tried for a light tone as she answered Sophia. "If your tabloids are anything like ours, they'll have you engaged to someone else within a week."

"Of course. When Alex abdicated in favor of Constantine, I suppose Stephan became the next spare. One brother should be as good as another. But I don't wish to be bounced from prince to prince until the public gets its next big romance."

She sighed. "I'm tired of being controlled by the papers. And by my family. And even by the king. I want a life of my own."

A sparkle of light snapped Sophia out of her wistful mood. She moved inside, ushering Gracie into a cool shaded corner. "Photographers. Tabloids. We're this week's entertainment."

"I see why you envy me." Gracie thought back to the way Prince Stephan had unwittingly deflected the press' attention from her. His arrogance became her blessing. Even today, she was nothing more than a blip on the media radar screen. "No one cares about the bride's brainy half-sister."

Gracie chewed her lip, remembering the peace she'd found when she finally slipped from the public eye. Everyone deserved a chance at that peace. Even a member of the Melesian aristocracy. "Do you ever want to just disappear?"

"All the time," Sophia replied, a hint of sadness shadowing her voice. "I've made plans to spend a year abroad with Princess Lydia at her home in Europe. After that, I'll join a Melesian goodwill tour scheduled to visit Europe and the Americas.

"The press will speculate I'm nursing my broken heart. If I'm lucky, I can stay away until the next heir to the throne is born. When your sister becomes pregnant, I'll have a measure of peace. I will never have the freedom that you do."

Gracie's mind raced and she considered ways to help Sophia. "What if you could be someone other than Lady Sophia for a few days? Someone like me?"

A flicker of interest lit Sophia's eyes.

"You said the goodwill tour is scheduled to visit the Americas eventually," Gracie continued. "If you could get away from the entourage while you're in the U.S., I could buy you a few days of freedom."

"Tell me." Sophia leaned forward, her attention riveted on Gracie.

"I'll be transferring to the Melesian Royal Academy for the fall semester," she began, grateful that her family and the school administrators had agreed to let her register under her mother's maiden name instead of the name Bradley, which she shared with her now famous sister. "I won't be making many trips back home."

Hours later, Grace Susan Bradley handed Sophia her driver's license and a detailed plan for escaping the goodwill tour for a day or two of freedom. Now all Gracie had to do was fade into the background, focus on her studies, and hope the world forgot her.

Again.

Chapter 3

September, one year later.

Gracie hurried into her room and tossed her books on the narrow bed, ignoring the clawing turmoil in her gut.

"*Laddos,*" she muttered.

"Hey, what's got you so upset that you're swearing?" Her suite mate poked her head through the bathroom that joined their tiny dorm rooms.

"English, Marta. My head hurts from the debacle in lab this afternoon."

"You need to practice your Melesian, Gracie," Marta replied, switching to English, nevertheless. "After a year of study you should have a better grasp on our language. And don't start stressing about getting into graduate school again. You're months away from graduation and at the top of your class. There is no debacle big enough to keep you out. Your biggest problem is learning the language and getting ready for work. We're going to be late if you don't hurry."

Marta disappeared and Gracie booted up the computer while she dragged on the black hose and shapeless tan dress of her work uniform.

For once, the sound of the ocean and the faint tang of salt air drifting through the window into her cramped dorm room didn't soothe her.

Ignoring the rest of her uniform, she plopped in her chair and accessed her online journal subscriptions. Feature articles from *American Scientific* and *Marine Biology Bulletins* flashed on screen, calming her in a way the sea breeze hadn't.

And the journals were in English. Gracie sighed in relief. Melesian business and academics all took place in English, but social venues favored the native language. A language Gracie couldn't grasp despite her repeated attempts.

Her head throbbed with the effort of having a single conversation in Melesian. Following half a dozen people at a party was more than she could handle. Besides, it was foolish to expect a normal social life here. Her halting language skills weren't to blame. She was.

She forgot her worries as she scanned a series of articles detailing the effects of environmental stresses on coral reef development. Mentally cataloging the abstracts, she outlined the research topic for her advanced field studies thesis.

"*Laddos,*" she muttered again, using one of the few Melesian words she knew. Gracie swiveled in the chair and searched through her books till she found the wrinkled photocopy of the dive team sheet. Five student teams had paired up for the research dives. Since she'd been late to class—thanks to her uptight Customs & Protocol professor—she'd been the odd woman out.

At least she wanted to blame it on the C&P professor. But she knew that wasn't the reason. She'd been a social misfit at the Clarkson Community College back home too.

You're the smart one. Jill is the pretty, popular one. Her mother's words—intended as encouragement—stung despite their truth. Her brains isolated her. Acing advanced calculus and theoretical physics didn't get her invited to parties. Not that she wanted to go to those kinds of parties. Primping and chatting with airheads versus spending the night with a good book? It was a no-brainer decision.

Gracie looked at the dive list again, her stomach lurching. She'd have to join the other teams as a third wheel on their diving expeditions. "*Laddos,*" she whispered past the tightness in her throat.

"You're swearing again." Marta rushed back into the room, securing her long, gleaming braids in a gold filigree clasp. Flashy jewelry was strictly prohibited while in uniform, but Gracie doubted anyone would mind. Marta, like her sister Jill, was a natural beauty.

"Why is it the first things people learn in every language are the swear words? Come on. Shut down the computer and finish getting dressed. I'm serious. We'll miss the ferry to Royal Island."

Gracie checked the clock and hurried back to her closet. She slipped into her low-heeled black pumps and tugged on an ecru smock embroidered in the national colors of green and gold. Marta stepped behind her to tie it.

"Good you're almost ready. The ferry always takes a few minutes to load. We'll still get on," Marta said, reverting to her native language.

"English, Marta, please. I don't have the patience for Melesian today."

"I'm glad you find it difficult to learn something or you'd be impossible. Everything else you soak up like a sponge. But you need to practice. You'll never learn the language if you insist on speaking English all the time."

"I'm not good at languages. My—" Oops. She'd almost said *my sister, Jill, is the one who excels in languages.* She gritted her teeth. Jill's influence had gained her admittance to the exclusive academy, but Gracie vowed no one would credit her success to her political connections.

She'd fought to enter the academy as an unknown, and she'd graduate as an unknown, despite her relationship to the new Melesian queen.

"Your what?" Marta prompted before Gracie's thoughts raced out of control.

"My patience is thin. I had a difficult time with the C&P professor today."

"First the lab debacle. Now Customs and Protocol. Something's eating you and it's not school. Besides, C&P's the easiest class in the academy. The whole purpose is to get you ready to be presented to the royal family. The gala ball at the end of the year is a little like your senior prom."

"I hated my prom." Gracie pushed the memory aside. Dancing. Laughing. The date who'd showered her with attention until she refused to help him cheat on his chemistry exam. The social isolation she'd suffered for the rest of the term. Her prom wasn't worthy of second thoughts. She tugged her hair into a ponytail, grabbed her cell phone, and pulled Marta out the door.

Half an hour later, they sat crammed into the commissary in the palace basement, listening as their supervisor explained the work-study program to the new students.

The Royal Academy required all students to work in public areas of the country. Gracie grudgingly admired the plan, which used both native and foreign labor, in lieu of heavier taxes and higher tuition.

Gracie's mind drifted as the supervisor droned on. She'd always been assigned to the palace on Royal Island where she cleaned, made up rooms, and sometimes gave tours. It was easy work, but it also brought her into closer contact with the royal family. It was another place she didn't belong. She squirmed on the hard bench of the commissary.

Her sister's fairy tale courtship and marriage anchored Gracie to the royal family like a barnacle to a boat. Attached, but not really needed or wanted. A foreigner, along for the ride.

Gracie couldn't understand the politics of an anachronistic government that should have been abolished a century ago. A government where leaders were born, not elected, to their positions. It conflicted with her American roots.

Besides, whenever she was in the palace, her thoughts turned to Lady Sophia. True to her word, Sophia had left Melesia after the wedding to stay in Europe with Princess Lydia for nearly a year. Then she'd joined a Melesian goodwill tour of Europe for several months.

When the tour made its way to America, Sophia had slipped away using the plan Gracie had outlined. But she didn't return in a few days like they'd agreed. And the press's reaction—or lack of—unsettled Gracie.

Public reports about Sophia didn't fit with the text messages she'd received from the woman herself—a woman who was in no hurry to return home. Gracie feared it wouldn't take much for someone to discover the other "Miss Bradley."

It helped that Gracie used her mother's maiden name at school. No one remembered her connection to the former Miss Bradley, now Queen Jillian. The name of Bradley seemed to have slipped from the public vocabulary.

The country accepted Jill as one of their own, almost forgetting her American roots. The weaker the connections between the United States and the royal family, the less likely anyone would be to look for Sophia in Jill's backyard. Literally.

Being invisible has its advantages. Besides, Gracie admitted to herself, she'd always been more comfortable in the background than in the spotlight.

When the orientation ended, Gracie gathered her wicker basket of cleaning supplies. Preoccupied with her thoughts, she headed toward the main palace entrance. The grand entry-way consisted of a cavernous marble hall with a luxurious, sunken sitting area on the ocean side of the room.

She pulled a cloth from the basket and focused on cleaning the nearly spotless tables scattered throughout the room, refilling conch shaped silver bowls with exclusive gourmet chocolates created especially for the Melesian palace by the Fantasy Fudge company. Another student replaced wilting tropical flowers in the vases with fresh varieties.

Stepping into the public areas of the palace transported Gracie from the twenty-first century to the eighteenth. No modern country was a working monarchy anymore. Except Melesia. Her brother-in-law could probably lop people's heads off if he wanted.

Thank goodness he hadn't insisted on touting himself as her royal sponsor at the academy. For better or worse, he and Jill had let her keep her distance.

If it wasn't for the beauty of the oceans, she'd have stayed home in the States, making do with a local university. But the Melesian school of marine biology was among the best with world-class field opportunities.

Finishing an undergraduate degree there put her miles ahead of the competition. And a degree from their graduate school almost guaranteed her whatever job she wanted. Gracie would have sacrificed anything to attend, even her pride.

And she had, because she could never be sure she would have gotten a scholarship—or even been accepted—on her own merits. Having accepted the gift of a scholarship, it was up to her to prove she deserved it.

No taking the easy way out.

No mistakes.

No failures.

An older couple moved into the marble entryway. "Oh, look, William! Where's my camera?"

"We're here for a week, darling. I'm sure there will be plenty of time for photos. And if things proceed the way I hope they will, we'll be invited back for some profitable business discussions soon."

Mentally reviewing the list of guests, Gracie decided this must be Dr. and Mrs. William Joyner, an American chemical industry leader invited for Prince Stephan's Energy and Industry Summit.

"It's like walking into a fairy tale." The woman swept down the marble steps to the sitting area, caught up in her own private story line. "That servant could be Cinderella waiting for a prince to rescue her."

"Be careful what you say, darling. These are student workers, not servants. You might be pointing at a future engineer who'll make me millions."

"I'm sure the engineers are assigned to more intellectual jobs than polishing furniture."

Gracie focused on her work and pretended not to hear. With any luck, they'd think she didn't speak English. She breathed a sigh of relief when an aide escorted them to their rooms.

She wandered to the center of the now deserted room where the top half of a two-story aquarium filled most of one long wall. Flanked by windows overlooking the ocean, it was designed to give the illusion of a vast undersea panorama.

Gracie methodically polished the aquarium glass, keeping her movements slow and flowing so as not to disturb the creatures behind it.

A green moray eel peeked out of a rock crevice, following the sweep of her arm, and disappeared into the depths of the aquarium, his supple body fluttering like a banner in the breeze.

Above her head, a group of cownose rays floated by, attracted by the food an unseen attendant dropped into the water from the top of the tank. Colorful tropical fish darted through the middle of the scene.

How could children's stories compare with the natural beauty of the island and the sea? Gracie lost herself in cleaning the glass and watching the show until the excited voices of children distracted her.

A group of children clustered together at the other end of the aquarium's expanse, pointing excitedly at the various animals and chattering in their native language.

A tousled, golden head in their midst clearly belonged to a much taller man who was crouched down to reach their level. They followed his motions, twisting to see where he was pointing and answering his softly voiced questions.

The giggles, smiles, and occasional excited whoops brought an answering laughter of his own. Occasionally Gracie saw the glint of metal as he pressed small coins into the outstretched hands of the children.

She listened to the melodious sound of the man's voice, not caring that she didn't understand many of his words. She continued her work, dividing her attention between the animals, the children, and the man.

"Children, time to leave for the mainland. Your parents will be waiting." The teacher's voice cut across the excitement, so calm and well-modulated that even Gracie could follow her carefully articulated Melesian instructions. "Be sure to thank His Highness, Prince Stephan, for allowing you into his home and showing you his aquarium."

His Highness, Prince Stephan? Gracie snapped her full attention back to the glass wall in front of her, longing to be invisible. They had only met once, briefly, at Jill's wedding where he'd dismissed her with barely a glance.

Gracie doubted he'd remember her since almost no one else did. Besides, she'd been so made up and decked out that she barely recognized herself that day. Nevertheless, the last thing she wanted was an encounter with the arrogant Prince Stephan, close advisor to the king and organizer of the country's first Energy and Industry Summit.

Especially if guests like Mrs. Joyner were in the wings watching them as if they were part of the entertainment.

She was grateful when the room grew silent and the children's voices faded in the distance. Prince Stephan must have followed them out. She sighed in relief.

"I should apologize for allowing the children to smear the glass. You've obviously worked hard to keep it clean."

At the sound of his voice Gracie whirled around, her hand at her throat. Recovering, she dipped into a quick curtsey. "Your Highness," she murmured, eyes lowered, hoping he would leave quickly.

Instead he spoke in a soft, lilting cadence, clearly asking her a question. Both her composure and her language skills fled. She looked up, sure confusion was written on her face.

Good heavens, but his eyes were the bluest she'd ever seen. Warm and clear like the Caribbean sky, with a hint of a sparkle in their depths. His lips curved into a smile and an unfamiliar tingle hit her right in the gut, like a jolt from an electric eel, only pleasant. The feeling wiggled around inside her, setting off little quivers in parts of her body that had never quivered before.

What happened to the cold, arrogant man she'd expected? She could handle her reactions to him. But this man…this look… It should be illegal, reducing a woman to a lump of jelly with just a look and a smile.

"I must apologize again," he said breaking the spell the tiniest bit. "I assumed you understood our native language, but you are clearly more comfortable with English."

Not really. Not when it carried that lovely island lilt and had soft warm tones that made her feel like she was being caressed instead of being spoken to. But she nodded anyway.

He took her elbow and turned her back to the aquarium. "I am intrigued by how in tune you are with the animals. They generally shy away from the glass when visitors are near. Not so with you."

"They know me. I'm always careful to move slowly and quietly. They can sense the noise and shadows as easily as we sense each other."

"Your heightened senses no doubt account for why I startled you a moment ago." His smile deepened a shade and Gracie felt the squishy, tingly jolts all over again.

She swallowed a giggle and cursed herself for acting like a giddy teen. "I was savoring the quiet," she said, aware that she was blushing. Fair hair and freckles were a curse sometimes.

"I understand what you mean." He didn't comment on her blush. Instead he released the light touch on her elbow and moved a step away. "Enthusiasm makes the young ones loud at times. I hope that by showing them the beauty of their country, they will grow to appreciate it as adults. They are a little young to be learning intricate details of marine life, but I'd be happy if they can tell the difference between a hammerhead shark and a swordfish."

"There are no hammerhead sharks in the tank, Your Highness. They would feed on sting rays." She peered into the water, but the rays had all settled near the bottom, out of sight.

His warm chuckle wrapped around her as he stepped closer to the tank and followed her gaze. "Your friends, the rays, seem to have disappeared. But you're correct, the sharks would prey on the rays in the wild.

"I'm hoping we can avoid that in captivity. As it happens, I'm introducing some bonnet head sharks into the tank next week. I promise to keep them well-fed and small enough to prevent attacks. I'm sure you are aware that they can be placid under certain conditions. You know your marine life. But then, I was told to expect that."

He turned from the tank and look directly at her. "You're Gracie Bradley, aren't you?"

"Smith, Your Highness. Gracie Smith," she said, automatically giving him the name she used at the academy.

His eyes turned from a friendly shade to a darker, almost stormy, blue. Tiny lines bracketed his mouth as he clenched his jaw tighter. "I see."

With the warmth gone from his tone and look, Gracie suddenly remembered he was a powerful and important man. Known to the world as the goodwill ambassador of Melesia, he also served as chief advisor to the king on matters of industry and technology. And he was the chancellor—the figurative royal representative—of the academy.

She'd forgotten all that the minute he smiled at her. But the knowledge rushed back an instant. She stammered, then snapped her mouth shut and retreated into a childish ritual, calming herself by mentally reciting the value of pi to the sixteenth digit.

It didn't work.

The silence between them pressed on her until she gave in to a spurt of nervous chatter.

"I'm a student at the Royal Academy, majoring in marine biology. I plan to do my senior research thesis on corals native to the area. I also hope to be admitted to the graduate program." She babbled, seeking refuge in a litany of facts including tidbits about the native marine life, the school's credentials, and a dozen other topics.

He held up a hand to stop her. A hint of a smile reappeared but didn't reach his eyes. "I can see that you are very knowledgeable."

Prince Stephan took her hand and bowed over it, brushing his lips across her knuckles in a courtly manner she'd only read about. "I would caution you, however, Miss..." he paused slightly, "...Smith, not to underestimate my intelligence.

Among other things, I'm known to have an excellent memory. Especially for faces and names." He nodded in farewell then strode away toward the private, family-only wing of the palace.

The pleasant quiver in her stomach turned to a leaden weight.

He remembered her.

Chapter 4

The security guard bowed as he passed, and Stephan greeted him with an automatic gesture. He dropped his smile when he entered the private wing of the palace. At least here, he didn't need to pretend to be charming.

He fisted his hands, wishing he could have throttled the girl. Her arrogant assumption that he would fall for a fake name and an innocent look rankled. Did she think he was stupid? Clearly, she had since she'd had the arrogance to lecture him on his own country and school.

But he couldn't lose control and give her a piece of his mind because courtly manners were critical in public areas of the building. The tourists demanded it. And protocol greased the wheels of public life.

Gracie Bradley, on the other hand, was a rusty nail in the wheels of public life. And since Jill and Constantine weren't doing anything about it, the duty fell to him.

As younger brother to the king, Stephan was happy to take on whatever duties he could to ease the burden of government. A modern king relied on advisors and specialists to give him information to make economic, cultural, and policy decisions.

So what if it meant his dreams of fostering appreciation of marine conservation through grants and lecture tours was put on hold indefinitely? Others could handle that.

Instead of focusing on the selfish pursuit of his research, Stephan put his interests and abilities to work as Constantine's science and technology advisor.

Which reminded him that he should be on his way to the Energy and Industry Summit to greet his invited guests. Instead he was on the way to the queen's apartments to try, once again, to get her to see logic.

He'd argued with his brother and sister-in-law about the wisdom of letting Gracie use an assumed name. And about letting her attend the university classes without a security team assigned to her.

She was—by virtue of Jill's marriage, if not by blood—a part of the royal family. She should be living on Royal Island, preferably at the palace, where her safety could be assured. Instead of public classes, he would see that she had the best tutors available. She could study everything she wanted, enough to challenge even someone with her academic records and IQ.

An acid rush hit his gut, causing it to clench in a painful cramp. He clawed in his pocket for the roll of antacids he always carried. He'd grown used to the chalky, gritty taste over the past months as his need for relief came more and more frequently.

He slowed, chewing the tablets and stepping onto one of the balconies that overlooked the private beach and the lagoon. The afternoon breeze filled with the scents of the ocean, and the native flowers soothed his ragged senses.

Security teams? Private tutors? No wonder Constantine had shrugged off his suggestions. He wasn't obsessing about providing security for the rest of Jill's family. They were safely tucked away in the United States, outside of his power and control.

Still, they were as closely related to the royal family as Gracie was. Logic dictated that if she was a target, they would be too.

No, his instinctive, protective stance toward Gracie was something more.

Sophia's image flitted through his mind. She was a Melesian noble, one of the sheltered few who'd had little contact with life outside the islands. And he'd allowed her to take his place on a recent international goodwill tour. Several weeks ago, when the tour came to America, she'd slipped past layers of security and disappeared from the entourage.

A week later, he'd received a note, purportedly from Sophia herself, begging him to understand that she wanted a few days to explore America. It sounded like something she'd ask for. Moreover, his security experts verified her handwriting, the Chicago postmark, and the Melesian consulate stationary it had been written on.

But while Sophia might have been foolish enough to think she could explore a city on her own, he doubted she'd been able to outwit a security detail and evade a search team without help.

God help her—and him—if she'd put her trust in the wrong people. Unease gnawed at his gut despite the full undercover search by his team of specialists.

He should have been adamant and gone on the tour himself. At the very least, he should have increased the tour's security detail. Instead, he'd amused himself by dabbling in science and organizing his summit.

Sophia's disappearance could mean trouble for his brother and for the country. Especially with the de Lyons relatives ramping up their efforts to have her to inherit the duchy. Relatives who, according to his sources, hadn't bothered to tell Sophia of their plans. Which meant they were using her—again—in an effort to gain power and influence.

The goodwill tour was a convenient excuse to put off addressing their petitions, but how long would it be before they began to wonder if he was deliberately keeping her away?

So far, he'd been able to distract and deceive the world, and her family, into thinking she was where she should be. But the ruse couldn't last for much longer.

Adding the burden of finding Sophia to his list of responsibilities didn't seem like enough to make up for losing her in the first place. Nor did his vow to never allow harm to come to another citizen—noble or common—under his protection.

Gradually Sophia's form blurred and shifted, turning into Gracie's. The physical similarities were unmistakable, but what intrigued him was the exquisite, fragile air that surrounded both of them. What Sophia hid with poise and polish, Gracie broadcast with the thousand-watt glare of uncertainty that shone in her eyes.

Both had secrets and vulnerabilities.

Both needed protection.

As younger brother to the king, it was his job to see they had it.

He'd failed once.

He wouldn't fail again.

Jill watched Stephan pace, his long strides eating up the expanse of the room. He openly displayed a frown, something her husband Constantine, King of Melesia, rarely allowed himself to do in public.

It was odd, in a way. Since her wedding and acceptance as new Queen of Melesia, Jill had learned to stop hiding her feelings. The masks she'd used to keep people at a distance weren't needed here, except on rare occasions. And it tore at her heart when she had to feign indifference.

"Stephan, please, stop pacing and sit. You're making me dizzy." She reached for a ginger butter cookie to settle the sudden unease in her stomach.

Stephan's searching look seemed to see more than she wanted to reveal, but he did as she asked. "It's wrong," he said finally, his tone as steely as her husband's. Despite their differences in coloring and build, the lanky, blond Stephan and the dark, imposing Constantine were alike in their passionate commitment to family and country.

"Your sister's attitude toward the family is wrong. You've done nothing but help her. She shouldn't shut you out of her life. Just now in the Grand Hall, she tried to give me an assumed name. How can she be so foolish as to think I wouldn't remember her?"

Jill's heart clenched as Stephan pulled half a roll of antacids from his pocket and popped a couple in his mouth. He'd changed so much over the past few months. He used to be relaxed and playful. His teasing and laugher had eased her through the stressful transition from commoner to royal bride. Lately, he only smiled in public for the visitors and the cameras.

"It's complicated, Stephan. Most of her life, Gracie's been a person who'd rather hide in her room with a book than do anything else. She's uncomfortable in the spotlight. And life as part of the royal family is one big spotlight after another."

"Life doesn't always hand you the things you want. Food served on silver platters can taste bitter, but it's wrong to disdain it while people starve," he said, quoting an old Melesian proverb.

"Meaning what, exactly, Stephan?"

"I could barricade myself in a room with books too. But I have a duty to my country, and my own selfish whims have to take a back seat. Constantine relies on me to keep the world aware of Melesian interests and to promote our economy, public health, and national interests. I can't do that from the library on my yacht."

"We have a duty, Stephan, but Gracie doesn't."

"Like it or not, Gracie has ties to us now. If she continues to live in Melesia, she'll have to bear the spotlight eventually. I've been distracting the press and protecting her from them since your wedding. I can't do it much longer. She must learn to adjust."

"Gracie would be grateful to you if she knew."

"I don't want her gratitude. If anyone has earned it, it's you. Considering the sacrifices you made, you deserve better treatment from her."

"They're not sacrifices if you love someone. Yes, I lived like a miser for years to save for her education. And yes, my actions almost caused an international scandal. But in the end, I fell in love with the man of my dreams. Gracie deserves a chance to be as happy as I am."

"But she won't even acknowledge you in public. If she didn't work in the palace, you'd never see her." He stood and resumed his pacing, more slowly.

Jill watched for a moment, weighing her thoughts, hoping to make him understand. "Stephan, Gracie needs things I can't give her. Years ago, she was an outgoing, vibrant child. All of that disappeared in an instant when her father died in the accident."

The memory assaulted her as if it happened yesterday, and she retreated behind her rarely used public face.

"He was your father, too, Jill." Stephan's voice was quiet. "You don't have to hide your feelings from me. We're family now, remember?"

Jill nodded. The lump in her throat made her voice shaky when she spoke. "I was almost an adult when he died. She was just a little girl. I can't give her the father she lost, but I can respect her choices just as he would have. She dealt with his death by hiding behind her books and pretending she didn't need anyone. Now that she's an adult, she has to prove to herself that she's capable of standing on her own."

"I don't understand it." Stephan still frowned, but his posture relaxed and some of the steel seeped out of his voice. "But for your sake, I'll accept that she may have reasons, however misguided, for her behavior."

"She needs this, Stephan, in more ways than she understands herself. She thinks it's just about succeeding on her own, but it's not. Living in anonymity in the dorms gives her a chance to develop the social skills she'll need to get by in life. We let her stay isolated for too long when she was a child."

"You and I both know that it's possible to be surrounded by crowds and still be isolated. According to my sources, that's exactly the position Gracie is in. Despite your noble intentions, she may never develop the social skills she needs without help."

"Gracie's a survivor. She'll do what she has to."

"I'm uncomfortable leaving her on her own. I don't suppose you'll let me post undercover bodyguards to watch out for her, will you?" He radiated a mixture of tension and resignation.

Jill shook her head, careful to hide her smile. "Gracie's not in any danger on Academy Island. No bodyguards. But if you want to look after her yourself, that's another matter."

If anyone could understand Gracie, it would be Stephan. The kind of protection her sister needed wasn't from physical danger. It was from emotional pain. And from herself. She could count on Stephan to protect her from those too.

He paused for a moment, staring into space with a still, thoughtful air that Jill associated with his private, intellectual side. "So," he said turning to her, "are you telling me that you wouldn't mind a little discreet interference on my part?"

"I'd be thankful for it."

"And if she refuses my overtures of friendship?"

"Then you're not the charmer I took you for."

Stephan laughed, his eyes showing a hint of a twinkle. It was the first unscripted laughter she'd heard from him in months. "I shall do everything in my power not to disappoint you. After all, I live to serve you, My Queen."

He clasped her hand and bowed over it in a courtly gesture that had her laughing as well. "But for now, I must leave you. I have to welcome my guests at the summit."

"Keeping up with a group of scientists for a week-long conference should keep you entertained," she teased.

Her intellectual brother-in-law favored her with a mock frown, but she saw the excitement in his eyes.

She hoped the summit would take his mind off the myriad of duties he'd insisted on assuming at Constantine's coronation. He'd grown too serious over the past year. Most of all, she worried about his obsessive desire to find the missing Lady Sophia. When she disappeared, so had the last of Stephan's carefree charm.

Though teams of specialists were working to locate her before a public and political scandal could erupt, Stephan seemed to think it was his responsibility alone. She didn't doubt that he'd handle the situation effectively, but she hated seeing the shadows in his eyes.

A sense of loneliness clung to him despite his attempts to hide it. His intellect and determination to shoulder more than his share of responsibilities tugged at her heart. It was a familiar tug.

"You have a lot in common with Gracie, and you don't even realize it." She paused until she had his attention. "If you want to know more about her, start by finding out why she won't accept gifts. When you discover her reasons, maybe you'll understand why she keeps her distance." *And maybe you'll both break through the shells that isolate you.*

Stephan absorbed her comment with an inscrutable look, but Jill knew he was intrigued. After he left, Jill relaxed against the sofa. She hated Gracie's self-imposed exile, but she wouldn't force her sister's hand. At least not in larger matters.

She still assigned Gracie to work in the palace so that they could meet more easily if Gracie chose to. And she insisted that Gracie keep her phone with her so they could have some means of contact. But everything else was up to Gracie.

Jill wondered how she'd react to the latest news. She nibbled another cookie and rested her hand against her stomach. Constantine was urging her to make a public announcement, but she couldn't tell the country about her pregnancy without first telling her sister.

For now, only she, Constantine, and the royal physician Dr. 'Oodsoon knew the truth. Jill wanted Gracie to be told first, then the rest of the family. After that, news of her growing child, heir to the Melesian throne, would belong to the world.

More than ever, she needed the little sister she'd lost that rainy October night. She only hoped Gracie stopped blaming her for their father's death long enough to forgive her when she needed her most.

Chapter 5

*P*regnant!

Gracie sagged in the corridor outside of the queen's drawing room. She was about to become an aunt. Of all the things she'd expected when Jill summoned her, it wasn't this.

Gracie wandered back to the ground floor and made her way to the ferry returning to Academy Island, glad that she'd missed the earlier boat with its full load of student workers.

She paused as she passed the aquarium. The serene, peaceful glide of fish through the still water calmed her as her thoughts wound their way through the minefield of painful memories and half formed hopes.

Jill's fragile image burned like a phosphorescent ghost in her mind. Gracie hadn't seen her look so vulnerable since those first weeks after their father died. The weeks when she and Jill had gone from best friends and closest confidants to distant siblings. Scenes from the past swam through the darkened aquarium bringing to life things she'd thought buried forever.

Gracie crept into the shuttered room, approaching the dressing table with the magical bottles of cosmetics, nail polish, and perfume. "Hi, Jill." She climbed into her sister's lap, careful not to disturb the cast that wrapped Jill's broken arm. "Are you feeling better today?"

Jill slid her uninjured arm around Gracie more from force of habit than in an embrace. "How was school, princess?" Jill's voice wasn't sparkly and warm like before. The flat tone scared Gracie.

"Okay." She studied her ragged nails. Only a few specks of pink remained. No matter how careful she'd been, the polish chipped away. Maybe her sadness and Jill's would chip away like the polish one day.

"Jill?" Gracie tried to turn Jill's face to her, but her sister didn't move. "When your arm is better would you paint my nails again? And fix my hair?"

Jill nudged Gracie off her lap. "That's not a good idea, princess."

"But I want to be pretty, just like you."

"No, you don't. That kind of thinking got Daddy killed." Jill turned away and swept the bottles off the dressing table and into the waste can with a crash.

Gracie jumped at the violent movement. The cloying scent of perfume rose from the broken glass. She wanted to run away, but Jill looked so lonely that she didn't. "I could fix your hair, if you want," she offered trying to make things better even though she knew she couldn't.

"No. I said it wasn't important." Jill's voice was sad again, not angry. She turned to Gracie. "Don't you have homework to do, princess?"

"Don't call me that." Gracie rushed to the door before Jill could see her cry. If she couldn't be Daddy's princess, she didn't want to be anyone's princess. Jill's words finally sank in, even though she didn't fully understand. Somehow painted nails and braided hair had killed Daddy.

Suddenly, she didn't want to be pretty ever again.

Over the years, Jill's confidence returned, but the closeness between them never did. Today, however, Jill had been dwarfed by the opulent surroundings of her suite. For the first time since Gracie could remember, her strong, vibrant sister had needed her instead of the other way around.

The image vanished when Constantine walked into the room and gathered Jill close, but Gracie couldn't shake the feeling that Jill was hiding behind a mask of happiness. She'd fled the suite after uttering a few words of congratulations.

"Hey, Gracie, what delayed you?" Marta detached herself from the shadows along the palace wall and walked with her toward the pier. "I knew you'd gotten another assignment, so I waited for you."

"Thanks. I finished up and took advantage of the chance to get in touch with my family."

"So what's going on at home?"

Gracie weighed her words, not ready to talk about all she'd learned, yet not wanting to shut out the only friend she had. "I spoke to my sister for the first time in a while. She seemed…lonely, I guess. I suppose it made me a little homesick."

"Why didn't you take the chance to visit home the last time we were on school break?"

"I tried to. It didn't work out." She shrugged, and they lapsed into silence.

The truth was she canceled her plans to go home the minute she'd received a text message from Sophia indicating that their escape plan had worked. She'd delayed applying for a new driver's license, using her passport for official identification instead. Nevertheless, she didn't want to risk showing up in the States with another Grace Susan Bradley on the loose.

Somehow, in trying to make things better for everyone, she made a muddle of it instead. She boarded the ferry in silence and walked to the railing to look out onto the night sea. The vast emptiness, which had always appealed to her before, seemed forlorn in the starlight.

"So if you don't want to talk about home, let's talk about our jobs." Marta closed the distance between them and chatted about her new assignment for a few minutes. "What about you? I know you were at the palace today, but did you talk to Miss Alia about transferring to the aquarium? You should be a natural, with your major and all of your knowledge."

Gracie shook her head. She knew it had been a long shot trying to get transferred to another position. Now, with Jill's pregnancy, she was almost glad she'd been asked to stay on the palace staff. "It looks like I'll be cleaning the grand salon and the royal apartments until graduation. Maybe if I get into the graduate program, I can transfer."

"If you get in? You're at the top of your class. At least you're at the top of your science classes, and that's including all the graduate level courses you're already taking. You still need to pass the language class."

"Language and C&P," Gracie said. The same professor taught both. And she didn't like Gracie at all.

A breeze kicked up from the ocean. As she turned her face into the cool evening air, Gracie let the sounds and smells of the sea wash away her worries.

Marta had a point. Her academic record was strong. She'd earned a place at the head of her class. Maybe she could relax. Maybe it was time to let go of her need for independence and give in to her need for family.

She was going to be an aunt. And a baby needed family to spoil her—or him. Even a royal baby. Especially a royal baby with half a family tree full of arrogant, powerful men.

"So," she said to Marta in Melesian, "I'd better practice my language and protocol." *Or else,* she added to herself, *I'll be learning them in the nursery with my niece or nephew.*

The child wouldn't be allowed to grow up on hot dogs, grilled cheese, and American apple pie. Like it or not, Gracie had another tie to the arrogant aristocracy.

The week passed swiftly with parades, public holidays, and fanfare as the nation celebrated the announcement of a new royal heir on the way.

Gracie buried herself in her studies, feeling more disconnected than ever. Back home, she might have planned a shower and learned to knit a baby blanket. Here, she watched from the sidelines and tried to read Jill's face for signs of fear or fatigue. Even if she'd known how to bridge the gap between them, the media fanfare made it impossible to try.

Her world had shifted. Her last refuge—the advanced marine biology field study class—wasn't the escape it had once been either.

"Miss Smith, please stay behind for a minute after class. I need to speak with you." Professor Pontileus caught up with her just before the opening bell rang.

Gracie nodded and made her way to a solo lab station. Everyone else was paired off. She pulled on a clean apron and latex gloves before turning to study the specimen in front of her.

"Ladies and Gentlemen," Professor Pontileus began, "who has an interesting story about their first research dive? Would anyone like to share?"

"Sheila and I found a great place," Derek began, gushing about the sights and discoveries in what Gracie had thought was a mundane dive.

She poked at the starfish in her tray, feeling as disposable as this poor creature that had washed up on the wrong shore. Derek and Sheila had tolerated Gracie on the dive but not included her.

She wished she could chart a solo course and hire a dive master on her own. She steeled herself to approach the professor with her idea.

The hour passed in a blur.

"So, Miss Smith, I've heard from everyone else in class. What did you think about your first research dive?" Professor Pontileus eased onto the stool next to her.

Gracie looked up, surprised to find the classroom deserted.

"You've been lost in your study of the specimen. A little too lost, it seems to me," the professor said. "You didn't even hear the bell. What's on your mind? The dive?"

"It was fine. I took photos and gathered a few specimens. But I'd really like to explore something a little more unusual. I'd like to see the corals off the remote islands."

The professor looked thoughtful. "Yes, I think the corals would be an excellent topic for you to study. And despite what you say—or don't say—I can tell that the first dive wasn't challenging enough for you. You don't like being the third person on a team, do you, Miss Smith?"

She shook her head. Maybe now was the time to ask him. Gracie put her specimen tray away and stripped off her gloves. "Would you consider letting me dive with a hired partner? I could charter a boat. The captain could make sure I'm safe."

"No, I'm afraid that is against school policy. I can't sanction a student diving with a paid dive master who might somehow influence your research.

"However, in your case, I can make some exceptions to the rules. As it happens, someone," he hesitated, and an odd look crossed his face, "a private citizen with university ties, has offered his services. He's an experienced diver.

"Of course, you'll still be responsible for all of your own sample collection and analysis. You'll be on your own for the labs, but he's willing to be your dive partner for the sake of safety. You can pick the dive sites. He'll act as your assistant."

The professor tugged at his tie and looked decidedly uncomfortable. "It's all highly irregular, but not against policy."

"Thank you, professor. If you think he's trustworthy, then I'd like that very much."

She thought the professor looked a little green. "Trustworthy? Of course, he is. He's— Never mind. In any case, I thought you might like the new dive arrangement." He locked the specimen cabinets and pulled off his lab coat. "Here's where you can meet him. Good luck to you, Miss Smith. I expect great things from this pairing."

With that, he ushered her out of the room and snapped off the lights. Gracie stood in the nearly deserted hallway and looked at the slip of paper he'd given her. She was scheduled to meet her new dive partner—whoever he was—at six a.m. the following morning at a remote pier.

She hurried to check out diving gear. Uncertainty gnawed at her gut. Professor Pontileus didn't seem concerned about her safety, but something about her mysterious benefactor obviously disturbed him.

It didn't matter, she told herself firmly. She was in charge of the dive, not the stranger who'd offered to partner her. So why wouldn't the nervous feeling go away?

Chapter 6

racie trudged along the rocky path that led from the bus stop to the pier. Her neoprene wet suit squeaked with each step, and inside it, her skin felt clammy. Sweat trickled down her back, despite the slight morning chill in the air, and she regretted changing into it so early.

Her bag of gear dragged her down, making each step slow. Her other bag, a duffel filled with maps, research notes, her camera, and extra clothing, bounced against her hip as she walked.

A single ship waited at the pier, but it was much more luxurious than any diving vessel she'd seen yet. She headed toward it, wondering if she and her escort were to meet here and travel elsewhere for the dive, but she didn't see any vehicles nearby.

Her footsteps slowed as she approached the end of the pier. Then she caught a flash of movement on deck and relaxed a bit. Until a lithe, muscular—and familiar—form hopped over the edge and onto the pier.

His blond hair was tousled by the wind, which tugged at his unbuttoned shirt, revealing tantalizing bits of muscled flesh.

"Your Highness." She dipped into a curtsey, feeling more foolish by the moment as her bags of gear threatened her precarious balance.

Prince Stephan let out a genuine laugh that echoed across the empty shoreline. "That looked appalling, Miss Bradley. Your courtly manners are not improved by the wet suit." He scanned the area and continued to chuckle. "At least no one else was here to witness it. It's a good thing I value my privacy enough to suggest a remote location and an early hour for our meetings."

He stepped forward and swung her gear bag out of her hand with no apparent effort. "I suggest we dispense with formalities while we're working together. It makes life easier for everyone involved. Come on, hop on board, and I'll introduce you to the staff."

Gracie stood frozen in place, staring at him. "You…you're my new dive partner? The private citizen who offered to work with me?"

"Does that surprise you? I do have a few useful skills, you know." His teasing smile was doing things to her again. The squishy feeling in her gut and the jellyfish knees were back.

She'd waited all her life to feel this excited by someone's smile. Why did it have to be him? A prince? He was an illusion, not a man. As an ambassador for his country, it was his job to make people feel good.

The wriggling pleasure in her gut proved he excelled at it. Why couldn't she feel this way about someone normal? Someone who didn't live in the public spotlight? Someone who wouldn't put the needs of his country above hers?

"But I thought you disapproved of—" she waved her hands vaguely, "me, and, um, things."

"Hiding your identity? I do disapprove. But for your sister's sake, I'm willing to suspend my judgement on the matter. Besides, it isn't an issue when we're alone, is it? And there's no one here except me and my staff. It might do you good to drop the charade for a while."

He tossed her gear on board. "Come on," he said, extending his hand. "Let's get under way. The longer we linger at the pier, the more chance some busybody with a camera will intrude. We can talk on board."

She took his hand, but instead of graciously helping her on board, he drew her up beside the ship, locked his hands around her waist, and lifted her over the rail as if she were no more trouble than her gear bag.

He followed and gave the order to cast off. Within minutes the crew had them on the open ocean, away from prying eyes and the safety of the shore.

"So, boss, where are we diving today?" Stephan sank down on a cushioned bench and stretched out, propping his head in one hand and regarding her with an unsettling twinkle in his eyes. The wind ruffled his hair, sending the wheat-colored strands into disarray. It tugged at his open shirt, too, giving her an unhindered view of his sculpted chest and the sprinkling of blond hair that covered the tawny expanse of his tanned skin.

She tore her eyes away from him and dropped to a seat on the deck, dragging her duffel bag in front of her both as a shield and as a distraction. She rummaged around it in for a minute before finding her map. The wind whipped at the edges until she spread it out on the deck and knelt over it, anchoring it with her knees and the bag.

"Last week my team only explored a fringing reef near the school. I thought we'd go further out today, to one of the barrier reefs near the southwest islands." She pointed to a cluster of islands just beyond the main residential centers.

"I'd really like to see the Great Neptune's Crown Reef, but that area is restricted." She shrugged. The local reef, famous for its variety of marine life, was considered a bit of a national treasure.

Stephan's soft chuckle drew her gaze from the map. "What a pity that you aren't diving with someone who could give you access to Neptune's Crown." The twinkle in his eyes rivaled the sun glinting off the water.

This was the charming man who'd been at ease with the children, not the cool prince whose penetrating look chastised her for hiding her identity. Gracie relaxed a bit.

"Could we go to Neptune's Crown?" She should have known. He was probably the one who'd designated it as a restricted area in the first place. Excitement pushed away any reservations she had about accepting special treatment from yet another member of the royal family. She sat up, clutching the map in one hand.

"If it pleases you, then, of course, we can go."

"Just like that?"

"Nothing would be easier." His carefree smile made her breath catch. The warm, squishy feeling lodged in the pit of her stomach again. "But as it takes over an hour to get to the reef even at full speed, I'd suggest you slip out of your wet suit and into something more comfortable for a while."

She followed him down the stairs into the belly of the yacht, grateful not to be looking into those dangerously seductive eyes. She focused instead on the gleaming, polished wood floors that led to a hallway larger than the main corridor in her dorm complex. Spacious rooms opened on either side.

"The main salon is aft, on this level. The guest rooms are this way." He pointed to a door on her right. "This is the guest suite. Make yourself at home. My suite is the next one down, at the end of the hall."

"Really, this isn't necessary. I'm happy to wait on deck."

"But that would make me uncomfortable. And I hope you are too polite and well-mannered to do that. Go on. Relax a bit."

She turned to the door. Eight feet of solid, carved teak stood between her and who-knew-what. The yacht, which looked normal from the outside—well, big actually but still relatively normal—threatened to overwhelm her. Behind her, Stephan was an equally overwhelming presence.

She felt trapped—claustrophobic—despite the high ceilings and spacious hall. Her wet suit, comfortable a second ago, now pinched and tightened, constricting her chest, squeezing breath from her lungs. Caught between the man and the door, there was no escape.

Stephan touched her shoulder, and through two millimeters of neoprene and a layer of cold sweat, she felt her skin burn. The man or the door? Coward that she was, she grabbed for the knob like a lifeline in a storm.

"Here, let me help you." His voice sizzled in her ear sending shivers in its wake. Cupping his fingers around her shoulder, he came half a step closer until she felt the heat of his whole body along her spine.

The rasp of a zipper and a touch of slightly cooler air startled her out of the spell. The feel of his knuckles gliding along her back, just below the zipper, pulled her into it again. His hand finally stilled, resting, warm and unfamiliar, on the swell of her hip. "It's murder, trying to unzip these things on your own."

Despite her one-piece swimsuit, she felt naked to his gaze. Naked and far too vulnerable. The events of the past half hour swirled in her head.

She wasn't diving with a private citizen. She was diving with His Highness Prince Stephan. Who looked far too human and touchable in his open shirt and loose shorts.

To her dismay, she couldn't summon a single bit of trivia to hide behind. Instead, she gripped the knob more tightly and chanted the multiplication tables to herself. The childhood habit soothed her nerves and focused her mind. Finally, she turned the knob, resigned to hiding out in luxury.

"I'll see you in the salon in ten minutes." His voice drifted back to her from several feet away.

Even from a distance, he had the power to unnerve her. Gracie fled into the suite and leaned against the door, eyes closed. For the first time in her life, she felt seasick.

Chapter 7

"This new girlfriend must be special if you are taking her to your private marine sanctuary, Your Highness," his steward remarked as he filled a cup with strong coffee.

Stephan glanced up at the weathered face of the man who'd been friend, mentor, and father figure for most of his life. He ignored the amusement hovering in those deep brown eyes, instead sipping his coffee and turning his thoughts to the last half hour.

He'd offered to look after Gracie for his own reasons. Despite her stubborn pride, she needed someone to do it. He'd steeled himself to cope with more of the arrogance she'd showed in their last, brief encounter.

Instead, his annoyance with her faded the moment she stepped onto the pier. The uncertainty that radiated from her dissolved his anger and roused something else. He'd mistaken her self-protective bluster for arrogance. Now he wondered what else he'd been mistaken about.

"She's not a girlfriend, Petros, she's a student at the academy."

"And when does your job as Chancellor to the Royal Academy include taking students to Neptune's Crown?"

"It doesn't. The chancellor position is purely ceremonial, as you well know. This is a private interest of mine."

"Indeed." Petros moved to the dumbwaiter and brought dishes of fruit and pastries to the table. "So, my friend, is there anything I should know about the girl?"

"Nothing." Stephan sipped more coffee and tried to forget the sliver of pale skin he'd seen before her baggy, ill-fitting bathing suit obscured his vision.

"Your Highness?" Stephan looked up, surprised to find Petros still hovering nearby. Worse, he detected a hint of laughter beneath his friend's slight deference. "The look in your eyes makes me wonder. Should I make up the guest suite? Or will the young lady be sharing the master suite while she's on board?"

Stephan set his coffee down with a sharp crack of cup against saucer. "What you should do, Petros, is mind you own business."

"As you wish, Your Highness." Petros bowed, a one-hundred-dred-watt grin lighting his lined face. "By God, but it's good to see you interested in something besides your books and those foreign businessmen. It is very good." With that, he left.

Petros was too observant, Stephan mused. His friend was one of only a handful of people who could see beneath the image he projected. After spending nearly two decades together, he supposed it was inevitable.

Stephan settled back with his coffee, his eyes trained on the entrance to the salon. It did feel good to be back on his yacht again. He'd forgotten how the wind in his hair could make him feel free.

On land, he was always Prince Stephan, conforming to duty and tradition. At sea, he was merely Stephan, unfettered by expectations. At sea he was, like his ancestors, just a man facing nature.

Legend held that the first settlers and rulers of Melesia had been exiled from Greece hundreds of years ago. They'd crossed the Atlantic Ocean and settled in the Caribbean islands through sheer strength of will, merging the Greek and native cultures to create what became the modern nation of Melesia.

According to some versions of the legend, they were thieves and murders. According to others, noble exiles whose idealism caused their downfall. But no matter which version was true, in the centuries since, they'd grown into a glittering example of a fairy tale come to life.

Stephan poured another cup of coffee from the carafe and plucked a piece of toast from the basket. At least here, on the ocean, he wasn't forced to play Prince Charming for the tourists. Neither was he required to be the intellectual advisor to the king. Here, he was just…

"Your Highness."

He looked up, visions of expectant tourists cluttering his mind. Gracie stood a few feet from his chair, clutching at the tie of a short terry cloth robe with white knuckles. Too bad she hadn't opted for the pale silk.

Stephan pushed himself away from the table and stood. "Miss Bradley." He gestured to a chair at the table and waited till she sat. "I'm disappointed. I thought we'd agreed to be informal, at least while we're on my yacht. I would like to consider you a friend. I'd like to call you Gracie. But I can't, unless you agree to call me Stephan. Would you be willing to do that for me, Gracie?"

She nodded, the move so slight it could have been unconscious.

"Are you sure? I wouldn't want to make you uncomfortable."

"It's just…I don't know. I feel caught between two worlds."

He poured a cup of coffee and passed it to her, waiting.

"In the U.S., we respect our leaders, but we don't owe them deference. They earn their positions, rather than being born into them." She took a swallow of coffee. "Oh dear, that didn't come out quite right. Thank goodness we'd agreed to be friends. Otherwise you might feel compelled to throw me overboard."

Stephan relaxed in his chair. This was the prickly girl he'd seen by the aquarium last week. The one who, according to his sources, might be the only person in the history of his country to fail the Customs & Protocol class because she preferred to debate forms of government rather than learn how to curtsey properly.

He liked the spunky side of Gracie. Especially when he had the pleasure of coaxing it from her. He liked it even more that she'd just called him a friend.

"It would take a lot more than a political disagreement to make me throw you overboard." He grinned at her. The shy blush in her cheeks was at odds with the stubborn set of her jaw. "You could probably make me do it, but not that easily."

"What would it take to push you to the limit?"

"You're a smart woman. You'll have to figure that out on your own."

"And what are the warning signs? I'd like to know when I'm close to the edge."

"You'll have to figure that out on your own too. Although if I unexpectedly hand you a life jacket, it might be wise to put it on."

"Chivalrous, even in the throes of anger. I admit, there's something admirable in that."

He saluted her with his cup. "Here's to finding admirable qualities in one another."

She returned his salute.

The silence stretched between then until it threatened the tenuous link they'd forged. "You seem different," she said at last, her voice quiet but slightly puzzled.

"How so?"

"It's hard to explain." She ran her finger around the rim of the china cup. "More of some things and less of others, I guess. Just now we had a conversation—like normal people. We never did that back…on…I mean, we never did that before."

"We never had a chance before. You raced home after the wedding and returned to enter the academy a couple of weeks later under a completely different name."

"You've known about my fake name from the beginning?"

"I am my brother's confidant, after all."

"How foolish of me." She lifted the cup to her lips and sipped the last of her coffee. Stephan could almost see her gathering her thoughts and weighing her words as she dragged the action out as long as possible.

"We barely spoke during the wedding festivities and whenever you looked at me, it was as if I didn't exist." She accented her words with a small shrug. "I honestly didn't think you'd remember me."

Stephan stood, covering his shock with the simple motion of pouring more coffee for her. He remembered every detail of her visit, from her first tentative steps into the palace foyer to the panic that shivered through her body whenever a member of the press tried to talk to her.

The only reason she was invisible to the public was because of his efforts to shield her. But invisible to him? Never.

"Perhaps," he said, returning to his seat, "the difference you feel simply reflects our change in circumstances."

"But they haven't changed. You're still a prince, and I'm still just plain Gracie."

"Those are circumstances of birth, nothing more. We don't control them. They influence, but don't totally define us either.

What I mean is that you're no longer playing the sister-of-the-bride role, and I'm no longer cast as chief ambassador and next heir to the kingdom. Here, we're acting as private people, not public personas."

"I've always been a private person. And we're still from different worlds."

"Sure, I'm still a god, and you're a mere mortal, like Eros and Psyche," he teased, masking his annoyance at her attempt to push him away, "but that doesn't mean we can't find common ground."

She blushed. No doubt she knew the myth the god of love piercing himself with his own arrow and falling for a mortal woman he was supposed to curse. He wondered if she knew the erotic details or the children's version of the tale.

"Their common ground started out with deception, and it wasn't a smooth path forward. Besides," her cheeks deepened to crimson answering his unspoken question, "we're not remotely like those mythological Greek lovers."

"So you don't think I brought you here to ravish you and prove my undying love for you?"

Her gaze flew to his, eyes wide with shock.

"That just proves how smart and perceptive you are," he continued, the teasing fading from his voice. "I brought you here so that we could get to know one another and so that you could have your choice of research opportunities. Nothing more."

Gracie nodded and downed the fresh cup of coffee, her features slowly returning to normal. "Thank you."

"It is my pleasure. And now, if you are finished, I'll give you the rest of the tour." He stood and offered her a hand. "I'd like to show you my library. There are sea charts of the entire archipelago. We can pull up the one for Neptune's Crown and you can tell me what you know of the reef and what you hope to gain from your research."

At the mention of the library, the remnants of tension and embarrassment left her shoulders and she nearly jumped from her chair. Stephan didn't bother to hide his smile. Her school records indicated she was intelligent. But the excitement in her step told him even more. It told him that he might, at last, have found someone he could talk to.

After all, a man couldn't spend his whole life teasing her. Or admiring the swish of her sassy backside, for that matter. Or could he?

Chapter 8

"I still can't believe you're not wearing a wet suit." Gracie stood on the dive platform at the back of the yacht and squinted at Stephan. He'd donned fins and a mouthpiece but dispensed with a wet suit. Only his open shirt offered protection from chaffing by the oxygen tank.

"We're just exploring the shallow shore zone. It's probably not deeper than about thirty to forty feet. I suggest we keep the dive relatively short, since we're still getting used to each other. But it's up to you. I'm just along for the ride."

"Okay, but don't count on me to warm you up if your naked body takes a sudden chill down there."

"Your concern for my naked body is touching." He flashed her a grin that weakened her knees, just a bit.

"Actually, I said no touching. No warming you up. No chaffing the chilled skin."

"No CPR?"

She shook her head, refusing to get more embroiled in this nonsense.

"Good thing the water's warm because you're acting rather chilly," Stephan muttered before jumping in.

Gracie stood on the dive deck a moment, stung by his tone. She'd been teasing—hadn't she? Yet too often her teasing fell flat. At parties, the laughter drifted around her, not aimed at her, but not including her either.

She made final adjustments to her mask and strapped her dive computer to her wrist. Biology was so elegant. Single cells dividing and multiplying. Simple organisms following an orderly plan for life and death. Physics and physiology.

But add psychology and the human element and everything turned chaotic and impossible to understand.

"Are you coming in, or waiting for the next tide?" Stephan's call interrupted her thoughts.

She looked at him, glad to see his grin was back. Maybe she wasn't as bad at teasing and flirting as she'd thought. Gracie plunged into the water after him.

The sudden change in pressure and the accompanying silence wrapped her in a cocoon of safety. Under water, everything was different. The magic of the deep soothed her, and the tension seeped out of her shoulders and neck.

Stephan swam just outside her sphere of solitude, close, but not intruding. She exhaled a little, listening for the sound of the air bubbles as they broke the silence, then she focused on the sights in front of her.

About thirty feet down, the fore reef came into view. Crenellated fire coral lay in pale clumps next to rough star coral and large cupped bolder coral. Gracie skimmed past the fire coral, careful not to scrape her hands against it. A school of parrot fish nibbled along the cups of the bolder coral, their teeth rasping as they grazed.

Life was different under water, colors more vibrant, shapes bigger and more real, sounds somehow both sharper and more muted. Sharper because she could hear the scrape of the parrot fish as they rasped against the coral; muted because there were no voices telling her what to do—not even her own.

She'd dropped out of dance class and started swimming at the local YMCA shortly after her dad died. You couldn't cry under water. And you couldn't hear people tell you not to. It became her haven, a place where no one else intruded.

Diving was even better than holding her breath and plunging into the deep end of the swimming pool. It was a world all her own with no painful memories. No one pried into her thoughts or emotions, no one asked anything of her. She would stay here forever, if she could.

A flash of color caught her eye. A brightly colored blue and green male parrot fish had joined the grazing females.

Gracie tugged her camera from its clip on her dive belt moving slowly so as not to startle them. Even so, they darted away only returning when she stilled. She poised the ultra-slim, waterproof digital camera so that she could shoot photos without much movement.

The camera, which by design didn't require a cumbersome case, had been an extravagant purchase to celebrate declaring her major in marine biology.

During her sophomore year at the Clarkson Community College back home, she'd scrimped and saved and pulled extra shifts at the Greasy Burger Barn to buy it, never dreaming she'd one day be in the Caribbean photographing the famed Neptune's Crown Reef.

Gracie snapped half a dozen photos of the fish before settling down to her research. She checked her dive computer for depth and oxygen tank information. She had at least half an hour before she had to think about surfacing.

She swam cautiously around the coral formations, photographing features and taking careful measurements. These untouched specimens would give her baseline data. Later, she'd compare coral next to waste effluent streams from the local municipalities and industries to see what impact they had on the formations.

A jackknife fish with its racing striped body glided across her field of vision, interrupting her analysis of the coral. She followed his languid movements as he skimmed along the rocky mountains of his underwater home until she saw it.

From the edge of her field of vision, a bony hand protruded from the sea floor, its skeletal fingers blurred by bits of debris caught in the eddies and currents. She gasped, the rush of air into her lungs and a panicked flutter of arms and legs causing her to shoot upward before she controlled herself. Exhaling, she propelled herself back down for a closer look.

Thin finger coral, commonly called "dead man's hand" stood innocently among the other specimens. Gracie chided herself for letting her imagination run away with her. In the watery light with shadows of the fish playing around it, it had looked real.

Gracie checked her computer again. Her heart thumped painfully within the skintight wet suit, reminding her that adrenaline still coursed through her body. Maybe it was time to begin the ascent.

She looked around for Stephan, aware that she'd all but deserted him the moment she entered the water. A good dive buddy would have kept track of her partner.

Guilt stabbed at her as she remembered how he insisted on diving in his shirtsleeves. Heaven help her if he had run into a problem. Her mind raced with images of everything from hypothermia, to a painful welt from scraping against the fire coral, to hypoxemia from oxygen depletion as she scanned the area. She turned in slow circles until a shadow above her drew her gaze up and to the side.

She approached slowly, not taking her eyes off the most amazing sight she'd seen today. Stephan's shirt billowed about him exposing his chest while his shorts hugged his body. The colorless mask he wore appeared almost invisible. Like Neptune himself, he floated, calm and unconcerned, as the fish swam around him.

Gracie sighted him in her camera's viewfinder and shot frame after frame as he moved with aquatic grace. Angel fish, soldier fish, trigger fish, and more swam about him in flashes of moving color. He stayed, nearly motionless, while they approached without fear.

A porcupine fish swam close to inspect him, and Stephan cupped a hand several inches under the fish's belly, almost as if in greeting. The fish blew itself up to giant proportions its spines prickling out all around him, but it didn't flee.

After several minutes, the fish relaxed, its spines drooping and his body deflating, no longer on guard against a predator. Man and fish seemed to understand one another.

She took more photos, mesmerized by his ability to communicate without sound or touch. She drifted close. Like the fish, she was drawn to him, at least here in the safety of the depths. The image of him as Neptune fit comfortably in her mind. The image of Eros and Psyche that he'd raised earlier burned. She wouldn't fall prey to its lure.

He looked over and Gracie clipped the camera back onto her belt. Motioning, she indicated they should begin their ascent. He nodded then gently fanned the water, sending the porcupine fish floating away.

Together they covered the distance to the surface. Halfway there, Gracie stopped as Stephan slipped his hand into hers. She turned to him and he pointed to his depth gauge. She checked her dive computer. Fifteen feet to the surface. They needed to stop the ascent to let their bodies adjust to the changes in pressure and to let the oxygen, nitrogen, and carbon monoxide in their bodies equilibrate.

She looked at him, aware that behind his mask and breathing regulator, his eyes twinkled. If he could have grinned underwater, she suspected he would have. She returned the look, letting her eyes speak where her lips couldn't.

For a moment, time stood still. He squeezed her hand, still clasped in his much larger one, and Gracie felt a surge of happiness at the simple human contact. Then he pointed upward, and they began the final ascent, away from the magical world and back to the real one.

Chapter 9

Stephan climbed onto the dive platform and shrugged out of his gear. Gracie followed, looking slick and sensuous in her skintight wet suit. Her eyes glowed with excitement, and he felt a ridiculous surge of pleasure, as if he'd created the coral reef, instead of just bringing her here.

Underwater it was as if the distance between them dissolved. On the dive, Gracie wasn't skittish or shy. She'd focused on her work, of course, ignoring him with the intensity of a scholar on a quest. But when he'd touched her hand on the ascent, she didn't pull away.

The feel of her hand in his reminded him of simpler times. Times when he'd been the less interesting, younger D'Malia brother, before Alex's abdication had thrust him into the temporary role of Crown Prince. On the dive, Gracie had responded to *him*. Friend to friend. Woman to man. Not awkward outsider to prominent prince. The thought warmed him.

"Let me give you a hand." He eased the tank off her shoulders. "If you climb onto the main deck, I'll pass the gear up to you. I'll send for someone to help me with the tanks later."

"I'll climb up, but only if you promise to give me the tanks too."

"I admire a woman with great upper body strength," he quipped, not taking his eyes off her slick backside as she climbed the ladder to the main deck.

"If I can't handle the equipment, I shouldn't be diving." Ice replaced the warmth in her tone.

Stephan hefted the depleted oxygen tanks up to her. The determined set of her jaw erased her earlier look of excitement as she hauled them onto the upper deck. He passed her the masks and fins, aware that the tension between them was back.

Gracie showed her spines at the oddest moments, creating an invisible shield of toughness as quickly and effectively as the porcupine fish. At least he understood why the fish viewed him as a threat. He hadn't a clue why the woman did.

Did she still think he was angry about her hiding her identity? They'd moved past that—or so he hoped. He climbed to the main deck, wondering what it would take to break through those barriers again.

He'd rather spar with her—wit to wit, keen observation to cool logic—than be shut out. Jill's warning about Gracie's hidden depths had roused his curiosity. The more he saw, the more fascinating the puzzle became.

"What did you think of the reef?" he asked casually. "Did it live up to your expectations?"

"It was even better than I'd imagined it would be. I shot some fabulous photos." A sparkle lit her eyes. She unhooked the camera from her dive belt and fiddled with it to select a shot. "Check out this dead man's hand coral. At first glance it scared a year off my life."

"Let's see." He stood next to her and peered over her shoulder as she paged through several shots, each one clear and vibrant. "That's a sweet little camera you've got there. I've not seen one that small before."

She grinned up at him. "It's probably the most expensive underwater camera on the planet. I nearly had to promise my first born to get something small and waterproof to the depth I needed."

He plucked it from her grasp and inspected the casing, ignoring the photo display even before it turned off. "It's a great design, but personally, I don't think I'd have paid more than an arm and a leg for it. A first born is far too pricey for me."

"The risk was all theirs. I don't plan on having a first born to barter with." The matter-of-fact tone in her voice warned him the spines were about to resurface.

He ignored her comment and flipped the camera back on, paging through the photo file in an attempt to restore her good humor. "Let's see what else you have on here. A jackknife fish, a school of parrot fish, some fire coral—"

"It's not all that interesting. Here, let me put that away." She reached for the camera.

Stephan started to hand it to her, but then noticed the next photo in the memory. "Well, well, well," he mused, turning his back on her and pacing a few steps away. "This is an interesting photo. Set of photos, actually."

Photos of him swimming with the fish took up more space than the research photos of the coral formations. And the close ups were revealing—in more ways than one. The chilly, prickly woman who'd claimed to have no interest in his naked body hadn't been snapping those shots.

He turned back to Gracie who stood rooted to the deck, her cheeks awash with more color than he'd ever seen in them. He was wrong about her. She wasn't chilly. Beneath those protective spines, he'd bet she was hotter than the sun-baked sand in summer.

"Stephan, could I have my camera back? Please?"

"Not yet." He slid down the waistband of his shorts, watching her eyes widen until she saw the edge of his Speedo. He tucked the camera into the snug band. "I want to take a closer look at these photos."

"It was just a couple of pictures." The uncertainty in her voice pricked at his conscience, but as long as he had the camera, her spines remained unfurled.

"You can learn a lot about a person by studying the things they find interesting," he said softly. "Why don't you go wash off the saltwater and change into something comfortable? It's a beautiful, calm day out here, and there's no rush to get back to the mainland. I promise, I won't let anything happen to your camera while you're gone. I just want to check out the reef shots again."

She disappeared into a changing area on the main deck before he could offer to help with her zipper.

Stephan stepped under a shaded canopy by the bar area and looked through the photos again, slowly this time. The shots she'd taken of him had captured something. A playful curiosity he thought he'd lost.

The man in the photos seemed years younger and a lifetime away from the person he'd become in the last twelve months. Maybe Gracie wasn't the only one who put barriers between herself and the world.

He summoned a crew member to stow the camera safely in the library. He'd ask Gracie's permission to download the photos later. If he ever lost touch with his soul again, the photos would remind him of where to find it.

Ambling back toward the open deck, Stephan shrugged out of his damp shirt and stretched out in the sun. The warmth seeped into his tense muscles, urging him to relax.

In the weeks since Lady Sophia had disappeared from the goodwill tour, he'd shouldered the responsibility of finding her in addition to all the other duties he'd taken on since his brother's coronation. Somewhere between worrying about his childhood friend and fabricating press releases to keep her disappearance from becoming a political fire keg, he'd nearly lost the ability to relax.

Today, for the first time in months, he had relaxed. And Gracie had captured the moment. He'd proposed diving with Gracie out of a need to understand her, to protect her if need be, and to find a way to mend bridges she and Jill had burned long ago. A peacemaker's mission. Like so much of his life, it had begun as duty to family and country.

But the moment Gracie stepped onto the pier in the dawn light, uncertainty etched on her face, something changed. Stripped of her bravado and forced to be alone with him, the real woman peeked out from behind the illusion that defined her. She'd shown him a dozen different faces, but the side of her that intrigued him most was the one he almost hadn't seen. The hidden part of her that connected to the missing part of him. The one who'd shot such insightful photos.

With a single click of a shutter, she turned from a project into something more. A woman. Someone who might be able to look into his soul and understand him. Someone he might understand too. No wonder Jill had tried to throw them together.

In coaxing her from her protective barriers, he'd become like the old Stephan. The man who knew how to laugh. How to play. Not the isolated, obsessed man who fell asleep pondering security team reports and woke shortly after to spend the rest of his sleepless nights reading technical journals.

Today, he felt like a free man. And he hadn't had a damnable antacid tablet in hours.

The slap of the waves against the side of the yacht and the gentle list of her in the water soothed him as he pondered what he'd learned this morning. Awkward, uncertain, little Gracie had passions that went beyond fish and coral, books and studying. She wasn't as cool or indifferent to him as she pretended to be. And he wasn't about to let her go back to pretending that she was.

"Stupid, stupid, stupid." The word echoed around the small chamber and reverberated in Gracie's head as she rinsed their flippers and masks in the utility sink of the on-deck changing room. Other pieces of gear were stowed in the room, clear evidence that Stephan wasn't the casual diver she'd taken him for.

Stupid. Why had she let him see those photos?

She twisted, stretching to grasp the zipper in the back of her wet suit. A few short hours ago he'd helped her with that zipper and the memory of his fingers sliding along her back was etched into her brain. So was the memory of him walking away, unaffected, while she was shaken to the core by his actions.

She peeled the wet suit from her body, glad for the rush of cooling air on her skin. The clammy feel of wet neoprene always left her wishing for a shower. Too bad she'd opted for the changing room instead of the guest suite. She rinsed the wet suit out in the sink, careful to remove all traces of the saltwater.

But it wasn't care for the school's equipment that kept her in the changing room. It was embarrassment. She didn't belong in this world. And Stephan was the epitome of all she disliked about it.

He lived in a protocol-dominated bubble and oozed privileged indulgence. Life came to him on monogrammed silver platters. She lived in the real world where people worked their way to the top or died trying.

Despite the differences between them, she'd flirted—or tried to—with a man she should have avoided. And she'd failed miserably. Her efforts annoyed, rather than intrigued, him. So she'd stopped trying. From the frowns he'd given her,

Stephan was even less impressed with her sense of responsibility and independence.

At least she'd stopped short of babbling about the potential impact of marine science on the human genome project. That kind of geek talk would have been enough to turn him glassy eyed with boredom before he decided to throw her overboard.

Gracie pulled the wet suit out of the sink and hung it to dry, knowing that she couldn't hide in the changing room for much longer. If only Stephan hadn't seen the photos she took of him, she could keep her discomfort under control.

Instead, reluctance lodged in her gut and slowed her steps, just as it had in third grade when her teacher caught her passing a note to a boy she liked. She remembered the way her voice trembled and her hands shook when Miss Simross made her read the note out loud to the whole class. And the boy—whose name she'd forgotten—avoided her the rest of the year.

Maybe it would be easier if Stephan avoided her, too, instead of looking at her with that sense of disapproval. She stepped out onto the deck, wishing again that she'd opted to clean up in the guest suite. She could have hidden there till they docked. Or at least changed into something other than her purely functional, basic, black swimsuit.

She spotted him, stretched in the middle of the open deck. Asleep. If she took her camera back now, maybe they could pretend she hadn't been ogling his body through her viewfinder.

She eased down next to him. Stephan's chest rose and fell in a slow, measured cadence. The golden cast to his skin intrigued her, as did the sprinkling of hair scattered across the smooth muscle.

This close, his body tempted her more than the glimpse through her viewfinder. *He's asleep,* her mind whispered. *You're safe as long as he's sleeping.*

Curious, she stroked her hand lightly across his skin, barely touching, aware of the tickling of those wisps of hair on her fingertips. She never dreamed she'd be so affected by the tiniest of unintentional touches.

Bolder, she pressed her palm to the warm skin and explored the smooth ripple of skin and muscle. His even breathing assured her that her explorations were private. Her heart pounded as she ignored caution, giving in to her newfound sense of daring.

The touch of flesh on flesh fed a craving for closeness she'd all but forgotten during her time in Melesia. A hunger for human contact. Until this moment, she hadn't realized how much she'd missed her mom's hugs and her brother's high fives—all of which paled next to the feel of her hand on Stephan's skin. Like an addict seeking a fix, she couldn't pull away.

Her fingers inched toward his waistband, tentative at first then more aggressive as she slipped unnoticed beneath the loose shorts and headed for the tight Speedo she'd glimpsed earlier.

"If you're looking for your camera, it's not there."

Gracie jolted. Her hand tangled in the fabric as she tried to free herself. Instead he stilled her movements and pressed her palm against his hipbone, his touch gentle, yet firm through the thin fabric that separated them.

"You're still welcome to explore."

His sleep roughened voice was warm and welcoming, not threatening. Yet Gracie felt censured, trapped between her own curiosity and his hand. She eased away from the danger zone, worming her way back up to the relative safety of his navel.

His movements followed hers, his grip encouraging her to keep touching him rather than to draw away. He brushed his thumb across her knuckles, and she gasped at the intimacy of hand against hand. Her craving for human contact intensified.

"I hope that means you like my touch." He gazed up at her, his eyes a sleepy, smoky blue, flecked with specks of gray she'd missed before. "Because I like the feel of your hand stroking me. I'm glad you changed your mind about not touching me. Not chafing my chilled skin."

"You're not chilled," Gracie murmured. The heat of their contact seared, burning from her flattened palm all the way to her chest. Each breath was a hot struggle that pulled her deeper into the inferno of sensation.

His fingertips followed the flash of heat. No longer trapping her hand, he brushed along the sensitive skin of her arm, sending shivers of pleasure in the wake of the heat.

"You're warmer than I first imagined too."

The brush of his hand was intoxicating, and Gracie relaxed against the deck and propped her head in one hand, the urge to flee seeping out of her muscles. She traced small patterns against his flesh with a single finger, meandering like one adrift in the surf.

Her discomfort and shyness burned away, no more substantial than the wisps of gray smoke that flitted through his blue eyes. "So, do you spend all of your days lounging on the deck of your yacht?"

Gracie's heart thumped as she waited for his response. Would he understand her attempt at teasing? Or had it come out like a barb as so many of her jokes did?

Stephan continued to work magic on her arm, trailing his fingers from knuckle to shoulder is a slow sweep. So far, so good. "I never waste time lounging around, unless a pretty woman tempts me into it."

"What's your excuse today, then?"

"You."

She reluctantly stopped stroking him and sat up, breaking the contact between them. "I'm smart enough to know I'm not a pretty girl."

"Woman," he corrected. "And whoever told you that you weren't pretty didn't look closely enough. Although, there is one atrocious feature that I'm struggling to overlook at the moment."

"What?" She turned to stare at him. Gracie was used to people ignoring her in favor of pretty airheads, but she wasn't used to them pointing out her flaws in such dispassionate tones. A sharp, unexpected hurt pricked her heart.

Stephan grinned. "That horrid bathing suit you're wearing. It looks like it was designed for a nun. Padding with fake attributes in all the wrong places. Baggy in all the places a suit should be revealing. It's like armor. Enough to send a lesser man fleeing before he could see the beauty trapped inside."

"You're being ridiculous. It's just a swimsuit." Warmth replaced the hurt of seconds ago.

"It looks like it came from your grandmother's attic." He tugged at her suit and frowned.

"Are you insulting my grandmother?"

Stephan laughed and pulled his hand away. "Ouch. You got me with that one. Serves me right for trying to tease a serious woman. I'll be better prepared next time we cross wits."

Next time. He wasn't so put off by her awkwardness that there wouldn't be a next time. Gracie smiled to herself, ridiculously pleased by the thought.

"Come, O Formidable One." Stephan stood and offered her a hand up. "I don't know about you, but I could use a shower and some lunch. The noon sun is a little too intense even for me these days."

Gracie let him pull her below deck, back to the luxury of the well-appointed yacht. But this time, given the choice, she wouldn't hide behind the closed doors of the opulent guest suite. This time, she'd risk the man rather than the door.

Chapter 10

Stephan leaned forward in his chair and frowned at the reports his team had e-mailed him earlier. In the weeks since Lady Sophia had disappeared, the investigation team had combed through every phone call she'd made and every speech she'd given.

They'd found no common links to anyone that could cause her harm. She'd spent all her time in the company of the entourage or her private staff. Until the day she disappeared.

He continued to receive periodic notes from her, some on scraps of consulate stationary others imprinted with a wax seal and an impression of a de Lyons signet ring. Each was posted from random cities throughout the States. Each leading to a dead end. They kept him balanced on a knife edge of tension, wanting to believe she was safe but more anxious than ever about returning her to her home.

He stared at the latest report. No matter how hard they tried or how deeply they investigated, they couldn't find evidence of wrongdoing. No ransom notes. No terrorist threats. Nothing.

It was as if she had wanted to disappear just as the notes implied.

But why would she want to stay away?

It didn't make sense. Sophia had no skills, no knowledge of how to survive in the real world. She should have tired of her prank by now, if indeed that is what it was. In any case, he needed to find her soon.

Stephan yanked the desk drawer open and grabbed his extra-large bottle of antacids. He jerked the cap off and chewed a handful of tablets, grimacing at the texture.

Knowledge of Sophia's disappearance could ignite traditionalist political factions that opposed Constantine. Her aristocratic pedigree underpinned their hopes to restore purity to royal bloodlines contaminated by D'Malia marriage practices.

First marriages to natives that mingled pale Greek to darker islander. Later, marriages of royals to commoners. All things that made sense to Stephan but infuriated the purist factions.

Should those factions fail to achieve their aims by manipulating Sophia, they might try to seize power through other means. A whispered word in the Council of Nobles, hinting at a D'Malia vendetta against the House of Lyons, might mean nothing now. But as Constantine's proposed reforms passed more power to the people, those in the nobility who opposed him could gain traction.

It was a tricky business in which Lady Sophia was an unknown variable. Stephan didn't like unknown variables. Especially when he, the king's righthand advisor, had introduced it into the equations.

He remembered every detail of the day Sophia begged to take his place on the goodwill tour. She'd first asked him as he escorted her from the press conference that announced Constantine's engagement to Jill. Stephan knew better than to think she suffered a broken heart.

Still, she'd been used by her scheming uncle as a political pawn for as long as he could remember. And the disgrace that the Duke de Lyons had suffered shouldn't be allowed to sully her life. Placing her on the government sponsored tour amounted to public endorsement by the king, something she badly needed.

Constantine had left the decision in Stephan's hands. And as Sophia knew from years of experience, he couldn't resist her big, soft eyes and pleading smile.

He'd gone along with her plan—despite his nagging doubts. Just like he'd given in to her requests over the years. Little Sophia schemed and manipulated as effectively as any sister. With years of successes behind her, adult Sophia refused to accept no for an answer.

Worry gnawed at him. Sophia was beautiful, cultured, and a prime example of the romantic illusion that made Melesia a favorite tourist destination. But she wasn't the kind of woman who could survive on her own.

Unlike Gracie.

The screen saver turned on and a slideshow of her photos came into view. Gracie not only survived, she surrounded herself with a minefield of do-not-disturb signals, a set of prickly spines for those who came close anyway, and an ugly black bathing suit for the remaining brave souls. So far, he'd breached all but the last barrier.

He reached for the bottle of antacids but paused with one halfway to his mouth. For once, he didn't need it. The excursion with Gracie had left him feeling less burdened, rather than more.

The memory of Gracie's fingers brushing against his naked flesh surged up in his brain, delightful and fleeting as the encounter with the porcupine fish that she'd caught in digital perfection. He turned to the images on screen, longing to be that carefree man for more than a stolen hour. And wishing he could have a photo of Gracie to complete the set.

Even now, thoughts of her pushed his demons aside and gave him a measure of peace.

"They told me I could find you here."

He looked up at the sound of the soft voice and quickly swept his medicine bottle out of sight. Gracie stood framed in the doorway dressed in pale blue shorts and a tank top sprinkled with sparkles.

"Everyone on the yacht knows to look in the library if they want to find me. But today I made sure they sent you here first."

His gaze skimmed over her, taking in the long, slender legs, the way her top clung in all the right places, and the shining fall of soft blonde hair that framed her face and cascaded over her shoulders. For the first time in weeks, she looked more like a woman than a science student.

"Did you find everything you needed in the guest suite?" he asked as he rounded the desk and leaned against it. "Enough towels and stuff?"

She nodded. "Every luxury imaginable. And a few I hadn't imagined before."

"Then I hope you made use of everything. I'd be insulted if you passed up the opportunity to wallow in luxury. Think of the suite as your home, at least until we've finished exploring the reef together."

"That's very gracious of you, but I wouldn't want to inconvenience your other guests."

She'd edged into the room, closing the distance between them one tiny step at a time. Until she halted at the mention of other guests.

"How fortunate for both of us that I rarely invite guests onto my yacht. In fact, you're the only one I can recall for a very long time."

"I thought the adjective *playboy* always went with the title prince."

It was his turn to laugh. Luxury. Prince. Playboy. A subtle verbal attack she used to keep him at a distance. Another instinctive barrier that kept the soft part of Gracie unharmed. Each new technique amused him because it meant he'd successfully maneuvered around the previous one. Two could play this game.

"Charming," he said. "That's the adjective you're looking for. Not playboy. At least not for me. That title belonged to Constantine."

Fire danced in her eyes, and he could sense the spines coming up, not to protect, but to attack. Gracie's reaction pleased him. Despite her self-enforced exile from her sister, she was ready to protect and defend her without a thought.

"Before you get riled, remember that I said *belonged*. Past tense." He watched as some the fighting urge melted from Gracie. "He never was as much of a player as the media made him out to be. And since he met Jill, I don't think he's even looked at another woman."

"He'd better keep it that way. King or not, if he hurts my sister, he'll have me to contend with."

"You'd have to fight for your place in line, Gracie. Along with me, and Alex, and Helena, and most of the citizens of Melesia. Your sister is a much-loved woman in the islands."

He draped an arm around her shoulders and steered her toward a table near the windows. "I took the liberty of having some food sent up to us. I don't know what you like, but we have conch salad, fruit, an assortment of breads and cheeses, olives..."

"It's lovely." She took a seat and sipped at a glass of cool water.

"I could send for something else, if you like. Anything. We're generally well stocked on board." He was babbling almost as much as she did when she was nervous. The temperature in the cabin seemed to shoot up without warning, plastering the back of his silk shirt against his skin. He should have stayed in his sailing clothes rather than dressing for work in his palace office.

"You don't have to try so hard, you know."

"At what?" Did she guess at how hard he worked trying to balance the economic and technical needs of his people with the desire to leave his country's pristine beauty intact? Or was she talking about his failed search for Sophia? As sister to the queen, she must know about it.

She interrupted his thoughts. "At being charming. I didn't mean to make you frown, Stephan. I—" She took another sip of water—a gulp, really—and cleared her throat. "I should apologize about the playboy comment. I didn't mean it. Those things just slip out at the wrong time."

Stephan sat across from her and filled a second glass with water. "I'm glad. I wouldn't want you to think that about me."

"I just don't know how to react sometimes. The idea of a real-life royal family freaks me out. I grew up in a small town in Ohio where the richest person in town was pretty much like everyone else. His wife shopped at the local grocery store, he had their car serviced at the garage, and they hired local kids to mow the lawn and rake the leaves. Here things are different."

"If it helps, I think you'd have the same culture shock if you went to Washington DC and had dinner with the president and the first family, or with one of his cabinet members.

"The difference is that we're trained from birth to lead our country. Your leaders don't decide what they want to do until much later. But politics aside, in the end, we're people with individual needs and interests and desires. That's the same everywhere you go."

"I suppose you're right." She toyed with the conch salad, spritzing it with a wedge of lime but not eating. "What interests you? What were you studying so intently when I came in?"

"If you must know, I was looking at your photos and thinking how insensitive it was of me to download them without asking your permission first."

"You downloaded my photos?" Her fork paused halfway to her mouth, and her green eyes went wide.

"I'll erase them if it bothers you. I promise. You can watch me do it. I didn't mean to pry."

"No, it's okay. You really don't mind that I took your picture?"

"Me? I'm not at all camera shy. Although I hope you don't plan to sell them. Maybe to *National Geographic* or a diving magazine, but please not the *Weekly World Stir* or other tabloids."

She shook her head. "Never. I wouldn't deliberately hurt someone I c— I mean, I wouldn't hurt a friend."

Someone she what? Cared about? Stephan busied himself with the bread and cheese, giving them both a bit of privacy. Gracie might not think she was capable of deliberately hurting those she loved, but he'd seen the shadows in Jill's eyes.

Gracie's quick defense of her sister proved that she still cared. But it was a one-way street with her. Gracie allowed herself to care about others, but she couldn't cope with them caring about her.

If you want to know more about her, start by finding out why she won't accept gifts. When you discover her reasons, maybe you'll understand why she keeps her distance. Jill's words burned in his memory. Gracie wouldn't accept gifts. Even kindness. Or love. The prickly spines that kept her safe also kept her alone.

His curiosity wrapped itself around the puzzle that was Gracie. She was a lot tougher to figure out than the Rubik's cube he'd conquered when he was six. That challenge had only lasted about fifteen minutes. Gracie promised a much greater challenge. And a much more enticing reward.

Chapter 11

"Some of you," Professor Mikolas said as she stalked down the aisles returning papers, "need to put a little more effort into your work."

Gracie peeked at a corner of the face down paper on her desk, unprepared for the ugly red scrawl that ran across the top. The rush of angry disbelief hit her like a punch from an invisible assailant.

It didn't matter that C&P was the most inane class on earth, she thought, fighting the urge to slam her books into her bag and leave. It didn't matter that all of the grades translated into a pass/fail system at the end of the semester. It only mattered that she was failing.

She never failed. Especially not in a segregated class filled with simpering girls who only wanted a chance to meet a prince. Marta was right. This was a semester long preparation for a party.

Gracie never failed at scholastic work. But she always failed at parties.

Her anger ebbed, making room for painful memories.

Professor Mikolas walked back to the front of the room, heels clicking on the floor. The haughty tilt of her head and the pristine perfection of her fitted suit snapped Gracie's attention back to the class.

Professor Mikolas gave her a hard, lingering stare as she surveyed the room. The normal chatter and excitement stopped as if frozen by the professor's icy glare. Subdued students quietly stuffed papers into book bags, eyes downcast.

"I realize that most of you ladies—especially the foreign girls—think of this class as a foolish waste of time. Or worse yet, some kind of preparation for a Cinderella-style ball. But here on Melesia we consider our traditions to be of the utmost importance.

"Our royal family is not a collection of cartoon characters, no matter what the tourists think. They are our leaders and our most precious national treasure.

"As students at the Royal Academy, you are among the fortunate few who are presented to the royal family. For you who were born here, it is a part of your heritage.

"For the rest of you," she paused and stared at Gracie again, "it is a chance to enjoy a civilized custom that you might never otherwise aspire to."

Gracie gritted her teeth and swallowed her urge to protest. The professor's attitude embodied everything archaic and unenlightened about the kingdom. But another voice sounded in the back of her mind, quiet, respectful and tinged with gentle humor. Stephan.

You'd have the same culture shock if you went to dinner with the president…or with one of his cabinet members. Put that way, the opportunity to meet the royal family did sound like a civilized custom that she wouldn't normally aspire to. Something to treasure.

"Furthermore," the professor said, "even those of you born and raised on the islands don't seem to grasp the importance of the recent changes within our government. Therefore, I am adding two new research papers to your course work.

"In the first, I want you to explore the impact of King Constantine's proposal to incorporate an elected parliament into the government. Discuss the pros and cons in light of both Melesian history and the current world political situation. This will give you a chance to compare and contrast the various world forms of government while learning to appreciate your own."

There was a touch of grudging respect in Professor Mikolas's tone. Gracie's opinion of her shot up. She'd been wrong to think the professor was hopelessly mired in the past. Maybe there was a middle ground between Melesia's archaic traditions and her own modern American views.

She resolved to try harder to understand the Melesian ways. After all, she owed it to her sister, her new niece or nephew, and to Stephan, who'd shifted all of her preconceptions within a single day.

A young woman from the other side of the room demanded the professor's attention. "I thought this class was supposed to teach us proper court protocol, not to discuss forms of government. It isn't supposed to be hard." A chorus of other voices chimed in, agreeing with her.

"You have Miss Gracie Smith to thank for that." The professor looked at her with a smile that bordered on a smirk. "She initiated the discussion on politics and delved into various forms of government in her most recent paper. I thought it…worthwhile…to explore the topic."

Gracie's surge of optimism plummeted as the room erupted into chaos. Students shot her nasty stares and tried to protest the additional assignments. Her stomach knotted as the verbal attack mounted.

Professor Mikolas wasn't interested in exploring new ideas. She was interested in seeing Gracie isolated and snubbed. But why? Her simple academic questions had provoked an unexpected, vicious response.

Gracie forced herself to remain calm despite the unwanted attention. Thoughts of Jill and Constantine flitted through her mind. If her fellow students and teachers knew about her connections, they'd be competing for her favor, not ostracizing her. But she refused to indulge in petty power plays.

Professor Mikolas let the students vent their frustrations for long, agonizing minutes before calling the class back to order. "The second paper is also courtesy of Miss Smith's interest in our leaders and their qualifications."

She gave Gracie a thin smile. "I want you to discuss the role of the newly announced future heir to the kingdom. For the purpose of this paper, I want you to assume that the parliament will not become a reality.

"The question is twofold. First, how would you design the young prince's education to prepare him for his future leadership role? Second, if the heir is a girl, discuss whether or not she, as the eldest child, should be allowed to rule the kingdom one day. I'm sure you understand the implications can be far reaching."

Gracie wanted to slink away, but her pride wouldn't let her. She stiffened her spine and turned her mind to her research thesis, going through the motions of the C&P class by rote.

"Now, ladies, it's time to turn our efforts to the protocol lessons. As Miss Lahala reminded us, there is a great deal to learn." Professor Mikolas began the lessons.

The next hour passed slowly as Gracie struggled to focus on forms of address and the proper way to curtsey in various situations. How to greet a member of the royal family when they met while walking. Or when they were formally presented. In public. In private.

"Ladies, it is highly unlikely that any of you will be asked to meet in private with a member of the royal family. Should the occasion arise, however, you must use your best court manners. Adhere to the most formal forms of address and behavior.

Be scrupulously correct. If given permission, you may become slightly more informal as the occasion demands."

Gracie swallowed a giggle at the memory of meeting Stephan at the pier. None of the forms of protocol they'd practiced in class covered meeting a half-naked prince while wearing a wet suit. No wonder Stephan had looked so aghast at her greeting.

"Miss Smith, please refrain from giggling. I'm sure even you will be thrilled to be presented to His Royal Highness Prince Stephan, but giggling is inappropriate."

"Stephan?" She'd heard that the former King Alexander was the one to whom the students were presented.

Professor Mikolas turned frosty. "Miss Smith, such informality is unacceptable. You appear to be struggling with the proper forms of address. I have an assignment that will help you remember."

She dismissed the rest of the class and led Gracie to the desk. "For the next class, you will practice your forms of address by handwriting the full proper name of our Prince Stephan one hundred times.

"I generally only give this type of assignment to children, but you seem to be having a difficult time with our protocols. No doubt it's due to your American background. Let's just say my methods have never failed to produce the necessary attitude adjustments."

"But Professor—"

"Make that two hundred times. Any other comments?"

Gracie clamped her mouth shut and shook her head, annoyed at being treated like a child but smart enough to know who held the power in this struggle.

"I didn't think so." Professor Mikolas took out a small, engraved card and presented it to Gracie. "Here is the example you are to follow."

Gracie nodded and stuffed the card in her pocket, her anger barely under control. She kept her head high until she left the room then fled to the biology lab. Halfway through her next class, curiosity made her pull the card out.

She shuddered. It was difficult enough to think of him as *His Highness Prince Stephan.*

But *His Royal Highness Prince Stephan Hercules Tantalus D'Malia* was impossible to reconcile with the images that danced through her memories.

The setting sun slanted through the window of her dorm room, washing the small space in vibrant color. Gracie shoved her papers aside and turned her attention to the computer on her desk. Scenes from her underwater exploration filled the screen.

But while the fish and the coral were interesting, the photos she most wanted to see were hidden in a password protected section of her hard drive.

Her fingers cramped with the effort of writing out the lines of C&P homework she'd put off till the last moment. And she wasn't close to finishing the task, even though it was due in the morning. *His Royal Highness Prince Stephan Hercules Tantalus D'Malia.* The stilted title and string of names didn't fit the man who'd swept her away to the private world of Neptune's Crown Reef.

She selected the photo files and tapped in her password—she'd assigned it to his initials in a fit of irony—*H R H P S H T D'M.* To get to the private Stephan, she had to go through the public rituals. To get to the photos, she had to remember who he really was.

In a way, the C&P teacher had done her a favor. After only a few days of exploring the reef with Stephan, it was far too easy to think of him as just a man—a rich man—but just a man, nevertheless. The silly assignment reminded her that no matter how down-to-earth Stephan seemed, he wasn't the kind of man who would fit into her life for more than a brief time.

She wasn't like Jill. She couldn't stand up to the pressures of public life. Or to the strangeness of island life. Her flag, her creed, would always be red, white, and blue. Stephan's would always be Melesian green and gold. No common ground there.

Her phone vibrated then played a jaunty tune, demanding her attention. "Under the Sea" blared from the speaker and a close-up photo of the porcupine fish popped onto the screen. Only one person had that combination. Stephan.

"Hi," she said, not bothering to hide the breathlessness from her voice. She smiled despite her determination to remain professional and detached. She always smiled when he called—which he had every day since their last meeting.

"Hello, yourself. I've been thinking about you. Did you get good feedback on your work at the reef?"

"Professor Pontileus loved the photos and my thesis outline. He agrees that we need a better understanding of the effect of industrial effluents on marine life. But he was surprised when I told him where we took the photos."

Stephan laughed. The warm sound of his amusement snaked through the phone and lodged in her stomach with the same jolt of pleasure that his smile produced. She looked at the pages filled with her cramped handwriting and felt like a teenager doodling her boyfriend's name, not someone completing a hated assignment.

"I probably owe the professor a trip or two to the reef to thank him for setting us up as dive partners. He's asked permission to research the formations before."

"And you didn't let him?"

"You're the first researcher I've allowed near the reef since I had it declared protected territory."

"But what about the photos in the biology texts, the maps and the displays at the National Aquarium? Who documented—" She broke off, chiding herself for missing the obvious clues. Stephan's extensive collection of dive gear. The way the yacht was set up for diving. His natural grace underwater.

"The reef has been my private diving and research site for years, ever since Petros took me on my first dives."

"Your steward? He's also your diving instructor?"

"We passed that distinction long ago, but yes, Petros is an old islander who took a curious, out-of-control boy and taught him to dive." Stephan hesitated and Gracie could picture him lost in thought, serious, despite the hint of amusement that seemed to thread its way through everything he did. "I learned a lot during those early trips. Not just about diving, but about people too. I'll tell you sometime if you're interested."

"I'd love to hear stories about your out-of-control childhood. I didn't think such a thing was possible." But it was all too easy to imagine him as a mischievous, charming child.

Again his laughter rumbled through the connection. "You have a lot to learn, Gracie. Speaking of which, we need to set up a time for the next dive. Same hour and same place as the last time, if it's okay with you. Let's pick the day."

Two minutes later they finished the conversation, but the warmth still wiggled pleasantly throughout Gracie's body. She studied her private photos, one at a time, savoring the images that only she had ever seen.

A knock on the adjoining door gave her barely a moment to close the screen before Marta entered.

"Gracie, you've got a grin a mile wide on your face. What's going on?"

The phone rang again. "Under the Sea." She hesitated and glanced at Marta.

"Go ahead. Pick it up. I'll wait." Marta wandered into the room and looked out the window, unconcerned about interrupting a private conversation.

The song continued. Gracie picked up.

"Hello?"

"I forgot to tell you something." The warm tingling feeling intensified at the sound of his voice. "I'm looking forward to our next trip together."

"Yeah, me too."

"Think of me until our next dawn meeting, beautiful one."

"I'm not—" The phone went dead.

Gracie flopped on her bed, phone still clutched in her hand.

"So that's who you were smiling about. The mysterious someone who can turn you to mush with a phone call. He must be special some guy."

"He's a cut above average, all right."

"Is he the reason you've been busy for the past couple of weeks? Pretending to study while you have clandestine meetings with Mr. Mysterious?" A mischievous smile played across Marta's lips. "You've stood me up twice this week alone, and I won't let you get away with it a third time. Tonight we're going for drinks, dancing, and some R&R. And you're going to fill me in on all the juicy details. Unless you've already got a date with the hunk on the other end of the phone."

"No, I don't have other plans. I really was studying those other times, but I'm taking the night off."

"Good. I want to hear all about the new boyfriend."

"He's not a boyfriend," she said, waving the phone in Marta's direction. "We're working on a project together. That's all."

"If you say so. Come on, you need to get out of this room for a while." Marta headed to her closet but stopped by the desk and picked up Gracie's handwritten assignment. "So you're Professor Mikolas's new victim. No wonder you're busy. She always picks someone to drill on the Royal Melesian heritage."

"Probably always the foreign girl."

"No, she's as likely to pick on a native girl. My cousin got on her bad side several years ago. Back then it was *His Royal Highness Prince Constantine Phillippe Ramon D'Malia.*"

"Before he became His Royal Majesty King Constantine Phillippe Ramon D'Malia, of course," Gracie added, picturing her imposing brother-in-law in his royal garb.

Marta nodded. "I think she wanted to squash any romantic illusions the students have about the princes. She's a traditionalist who still advocates arranged marriages for the royal family. Bloodline purity and all that. It must have been a shock to her when the king married an American woman."

Gracie sat up, her mind snapping out of its dream haze. "Oh my God."

A traditionalist had tried to kill her sister and force a marriage between Lady Sophia and Constantine. She was glad that Professor Mikolas didn't know her real identity, and not just because she wanted to make it on her own. A traditionalist might not attack their new queen, but she could make Jill's life miserable through Gracie. Or worse.

"Gracie? What's wrong? You look paler than normal."

Gracie clutched her phone, an unnatural coldness settling in her gut. How far would the professor go to get even with the Americans who she thought symbolized corruption in the monarchy?

She wondered if she could convince Jill to see her tonight. It was probably nothing, but the thought of her sister's narrow escape before her engagement to Constantine nagged at her.

"I forgot about work," Gracie said, hastily inventing an excuse. "Could we go out tomorrow, Marta? I requested permission to put in a few extra hours of work tonight. Between the new C&P class assignments, the research dives, and my other studies, I'm swamped next week. The director of student employment is letting me trade shifts to make up the difference."

"I could help you with the work," Marta offered. "We could still go out later."

Gracie almost gave in. Marta was her only friend and she'd been ignoring her for too long. But Jill was her sister, and the image of Professor Mikolas wouldn't leave her alone.

"Let's go for a drink and a quick dinner first, Marta. I'll pack my uniform and pull a late-night shift if I can. Give me a minute to change."

Gracie shoved her uniform into a bag and pulled some clothes out of her closet. As soon as Marta left the room, she grabbed her phone.

For the first time in months, she dialed Jill's private number of her own accord.

Chapter 12

"You look distressed, *Ba'hona-mei*." Constantine's concerned voice broke through Jill's musings. "Is something wrong?"

Her heart did the same little flip it always did when she heard him call her his beloved spouse. *Ba'hona-mei*. She never tired of hearing that particular endearment from his lips.

He shrugged out of his formal jacket and unknotted his tie as he eased down on the couch beside her. "I hope my late nights with the diplomatic corps haven't upset you. I promise, it won't last for much longer."

"Not at all. I'm surprised that you're home already." Jill snuggled into her husband's embrace and gave a contented sigh. "Gracie called a little while ago. She wants to see me. She sounded…thoughtful, and a little anxious, but she assured me nothing was wrong."

"Maybe you've finally convinced her to loosen up a bit. I confess, I didn't think your strategy of giving her time would work, but I'd be happy to be wrong."

He nuzzled her hair and ran his hands over her back. The warm, comforting feel of his embrace soothed the last of her worries.

"I'd planned to use the rest of the evening to seduce you." Jill wrapped her arms around her husband's neck and kissed him, drinking in the essence of the man she loved. "But I promised Gracie we'd meet her in my private salon. She'll be here shortly. The seduction will have to wait."

"We?"

Jill nodded. "She said you might want to be there too. That's why I'm glad your meetings ended early tonight. It's all much more mysterious than Gracie's usual manner."

"Whatever it is, we'll find out soon." He stopped her answer with another slow, leisurely kiss. The rush of passion from their early courtship blended with the sweet knowledge that they had a lifetime together to share.

Ten minutes later, they awaited Gracie in their private salon. She entered after a brief knock, unannounced and without her uniform, as if she were unconcerned with appearances. Jill rushed to envelop her in a hug.

"Gracie, you look pale. What's wrong? Has something happened at home?"

"No. Everyone's fine." She pulled out of Jill's embrace but didn't step away. "I just needed to see you. Both of you."

"We're here for you, whenever you need us." Constantine sat in a wing chair and waved Gracie and Jill toward the couch. He was holding back a frown, and his eyes turned deep aqua.

Jill knew the look, knew that he was steeling himself for trouble. She settled down on the couch next to her sister.

"Gracie I—"

"Jill, I'm worried about you. It all started with my protocol class. I'm not complaining, and I don't want you to intervene on my behalf," Gracie gave both Jill and Constantine a fierce look, "but some things don't add up."

Gracie talked about her class, using general terms, but it was enough for Jill to see she'd been singled out by the instructor for some reason.

"I thought the professor just disliked me," Gracie continued, "but Marta told me today that she holds to traditionalist politics. They say she's still in favor of arranged marriages and that your marriage caused an uproar in her classes at the time. I think she hates all foreigners."

"That may be, but the time for protests is long past." Jill laid a hand on her stomach and thought of the life within. "Our pending marriage was sanctioned by both king and church before Constantine took his oath of office. And the people blessed us at the wedding. Our future heir is on his way, and even the protestors wouldn't dispute his bloodline. At least on the father's side."

"Jill, de Lyons was a traditionalist and he tried to kill you. He could still have followers who wish you ill."

"Enough." Constantine silenced them with his low commanding voice. "I won't have Jill upset by talk of conspiracy. There has been a traditionalist faction protesting the bloodlines since before my father married a half-American woman who gave birth to me. It dates back to the founding of the kingdom when D'Malia ancestors married native islanders. The traditionalists have a voice, but, except for the duke, they have never been dangerous."

"I wouldn't put it past Professor Mikolas to try to cause trouble. She—"

"Mikolas?" Constantine's voice, while still low, held an edge that made Jill shiver with unease. "Dorinda Mikolas?"

Gracie nodded.

"That puts a different spin on things. I still don't think Jill or you are in any danger, but Dorinda has a vindictive streak. She might try to stir up unrest. Just like her mother, who's been needling me about various issues for months."

Constantine stood and paced slowly about the room. His dangling tie and loosened shirt neck gave him a dangerous look, the look of a predator laying a trap for an unwary prey.

"Dorinda Mikolas is the daughter of Ophelia de Lyons and Gregor Mikolas," he said at last.

Jill understood the implication immediately and turned to explain to Gracie. "Ophelia is the disgraced duke's sister. Constantine's father first married in a traditional arranged marriage, but his wife died shortly after Alexander was born. When he remarried, the traditionalists expected Ophelia to be his next bride."

"My father had other ideas and, as you know, there have been battles of ideology ever since. Traditionalists believe that the nobility should not mix blood with the commoners. They sought to remove the taint from my blood by marrying me to Sophia. It would have ensured that my heirs were more fit to rule than I."

"What of your child now?" Gracie asked. "Will he—or she—be considered unfit to rule?"

Constantine shook his head. "Few people follow the traditionalist line of thought today. But Dorinda bears watching. Her mother, Ophelia, is unhappy and bitter in the marriage she eventually made to a minor nobleman. She raised Dorinda on stories of how her birthright was stolen when my mother twisted the king's mind. Dorinda believes she should have been a princess."

"So, she is a threat?"

"No, I don't believe so. She is bitter, but without power." He stopped his pacing and turned to Gracie. His eyes narrowed as he chose his next words. "Although, for the first time, I believe there is some wisdom in your decision to enroll in the academy under an assumed name. It minimizes her chance to make easy mischief."

"And she might have tried to hurt Jill through me."

"Despite your intelligence, you are not politically savvy compared to someone like Dorinda Mikolas. She would use you to try to drive a wedge between Jill and the rest of the country if she could. She'd be delighted to see public opinion—if not the Council of Nobles—force me to choose between my throne and my wife. As an American, you might figure into her schemes, but your anonymity lessens the impact she could have. You must be careful around her."

Gracie nodded. "Since she doesn't know me, I could act as your eyes and ears around her and let you know if anything else doesn't seem right. At least the eyes part—I'm good at making observations. I'm less good at following Melesian conversations, but I could try."

"Careful, Gracie," Constantine added, a hint of a smile tugging at his mouth. "That sounds suspiciously close to giving up your democratic principles to aid what you dubbed my *anachronistic government that should have been abolished a century ago.*"

"It should have been," Gracie mumbled, averting her flushed face. "But since it hasn't, I can't think of anyone better to run it than you. Besides, this isn't just about your government. This is about family."

"Thank you for your vote of confidence. And I shall strive to continue to live up to the faith you place in me. As for being an extra set of eyes for me, I accept your offer. You may report back to me about anything that raises your suspicions.

"You are not, however, to snoop or gather information other than what you would during the course of a normal day. No going out of your way to see or hear anything. No raising suspicions. Is that clear?"

"Yes." Gracie paused, a frown creasing her forehead. "Are we in danger?"

"If trouble occurs, I will bring you to Royal Island and under my protection immediately." His uncompromising tone seemed to calm Gracie's fidgeting, despite the threat to her independence.

Constantine sat on the other side of Gracie and took her hand in his. "Believe me when I tell you that I would never let harm come to your sister or to you, *Mi'cochida-ba*. I would protect you with my life, if need be."

The sight of Gracie's small pale hand engulfed in her husband's sent a bittersweet pang through Jill's heart. She missed her father and all the moments they had shared, but Gracie had almost no memories of him. Her sister never had a strong male presence to lean on during most of her life.

As Constantine cupped Gracie's hands in his and reassured her, calling her *Mi'cochida-ba*—beloved little sister—Jill could see Gracie fighting her emotions. The longing in her eyes contrasted with the set of her chin, and Jill guessed that Gracie's lip would quiver if she hadn't held it clamped between her teeth.

She rubbed Gracie's back, not letting her hide the need behind a wall of indifference. When Gracie clutched Constantine's hand and leaned her head on Jill's shoulder, Jill felt a weight lifted.

She had a second chance to be friends with her sister after all.

Chapter 13

racie sat cross-legged on the deck of Stephan's yacht, staring into the ocean. A breeze whipped the surface, sending sprays and ripples chasing across the watery expanse to the horizon. The ocean looked as restless as she felt.

Overnight, everything changed. Her advanced studies no longer gave her pleasure or escape from her worries. Protocol class had gone from a trivial annoyance to a potential minefield. She'd transformed herself into a model student, silently enduring veiled insults and character slurs from Professor Mikolas, while reporting everything to her sister and brother-in-law.

She imagined traditionalist spies around every corner. It was war, and Gracie was just a pawn, trying to protect the queen. Trying to protect her sister.

Her stomach lurched when she heard Stephan's footsteps. Tension knotted her shoulders, neck, and back when he settled onto the deck. She could almost sense his movements as he stretched out behind her.

Gracie drew her knees up to her chest and hugged them, wishing she'd worn her old bathing suit instead of the new pink two-piece number she'd impulsively bought. Both her emotions and her body were more naked than she'd ever been.

"You seem distracted." His quiet tone didn't fool her into thinking it was a careless comment. He was demanding an explanation.

"I'm sorry for what happened on the dive today. I was careless." She'd jumped at every shadow, imagining spies and threats lurking even in the serene waters around Neptune's Crown Reef. She kept seeing the broken stalks of decades-old Staghorn and Knobby Candelabrum coral fall as she flailed in the water. Her gut lurched and nausea threatened as she relived the moments of destruction.

Even diving no longer provided an escape. She swallowed the nausea and the lump in her throat. "You probably won't let me come here again. I understand."

Silence greeted her confession. She stared out into the ocean, the tension in her body grew almost painful as she waited for his response.

The gentle stroke of his knuckle down the side of her spine wasn't what she expected.

"Gracie, you weren't yourself today. You seemed distracted during the dive too. You were in the middle of one of the largest fire coral formations for miles. Did you get hurt? The sting can be painful, but I have some medicine for it."

"No, I didn't get hurt. The wet suit protected me. Too bad it couldn't protect the coral."

She focused on the surf and mentally chanted multiplication tables, trying to keep her emotions in check. Seeing Jill earlier in the week had broken through her defenses. Fear, worry, and concern about her sister opened the door to feelings of loneliness and isolation.

Now just about everything, from seeing Stephan looking handsome and professional in his wet suit, to her destruction of the coral, wrested more emotions from the place where she'd hidden them.

It was a Pandora's box full of unruly reactions and feelings that defied her cool logic.

"Thanks for loaning me the new wet suit and gear," she said, hoping her voice didn't betray her struggle. "It's much better than the school's gear. More convenient too. It's nice not to have to transport everything from school to here."

"Keep them if you like."

"No, thank you." Gracie shook her head. "I couldn't. It's too much."

"Jill told me you didn't like to accept gifts. I was hoping you'd make an exception for me."

The feel of his hand gliding along her bare skin tempted her to give in, to break the iron rule she'd held for so long. But fear of the consequences kept her from yielding.

"I can't. It's a long story. I lost…" She took a painful gulp of air and silently recited a list of the first thirty prime numbers before she felt able to talk again. "I'd rather not talk about this now."

"We could talk about how much I like the new bathing suit. It's a definite improvement over the black battle gear. And even if you won't accept the wet suit as a gift, please continue to use it while we work together."

"Does that mean you're not angry about the reef?"

"What do you think?" His touch remained gentle, but instead of soothing her, it sent shivers dancing across her skin. He traced a path on her lower back, just above the line of her bathing suit before inching his way up her spine again.

"I don't know." She felt like she was picking her way through a sandbar full of jellyfish, not sure if her next step would bring safety or a stinging surprise. The sleepless nights and emotional wrestling matches had taken a toll on her logic and her clarity.

Two, three, five, seven, eleven, thirteen, she chanted again mentally, trying to find calm in the mathematical sequence.

His hand continued to work magic on her back while his silence demanded an answer.

"You should be angry," she said finally. "You could forbid me to dive here. I ought to go back to working with the student teams, so I don't create any more damage."

"I should do this. I could do that. You ought to do something else. All kinds of terrible things are bouncing around in your imagination. But what *am* I doing?"

His hand stilled resting lightly on her hip. The warmth made it hard to think. Gracie hugged her knees more tightly to herself and remained silent.

"Could it be that I'm more concerned about you than the reef? That damage to a few square feet of coral in miles of reef isn't as important as what's causing you to make mistakes?"

This time Gracie did sense a touch of anger in his words.

"Could it be that I'm not the ogre that you take me for?" he asked more softly than before.

She'd been wrong. It wasn't anger. It was hurt that she heard in his voice. "I'm sorry," she said again. "I didn't mean it that way. I feel guilty about abusing the privilege of diving here. I repaid your kindness by destroying an untouched national treasure."

"Gracie, you know as well as I do that the reef sustains plenty of natural damage every day. The impact of a single diver means nothing. That reef was here before we were born and will be here long after we're gone. I'm protecting it from tens of thousands of overly eager tourists. Not one researcher."

He ran his hand across her back again. The tiny calluses on his fingertips and palm sent pleasant, unexpected tingles through her, melting some of her tension and most of her resistance.

"I can't think when you do that."

"Good. You think too much. You worry too much. You need to let the barriers down once in a while. Show your soft side."

"I don't have a soft side. Ask my classmates. They think I'm made of granite."

"If you didn't have a soft side, you wouldn't need to put up so many walls to protect it. Let me in, Gracie, just a little."

Gracie didn't want to think about the protective walls, but Stephan seemed intent on scaling them. Poor man. Once inside, he wouldn't like what he found. She wasn't a sleeping beauty waiting to be awakened by his charm. She was brainy, awkward Grace Bradley, destined to send any man running if he got too close.

"Awkward Grace," she whispered.

"What?"

"The kids in middle school called me 'Awkward Grace.' They thought it was funny. The name stuck. It wasn't easy trying to live up to the image of beauty and elegance that the name Grace conjures."

"Try being named after a Christian martyr, a Greek hero, and a mortal doomed to be forever tempted yet never satisfied."

Gracie turned to him. A glimmer of amusement lit his eyes, and for the first time in days, the foreboding that had dogged her lightened. "I never thought of it that way. Stephan Hercules Tantalus D'Malia. I could write your name in my sleep after the C&P assignment, but I still didn't get the irony."

"So you'll concede that there are worse things than being called Grace. But I'm curious. When did I turn into a class assignment?"

Gracie felt a rush of heat on her cheeks. "I shouldn't have mentioned it."

"But?" He grasped her hand to keep her from turning away.

"The C&P professor was drilling us on proper etiquette and forms of address for the Presentation Tea. When she mentioned you, I kind of slipped up." She waved her free hand, uncomfortable with the retelling. "I forgot to refer to you with all of your titles and extra names. It was unforgivable for a common foreigner like me."

Stephan burst out laughing, his eyes crinkling in amusement. "I don't believe it." He flashed her a brilliant smile. "You finally decided to ignore the huge, impassible social gap that you think exists between us, and you did it in front of your *protocol* teacher? That's priceless, Gracie."

"Laugh all you want, but Professor Mikolas didn't see the humor in it. I spent the days filling half a dozen pages with the words *His Royal Highness Prince Stephan Hercules Tantalus D'Malia*." The memory made her hand cramp, and she flexed her fingers within his grasp.

"Ouch, that must have hurt," he said, sympathy replacing the humor in his voice. Stephan sat up, a look of concern in his eyes. "Let me see."

He opened her hand and sandwiched it between both of his, carefully caressing her fingers before kneading her palm with his thumbs. "That explains why you're favoring this side of your body. It also explains at least part of your problems during the dive."

Gracie nodded. Physical pain was easier to admit to than the emotional turmoil she'd fought. The warm, soothing feel of his hands on hers pushed aside the darker emotions.

He cupped his fingers around each of hers in turn and tugged slightly, massaging from the base to the tip. "You hold your pen with a death grip. There's a callous here," he rubbed the knuckle of her second finger, "and the tip is slightly bent. Which means you've probably been doing it since you first learned how to write."

She nodded, not wanting to break the spell his touch created. The squishy feeling in her gut was back. She could swear tingles shot from the tip of her right hand straight to her toes, touching everything in between.

"It's hard trying to be perfect," he continued. "Perfection is another type of wall that keeps people from getting too close." He worked his way up to her palm, kneading again until he hit a tender spot near the base of her thumb.

She winced. "It's sore there."

"From too much web surfing for your research papers, no doubt. Unless you spend your days text messaging your friends stateside."

She squeezed her eyes against the sound of his soft chuckle. The only text messages she shared were from Sophia—and she didn't want to think about Sophia now. Especially since palace insiders whispered that Stephan was in charge of the search for the missing niece of Duke de Lyons.

Guilt nagged at her. At the time, helping Sophia escape the glare of the press and the machinations of her family seemed like the right thing to do.

But now, she wasn't so sure. Sophia was kicking up her heels in America, nearly drunk on the freedom she'd been denied most of her life. But the royal family members, especially Stephan, all wore worried looks whenever her name was mentioned.

She didn't want to face Stephan's anger, or worse, his disappointment when he learned of her role in Sophia's disappearance. If only she could convince Sophia to return on her own, things might work out.

Gracie pushed the thoughts aside and focused on the way Stephan's fingers slid up her arm, circling her wrist and gliding to her elbow and back with a gentle pressure.

"It's tight here." He deepened the pressure, giving her a few long, pleasurable strokes before digging into the area near the elbow.

She winced again and cried out at the sudden sharp ache.

"I know, *mi'hona*. I know, sweetheart. It's tender there," he murmured as he worked. "I know it hurts. But we've got to work the stiffness out. Just a little longer and the painful part will be over. Try to relax."

Gracie held on to the sound of his voice, soaking in the tender tone and endearments as he kneaded the sore spot near the bone. She loosened the fist she'd unconsciously made and opened her palm, trying to make her arm heavy.

Stephan cradled the weight in his hand. "That's good, *mi'hona*. Relax."

Her palm brushed his thigh and she rested it on his hard muscles. The soft sprinkling of hair tickled her hand in a pleasant way. When he switched from the deep massage to the long soothing strokes again, she gave a sigh of relief.

"Better?"

She opened her eyes slowly, feeling drugged by pleasure. Stephan's smile was more tender than teasing and her heart squeezed at the sight of him. "Much better. Thank you."

"You know," he said, his voice serious, "you've likely stressed the neck and shoulder too. I could do a much better job of this if you'd come below deck and let me find some massage oil." He trailed a finger along her cheek and down her neck, outlining her shoulder as he spoke.

The image of him sliding oil-slick hands across her body flitted through her mind, tempting, but impossible. They were from two different worlds. She was like Hans Christian Anderson's little mermaid, who turned to foam on the sea when her prince rejected her.

Despite her magically created legs, she couldn't live in his world. Gracie would fare no better. "I don't think so. You've done more than enough for me already."

"Are you sure?" Stephan switched his attention from her neck to her palm, his touch lighter than before.

Gracie giggled and tried to pull away, but he kept her hand firmly in his and ran a tickling finger across the palm, over the base of the fingers and back to her wrist. The sensations set her nerves on fire and sent a shower of goose bumps up her arm. The involuntary giggles left her weak, but she couldn't stop.

"That's an interesting reaction. An out-of-control Grace Bradley. That's something I thought I'd never see." His touch grew firmer and Gracie took a deep, shuddering breath.

Stephan pressed a kiss to her palm. "I think I've found a chink in that wall you hide behind. I'd like to find more. Are you sure you won't let me work on your shoulders and neck? I promise to be good."

"I'm sure you would be." *But good at what?* Gracie stood and started toward the stairs, reluctant to leave the ocean, but knowing she should go before he brought her emotions back to the surface. "I'm not used to this kind of self-indulgence. Too much luxury is bad for me. I should just shower and change."

"Gracie?" Stephan stopped her with a single word.

She turned back to him.

"What are you afraid of? Luxury? Or me?" The breeze ruffled his hair making him look wild and tempting. "Or are you afraid of yourself? Of what might happen if you let go?"

"Yes," she said. But she didn't know if the word was an admission that she feared everything he'd said, or an agreement to let him lead her back into dangerous territory.

"I promise, *mi'hona,* I would never hurt you."

When he took her hand and tugged her toward the stairs, she followed.

Chapter 14

Stephan sorted through the images and information in his mind in a rapid-fire analysis while maintaining a languid, easy stride that hid his inner turmoil. Gracie with dark circles under her eyes. Gracie flailing about in a panic underwater. Gracie dropping her tank and flippers on the dive deck and racing for the changing room.

Gracie huddled on the deck, not a single prickly spine in sight as she lashed herself with recriminations.

Gracie, flinching from his touch.

It tore at his heart to see her broken down and wounded. Yet, the confessions that poured through the gap in her defenses were better shared than hidden in the dark. And when she finally let him offer her comfort, it had been a victory, of sorts.

She was learning to trust him. Despite the tears that seeped out from beneath her eyelids, she didn't pull away, even when his ministrations caused her pain.

She hadn't pulled away from the emotional pain, either, when he'd touched on tender spots.

Tomorrow she might analyze the situation to death, but today, she trusted him.

Stephan paused at the door to his suite. Gracie had followed him this far, not resisting, but not quite enthusiastic either. Her green eyes clouded, skittering between his door and the door to the guest suite. He dredged up his most reassuring smile and overlooked her distress as he opened the door.

"I won't hurt you," he repeated as he led her into the room "and I won't force you to stay against your will. You can leave any time you want."

Her eyes widened as he clicked the lock into place, but she didn't say anything.

"Don't worry, Gracie. It unlocks as easily as it locks." He flipped the lock open then closed again. "I want to give us some privacy, but if you decide to leave, you can go at any time. Since we're in my suite, you don't have to ask me to leave and wonder if I'll go or not.

"You don't have to say anything at all, for that matter. Just open the door and leave. There's also a connecting door between the suites in the bathroom, if you prefer. My side is always unlocked. Your side is yours to do with as you will. Satisfied?"

"I wasn't afraid." Her jaw pinched shut with the mutinous look he was coming to adore.

But the word afraid lodged in his gut. Most women her age would have acted with enthusiasm at his suggestions, taking what he offered and much more. Most would have attempted to seduce him, not bolt at the thought of his hands on her. But Gracie wasn't most women. She was a special someone—*hona* in his language—a person deserving of great care and consideration.

He'd teach her that she never needed to be afraid, even if it took every ounce of self-control he possessed.

"Let's test that theory." He plastered a cocky grin on his face and sauntered over to the bed, tossing aside the quilted royal blue and silver cover. "Are you brave enough to come over here and lie down?"

Fire flashed in her eyes. "Really, Stephan, it's just a massage. Why make it into such a big deal?" She marched to the bed and threw herself down on the pristine white sheets.

"Precisely my thoughts." He kept his voice cool and dry. Lucky for him she had her face buried in the pillow. He didn't have to hide his amused looks. Give Gracie a challenge and she rose to the occasion.

Stephan settled on the bed next to her and ran his hand lightly down her back. She giggled. He deepened the touch, reminding himself that he'd promised to be good and not torment her. At least not now.

"Let's see what's going on here," he mused half to himself, reverting to his native tongue. He ran his hands across her shoulders, feeling the tension in the bunched muscles.

"Stephan?"

"Yes, *mi'hona*?"

"Could you speak English? Please? I haven't got a knack for languages."

"Then let me take the opportunity to tell you that you are delectable, intelligent, high-spirited, and the most pig-headed woman that I've had in my bed for a long time," he said in Melesian before switching to English. "I'll do my best."

"Thanks. Even with over a year of study, I can't speak your language."

He rubbed oil on his hands and started to warm up the tense muscles in her shoulder. "You can, but you don't want to," he said softly in his native tongue.

"What?"

He repeated himself in Melesian, giving her a moment to translate and understand the words before repeating them a third time, in English. "You don't want to because you're afraid of making a mistake. Of being less than perfect."

Stephan moved his hands to her neck, sliding beneath the halter style top of her bathing suit and unfastening it in a move so smooth she barely twitched. He continued the sensuous slide across her slender neck and down again to her shoulders.

"I make too many mistakes," Gracie muttered into the pillow. "I feel stupid trying to search for words. My tenses come out garbled. My pronunciation stinks. My—"

"Excuses." He pinched a bunched muscle between his fingers, and she let out a hiss. "Easy, *mi'hona*, it's just another very tight spot. We need to convince these muscles to relax."

He soothed her with his other hand and picked up the discarded threads of their discussion. "You were probably too brilliant as a child to realize this, but mistakes are all a part of learning. They are nothing to be embarrassed about."

"Listen to you with your perfect English, lecturing me on languages. You're just like Jill."

He laughed. "There are many, many ways in which I am different from your sister. Shall I expound on them? For starters, there are the basic differences in anatomy."

"I don't need an anatomy lesson, thank you."

"Too bad. It was one of my favorite subjects." He eased the pressure on the tight spot and slid his hands along her shoulder blade, coaxing the muscles to relax, teasing them with a variety of firm, then light, strokes until he felt her entire body begin to go limp.

"You're very good at this." Gracie let out a contented sigh and sank deeper into the mattress. "How did you learn to give such a good massage?"

"Like I said, anatomy was one of my favorite subjects. I had a tutor once who helped me understand the muscular-skeletal system by teaching me the basics of massage. Years later, it made me very popular with the ladies."

"I can imagine."

"Can you?" He rubbed more oil in his hands and moved to her lower back, wishing the remaining strap of her bathing suit didn't block his way. "The good thing is that I enjoy giving pleasure as much as I do receiving it."

"That's a classic pick-up line if I ever heard one."

Her stilted, uncertain teasing hit the mark—somewhere near his heart. What he'd once mistaken for prickly spines of self-defense, what had caused her friends to think her untouchable and awkward, was so much different. He wondered how many times she'd been rebuffed, driving her further into her shell.

"I've got others if that one doesn't suit," he teased back. "How about these? Heaven must be missing an angel, because you're here with me. Or, do you want me to call you in the morning, or just nudge you?"

"Stop. Please. They're getting worse." Laughter rippled through her, making her quiver under his hands.

The satiny texture of her skin coupled with the litany of corny lines had him thinking with the primitive parts of his brain. His body was tighter than hers and hard.

She, on the other hand, was toned, but soft in all the right places. Or at least she looked soft. He still had enough control to know that pushing her too far and too fast would destroy the tenuous link between them.

He watched the rise and fall of her breathing as he used the heel of his hand to ease the tension in her lower back. A few inches lower, and he'd test out his own theories, both about the softness of her curves and the intensity of her reaction to him. But it was too soon to experiment with her.

"So, Miss Bradley, what makes you such an expert in pick-up lines?"

"Oh, dear. Are we back to being formal again? Stephan Hercules Tantalus D'Malia is such a mouthful."

"Careful, *mi'hona*, or you'll be nominated for the worst pick-up line ever." He felt her still beneath him, then gasp as she caught his meaning. But she didn't try to leave. He pressed his luck. "Still having second thoughts about staying? Or do you trust me a little more now?"

"I trust you."

"Enough to let me undo this?" He ran his hand under the offensive strap, caressing her bare skin.

She nodded, but the minute he unhooked the slender pink barrier, she tensed. He pretended not to notice, moving his hands up and down her body in smooth gliding strokes until the tension ebbed again.

"Why Tantalus?" she asked, her voice warm and thick as the pleasure melted her resistance. "Stephan and Hercules, I understand. Both were examples of the best of their culture. But Tantalus?"

He stilled his motions, surprised by the question. "Why not? It fits." His fingers drifted across her soft, slick skin, enticed by the feel of her. No longer kneading or massaging. Just touching. Enjoying.

"Do you remember your mythology?" he asked softly. "Tantalus offended the gods and for punishment he was trapped forever in paradise surrounded by succulent fruits and streams of the purest water imaginable. But whenever he bent to drink, the streams receded. And when he tried to eat, the fruit moved just beyond his grasp. He was surrounded by the illusion of plenty, but he had nothing."

"That doesn't fit you. You are surrounded by plenty and you enjoy it all."

"Yet I have a beautiful and enticing woman with me who shies away at the barest hint of intimacy." He slipped his hand just under the elastic of her bathing suit bottom to touch the softly rounded curves. She tensed.

"See what I mean?"

"I'm not beautiful or enticing, Stephan."

"But you do shy away from my touch." He traced the line of the suit with a single finger, easing it down by mere millimeters. He caught a tempting blur of color at the base of her spine, but he put off investigating until later. There would be other times. He'd make sure of it.

Her breathing deepened, and she fisted the sheets, but she didn't move away. "Don't forget. You can leave at any time."

"I don't want to leave." The drowsy admission sent a quiver of tension racing through her body that belied her words.

"Stay as long as you like." Stephan eased himself farther onto the bed beside her and stretched out, still running a soothing hand along her back until she adjusted to the new positions and let her defenses sag again.

The weight of his body caused the mattress to dip and she rolled closer to him, giving him a tantalizing glimpse of the curve of her breast. For now, he contented himself with looking and imagining.

He stroked down her back until his hand rested on her Lycra covered butt. He caressed the bare skin above the waistband with a thumb while enjoying the lush feel of her soft curves beneath his palm and fingers. Today the gods were being generous with him.

"You are far more tempting than you realize." The feel of her back pressed to his naked chest and her butt fitted snugly between his hand and his groin teased his hardness in a way that tormented him with the promise of great pleasure — eventually.

Gracie's budding trust in him could develop into so much more if she kept her defenses down. He could easily envision a future together at some point, once he'd solved the current batch of problems laid at his feet. It was something he'd never thought of with other women. He and Gracie shared common interests. Intellect. Attraction. It was more than many royal couples had. But he was getting ahead of himself.

He'd thought that earning Gracie's trust, breaching her defenses, and getting close to the woman inside required baby steps. A thousand baby steps from now…who knew what could happen?

But the way she pressed against him felt more like a leap than a baby step. Despite the intimacy, she didn't run. Nor did she flinch when he kissed the back of her neck and pulled her closer.

Out of the corner of his eye, he saw afternoon sunlight glinting off the water, sending a thousand twinkling shafts of light through the seaward windows of his suite. It was as if the gods were winking and laughing among themselves at his folly.

It was then he realized the luscious fruit he thought he'd grasped had receded out of reach after all.

Gracie was asleep.

Chapter 15

For the first time in days, her dreams hadn't disrupted her sleep. Gracie stretched under the covers, luxuriating in the softness of the sheets and the faint sounds of the ocean outside of her window. She snuggled deeper into the bed, not wanting the alarm to pull her to full wakefulness.

The scrape of the satin cover against her bare breasts felt unfamiliar. No, not unfamiliar. Wrong.. Something was wrong with her room. She didn't own a satin bed cover, and she didn't sleep naked. Wakefulness surged through her as she sat up letting the blue and silver cover fall to her waist.

Outside the window, the sky was painted with a purple-blue tinge that signaled the onset of evening. Inside, she was surrounded by an opulence that didn't fit her dorm room. The maroon and gold furnishings told her she was in the guest suite of Stephan's yacht. The blue and silver cover pooled at her waist reminded her that she had been in his room.

The memory of his touch was imprinted on her body, even hours later. She'd followed him to his suite in the daylight and awakened in hers—no, not hers, but his other suite—at twilight.

She got out of bed and padded across the floor to stand at the window. No land was in sight. They weren't docked. Odd.

Her gritty eyes blurred her vision and her hair clung to her neck in ratty clumps as she headed to the shower. The tiled enclosure circled in a nautilus shell pattern until she reached the spacious expanse filled with multiple shower heads. The earth shaded tiles exuded warmth and comfort. But as she turned on the water, she was reluctant to wash the feel of Stephan's hands from her body.

Gracie hastily washed her hair then ran soapy hands over her skin, not bothering with a washcloth. She paused, caressing her breasts as she washed, wondering if Stephan had touched her there while she slept. She hoped not. She didn't want to miss the experience of his hands touching her breasts for the first time.

Of anyone's hands touching her intimately for the first time.

She slid her soapy hands over the rest of her body, touching the places where she'd only washed before. Skin on skin, without a barrier roused strange images and thoughts in her mind. The utilitarian necessity of a shower became a private, awakening experience.

All because of Stephan.

She shook her head at the strange thoughts and turned off the water. Since when did she, awkward, brainy, reclusive Grace Bradley, entertain herself with thoughts of a man caressing her body?

Hadn't Jill warned her years ago about letting her desires get in the way of her studies? Overnight, her sister had gone from helping her primp and play princess to urging her to avoid boys and stick to her books.

And overnight, she'd agreed. The ache of losing her father couldn't be soothed with the antics of hormone-crazy boys. If she'd found one of them who lived up to her father's image, she might have considered it, but none of them did.

But now, everything was different. Her sister was in love and expecting a child. And Gracie had fallen asleep in the bed of a handsome man who'd called her beautiful. She replayed the words in her mind, savoring the unfamiliar thought. Coming from him, the words sounded nice.

His smile was nice too.

His voice was lilting and beautiful with an accent to make girls melt.

His touch was more than nice. It was addictive.

Gracie wrapped herself in the terry robe and pulled a comb through her hair, reliving his touch, feeling her skin tingle at the memory.

But he'd left her. Banished her to the guest suite and wandered off. For the first time in her life, she regretted her decisions to follow Jill's advice. If she'd been as experienced as women her age were supposed to be, he wouldn't have left her.

If she'd given in and followed Barney "Brains" Baker to his home after the Math Team Championship Match in high school, she might have known how to react. But Barney hadn't tempted her. His kiss—a flat press of lips against hers while he held her with sweaty hands—didn't rouse her enthusiasm. She'd been more interested in calculating sine wave functions than in making waves with him.

None of the other boys in her past tempted her either. So she'd learned the basics of procreation from books and avoided any practical experience. Sex was messy. Illogical. Unnecessary—for her at least.

And for the first time in her life, it was tempting.

She finished her hair, dragged clothes from her duffel bag and went in search of Stephan. He didn't answer her knock on his door. He wasn't in the library. At last she found him on deck.

He stood, silhouetted against the evening sky looking out over the waves. The elegance of his simple slacks and shirt underlined her awkwardness. Her wrinkled shorts felt too casual, the tank top revealing. No wonder he'd relegated her back to the guest suite.

She drank in the sight of him from where she stood rooted a few feet away. Then he turned, almost as if he could feel her eyes on him.

"Hi, beautiful. I hoped you'd wake up soon."

"I'm not—" She clamped her mouth shut on the automatic denial. Why not enjoy the illusion for a few minutes? "Hi, yourself."

Stephan crossed the deck and took her hand in his. He led her to the deck rail. "I see your manners are improving." He flashed her a teasing smile. "I was getting a little frustrated having you contradict me every time I called you beautiful."

"I suppose the protocol teacher would have a fit if she learned about that."

"Undoubtedly. But I'm more interested in learning why you can't accept a compliment."

"I'm out of practice?" she ventured, hoping he'd let her joke her way off the subject.

"Then I consider it my duty to help you brush off those rusty skills. Besides, I mean it. There's something special about you, Gracie. Beauty isn't just about the shape of your face or the color of your hair. It's about the way you move and think. Your laugh. The way your eyes tell me a thousand things that your lips won't, and the way you come alive when you're underwater. It's about the whole package, not just the parts."

The warmth from his body surrounded her. His scent carried on the breeze that stirred the air between them. In the increasing darkness that surrounded them, nothing mattered except the connection she felt. She edged closer to him. "Wow. When you put it like that, it doesn't seem so bad."

"When did you start to think being beautiful was a bad thing?" he asked quietly.

"It's just that…" Gracie stared off in the distance, not wanting her past to interfere with the present. She waved her hand in a dismissive gesture and tried for a light tone. "Why primp when you can read?"

Behind them, someone cleared his throat. Stephan turned.

"Your Highness? Shall I serve dinner now that Miss Bradley is here?" Petros stood on the deck, waiting.

"Hungry, Gracie? Or shall we wait?"

She just stared, hopelessly ensnared by the look in Stephan's eyes. Her insides melted to mush, and it was all she could do to shrug. "Whatever you like."

"What I like is you. What I think we should do is eat." He nodded to Petros who disappeared below decks in an instant. "I hope you don't mind that I made the decision to stay out on the ocean tonight. We could dock if you'd rather, but I thought you might enjoy spending the night here and getting an early start in the morning."

"Spend the night?" Her confidence faltered.

"Don't worry," he said, his voice as soft as the evening air. "I've instructed Petros to refresh the guest suite for you. I promise, all I'm offering is a quiet evening, a little romance, and *separate* beds." She followed the movement of his throat as he swallowed. "Under those conditions, will you stay?" He rubbed his thumb along her knuckles sending shivers through her.

"Yes. Yes, I will." The smile that leapt into his eyes at her response made her hot all over. She'd spend the night leaning on the deck rail holding hands if she could. Or doing anything else he asked her to do.

It was crazy, dropping all her inhibitions for a single, romantic night, but she'd never had one, and she deserved it. Besides, the giddy rush carried her along as surely as if she'd been adrift in a dinghy during a storm. It was time. And she'd rather have one fantasy night with Stephan than a lifetime with a brainy, boring scholar.

She didn't fool herself into thinking that he'd want forever. He didn't even want to share her bed. They were from two different worlds. He was a polished diplomat—a player on the international stage. She was a reclusive researcher at heart.

It didn't require complex statistics to calculate the odds on a future for them. Besides, even if they moved beyond the other hurdles, she refused to spend a lifetime hiding her intellect to protect a male ego.

Common wisdom—and her own experience—had shown her that attractive men and smart women were oil and water. They didn't mix well and never stayed together.

But her intellect didn't make her tingle the way Stephan's touch did. It didn't make her melt like his smile did. It was something she was willing to sacrifice for the sake of tonight.

Several hours and a bottle of champagne later, Gracie leaned back in her chair and stared at the stars. The islands were truly paradise with stars that blazed rather than just shone.

"This has been a wonderful evening," she said in halting Melesian. "Thank you for inviting me." It wasn't quite what she wanted to express, given her limited vocabulary, but it was close.

"What?" Stephan leaned toward her, looking shocked, until she saw the crinkle of amusement around his eyes. "Did I just hear my native language from your lips?"

"I probably butchered it. But I—"

"Say it again." The low soft command sent shivers of pleasure up her spine.

Gracie complied.

"Good," he praised, his voice warm with approval. "It was brave of you to risk mistakes." He stood and motioned to her. "Come here, Gracie."

"Why?" Unconscious power and arrogant sensuality radiated from his stance, turning her knees weak, and her insides liquid. But she walked toward him anyway.

"Courage like that deserves a reward, don't you think?" He wrapped his arms around her and threaded a hand through the hair at the nape of her neck. She was immobile. Imprisoned. But willingly so.

"I'm proud of you," he whispered, his lips hovering near hers. "It pleases me to hear you speak my native language."

Gracie felt, as well as heard, his words. They shimmered, hot and vibrant between them until the words turned into the tangible press of his lips to hers.

His hands touched her back again, awakening memories of how he'd worked oil into her skin hours ago. And his lips played over hers in a warm, moist, magical way. This was the way kissing should be. Lips, and hips, and toes touching and melding. Swirling, squishy warmth surging and tingling in an electric web of excitement. This was worth waiting for.

"So, do the rewards outweigh the risks, *mi'hona?*"

"*Aaya,*" she replied in his tongue. "Yes."

"Good. Practice your language skills with me anytime. I promise even better rewards as your proficiency progresses."

Heat surged to her cheeks, but she didn't care. "And if I make mistakes? What then?"

"Ah. Mistakes. Mistakes have consequences. Too many of them and you'll have to pay a penalty."

"Such as?"

"You'll have to return the kisses you earned earlier." The starlight wasn't bright enough for her to see his expression, but she heard the smile in his voice.

"I think I can handle it."

"Good." One hand played at the nape of her neck, sending shivers down her spine to where he held her close with the other hand.

"Kiss me again," she murmured in Melesian.

"Very good, indeed." His lips whispered the words against her, and again, the words turned to touch, and the touch turned to fire.

And Gracie turned to lava.

Without the courage to ignore his self-imposed limit, this kiss would have to last her for a lifetime.

Chapter 16

Several days later, Stephan sat in his palace office. Only the quiet bubbling of his private aquarium, which took up an entire wall of the office, broke the silence. Home to the specimens he collected on his research dives, it looked forlorn and nearly empty now that he spent most of his days stuck on land. Except for the stolen hours with Gracie.

Someday, when the current crisis passed, maybe his time would be his own again. He looked forward to the time when he could immerse himself in his coral reclaim, wildlife breeding, and education programs. But for now, he had matters of national importance to attend to.

He logged on to the security team's encrypted site and scanned the latest news in the search for Sophia, hoping for a break.

Ophelia had cornered him recently with a change of tactics. Instead of discussing Sophia's inheritance of the de Lyons titles, she'd hinted that Stephan should find the tour and escort her home. She'd also made broad, sweeping statements about how Sophia had always enjoyed his company. Then, with a wink and a nod, she'd inquired about his love life.

It wasn't a conversation he wanted to repeat. Ever.

He scanned the site, pleased to see the latest diversions were buying him time to continue the search. Because the Melesian royal tours always included their own private press corps, he'd been able to keep her disappearance quiet. Only the other tour members, the royal family, and his staff knew of it at the moment. By splintering the group into smaller segments and moving them about, he'd created the image she was with one of the groups.

Reports of Sophia visiting remote locations peppered the international news from time to time. A digital photography expert in the press corps had satisfied the AP with a string of realistic looking photos of Sophia at various public locations.

Eventually, he'd dispatched most of the Melesian representatives to various consulates throughout the United States. Their presence might make it easier for the real Sophia to come to the consulate if she needed help.

But as more time passed—still without ransom notes, terrorist threats, or any evidence of foul play—the idea that she didn't want to be found seemed more likely than ever. Especially when the team checked into the de Lyons finances.

She'd left the country with thousands of dollars' worth of American money, plus she'd cleaned out most of the family jewels.

Stephan's undercover teams had located some of the jewels in pawn shops scattered around the Chicago area where she'd disappeared. They were searching other major cities for more, hoping they could track her movements.

They also searched the obituaries, looking for unidentified females that fit her description. Thank God nothing and no one had turned up.

He pulled up the file of pawn shops and entered their locations on a map while he chewed on a couple of antacids.

Nothing new.

A headache threatened, building behind his eyes. He massaged the spot between his eyebrows, seeking relief. The walls of the office closed in, turning the spacious office into a hot, airless chamber. He needed to walk around the grounds to feel the sea breeze.

After updating his instructions to the search team and logging off the site, Stephan locked up his notes and left the confines of the office. Outside the door, Nikki, his young page, snapped to attention.

"Can I do something for you, Your Highness?"

"*Aaya,*" he replied, "you can. Please find your father and have him report to me." Stephan smiled as the boy darted off, confidence and pride evident in his step. Letting the children of his staff members run his errands gave them a sense of their own importance in the kingdom. As long as their studies didn't suffer, he let them "work" for him, earning treats and other rewards.

Outsiders rarely understood the workings of the monarchy, Stephan mused as he waited for Nikki to return. Even Gracie, who should have known better, thought it a useless entity dedicated to indulgence. Most failed to understand that, as a prince, he was more servant to his people than the other way around. Their safety and prosperity rested on his shoulders.

The young ones reminded him that the sacrifices of his time, energy, and privacy were worthwhile. Their enthusiasm lightened his burdens.

When Nikki returned, Stephan left Nicholas Senior posted outside his office. Located in the public area of the palace, the office required extra security, but it also allowed him to entertain business guests without disturbing the family.

Satisfied that all was in order, he left the wing, crossing through the queen's private shopping gallery and into the grand salon. It was empty. He exited onto an open walkway that stretched beneath the royal apartments located on the upper floors.

He drank in the familiar, yet welcome, sight of his home. As a child, he'd scrambled over the wide porticos and often laid flat on his belly peering into the decorative ponds, watching the fish. He'd climbed the terraced walkways, pretending to search for hidden treasure, his imagination turning the sculpted fountains, trickling waterfalls, lush gardens, and private pools into a villain-infested jungle or a pirate's private paradise.

As an adult, he'd grown to appreciate the serenity of the landscape. The ocean with the private beach and lagoon lay just beyond the manicured water gardens. A fresh ocean breeze wafted past, and he let go of his worries while he inhaled the scent.

Stephan wished he could shed his suit jacket and with it his formal bearing, but he couldn't. Royal Island allowed occasional private tours to carefully screened groups of tourists. Today several groups on guided excursions milled around the pools and crowded the pathways.

They expected a prince, and a prince he would be. With jacket. And tie. And appropriately aloof attitude.

He crossed the patios to a bridge overlooking the largest marine pool, aware of sunlight glinting off the screens of cameras recording his every move. Pausing on the bridge, he watched as a flock of stingrays glided beneath him, their flat, diamond shaped bodies undulating in the water in a perfect V formation. A swordfish flashed by along with a school of smaller fish.

"Prince Stephan! Prince Stephan!"

The clamor of childish voices and the thunder of small feet on the bridge startled the fish and pulled his attention away from the water. So much for being aloof. He turned to greet his young supplicants.

"Guess what we learned in school today. We studied—"

"No, me first. I saw him first."

"Miss Jasmine, Master Jacob," Stephan interrupted the argument before it gained traction, "don't forget your manners. We have guests." He nodded to the tourists.

Six-year-old Jasmine immediately stilled then dropped into a perfect curtsey. "Your Highness," she said then popped back up. "Did I do it right?"

Stephan went down to one knee bringing himself closer to her level. "That was very good, but next time, you must allow me to take your hand and assist you." She curtsied again and this time waited until he bowed over her hand. She giggled with pleasure.

Her older brother followed suit, bowing correctly. All around, cameras clicked while Stephan chatted with the children. He asked them questions then gave them each a small coin as a reward for sharing their lessons with him.

He stood, turning to continue his walk. And found himself face-to-face with Gracie and a friend. Dressed in work uniforms, they were clearly returning from a break.

Gracie eyed the children then gave him a smile that sent shock waves careening through his body, jarring every bit of him into heightened awareness. He thanked his luck that the suit jacket hid his more private reactions from the cameras.

A tug on his slacks pulled him out of his trance. He looked down into Jasmine's serious little face. She reached out with her other hand and tugged on Gracie's skirt, gaining her attention too. "Don't forget your manners, Prince Stephan. We have guests."

"Thank you, Jasmine," he whispered. Beside Gracie, her friend was frozen in a deep curtsey. A pang of guilt stabbed Stephan for ignoring her. He reached for her hand and scanned his memory for her name. Marta Ohanii.

"Miss Ohanii. It is a pleasure seeing you again." He bowed over her hand and helped her stand.

"Your Highness."

Stephan turned to Gracie, who dropped into a curtsey as well. Her face, so full of joy a moment ago, was frozen in rigid lines.

He took her hand and squeezed lightly, trying to ease her discomfort as well as his own. Tension replaced her earlier ease. He felt its whipcord sting through his body when she didn't respond to his unspoken message.

He couldn't wink with her friend standing near. Couldn't tease with the crowds of tourists gawking and pointing. Couldn't do anything but retreat behind correct behavior. So he bowed over her hand, murmured her name, and excused himself as quickly as possible.

Stephan wandered through the tourists, welcoming the groups to his island home, and answering questions. Each handshake with a curious stranger brought him one step closer to his office, which suddenly seemed more haven than prison.

One step closer to the roll of antacids and bottle of aspirin that beckoned, promising relief for his throbbing head and burning gut.

"How did you adjust? There must be hundreds of rules governing behavior. It's impossible to keep up with." Gracie kicked off her shoes and sank onto the couch next to Jill. She turned to her sister, ignoring the plates of refreshments on the table in front of them. "You're as independent as I am. Didn't it make you crazy kowtowing to Constantine in public all of the time?"

A jolt of excitement surged through Jill at the sight of her sister, curled up next to her. Once they'd talked about anything and everything on the battered old couch in the family room back home. The look in Gracie's eyes held a hint of the old warmth.

Gracie continued to chatter about her frustrations with the palace regulations, but underneath, Jill sensed something else nagging at her sister. Even though she was twenty-one going on twenty-two, Gracie showed all the signs of a sixteen-year-old in the throes of first love.

Gracie wasn't even aware of how often Stephan's name popped up as she talked about school, research, and work. But Jill caught every reference. And she saw the look of adoration in her sister's eyes.

"My circumstances were very different from yours. Constantine and I…" Jill paused, suddenly feeling sixteen herself. "We knew each other very well before he told me who he really was."

Actually, he hadn't told her. She'd discovered it on her own right after the first night they made love. And she'd flown into a rage, throwing everything she could get her hands on at his head. No, propriety and protocol hadn't been a part of their relationship.

"But when you left Chicago and came here, didn't you have to abide by the local customs?"

Jill answered the question her sister hadn't asked. "Learning that Constantine was a crown prince instead of an import/export specialist was a shock. On top of that, I'd been used as part of a plot to discredit him. I didn't know what to think for days. I couldn't get used to using his real name, and the enormity of who he was terrified me at times."

"How did you cope?"

"Whenever I thought of him as the crown prince, I panicked. But when I thought of him as just a man—and a man that I loved—everything fell into place."

"It's hard to concentrate on the man when you're dressed like a servant and forced to curtsy like one." Gracie picked at the embroidery on her apron, loosening the threads as if she could unravel the tangle of her life by unraveling the stitches on her uniform.

"How do you think Stephan feels about it?"

Gracie's eyes flew to hers and she turned pink. "I didn't mean… It's not… We're not…"

"Of course, you did, Gracie. And it's okay." Jill reached for her sister's hand. "He talks about you almost as much as you talk about him. Since you've been diving together, he smiles more than he used to."

"Really?" The pink tinge on Gracie's cheeks increased, and her eyes glimmered with a soft light instead of the uncertainty of a moment before.

"Yes. I've been worried about him. Since Lady Sophia disappeared, he's not been the same. He blames himself and he worries about the political repercussions if she's not found soon."

Gracie focused her attention on tracing the apron's embroidery, lost in thought. A frown etched her face with worry. "What political repercussions?" she asked finally.

Jill waved her worries away, not wanting to burden her sister with any more worries about the traditionalist factions. Like Constantine and Stephan, she knew if Sophia's disappearance became public, the traditionalists could try to accuse the king of foul play in an effort to discredit—and perhaps depose—him.

But she also believed the D'Malia family was more than able to handle the traditionalists while maintaining the peace and security of Melesia.

"It's nothing. You asked me before how I adjusted to life in Melesia. Stephan helped a great deal. He never took himself too seriously, and he encouraged me not to take everything seriously, either. Back then, he saw humor in everything. He helped me see that island protocol is nothing more than a combination of good manners and a dash of fairy tale illusion."

"Formal manners, like you might use if you met the president," Gracie murmured.

"Something like that. But also simple manners and courtesy that everyone took for granted generations ago, even in the United States. That's changed at home but not here in Melesia.

"As for the fairy tale illusion piece, that's just another national product, like flower extracts or exotic fruit or marine life exports. It encourages tourism. Your work in the palace, your uniform, and your formal court manners are an important part of the national economy."

"It still feels strange—like being a servant stuck in another century."

"I don't have much insight on that, Gracie. I didn't have a student job here. I came to Melesia as a guest."

"And stayed on as a queen."

"Eventually. My role changed when I became engaged. Believe me when I tell you that being bowed and curtsied to isn't fun, either. But I belong to the people now, as much as if I'd been born into the royal family."

"Was it worth the sacrifice?"

Jill gathered her sister in her arms. "Honey, love is worth any sacrifice it requires of you. You'll understand someday." *Sooner than you might think, mi'cochida-ba, sooner than you might think.*

racie lingered in the grand salon, needlessly polishing the aquarium glass as she watched the setting sun streak the sky with orange and red. Without the crisp air of autumn, only the early end to the days told her that it was nearing the end of October.

She missed the seasons, missed the rest of her family, but as she stared out over the ocean, she knew, for the first time, that she'd miss even more if she were to leave Melesia.

Not that she was in love, as Jill seemed to imply. It took more than a couple of diving excursions to fall in love. More than a romantic dinner at sea.

More than a single kiss.

Or even two.

It took laughter. And friendship. Intelligent conversation. Common interests. Trust. But Stephan had given her all of that. He'd wrung confessions from her—things she'd never told anyone else.

Gracie dropped her cleaning supplies and stared out over the ocean. *It took passion*, she argued to herself. But the memory of her body awaking under his touch told her that they had that too. He'd caused her heart to flutter and her knees to go weak with only his smile.

The thought of loving someone—someone she could lose—terrified her. Attraction itself was an overwhelming emotion. But love? She struggled to come up with a reason why she couldn't love him.

Love took time. More than the few days or weeks that they'd shared.

"Miss? Miss Smith?"

She looked down to see a young boy, his hand resting over the one she'd unconsciously fisted in her apron. "Yes?"

"Prince Stephan sent me to ask if you would come and clean the glass on his private aquarium. You're the only one left for the night."

"He sent you?"

"I'm Nikki, his page."

"Aren't you a little young to be a palace employee?" She bit back a smile. Stephan always seemed to be surrounded by adoring children when he was at the palace. Her heart melted at the thought.

"Prince Stephan says I'm very responsible and mature." Nikki said, his voice full of importance. "He trusts me. So, will you come? I promised him I'd bring you."

Gracie nodded and followed Nikki, her heart thudding at the thought of seeing Stephan again. *Not love, not love, not love,* she repeated with each step. But her heart didn't listen.

At the door to his office, she paused. *Formal manners and fairy-tale illusion are national products,* she reminded herself, steeling her mind for another formal encounter.

Nikki urged her to go in unannounced.

Gracie took a deep breath and opened the door. He wasn't in sight. She took a few tentative steps into the office, ready to call out. The door closed softly behind her.

"Hey, beautiful."

She whirled, right into his arms. And banged his shin with her basket of cleaning supplies.

"Ouch. That thing is lethal. Put it down."

She dropped the basket and plastered an insolent grin on her face. "Your errand boy said you needed someone to clean the glass on your aquarium."

He gathered her closer and leaned back against the wall. "When I saw you were still here, I sent Nikki for you. I didn't what to suffer through another public encounter. This afternoon was difficult enough."

"So, you don't want anything thing cleaned?"

"Gracie," he frowned at her. "Nikki's eight. I didn't think he needed to know my real reasons for wanting you."

"Which are?"

Stephan cupped a hand around her neck and drew her close until she could feel his breath across her lips. "Which are exactly the reasons why you wanted to come here. I hope."

He kissed her with the same tenderness they'd shared on the yacht. Gracie clung to him, her arms tight around his waist, savoring the feel of his strength beneath her palms.

"Yes," she whispered against his lips. "This is what I wanted."

His touch, his taste, his warmth and breath mingled with hers, all of it was what she craved. Her knees buckled like sea legs unused to walking on land. She broke the kiss and rested her head on his shoulder as he cradled her in his arms.

"I'm sorry about earlier today." He rubbed her back, pressing her closer to him so that she could feel his heartbeat.

"I acted so stupidly. A little girl had to remind me how to behave."

His laughter rumbled through her body as well as his. "Actually, she was reminding me, and showing off a little bit too. I completely ignored your friend—who probably thought I was unforgivably rude."

"I don't know. I was too embarrassed to talk to her about it."

"That's the problem, Gracie. I grew up with court manners. So did nearly everyone else on the islands. To us, formal greetings are as natural as shaking hands or saying hello. To you, it's demeaning. I hated making you feel that way. It tore my heart out to see your smile fade and the light go out of your eyes."

"I'm sorry." Gracie traced the length of his tie, then slipped her hand under it to touch the buttons on his shirt. The warm feel of his muscles comforted her with memories of their time together on the yacht. "I didn't mean to hurt you either. And I think I understand a little better now. Jill helped me see things in a different light."

"Is that why you are here so late? Spending time with Jill? I'm glad, Gracie. She misses you."

Gracie felt her throat tighten at the thought of the years she'd missed with her sister and the first steps toward reconnection they'd made.

"The whole issue of formal greetings and court manners could all disappear if you took your place as her sister instead of hiding behind the name of Smith."

"I wish—" Gracie paused, weighing her need for family against her need for independence. But her promise to be Constantine's eyes at the academy meant that she couldn't change course now, no matter how much a part of her longed to. "I can't. Not just yet."

She leaned against Stephan's chest, absorbing his warmth and listening to the steady, calming beat of his heart. If she told him her new reasons for wanting to stay anonymous, he'd try to change her mind. And she didn't think she could resist his methods of persuasion.

"Take all the time you need," he whispered into her hair. "When you're ready to come out of hiding, I'll support you. Meanwhile, we could try to avoid each other in public, *mi'hona*, but that won't be easy."

"We'll just have to play our assigned roles. But I want you to know that I hate having to keep my distance from you." She pushed away from his embrace, grateful to have avoided more serious topics. "I hate the formal rules we have to abide by in public."

"It isn't easy on me, either, Gracie. I've had a lifetime of practice, but it's different when I'm with you. No matter what the circumstances, the first thing I see is the woman. The friend."

"That's the only thing I want to see too."

"Then look at *me*. See *me*. Not the situation." He cradled her hand in his and leaned close again. "I'll tell you a secret. I hate shaving, but I do it because it's part of my image. Next time we meet in public think about that. And if I do this," he stroked his thumb across his jaw, drawing her gaze to the movement, "it's my way of reminding you that I hate the distance and formality between us too."

She nodded, warmed by his need to reassure her. "At least you can pick out your own suits and ties. I have to wear this horrible, drab, scullery-maid uniform every single day. I hate it."

She stepped to the center of the room and twirled, disdainfully modeling the tan dress and embroidered full length apron that all the palace workers wore. Stephan's soft chuckle stopped her in mid spin.

"I can fix that." He leaned against the wall, his gaze searing her despite the distance between them.

"How?"

"Take it off."

"What? You can't be serious."

"I can be. I am. Take it off." His voice held a hint of command and a husky undertone of seduction that melted her will power and quickened her breathing.

"Stephan, we're practically in public. I would never do something like that."

He strode to the door and Gracie heard the snick of the lock falling into place. "Problem one solved. We're alone and no one is coming in without permission."

He prowled across the room, the gleam in his eyes making her take a step back. Not out of fear. But something made her heart pound.

"Take it off, Gracie. Shed the symbol of your oppression. Like I do." He shrugged out of his suit jacket and tossed it aside.

Another step forward for him.

A smaller step backward for her.

He loosened his tie and dragged it from his neck, letting it slither onto the carpet in a silken heap. "Be free," he whispered.

Another step and he captured her in his embrace. His lips were as gentle as before, yet subtly different. More demanding. He pulled the elastic band from her hair and tangled his fingers in it at the nape of her neck, urging her closer.

She felt a tug on her apron tie. Felt his hands work their way under the loosened fabric while the bodice flapped about her like a useless bit of trim on an unbecoming garment. "Be brave, Gracie. Take it off."

He tugged again on the smock-style apron, and Gracie let it slip from her arms to pool on the floor between them.

"Good," he whispered between kisses. "Keep going."

Stephan slid the zipper on her dress down a few inches and traced her exposed back with one finger. Electric desire tingled and snapped in his wake. Gracie wrapped her arms around his neck and returned his kisses with a fervor she didn't know she had, lost in the tingling, swirling void that sucked common sense away.

Another few inches and his palm spread across the middle of her back. Memories surged. His touch on the sunlit deck of the yacht. His touch as she sank into the cool sheets of his bed. Then, he'd been a friend. But now, with his lips playing against her and his tongue sweeping into the recesses of her mouth, he was something else.

When he lowered the zipper farther, she moved her hands to his waist clutching him for support. "Stop. I shouldn't." Everything was too fast, too new. She pushed, separating herself from him by mere millimeters. "I can't do this."

"No?"

"No. Not now." Visions of equations flashed through her mind, but she pushed them aside. "I'm not ready."

"So much for shedding the symbols of oppression," Stephan said as he slid the zipper back in place. His free hand remained on the curve of her spine, warm and tempting, but restrained. "I'd hoped you'd let me see your tattoo."

Gracie pulled back, far enough to look him in the eye. She didn't want to break the contact completely. "How did you know about my tattoo?"

Stephan nuzzled her cheek, his kisses less demanding but still enticing. "I saw a tiny bit of it the other day on the yacht. Just a flash of color. It's haunted my imagination ever since. Will you show me some day?"

"I don't think—"

"That's right, don't think." He kissed her temple, her ear, her neck in a slow series of drugging kisses that stole both her breath and her resolve.

"It's a butterfly." She gasped when he kissed a sensitive spot on her collarbone. "I got it when I was fifteen. I thought it would make me fit in with the other kids."

"Gracie, you'll never fit in. You were made to stand out. Don't hide your beauty."

"I'm not—"

He nipped the tender spot. "And don't contradict me. Or else I'll issue a decree making it illegal for you to do so."

"Oh my." Gracie ran a hand across the hard muscles of his chest. "That sounds ominous. I'm trembling with fear."

"That's not fear, and you know it." He nibbled his way back up to her ear. "But the idea of locking you up indefinitely does have its appeal."

Gracie pressed against him, grinding her hips to his. Physiology and health classes taught her to expect the swollen hardness between them, but they didn't teach her about her own itching, clawing desire to respond. That was new. Unexpected. And, embarrassed as she'd be to admit to it out loud, a little frightening.

She pulled away, overwhelmed by inadequacy, vulnerability, desire, and a myriad of other feelings she didn't understand. She wanted to run. She wanted to stay. She longed to fly free like the butterfly etched on her lower back, but she was fettered by a cocoon of safety. Unbidden tears threatened.

She drew a shaky breath and recited the equations for sine, cosine and tangent functions, the mathematical precision helping keep her tears at bay.

Almost instinctively, Stephan drew her close again, but gently. He didn't kiss her but rested his chin on her head. Tenderly, he stroked her hair. "It's okay, *mi'hona*. Take it easy. I promise, I would never hurt you. We have time. As much as you like." The rest of his words were a blur of Melesian, sprinkled with ones she recognized and many she didn't know. But his tone soothed and calmed her.

Her breathing slowed, and her heartbeat returned to its normal pace. "I'm sorry," she stammered, horrified to discover her voice was still shaky.

"Don't be," he whispered in English. "Don't be sorry for anything. I'm not."

Hours later, on the last ferry to Academy Island, Gracie gazed at the velvet blue sky wondering how different the evening would have been had she listened to her desires, instead of her fears. But the night stars held no answers.

Chapter 18

"Gracie, we're going to the opening bash for the main island's hottest new club. My cousin is their opening night DJ and even he had trouble getting us VIP tickets to Paradise Cove. You will *not* wear that."

Marta threw her a disgusted look and dug through her closet. "That outfit is only slightly better than the work uniform that you constantly complain about. Don't you have anything that doesn't look like it came out of your grandmother's closet?"

Gracie winced at the comment, remembering how Stephan had teased her about her black bathing suit. Maybe it was time for a serious shopping trip. She'd always picked her clothes for practicality and comfort, but now… So many things in her life were changing that maybe her wardrobe needed to change too.

"You know, I have something that might work." Marta disappeared into her adjoining room pausing to turn up the radio as she passed it. "This should get us in the mood for club hopping." She reappeared with a short turquoise wrap dress and thrust it at Gracie. "This will look much better on you than it does on me."

Marta pushed Gracie into the bathroom. "Go. Change," she shouted over the music. "And leave your hair loose for tonight. It's time you shed your inhibitions and had some fun."

Gracie slipped out of her basic black dress and shimmied into the clingy turquoise number. It was tighter than it looked. She checked herself in the mirror and burst into giggles at the sight of her white bra straps sticking out over the strapless bodice. Her mind wasn't on the evening ahead.

It was on her recent encounters with Stephan. As she unhooked her bra the memory of him opening her bathing suit strap with a mere flick of his fingers caused her skin to tingle. He'd stroked the same spot on her back last night and in her dreams, she'd followed his lead rather than running from it.

She wiggled back into the dress, letting the cool fabric mold to her breasts. Elegant shirring accented her curves without quite revealing everything.

As an afterthought, she slipped off her panties and let them join the discarded heap of clothing on the floor. Now nothing stood between her and the sleek second skin. Nothing but the memory of Stephan's hands which seemed imprinted on her restless body.

How would he react to the dress?

Take it off. His teasing words sizzled in her brain. *Take it off.*

She looked again into the mirror. The brilliant turquoise color—or the uncensored direction of her thoughts—transformed her face from plain to something else. She added a hint of coral to her lips and dusted her face and décolletage with a shimmering, translucent powder, her mind turning the touch of the soft brush into the sweep of Stephan's gentle fingers.

When she pulled the band from her hair, it fell past her shoulders, long, straight and somehow more golden than she remembered. Maybe it was the dress. Or the hours in the sun. But what she'd always considered a mundane feature now gleamed. She ran a brush through the mass, remembering how Stephan's hands had stroked her hair, her back.

Everything, from the touch of silky fabric to the hot salsa and steel drum music pouring from the radio reminded her of him. Gracie flushed and hurried from the bathroom, hoping the night with Marta would give her something else to think about.

"Big improvement. That dress looks like it was made for you." Marta waved Gracie's cell phone in front of her face. "By the way, the *hono* called while you were changing."

Gracie stared at her, confused.

"You know, the *hono*, the boyfriend. I told him you'd call him in the morning."

"What? You answered my phone?" Gracie snatched it from Marta's hand, her heart thumping as if she were a child caught with her hand in the cookie jar. Marta and Stephan.

"After he called three times in a row, I thought it might be urgent, so I picked it up. I was going to bring the phone to you, but he told me not to bother. I wasn't moving in on your territory, Gracie."

Gracie's momentary surge of anger ebbed to irritation. "I know you weren't. But I'm a very private person."

"When it comes to him, Gracie, you aren't just private, you're positively secretive. I know I shouldn't have answered your phone, but honestly, I'm a little worried about you. Some Melesian men think playing American women is a game. I didn't want you to fall in with one of them. All of your secrecy was setting off warning bells and whistles in my head. I wanted to make sure he wasn't a perverted jerk."

"You can tell that from a short conversation?"

"Well, no, not exactly." Marta fidgeted and looked away, not meeting Gracie's eyes. "But now he knows you have friends who'd turn him into lobster bait if he hurt you."

"You didn't."

"Funny thing was he seemed to appreciate the warning. He said he was glad you had such loyal friends. I think he's okay, Gracie."

"Of course, he's okay." Gracie shoved the phone into her clutch bag along with a tube of lipstick and a mirror. "He's... I mean, I'm not that bad a judge of character."

"Maybe not. But come on, tell me a little about him. All I know for sure is that he took my warning in the right spirit and he's got a sexy voice. If he looks as yummy as he sounds it won't be long before you'll have more than phone calls at midnight. Before that happens it's only fair of you to spill some details. I'm your best friend."

"There's not much to tell. He's just a guy."

"How about his name, for starters?"

"His name? It's, uh, it's Steve." The name sounded hollow and toneless to her ears, but even if she'd wanted to, how could she explain Stephan Hercules Tantalus D'Malia to Marta?

"Gracie, my warning signals are starting to sound again. What's his last name?" Marta crossed her arms and leaned against the door narrowing her eyes. "We're not leaving for the party until you tell me something concrete about him."

"Fine. You're the one who wanted to go to the club opening party, not me."

"I'm also the one with brothers in the security business. I swear I'll have one of them follow you if I don't get a little more information about this guy from you. If it's not a big deal, why won't you tell me?"

Gracie sank down on her bed and studied her fingernails for a moment, gathering her thoughts. It wasn't just who he was that had her tongue tied. It was what he was, or rather what he was becoming to her. The *hono*.

"Look, Marta, there's nothing wrong with him. Professor Pontileus vouched for him when he hooked us up as dive partners, so put your worries away."

Gracie kept her eyes glued on her hands and forced the next words out. "It's just that I never really had a boyfriend before, and everything feels strange. Like some fairy tale that could disappear in a minute if I talked about it. Like a birthday wish that you have to keep secret."

"Oh, Gracie." Marta crossed the room in a swish of tangerine silk and sat by her. "Boyfriends don't melt away if you talk about them. If they're the real thing, they just get better with time and girl talk. Besides, if he's a Melesian guy, you'll need my help to keep track of the relationship."

"I think I'll know when he's turning up the heat."

"You think so? Well, I can tell you a thing or two about our Melesian love language that I doubt is covered in your language class."

Gracie shuddered. "I'm sure of that. Professor Mikolas doesn't strike me as the type to have much interest in love lives."

"Protocol class is bad enough for you without having her for language too. No wonder you have a difficult time."

"It's getting better. St— Steve is tutoring me a little." The memory of his kiss rewarding her for her halting Melesian sizzled in her mind. "So, what do I need to know about love languages?"

"First, you need to know that we have at least half a dozen terms for what you Americans call boyfriend or girlfriend."

"I already understand the gender specific terms. *O* for male, *A* for female. Hono/hona. Boyfriend/girlfriend. What else is there to know?"

Marta shook her head. "This could take a while. Come on, Gracie. I'll tell you over drinks at the club. But don't think I'm going to stop pestering you for information about Steve Whatever-His-Name-Is. I still want to know all the juicy details— like why he makes you go all soft and mushy. Now, let's hit the road and party."

Gracie and Marta mingled outside the club with a crowd consisting mostly of wealthy American tourists, a smattering of international celebrities, and hordes of paparazzi. High masts flying tattered banners rose stories above their heads.

The club, built to look like two cracked halves of a sunken pirate ship from the outside, cast an eerie ambiance over the crowds. At last they approached the door, crossing over a rickety looking rope bridge suspended above an artificial lake.

"It doesn't look like there are many locals in the crowd," Gracie whispered to Marta in Melesian.

"There never are at the newest attractions. The idea is to attract the tourists. The local customers usually take over once the hype dies down. You won't have to worry about having any language barriers tonight."

"Just when I'd come prepared to practice my Melesian." Gracie handed her pass to the attendant at the door.

"You can still practice." Marta grinned at her. "Let's start with that lesson in love languages."

As they passed into the interior of the club, all thoughts of language—love or otherwise—popped out of Gracie's head. The entire floor, most walls and even parts of the ceiling consisted of thick Plexiglas barriers where a variety of tropical fish swam beneath, beside and around them. Any solid supports and fixtures were cleverly disguised as part of a coral reef or the sunken ship.

It was a wonderland of illusion, almost like the magical world where she and Stephan dove off Neptune's Crown Reef, only here she walked through the world unencumbered by oxygen tanks or wet suits.

A tingle shivered down her spine as she raised her eyes and saw a second level balcony, covering a portion of the room and appearing to float over the dance floor. "What's up there?" she asked Marta.

"The biggest fish of all, I'd guess. Usually when there's this much interest in an attraction, someone from the royal family or the ranking nobility sponsors the festivities. The tourists love it."

As if on cue, Stephan stepped to the railing of the second floor and smiled down at the guests. The Melesian nobles at his side faded into insignificance as Gracie caught his eye across the crowd. Her heart beat faster and warmth flooded her when his glance touched on her, creating a physical sensation as real as if he'd run his finger along her cheek. Or at least she thought he'd seen her, but looking out over the crowd, how could he pick her out?

He drew his thumb slowly across his jaw in the secret sign that he was uncomfortable with the distance between them. Gracie's skin tingled at the movement, but when he turned to the man next to him, she wondered. *Was* it their secret sign? Or just an unthinking action on his part?

She tried to shrug off her reaction. From that distance, it was no more intimate than the gods peering down on the mortals from Mount Olympus.

I'm still a god, and you're a mere mortal, like Eros and Psyche. Stephan's teasing voice echoed in her memory. She'd dismissed his reference the day they first met on his yacht, but in the weeks since, hadn't it become more applicable?

He'd reached down into her world and, against all probability, found her desirable. She shook her head at the notion. Gracie Bradley didn't belong anywhere near the glittering stars of his world.

But wasn't that, too, a part of the myth? Eros desired the mortal Psyche because he was ensnared in a web of his own making. And only by facing impossible tasks could she prove herself worthy of him.

The thought sent a wave of reality crashing over her. What webs might Stephan weave if he so desired? And could she face the impossible tasks his world would demand of her?

"I told you it was a big fish," Marta murmured in her ear. "The biggest catch in the islands these days is the Bachelor Prince. I bet at least half a dozen American tourists will drop into a swoon over him tonight.

"Another three or four will try to stuff an article of clothing in his pockets. Not all of them single. And not all of them women, for that matter. Let's get a table near the dance floor and prepare to watch the show."

"Marta, that's cruel. The prince isn't a piece of meat to be fought over by a gaggle of women."

"Maybe not, but that's what always happens. And marriage only slows them down. King Constantine still has women throwing themselves at his feet begging for attention. I feel sorry for the royal family when they deal with masses of tourists. At least most Melesians have some respect for their privacy."

"It must be awful. Like being married to a rock star. Or being the rock star. Maybe that's why formality and protocol evolved, to give them some breathing room."

"I suspect you're right. I can't imagine being hounded by drooling, drunken fools trying to get my attention."

As Gracie and Marta made their way to a table, Gracie felt a stab of pity for Stephan, imagining him at the mercy of the party crowd. But when she searched out his gaze again, he'd turned from the railing, effectively, if temporarily, shutting out the masses below.

"We're in luck. Here's a spot." Marta pulled her to a pedestal table near the edge of the dance floor and flagged down a passing waiter. After putting in their drink orders, she turned to Gracie. "Now, let's get back to your boyfriend, and the love languages. For starters, what does he call you now?"

"Well, other than my name, he calls me *mi'hona*. I didn't stop to think about what it meant until tonight. That means girlfriend, doesn't it?"

Marta hesitated, as if choosing her words. A tiny frown line puckered her forehead. "Gracie, don't fall too hard for this guy yet. The prefix *mi* is short for *mico*, which means little or small. *Mi'hona* roughly translates into *little sweetheart*. It's affectionate, but not too serious."

Gracie's heart twisted a little. In the last hour, she'd convinced herself that his words of endearment meant more. "So it's a term someone might use for their friend's little sister?"

"It's not quite that bad. Besides, men are usually slower than women to put their feelings into words. He may just be taking his time, Gracie.

"If he starts to call you *hona-mei*, my sweetheart, that's a lot more intimate. And *er'hona* and *er'hona-mei*," Marta fanned herself and cracked a mischievous grin. "*'Er'* comes from the Greek word *Eros*, meaning erotic love. *Er'hona-mei* is *my desirable one*."

"Like Eros and Psyche," Gracie murmured. The image of entwined lovers was at odds with the tame endearments he'd showered on her.

"Exactly. But it usually takes an islander a long time to work up to calling a woman his *er'hona-mei*. It's a big step and a commitment for them."

"So that's at the top of the list?"

"No." Marta's eyes grew misty and she stared off into space. "The top of the list is *ba'hona-mei*. The closest your English can come to capturing the meaning is *my beloved one, beloved spouse*, or *soul mate*. It's really so much more than that. I can't describe it. But every woman dreams of being *ba'hona-mei* to someone in her life."

Ba'hona-mei. The word echoed in Gracie's mind just at the edge of her imagination. *Ba'hona-mei. Ba'hono-mei.* Her eyes followed the fish swirling around beneath the dance floor and in the wall-sized aquariums around her as the words tumbled over and over in her mind like driftwood caught in a whirlpool.

Ba'hona-mei. Jill. That was what Constantine called Jill. Her imposing brother-in-law, King of the Caribbean Archipelago Nation of Melesia and formidable international statesman, got soft around the edges when he looked at Jill and called her *ba'hona-mei.* Recalling the look in their eyes, Gracie knew exactly what it meant.

And she knew she wanted someone to look at her that way. To love her. She eyed the balcony. Could Stephan, would he… Surely, that was a foolish thought. But even as her mind pushed the thought away, her heart held it close.

"Ladies, if you'll excuse me." The waiter appeared at the table, pulling them from their thoughts as he placed a bowl of pineapple, strawberry, coconut and kiwi in front of them. "A gentleman guest of the club asked me to bring this to you. I've been instructed to keep your glasses full for the duration of the evening."

He presented a bottle of champagne and popped the cork. After filling two flutes, he turned to Gracie and, with a bow, presented a note to her. "The gentleman also asked me to give you this. Ladies, enjoy the evening."

Gracie opened the note, savoring the feel of each crisp fold, prolonging the moment. Only one person would have sent it. His handwriting, she realized, was unfamiliar. Yet the note left no doubt.

The gods tantalize me tonight with your beauty, near at hand, yet ever out of reach.
An Admirer

"Gracie, let me see." Marta leaned over to inspect the note. "Wow. I think your *hono* is going to have some competition."

Heat washed over her, and the mythical lovers' image rose unbidden in her mind as Gracie glanced at the balcony. He was there, watching. And this time she knew his gaze wasn't fixed on the crowd, but on her. Acting on instinct, she took the note, refolded it and slipped it into the bodice of her dress in the warm, tight space between her breasts and the shimmering folds of material. Even without watching him, she knew he followed her movements.

Gracie reveled in the surge of power unlike anything she'd ever experienced. Pure, strong feminine power pulsed through her with each breath. Each heartbeat. She plucked a strawberry from the bowl and swirled it in the chilled champagne before raising it to her lips and slowly sucking the cool juice from its flesh.

She bit the fruit, enjoying the burst of sweetness along with the tang of the champagne. It was intoxicating, knowing that he followed her every move.

Even as Marta pulled her back into the conversation, exchanging bits of gossip and flirting with the other guests, a part of Gracie's mind remained on Stephan, hovering on the edge of her awareness, doing his royal duty, but regarding her with an intensity that belied his cool exterior.

She angled her body and crossed her legs, letting the dress slide up her thigh to expose a bit more flesh. Another strawberry. More champagne sucked from the fruit. And for the first time in her life, she felt like a temptress.

Chapter 19

Stephan gripped the railing of the balcony and smiled down on the crowd, careful not to let the tension that ripped through him show in his face. He could have sworn that Gracie didn't have a single manipulative cell in her body, but the seductive tricks she pulled out tonight proved him wrong.

Where in the hell had she learned to tease and torment a man from across the room? Those weren't things a woman learned from a book.

His knuckles turned white and his hand cramped, but he didn't ease his strangle hold on the railing. If he were any other man, he'd drag Gracie out of the club into the nearest grove of palm trees and kiss her senseless.

Not the tame kind of kisses they'd shared up to this point, either. No—he'd indulge in hot, reckless, ungentlemanly kisses. The kind of kisses that led to more. Much more. To exactly what Gracie was begging for with her lips and tongue and teeth as she toyed with that bowl of fruit.

And he wouldn't stop till he'd peeled that indecent turquoise dress from her body and devoured every last inch of her. If he were anyone else, he'd teach her the consequences of flirting with fire.

But he wasn't any other man. He was an icon. A tourist attraction. A member of the royal family. And tonight it was his duty to welcome the tourists that brought prosperity and wealth to his people.

So, despite the image of Gracie that seared his mind, he cooled his passions to a simmer. Tonight he was a prince. Later, when he was alone with Gracie, he'd be the man he longed to be. And neither of them would ever be the same.

"Careful, my friend, or the guests will see that something's eating you." Apollo Mikolas leaned against the railing and eyed the crowd below, his smile warming as he assessed the women. "You wouldn't want to disappoint the American beauties. Our Queen Jillian is quite possibly more popular in her birth country than Monaco's late Princess Grace.

"Every American woman down there wants a chance to be the next royal bride. The D'Malia charm is almost as profitable as pearls and perfume extracts to our national economy."

"It may be profitable, but it's in short supply."

Apollo snagged two glasses of champagne from a waiter and passed one to Stephan. "Being the heir to all those romantic illusions can't be that bad. Relax and enjoy yourself for once. Most men dream of nights like this. You could have your pick of any of the swarming beauties."

"You're the party type, Apollo. You should be charming the ladies, not me."

"You always were out of step with Constantine and the others. You're a blond-haired, blue-eyed changeling."

"I may not have my family's coloring, but I'm no less a D'Malia than my brothers." In his present mood, Apollo's jibes didn't roll off his back the way they always had in the past.

Instead they awakened centuries of inbred arrogance. Stephan felt a dangerous ripple of anger pass through his body as he stared the other man down.

Apollo laughed, apparently unmoved. "Take it easy, *Your Highness*. Unlike my dear Aunt Ophelia and Cousin Dorinda, I wasn't questioning your legitimacy or your bloodlines. Just your taste. You're the only member of the entire Melesian nobility who prefers a library full of books to a room full of women. It's not natural, Stephan."

The anger drained from his body, taking with it his lustful fantasies of hot sex in the palm grove. He glanced down at Gracie, now engaged in conversation with her friend. Her tight little body still stirred him, but he remembered a dozen other equally enticing attributes.

"What's so wrong about wanting a woman with a sharp mind as well as a beautiful body? Don't you ever want to have an interesting conversation with a woman?"

Apollo sipped the champagne and continued to peruse the dance floor. "Come to think of it, no." He shrugged, avoiding Stephan's gaze. "I don't stay with one woman long enough to crave conversation. And trust me, unlike you and King Constantine, the last thing these women want from me is a dissertation on the economic challenges facing Melesia in the coming decade."

"Maybe that's why you don't stay with them."

"Ah, but that's the proverbial chicken and egg question, isn't it? In any case, I'm not the one with a strangle grip on the railing and a smile that looks like it's about to crack into a million pieces. So, is it a woman that's got you in knots? Or something else?"

"It's a woman." Stephan turned from the railing and led the way to a private table at the back of the mezzanine floor.

"Lucky for you I came along. My expertise is at your service. Tell me about the woman. Then I'll tell you how to forget about her while the party girls below untie those knots for you."

Stephan discarded his untouched champagne flute and signaled the waiter. He downed a handful of antacids from his ever-present stash and discretely ordered the waiter to bring him only non-alcoholic drinks. He needed to keep a clear head. And a calm gut. It was going to be a long night.

Gracie lost track of how many times the waiter refilled their glasses as he wound his way among the crowds of patrons. Wealthy tourists might have to wait for their drinks, but Prince Stephan himself had asked the waiter to keep them happy. Apparently, the man took the request literally. If Marta wondered at the excellent service, she didn't mention it.

Gracie shot a look toward the balcony. Stephan had disappeared into the shadows. She settled into her high-backed chair and turned to Marta. "So, how do I get Steve to see me as more than just a *mi'hono*?"

Marta giggled and pushed her drink aside. "Gracie, that's funny. You almost had me spewing champagne everywhere."

"I didn't mean anything funny—"

"That's why it was funny. For starters, don't call a man *mi* anything. *Mico*—small. *Maco*—big." She mimed her words with gestures, still giggling. "All men like to think they're big. Big income. Big, important job. Big muscles. Big…ego. You get the picture. Big. Special. Person. *Ma'hono*. Don't spoil their illusions."

"Okay. Rule number one, don't step on the ego." Privately she doubted Stephan's ego would respond to anything she said or did. He was too self-assured, too calm. He didn't need ego. He was the real thing. "*Ma'hono*," she said carefully articulating the words in Melesian, "is a big man with an important job, a killer smile, and eyes that could make a girl melt."

"If your *hono* is so perfect, then why did you tuck the secret admirer note into your bodice? I think the jury is still out on your *hono*."

"A secret admirer is just that. Secret. A fun fantasy for a night. But St- Steve is more than a fantasy lover. He's real."

"As in really your lover?"

"Not exactly," she hedged. "I mean we haven't...I haven't... He's— Not yet."

Gracie grabbed her champagne flute and gulped, suddenly overheated. It was the packed club. That had to be the reason she felt flushed. The music's volume suddenly increased and people surged past them onto the dance floor.

The crowds, the built-in aquariums filled with darting fish, and the pulsing change in the lights around the dance floor made her dizzy. She pressed the cool glass to her temple and focused on Marta. "I mean he's my real *hono*. My *hono-mei*. *Mei-hono-mei-hono-mei*. Oh God, it's like some Melesian tongue twister."

"Tongue twisting can be good. Really good if the *hono* knows what he's doing." Marta giggled. "So what do you guys do when you're not diving? That can't be the only time you see him. Does he work at the palace? Is he the reason you're suddenly pulling extra shifts and staying until the last ferry?"

"He shows up on Royal Island once in a while. But that's not the reason I'm working extra shifts." Gracie looked at her friend, suddenly sick of all the secrets and intrigues that defined her life. The fuzzy comfort of a champagne-induced haze made her want to confess everything. "Marta, do you have any sisters?"

"Me? No. Just brothers. Why?"

"I have three sisters. One older and two younger. They're all so sure of themselves. So outgoing. My older sister is especially beautiful. She has everything—a loving husband, a child on the way. And the girls are growing up to be just like her.

I'm the middle sister that no one ever notices. The brainy, invisible one."

"You only think you're invisible. You hide behind your books and pretend no one can see you. But look at yourself tonight. I'm not the one with a secret admirer. You are. He thinks you're special. So does your Steve. You're the only one who can't see it."

"Thinking of myself that way feels strange. Foreign. It's hard to believe it's real."

"If you don't believe me, maybe you'll believe him." Marta shot a glance at a tall, dark figure headed across the dance floor toward them.

Gracie barely had time to assess the arrogant set of his stride and the slight condescending tilt of his head before he stood beside their table.

"Ladies," he said in Melesian accented English, "it's a shame to see two such beautiful women drinking alone. Would you do me the honor of this dance?" He held out a hand to Gracie.

"I'm sorry. I don't dance."

His brow crinkled, and he made an impatient motion with his hand. "Of course, you do. Everyone dances. Especially at a club opening."

"No," Gracie said more firmly, twisting to show him her profile. She fiddled with her glass, staring at the empty flute. "I prefer not to."

"Then perhaps your companion will ease my wounded pride." He smiled at Marta, a smooth, polished demeanor replacing his frown.

Gracie sighed in relief as the couple headed to the dance floor. Dancing had been the farthest thing from her mind when she agreed to accompany Marta to the club. Now she realized her mistake. At least the upbeat steel drum and calypso tunes didn't evoke the same memories as the classic 1940's dance tunes.

Her gaze flitted over the floor, absently taking in the couples until she saw Stephan partnering a slinky brunette. The music changed and a stocky blonde replaced the brunette. Stephan's smile didn't waver, but Gracie detected a stiffness in his movements. His partner edged closer to him even as he moved away in time to the music.

"Gracie, what's wrong with you?" Marta hissed as she eased back onto her chair. "Do you know who that was asking you to dance?"

She shook her head.

"That was Apollo Mikolas, the next Marquis of Elonyia. Next to the D'Malias and the de Lyons, he's from one of the most influential families on the islands."

"Is he related to Professor Mikolas?"

"Of course, he is, but that's not the point. He's gorgeous, wealthy, influential, and he could be your secret admirer."

"I don't think so. Besides, if he's related to Professor Mikolas, it would just spell more trouble for me." Gracie's head cleared a bit as a jolt of adrenaline shot through her system. This could be a chance for her to learn something that might be useful to her brother-in-law. Maybe she could force herself to flirt with Apollo.

"From what I've heard, the professor's relationship with the rest of the family is frosty at best," Marta said, answering her unspoken questions. "It's the same with the rest of the nobility. For as much as she defends tradition, she defied the king and refused to attend the royal wedding. Of course, she claimed an illness, and he graciously overlooked it, but no one really believed her story."

"So Apollo isn't politically opposed to the American queen?"

"I doubt it. But who knows? Why are you suddenly so interested in island politics? You always seem determined to avoid discussion of the royal family at all costs. What's up?"

Gracie filed the information on Apollo away for later reference and pasted a sufficiently bored expression on her face. "I was just curious, that's all."

"It doesn't have anything to do with Apollo possibly being your secret admirer, does it?"

"Not at all. Besides, him being my admirer is about as likely as snow on the beach."

"Don't discount it, Gracie. Think about it. That note made veiled references to mythology. Who else would send it but someone named after one of gods? Besides, it explains why our waiter was so solicitous. Who wouldn't be for a future marquis? It all makes perfect sense. Up until the part where you refused to dance with him."

"He doesn't look like he's suffering." Gracie pointed to where Apollo stood surrounded by half a dozen preening women. "Maybe he's everyone's secret admirer."

"Cynic." Marta turned back to her drink.

"You're the one who told me the nobility were nothing more than tourist attractions at these openings." Gracie scanned the room searching for Stephan. A new woman clung to his arm.

Marta's exact words surfaced in her memory. *At least half a dozen American tourists will drop into a swoon over him tonight. Another three or four will try to stuff an article of clothing in his pockets.*

As if on cue, Stephan fished something out of his suit pocket and dropped it on the tray of a passing waiter while turning his attention to a new partner.

They twirled within a few feet of her table and Gracie saw the shuttered look in his eyes. She flashed him a smile, and he seemed to soften, ever so slightly.

"So why didn't you dance with him?" Marta's voice broke into her thoughts. "Are you really that stuck on your *hono*?"

"I just don't like to dance. A long time ago, I—"

"Gracie," Marta hissed, directing her attention over Gracie's shoulder.

"Dance with me?" Stephan stood at her shoulder, a hint of a real smile lurking beneath the façade.

"I, uh…" She hated dancing and the memories it evoked.

"Please?" The softly uttered word voiced the entreaty in his eyes.

After watching him be eaten alive by the tourists, how could she resist? She swallowed the lump in her throat and put her hand in his. The music started again as they reached the dance floor.

"Thank you," Stephan murmured in her ear. "Besides, they're playing our song."

The calypso rhythm of "Under the Sea" resounded in her ears as he sent her whirling across the floor. Above her head, beneath her feet and all around, tropical fish swam in their aquariums. A spotlight and disco ball drowned the room in flickering blue light, and for a moment she was swimming with him in their own private, carefree world.

Stephan grabbed her hand and led her in a series of turns and dips that she'd never thought she could do. Following him was easy, and as she relaxed into the dance, she forgot her anxiety.

Gracie laughed at the joy of moving in rhythm with him on the dance floor. Stephan's answering smile—real, not contrived—touched her heart in a way that little else could.

All too soon the song drifted to a close, but instead of releasing her and moving on to charm another club guest, he pulled her close and swayed in time with the musical interlude.

Gracie savored the closeness, oblivious to everything but him. "How did you know that was our song?"

"Your friend told me about the ring tone on your phone when she answered it earlier tonight." A chuckle rumbled through his chest. "Right before she threatened me."

"I'm sorry about that. Marta's developed a protective streak since I've started seeing what she calls my mystery man. She told me she'd turn you into lobster bait if you hurt me."

"Not all of me," he put his lips close to her ear so that his breath teased her as he spoke. "Just certain parts. Ones that I'm rather fond of."

"She didn't!"

"She did. But she didn't need to. I would never knowingly hurt you, *hona-mei*."

The lights dimmed. "Let's slow things down," the DJ announced in a smoky rasp. "Here's a classic tune for lovers from the American golden age of music."

Stephan tucked his hand at the small of her back and led her deeper into the crowd of dancers. But as she followed his lead, the music and the words suddenly touched a raw spot in her memory.

A sultry rendition of classic Gershwin poured from the speakers, sucking her into the undertow of emotion.

I'm a little lamb who's lost in the wood,
I know I could always be good,
To one who'll watch over me.

Her father had crooned those words to her all her life. They'd danced to the tune for as long as she could remember, from the time he'd swayed with her in his arms to the time she balanced on his toes and whirled across a dance floor with him at Aunt Edna's wedding. To the time when she'd danced with him for real, on her own two feet. The day she'd tried out her fledgling feminine power as she begged him for a new dress to wear to the father-daughter dance at school.

Gracie choked back tears as she fought her way out of Stephan's tightening grasp. Try as she might, she couldn't picture her father's face when he'd danced with her. She could only see him as he lay, still and waxen, in his coffin two days later.

"*Hona-mei*? Are you all right?"

"I have to go." She pushed against Stephan, struggling to breathe despite the guilt that threatened to suffocate her. "Dance with Marta. Then tell her I went home."

Gracie ran from the club, all but blinded by the tears she tried so hard to hold back. She ran until she reached the safety of her bed and collapsed beneath the weight of pain and guilt.

Loving someone meant you could lose them. And losing someone you loved caused a wound that never healed. Look at how easily a song had ripped the scab off her heart.

I would never knowingly hurt you, hona-mei. Stephan's words whispered themselves in her heart, but the memory only intensified her hurt. How would she feel if she lost him? A million things might tear them apart. Another woman. His royal duties. Her fears. Death.

Even the sound of her cell phone repeatedly jangling "Under the Sea" couldn't pull her from her misery.

She was in love with him.

And love sucked.

Chapter 20

racie shifted her beach bag to the opposite shoulder and readjusted her grip on the bus strap as a woman jostled her. The oversized sunglasses and hat she'd pulled on to hide her puffy eyes and blotched face shielded her from the curious stares of the other passengers. Since when did the early morning bus have standing room only?

"Does anyone know who the woman at the Paradise Cove club was?" called a voice from a few rows behind her.

"We only know that he danced with her more than once and that she left abruptly."

A shiver crawled up Gracie's spine. Something was wrong.

"I, for one, think the Cinderella antics were a bit over the top. Does she think the prince will chase after her?" asked the first voice. "The woman went to ridiculous lengths to try to grab his attention."

"Unlike you, getting up at the crack of dawn to primp before climbing on a bus to search out the location of the prince's yacht." The second woman's good-natured jibe only increased the chatter on the bus.

Gracie shifted slightly, to get a better view of the other passengers. From their painted toes and their perfectly tanned bodies to their expert makeup and carefully chosen accessories, they looked more like models going on a photo shoot than tourists.

"In any case, the disappearing debutante wasn't the last woman he danced with. I was."

"You were not. I was."

While the women argued over who danced when, Gracie stared out the window at the familiar route. Their voices faded into an indistinct hum as she pondered her options. Stephan would have his yacht docked at the pier waiting for her, not suspecting that a bus load of royal seekers would be descending on the pier too.

Should she risk calling him from the bus? Get off at an earlier stop and call from there? Try to blend in with the crowd and distract them? Or simply march up to the yacht and board it as if the others weren't there?

Gracie dismissed the last option. Drawing attention to herself would only cause photos to snap and tongues to wag. Despite her aching head and red eyes, her thinking was clear this morning.

Revealing her political connections to Marta in the privacy of their friendship was one thing. Having them ferreted out and splashed across the news sheets and entertainment journals was something else entirely.

She might still be able to continue her studies from the confines of Royal Island, but she'd never again be "just Gracie" to her classmates, professors and friends. She'd be a public figure.

Just like Jill. And Constantine.

And Stephan. She felt a stab of sympathy for him, wondering if there was anywhere he could go to be *just Stephan*.

The bus rolled to a stop and Gracie was pushed along with the stream of women pouring out of its doors. Next thing she knew she was following them down the rocky path leading to the pier. So much for options one and two.

"Hi," said a woman walking next to her. "I'm Joanne. This is my friend Melody." Joanne's smile was warm and open, despite her picture-perfect looks.

"Um, hi," Gracie managed.

"You're probably the only one on the bus who isn't part of one of the tours," Joanne continued. "So are you trying to catch a glimpse of the prince too? Or are you here for something else?"

"I'm a student. I'm here to do some research on the local marine life."

"Well, good luck finding a charter to take you out. I think the tour guides booked every available boat in the marina. Of course, if the prince's yacht is docked here, I doubt that anyone will want to wander far from the pier." Joanne laughed. "Otherwise we might miss our chance to be the next Jillian Bradley."

Gracie answered with a ghost of a smile. It was strange, having other people refer to Jill as some kind of icon. "This pier is usually deserted. There's no good place to sit and relax. If you're looking for the royal family, you'd have a better chance of seeing them by sitting at a café on the main island or trying to book a tour on Royal Island."

Joanne shrugged. "You're probably right but think of the adventure we'd miss. None of us really believes we'll get anything more out of this than a story to share with the friends back home. But it's fun. Anyway, we'd better hurry to catch up with the others." She stuck out her hand. "Good luck with your studies."

"Thank you." Gracie walked in silence, her steps slow to avoid the crowds. As she neared the pier, she was astounded at the sight of limousines, cars and even horse-drawn carriages all teeming with female tourists.

The women on the bus might be out for adventure, but some of the ladies on the pier looked like they were out for blood. Or a wedding ring. She wondered idly if any of them had brought along her own justice of the peace. Or maybe that was what the charters were for. Captains still married people, didn't they?

Only one thing was missing from the scene. Stephan's yacht. Gracie sighed with relief. No doubt his calls last night were to warn her and cancel their meeting. Too bad she'd been so rushed this morning that she didn't pick up her voice mail.

Despite Stephan's absence, boats of all kinds crowded the pier, and several vessels were already under way heading for the open bay. Joanne had been right. Every charter on the islands seemed to be waiting to board the ladies bent on catching a glimpse of the prince.

She wandered aimlessly down the pier, gazing out over the water, longing for the peaceful atmosphere she'd found here over the past weeks.

"Charter a boat, miss?"

Gracie started at the sound of the heavily accented voice until she turned and recognized its owner.

"Petros!"

"The boss and I," he winked at her "thought you might enjoy a little jaunt in the motorboat before settling down to do your work."

"Oh, thank you." She threw her arms around the weather-beaten islander who served as Stephan's steward, teacher, and friend. She'd get to see him today after all.

"Are you all right, Miss Gracie?" Petros disengaged himself from her hug and led her to the dinghy tied up at the pier. "We were worried about you after what happened last night."

So he knew. "Yes, I'm fine. I'll tell you later." She owed Stephan, and Petros, it seemed, an explanation of her behavior last night. But the time for spilling her guts was later. Now she just wanted to be away from the crowds.

Once she was settled into the boat, they sped out into the open ocean, and Petros radioed back to the yacht. "We're on our way. We'll lose the tourist boats then head to the ship. And don't worry. She's okay."

As they meandered through the surf, taking their time, the other boats veered off in various directions. Gracie relaxed. "I'm glad Stephan wasn't docked at the pier this morning. Some of those people looked like they'd try to commandeer his yacht."

"Public appearances during tourist season always bring out the royal watchers." Petros broke into a smile, the dark planes of his face crinkling into well-worn wrinkles. "He has learned to be careful."

"You've known him for a long time, haven't you, Petros?"

"*Aaya.* Yes."

Gracie waited but he kept his eyes trained on the expanse of water ahead. She probed for more information. "He told me you were the one who taught him to dive."

Affection and pride lit the older man's eyes, transforming him from taciturn to animated. "He was an easy child to teach. At least for me."

"Something tells me there's more to the story. Stephan told me he was—and I quote—a curious, out-of-control boy. Is it true?"

"That one was a trial to his teachers from the start. Never sitting still. Hardly listening to the lessons. Disrupting the other royal children. The old king hired private tutors, but he went through them like other kids go through candy. Not even the prestige of being a royal tutor or the generous salary could hold them after a few weeks with our Stephan."

"I gather he wasn't a good student." He'd grown into a re-markable man despite his academic difficulties. Still, a hint of disappointment tugged at her. He seemed to know so much about the islands and the oceans that she'd hoped he, unlike the others in her life, wouldn't be frightened off by her IQ and her pursuit of advanced academics.

"I don't know much about his formal studies. Just that the teachers came and went a lot more often than with the other children. They said there was nothing they could do for the boy, but I knew better. Young Prince Stephan and I met when I fished him out of one of the decorative ponds on Royal Island."

Petros chuckled. "Such a mess you never did want to see. Dripping wet and stinking of fish and algae, yet he stood in front of me like he owned the place. Not that he was arrogant." Petros flashed her a glance as if to emphasize the point.

"He fully expected to be punished for running away from his studies. But he didn't whine or beg or treat me with anything but respect. And he didn't cower. Lectured me on the habits of the fish, he did. Told me he wanted to see them up close to study them.

"After that day, he sought me out as often as he could to talk about the fish. Eventually I asked for permission to take him diving. We've been together ever since, except for his stint in the military."

"He seems very fond of you," Gracie said quietly.

Petros flushed a deep shade of red beneath his dark skin. "He was always a good boy. He's grown into a good man." He hesitated, staring ahead into the waves before speaking again. "You're a blessing to him, Miss Gracie. He smiles more since you came into his life. When King Alexander abdicated, Prince Stephan lost himself in his public role. He forgot how to smile for anything but a camera."

Petros shifted the boat into a lower gear and slowed, turning their course in a new direction now that the crowds were lost behind them.

A comfortable silence wrapped around them as Gracie leaned against the seat and let the warmth of the sun seep into her bones. Funny, but she'd always considered Stephan the strong one in their relationship. The one with everything to give and nothing to lose.

But listening to Petros and remembering the look in Stephan's eyes when he'd asked her to dance last night made her reconsider. She had something to give him after all. Warmth. Understanding. And a chance to be *just Stephan* if only for a stolen moment.

Stephan scanned the calm ocean and strained to hear the sound of the approaching motorboat. He checked his watch. Two minutes later than the last time he'd checked it.

He needed to see Gracie. To make sure she was all right. He'd sent one of his bodyguards to follow her last night. Then he'd taken a gaping mouthed Marta into his confidence and bullied her into calling him to assure him Gracie made it home. And Petros had just radioed to tell him she was all right. But he needed more.

She was physically fine, but why didn't she take his calls? What had caused her to burst into tears and run from him at the club?

She was safe. But what had he done to make her so miserable?

The tightness in her voice as she pushed away from him echoed in his dreams last night. And the only thing that had changed from their first laughter-filled dance to their final tear-filled parting was that he'd held her closer, danced more slowly, and called her his *hona-mei*.

She should have known his feelings for her ran deeper than friendship. She would have expected him to voice the difference soon. Wouldn't she? Unless…

He'd assumed her feelings for him had been the same. God, she'd given every indication that there was something simmering beneath the surface that was more passion and less friendship. The kisses they'd shared on the deck in the moonlight. The way she'd responded to him in his office. The seductive appreciation she'd shown for his gift of champagne and strawberries last night. The way she'd turned down every offer to dance except his.

He couldn't be wrong about this.

But he'd been wrong in the past. Even before he'd been thrust into the role of next in line to the throne, there had been a few women who thought consorting with a prince was a stepping stone to landing a rich husband.

He'd never put Gracie into the same category as them. She wasn't out to snare a rich man or enhance her public image. But there was one thing she did have in common with them. They'd all viewed him as fun but not obtainable. What if Gracie felt the same?

What if she never made peace with the reality of being more than friends? More than lovers? Was he always going to be a remote in-law that she didn't quite know what to do with?

His gut cramped at the thought. But the conclusion was inescapable. She hadn't pulled away from him until he'd made his intentions clear by naming her his *hona-mei*.

Stephan scanned the quiet ocean again.

He had to see her.

Chapter 21

Forty-five minutes later, the sound of an approaching motorboat broke the silence. Stephan strained his eyes as the boat came into view.

For a moment, all his royal training pushed aside his personal concerns. He was a prince and an ambassador. He was trained to handle the unknown.

First assess the situation. Gauge the mood of the players. Focus on the desired outcome. Take action.

Then he saw her, sitting motionless beside Petros, shrouded in her oversized sunglasses and floppy beach hat. She clutched a canvas tote to her chest like a shield against unwanted advances.

All of his training fled, leaving him naked, vulnerable, and in love without a clue as to how she felt.

His crew leapt to secure the boat and she accepted their help disembarking. She paused on the dive platform and tilted her head upward. He smiled in greeting and was relieved to see her smile back. A small smile, but genuine.

He was at her side by the time she reached the main deck. He pushed away all of his intentions of giving her time and swept her into an embrace.

Stephan pushed her hat aside and buried his face in her hair, savoring the scent. He memorized the feel of her body molding to his, just in case it was the last time.

"Oh, sweetheart, I've been so worried."

He pulled back far enough to thread his fingers through her hair and push the sunglasses up with his thumbs. One look in her eyes and he knew he couldn't resist. He cupped her face in his hands and kissed her. Deep and long with as much passion as he dared show to one who looked so wounded.

His lips outlined hers; his tongue traced the delicate skin of her inner lip, and he poured all the love he could muster into the kiss. As if by kissing alone, he could heal all her aches.

But how could his kisses heal her if he were the cause of her pain?

He broke off the kiss and leaned away from her. "I'm sorry *hona-mei*—I mean Gracie. I shouldn't have done that."

"So I don't get to be *hona-mei* today?" The slight catch in her voice caught him off guard.

"Do you want to be?" He couldn't read her face. "Last night the words made you run away. I wasn't sure you'd come this morning. I can't take back my words, but if you want to be just—"

"Oh, Stephan." Gracie wrapped her arms around him and leaned against his chest. "That's not why I left last night. It wasn't you. It was me."

"This sounds like a classic break up line," he mumbled.

"It's not. It's something I need to share with you, but it's not about you. It's, well, it's not easy to talk about, especially after a night without sleep. I need coffee." She pulled out of his arms and dragged the sunglasses back over her eyes. "And aspirin. My head is throbbing."

"You were supposed to sip the champagne, not guzzle it."

"You're at fault, too, you know. The waiter was so eager to please you that he never let my glass get more than half empty."

"Someday I'll teach you the fine art of drinking without paying the price. But for now, coffee and aspirin it is."

Two cups of coffee, one glass of water and three aspirin later, Gracie curled up on the sofa in the lounge and rested her head in his lap one hand curled protectively around his thigh just above his knee.

She seemed more affectionate, more physical, and yet oddly more emotionally distant than he'd ever seen her. Confused by the contradiction, Stephan merely stroked her hair and her back and waited for her to give him clues.

"I'm sorry if I pushed you into anything last night," he began. "I know the situation at the club was awkward. Believe me, I was delighted to see you there. If I thought you would have accepted, I would have invited you upstairs."

"You were busy working. I know part of your job is to charm the crowds of tourists."

She traced provocative circles on his inner thigh and Stephan sucked in a breath. If he believed she were doing it on purpose, he'd haul her into his cabin without further thought. He eyed the passageway, mentally judging the steps from the couch to his bed. Too many.

"Stephan?"

"Hmm?" He pushed the thoughts of his bed aside and concentrated on her.

"I don't dance."

"Your actions proved otherwise last night."

"I mean, I don't like to dance. I haven't since I was eight years old." She took a deep, shuddering breath that he felt catch as he stroked his hand slowly down her back. "You're the first person that… The last time I danced—"

Stephan felt a damp trickle on his leg and instinctively pulled her to a sitting position, holding her on his lap, tucking her head into his shoulder. He wrapped his arms more tightly around her as her tears wet his shirt. "It's all right, Gracie. You don't have to talk about it, *hona-mei*."

He continued, muttering soft nonsense in his own language, most of which she probably wouldn't understand. But she stilled against his shoulder and seemed to calm.

When she spoke again, her voice wavered, but this time the quiet flow of words didn't dissolve into tears.

"When I was a little girl, my father taught me how to dance. He always danced with me at special occasions. All of us, actually. I used to watch him with Jill and dream of the day I'd be old enough to really dance, not just twirl in circles as he held me up. He called me his little princess."

"I'm sure you were a beautiful child."

She answered with a tiny laugh. "I thought so. Jill used to paint my nails and fix my hair. She let me play with her makeup brushes and old cosmetics. Mom didn't like it much, but Daddy always complimented me.

"Anyway, Daddy and I danced together a lot back then. We even took classes at the local studio. We were getting ready for the first father-daughter dance at my new school, and I wanted everything to be perfect.

"I remember feeling so grown up, even though I was still a little girl. I was taller than his waist. I thought if I just had high heeled shoes I could lean on his shoulder and everything would be just like it was in my imagination. Perfect."

She fell silent, burrowing deeper within his embrace, wrapping her arms around him as if holding him gave her strength. Stephan prayed it did.

"On the night before he died, we practiced our slow dance. I wore my prettiest outfit. Jill had helped me with my hair. She gave me a special pearl necklace to wear. I told her about the shoes and the dress I wanted for the dance. She said if I asked Daddy for them he wouldn't be able to resist, especially since I looked so pretty that night.

"So I did. I asked. I practically begged." Her voice grew even softer as she lost herself in the memory. "The dress was a blue and silver gown just like the one my collector Barbie dolls wore. And the shoes were silver with little heels. He smiled and promised to get them for me. Then he told me he'd always be there for me, no matter what happened. That I'd always be his princess and he'd always be my knight in shining armor."

"It sounds like a wonderful memory."

Gracie turned to him, her eyes snapping with anger, and something else. "You're wrong. It isn't a good memory. The next day Daddy came home with the dress and shoes and I thought I had everything I'd ever wanted. Mom took tons of photos of us dancing together. But later I overheard him tell Mom he'd put off having the brakes on the car fixed so he could bring my special presents home that night."

"Gracie, you can't think—"

"It was my fault he died. The car slid out of control later that same night. If he'd checked the car instead of spoiling me, he'd be alive today." She tore out of his arms and paced the length of the salon, her tone turning from strident to scathing. "I was a selfish, spoiled, little brat of a princess who expected the world to put my needs above everything else. My vanity killed him."

"Gracie, you couldn't have known." Stephan intercepted her pacing and locked her in his arms, holding her while frustration, anger and guilt poured out in words of self-recrimination.

He held on until the anger left her limp and drained. "You didn't cause the accident that killed him. He didn't die because he bought you a present. You can't control the roads, or the weather, or any of a thousand things that could have gone wrong."

Her anger turned to tears, then sobs. He rocked her gently, trying to soothe away years of pain. He'd known about the accident that killed her father. He'd watched Jill torture herself with guilt over asking her father to pick her up from a party on the rainy October night he died. Now, as he watched Gracie turn the same guilt and anger on herself, pieces of the puzzle fell into place.

Two sisters, once so close, torn apart by guilt and pain. Each blaming herself. Each, maybe, secretly blaming the other. While the years eroded away pieces of their souls.

"Gracie, *hona-mei*, it wasn't your fault." He lifted her and carried her back to the couch feeling her sag in exhaustion against his body.

"After that night I vowed never to ask anyone for another gift, ever again. I don't deserve them. And the price is too high. I won't risk that again."

"Don't let your memories shut you off from the people who care about you, sweetheart."

She was silent for so long, he wondered if she'd fallen asleep. He almost hoped that she had, hoped he'd given her enough comfort to keep the demons at bay for an hour or two.

A heavy sigh escaped her lips, ruffling the front of his shirt in its warm breeze. "It's hard, Stephan," she murmured, "so hard to love someone and lose them. Sometimes, when I try to picture his face, I can't do it. It's like he's lost forever. And he promised me. It was supposed to be just like the song we always danced to. He was supposed to be *someone to watch over Me*. And he's gone."

He's gone, Stephan thought as he soothed her into sleep, *but I'm here. And I'm not going anywhere.*

Chapter 22

"Feeling better?"

Gracie cracked her eyes open, grimacing at the gritty residue that clung to them after her recent bout with tears. She blinked a few times before she could clearly see Stephan sitting at the edge of the mattress.

"Where am I?"

"I brought you back to your suite after you fell asleep." He reached over to the bedside table and passed her a glass of water. It was cool to the touch. "It's time for a couple more aspirin and some water."

She nodded, inching her way up in the bed to take the offerings. "How long did I sleep?"

"Long enough for us to get to Neptune Island and drop anchor. We're on the opposite side of the island from where we usually dive. I thought you'd enjoy seeing some of the underwater caves."

"Sounds great. When can we start?"

"Not until I'm sure you feel up to it. There's no rush."

"Planning to stay out overnight again?"

"If you like." He took the empty glass from her and settled more comfortably on the bed.

"I'd like to. But after last night, I should probably tell Marta that I won't be coming home. Running out on her at the club wasn't a nice thing to do."

"Gracie, before you contact her, you need to know something. Last night, I asked Marta to call me and let me know you made it home safely."

"So she knows about us?"

"Under the circumstances, I thought it best." He sent her a cocky smile. "Even at the risk of my manhood becoming lobster bait."

Gracie felt her anxiety melt under the weight of that smile and the lingering concern in his eyes. "I suppose you're right. But I doubt she'll carry through on her threats now that she knows who you are."

"You might underestimate her resolve, but I'm not taking any chances. Seriously, though, I think you can trust her with this."

"Actually, I think I can trust her with all my secrets. It's getting harder to keep everything inside."

He rose and paced the length of the suite. "You can end the charade at any time. You know that. Either way, I'll respect and support your decisions for as long as I can."

Gracie nodded but didn't answer him. Instead, she swung her legs over the edge of the bed and padded toward the bathroom. Hadn't she considered the same thing last night? And this morning? But the reasons that made her dismiss the thoughts were the same as hours earlier. Now wasn't the time.

She brushed her teeth, splashed cold water on her face and combed the tangles out of her hair, feeling more human by the moment. The headache was gone, and the puffiness around her eyes had receded a bit.

The gut twisting emotions had also receded, leaving a calm she'd rarely experienced. Still, she needed some time to herself to regain her equilibrium. And she knew just the way to get it. She squared her shoulders and marched out of the bathroom.

"Stephan—let's dive."

The hours underwater did the trick. After stepping from the shower, Gracie looked, and felt, like herself again. That is, the weight of grief and guilt wasn't pulling her under the way it had a few hours ago.

But as she dressed, she realized she wasn't quite the Gracie of only yesterday. Not the plain, scholarly, familiar woman she was used to. Instead, some trace of the provocative woman who'd sucked champagne from strawberries last night remained.

The painful memories she'd shared today flashed through her mind, settling into patterns as new and unfamiliar as the creature she'd become in the Paradise Cove club. She'd always believed her father died because of her selfishness. But now she saw it in a different light.

Unconsciously over the years, she'd shied away from anything that smacked of that eight-year-old child's desire to look pretty. Stephan and Marta both joked about her wardrobe, but both had hit on the essential truth. She dressed to hide, as if by blending into the background she could keep tragedy at bay.

Last night she hadn't hidden. She'd dressed to impress, and nothing had gone wrong. The hours leading up to that last dance had been pleasant. Yes, the song had triggered painful memories, letting loose toxic emotions like a wound allowed to fester before being lanced. But today even the pain was a little more bearable, simply by sharing it.

Or perhaps it was the one with whom she shared it.

For once the differences between them didn't matter. Education. Politics. Countries of origin, circumstances of birth, life expectations, and even language didn't make a difference.

Such things might stand in the way of a future together, but they couldn't stop them from having a *now*.

The desire to see Stephan, to be with him, to share everything they could share for as long as they could share it pushed everything else aside. Even the pain and memories that had held her prisoner for so long. And the pain that would come when they parted.

Gracie brushed her hair slowly, letting it fall to her shoulders and slide across her skin. This was the woman she'd been yesterday. Seductive. Aware. Desirable.

Except she didn't know how to be desirable. If she tried, she'd fail. Last night had been a magical accident, something born of instinct rather than analysis.

So, she closed her eyes and followed her intuition. The tugging at her scalp as she pulled the brush through her hair became more. The swish of the strands against her skin seemed different, new. And the image of Stephan's eyes, glowing with humor, approval, and pleasure awakened the magic.

As a last thought, she pulled the simple white blouse from her shorts and unbuttoned the bottom. With a tuck and a twist, she knotted it between her breasts, exposing her stomach and accenting her curves.

She headed to the library, a surge of confidence lightening her step. She'd tapped into the core of her own femininity. A woman's power, not a child's fantasy. She knew exactly what she wanted. Warmth. Closeness. Laughter. And that thing that sizzled between them whenever he touched her.

She rapped on the door, opening it even as she heard his terse invitation to enter.

His back was to the door, and he was engaged in something on the computer. Even though he was dressed in his casual half buttoned shirt and shorts, everything about him radiated business. He shifted in his chair and asked a question in Melesian, his tone rapid and authoritative, before popping a couple of antacids from a large bottle as he waited for an answer.

Gracie closed the door and leaned against it, turning his words over in her mind. Papers, maybe. Or documents and communication. She wasn't sure what he wanted, but she knew he was expecting someone else.

"Well?" he demanded. That word was clear, even to her.

"I'm sorry, but if you want something from me, you'll have to repeat that in English."

The set of his shoulders softened, and he turned to meet her, a smile playing across his lips. "I think not," he said softly, clearly enunciating the words so that she easily understood. "*Naaya*. No."

"No?"

He walked to her, every step more relaxed than the last. "No," he said, switching to English when he stood in front of her. "There are new rules on board, *hona-mei*. No more English unless I give you permission."

"That's a little overbearing, isn't it?" The flirtatious jibe popped out of her mouth before she could think about anything but the mushy, warm way his words lodged in the pit of her stomach.

He shrugged, the movement careless and fluid. A gentle glow lit his eyes, not quite teasing, but something that made her insides tingle. "My ship. My rules."

"But I—"

"*Naaya*. No English." He placed a finger on her lips, silencing her protest and spoke softly to her in his own language.

"I don't understand," Gracie replied, not quite able to work through his unfamiliar words. It wasn't a textbook case of repeating known phrases, but an attempt at conversation, which always challenged her knowledge.

"This is your chance to practice," he repeated more slowly and quietly.

Understanding dawned. She smiled. "When Americans try to help a foreigner understand English, they speak louder."

"Do I need to shout?" If possible, his words were even softer than before. He trailed the finger from near her lips to caress her jaw.

"*Naaya.* I understand." The words felt clumsy on her tongue, but the light in his eyes encouraged her.

"Good." He kissed her lightly, then moved away. "I wasn't expecting you yet. You don't usually pound on my door. Is everything all right?"

"*Aaya.*" Yes. So far, he'd chosen simple words, ones she could understand from context or from the slight motions he used to accompany them.

"Do you still have a headache?"

"*Naaya.*"

"Are you hungry?"

"*Aaya.*"

He shook his head, frowning at her despite the twinkle in his eyes. "*Aaya. Naaya.* You must learn to speak more than these words. What would you like for dinner?"

He'd left her no simple answers to hide behind. She tried to remember her lessons. Food hadn't been a topic they'd studies much. "Tea?" she finally suggested, knowing the word from the many discussions about the Royal Presentation Tea that all the students would eventually attend.

"Nothing else?"

"I don't know many words for food," Gracie admitted in English, feeling foolish. She shrugged. "I'm sorry," she added in Melesian.

"No need to be sorry. And no need to be hungry either." He went back to the desk and picked up the phone. A rapid barrage of words followed that she couldn't begin to understand. When he hung up, he turned and beckoned to her.

She followed him to the couch and sat beside him, curling into his embrace when he wrapped an arm around her. They looked out the windows onto the sunlit water as he caressed her. "I ordered a few things that you might like. In a couple of hours, you should know enough new words to keep you from starving."

At her puzzled look, he alternately pantomimed and translated, repeating the words until she understood.

"I don't think you will let me starve," she ventured, settling deeper into his embrace.

"I might." Despite his words, there was laughter in his voice. "I warn you that you're going to have to earn your dinner tonight."

"I think I can do that." Gracie placed her palm on his jaw and caressed it. A primal reflex caused her to trail her fingers down his neck and along the open vee of his shirt.

"You'll have to do more than just that." His voice sounded strange, strangled.

Gracie smiled to herself and opened a button on his shirt, letting her fingers and nails caress his bare skin. "Like this?"

"That's pleasant," he managed through gritted teeth. "But not what I had in mind."

"Trust me, I have a lot more than this in mind." The words flowed easily off her tongue for once. She popped another button and slid her hand lower. "I thought I might—"

His kiss silenced her as he dragged her across his lap and took control of the situation. Gracie relaxed, her body limp in his embrace, but her heart pounding.

She'd done it.

Pushed him over the edge of chivalry into something more.

His lips played against hers, possessiveness adding an edge of roughness to the kiss. His hands roamed her back, pushing her closer. He captured her hip, cupping it in one large palm as he gave her a firm squeeze. The heat of his hand burned as if he'd touched bare flesh instead of thin cotton. She gasped at the intimacy of his hold

"*Aaya*, yes," she murmured when he let her take a breath. "More."

"*Naaya*. Not this way." He pushed her off his lap and back onto the couch with the same swift assertiveness that he'd used to drag her to him before.

"But Stephan," she cajoled, playing her role with gusto, "you told me to earn my dinner."

"Not that way." His words were ragged, but he took a deep breath and captured her hand. He pressed a kiss into her palm. "Not yet. First, you'll earn your dinner with words."

"But my way is so much more fun." She ran her other hand along his thigh from knee to the place where he captured it too.

"*Naaya, shakak.*"

"What?" The sharp new word didn't sound quite like an endearment.

"*Shakak*. It means pest. Little shark." He translated quickly, punctuating the concept with a series of tiny, tickling pinches on her ribs, belly, and every bit of exposed skin to drive the point home. Annoying, but endearingly so. "*Shakak-mei.*"

Gracie giggled and slapped at his mobile hands. "Bad *hono*," she scolded. "*Hono-mei.*"

"*Hono-dei*," he agreed. Your *hono*. He stopped tickling and soothed her instead, encouraging her to rest her head on his shoulder.

Language class had never been like this, Gracie mused as she searched for a new topic of conversation.

Her gaze fell on a wall plaque with the ugliest fish she'd ever seen and the words *you shouldda seen the one that got away* inscribed beneath.

"What's that?" she asked in halting Melesian.

Stephan laughed, his eyes sparkling. "It's a souvenir from Chicago. A gift from Constantine. He found it when he was courting your sister. It's far too ugly for the palace."

"It isn't much better here."

"*Naaya.* But one can't refuse a gift from the king."

"Especially when he's your brother."

They continued for a while, speaking quietly for a few moments at a time before lapsing into comfortable silence. Stephan paced their conversation as if he understood how easily she tired of searching for words. Each break renewed her until she stopped wondering if she could convince him to switch to English and began to enjoy their fleeting exchanges in Melesian.

When a knock interrupted them, Gracie glanced at the clock while Stephan opened the door for Petros and a cart full of trays filled with various foods. Several hours had passed, she realized with pleasure.

Petros placed an elaborate arrangement of food on the table while he and Stephan chatted easily. Gracie marveled at the camaraderie between the two men, separated by both age and station in life. The prince and the islander chatted as if they were old friends. How different from her early image of Stephan as distant and aloof.

When Petros closed the door behind him and left them in silence once again, Stephan took Gracie by the hand. "Time to study." He led her to the captain's chair at the head of the table and pulled her onto his knee for a quick kiss before settling her into a chair beside him. "You're doing very well with your lessons. Let's see if we can expand your horizons."

He gestured to the table laden with dishes of all kinds, some of which she recognized and some of which she did not. "We have a bit of everything here from classic cuisine to island specialties."

She nodded, understanding his simple words more easily than she'd thought she would.

"We also have—" he lifted the lid on a dish and quickly put it back "—some interesting items that Petros dreamed up for us."

"He's a chef too?"

"No, but he thinks he's a *honiimakker*—matchmaker," he translated into English before lapsing back into Melesian. "He obviously instructed the chef to add some special touches to the selections I ordered."

Stephan angled his chair near hers and captured her, his knees on either side of her own, his hands cupping her face before sliding down to rest on her shoulders. "Ready to learn?"

She nodded, not resisting when he pushed her gently back against the chair.

"Good. Your job is to focus on the words. Let me take care of everything else. Everything is yours for the asking. But remember my rule: no English."

"Your ship, your rules," she murmured, willing to try anything to please him.

His answering smile made her heart thump.

The table stood an arm's length away from her, so she watched as he reached across it, his fingers slender and graceful, yet strong as he selected something from the dishes.

Stephan swirled a piece of bread in olive oil and held it out to her. "Bread. With olive oil." Easy Melesian words she could understand.

She repeated after him and he touched the morsel to her lips. When she reached for it, he wrapped her hand in his. "Let me," he whispered, slipping the bread into her mouth. "Eat from my hands. Learn from my lips."

Gracie nodded, unable to speak past the feelings that welled up in her throat. Her entire body felt alert, attuned to the slightest touch of his knee on hers, his finger near her lips or his gaze locked on her.

When he selected a skewer of grilled shrimp and squeezed a wedge of lime onto the gleaming surface, she watched, her heart as hungry for his movements as her belly was for the food.

"Lime and brandy basted prawns," he said softly, gesturing, reiterating, and occasionally translating until she understood. When she repeated his words, he slid a bit of the prawn across her lips. Gracie licked the sweet and spicy flavor, slowly indulging her taste buds before nibbling on the offering.

"This is wonderful. May I have another?"

Stephan's eyes sparkled at her request. "Would you like to try it with honey mango sauce?" He pointed to a pot of honey and a mango, waiting until she said the words before picking up a small bowl of sauce topped with toasted coconut shreds. He dipped his finger into it. "Or would you prefer to try the sauce by itself?"

Without thinking, Gracie sucked his finger into her mouth, swirling her tongue around it and licking the sweet, sticky, slightly warm mixture. A hint of something exotic tingled on her tongue as he slipped his finger free.

"They say the touch of cinnamon acts as an aphrodisiac in this sauce. They might be onto something." He grinned at her.

Gracie somehow caught the meaning of his words, even though she'd never heard them before. The look in his eyes made his intent clear. "You eat some too." She swirled her finger in the concoction and offered it to him. The feel of his lips closing around her finger and the warm, wet suction of his mouth tugged at places that only Stephan had ever awakened.

"Yes, they are definitely onto something," he murmured before trailing his lips across her palm and down to her inner wrist. "I'll have to come back to this later."

Gracie almost sighed in disappointment when he pulled away, but moments later, he was offering her another delicacy on the end of a silver fork.

"Island ambrosia. Intended for lovers."

Her heart pounded as she repeated the words. *Ambrosia. For lovers.* The deep red color of the mixture was at odds with the nutty, spicy flavor. "What's in it?"

"Minced baby shrimp flavored with lemon pepper—for stamina. Strawberries—for sweetness. And pine nuts—to enhance nesting instincts and fertility." He translated the more complex words, mixing English with Melesian as he fed her another forkful. "Or so the legends say."

"There are lots of legends about Melesian food."

"And all with a grain of truth, *hona-mei.* Shall we see what other legendary foods Petros has seen fit to bring?"

And so they continued, each food accompanied by stories of the gods, mortals, heroes, and lovers of Greek, Caribbean, and Melesian origin.

Coriander and nutmeg dusted asparagus tips. Grilled pineapple wrapped in thin slices of ham. Baked goat cheese on crisp flat bread. Calamari sautéed in garlic butter sauce. Sweet fruit wine flavored with honey and spices. Cool to the tongue, but warm to the senses.

Stephan's eyes caressed her face as he offered her tastes from the fork. His fingers lingered on her lips when he fed her tidbits. And he licked his own lips as she drank the wine.

"More," she said, drinking deeply from the silver cup.

"More what?" He indicated the table full of tasty delicacies that they'd shared.

"More you." Gracie rose from her chair and put the cup aside. She leaned over him and locked her lips to his kissing him, demanding entrance, following the passion that built to a painful pressure inside her.

When he locked his hands on her waist and opened his mouth to follow her lead, Gracie moaned. Maybe it was the wine, or the spices, but she didn't think so. It was just the man. The one who called to her and dared to reach past the barriers that she'd thrown between them.

Well, he'd won. She didn't want to fight her desires anymore. She didn't want to sit by and watch life. She wanted to live it. Experience it. With him.

She was in his arms before she knew it, feasting on his kisses this time. She let her body sink into his, anchoring herself to his strength, following both her instincts and his instructions.

"Wrap your arms around my neck," he murmured in English as he kissed her throat, working his way to her collar bone.

"This is what I've wanted since I saw you in the club last night." Her words came out in a rush, an odd jumble of Melesian and English. She didn't care.

His laughter was warm against her skin. "Now she speaks without shyness or hesitation. I see I'll have to change my tactics."

He pulled away so that she could see his eyes. His deep ocean-blue gaze left her hot all over. "In the past," he said returning to Melesian and carefully enunciating the words, "I have rewarded you with food. Now, I am rewarding you with kisses."

"And in the future?" The promise of kisses made her willing to stumble through the Melesian phrase.

"In the future, I shall reward you with much, much more, *Er'hona-mei*. My desirable one. What do you wish from me?"

"Everything. And nothing held back."

His kiss was swifter this time. And deeper. He ravaged her, stroking the roof of her mouth with his tongue, tickling the delicate inner flesh of her lower lip. Pressing her into his lap to feel the evidence of his passion.

Gracie took it all in and demanded more. She threaded her fingers through his hair, drinking in his kisses as if they were life-giving nectar. As if they were water, air.

When he cupped her breast, the unfamiliar warmth sent her into overload, senses reeling. The lightning-swift jolt of pleasure as he stroked her nipple made her gasp. And the deep tug of want that shot in moist electric throbs through her body burned away all coherent thought.

"*Er'hona-mei*," he whispered. His hand trailed down her body, across the exposed skin of her belly, to a brief, fleeting touch between her legs. Barely even a touch, it still seared through the thin material of her shorts, bringing a firestorm of aching, melting pleasure.

He stood, bringing them to their feet. Then he released her. The warmth of his touch shimmered across her nerve endings even though he stood inches away. His eyes were solemn, studying her, almost weighing her reactions. "If this is truly what you want," he said in soft English that left no room for misunderstanding, "bring the wine and follow me."

He grabbed a small covered platter from the table and walked from the library, not looking back.

And like a woman enthralled, she did his bidding and followed.

Chapter 23

racie's legs shook as she clutched the cool pitcher and goblet to her midriff. She knew what she wanted beyond a shadow of a doubt, but knowing didn't calm the nervous flutter in the pit of her stomach.

The short walk to Stephan's suite cooled her passions just enough to let doubt creep in. If she'd been a normal girl, she wouldn't be hesitating. She knew she'd never be the kind of woman to take lovemaking lightly, but a normal person wouldn't be standing here with her knees knocking at the thought of her own inexperience.

She should have stepped out from behind the books once in a while. It would have given her more confidence. But at what cost? Being here, now, with Stephan had a feeling that was special. Right. Worth waiting for. Worth even the self-doubts careening through her mind.

"Having second thoughts?"

Gracie shifted her gaze to the bed where Stephan lounged against the blue and silver coverlet. His tone was neutral, his body still, neither enticing her to come closer nor encouraging her to leave. And she understood in that moment that he was asking her to make her own choice. Again. To come to him of her own free will or not at all.

She refilled her wine goblet and put the pitcher on a table by the door. The spicy, sweet scent teased her nostrils and Gracie indulged in a sip to ease the dryness in her throat. She turned away from Stephan long enough to lock the door before facing him again.

"No second thoughts." She took a step forward.

"No urge to recite the multiplication tables? Or to entertain me with scholarly trivia?"

She shook her head. And took another step.

"If you're sure, *Er'hona-mei*, come to me."

Gracie closed the distance between them, letting her desire for Stephan overwhelm her insecurities. Allowing a strange, unfamiliar tug in her heart that she dared not name, guide her steps. She placed the goblet on the bedside table and eased down beside him.

Stephan drew her into a kiss that was gentle and enticing, a sharp contrast to his hungry, demanding kisses in the library. Had the aphrodisiacs really pushed them into a mating frenzy before?

But as his kiss continued and she melted against his body, passion stirred again in her. The build was slower this time, the hunger no less intense, but somehow less immediate. The taste and scent of the spices lingered on his lips, but it wasn't the spice that enticed her.

She searched her feelings, gathering what was left of her logic before it melted under his attentions. No food or drink could have caused this desire. No spice or drug. It was Stephan's tenderness and laughter that created the desire. The way he skirted her defenses and encouraged her to feel again. It was a thousand things, but her mind could no longer grasp the reasons. She could only feel the results.

Stephan shifted, pinning her beneath the weight of his body as he kissed along her jaw and down her throat. He wedged a knee between her legs, the sprinkling of hair on his calf tickling the sleek smoothness of her own.

"You are beautiful to me, Gracie, in every way a woman can be beautiful. Your wit. Your courage. Your trust. All wrapped up in a package to entice me."

He kissed lower, tracing the outline of her open neckline with his tongue before tugging at the knot on her blouse.

I'm not beautiful. The words she'd repeated without thought for so many years sprang to her mind, but they never left her mouth. Because tonight she felt beautiful.

Stephan burrowed beneath her barely-there shirt to caress her breast as he nuzzled aside the fabric to kiss his way along its other edge and she felt more than just desire welling up in her. More than just the tingles and tugs and squishy gushes of excitement in her gut. She felt not only desire—she felt *desirable.*

Every sweep of his tongue and each tiny nip and kiss that he planted on her skin proved it. The heat and hard press of his body against hers proved it. And the dark, pleasure-drenched look in his eyes when he raised his head took her breath away.

"I've never been enticing before."

"If only you knew," he answered softly. "I doubt that I'm the only one with eyes to see your beauty, or the wisdom to appreciate it. But I'm glad I'm the first to make you see yourself as I do."

He dipped his head again, nudging her shirt aside with kisses and sweeps of his tongue. Gracie shivered at the cool air that whispered across the moist trail of his kisses, and the thought of being exposed completely to his eyes and his touch. He locked his lips on her nipple and sucked.

Gracie bolted up, bracing against the mattress at the intensity of the arcing pleasure pouring from her nipple to her belly, and lower. Heat sizzled through her breast at each tug. He rewarded her panting with the scrape of his teeth and the flick of his tongue, drowning her in pleasure so deep she could barely breathe.

He moved over her, wedging himself completely between her legs, pushing them wider to accept his bulk. Gracie swallowed a moment of panic as he shifted her into the new, defenseless pose. Then, instinctively, she wrapped her legs around his waist, pulling his hips against hers until he settled into place, the nudge of his penis warm against her own vulnerable flesh, despite the thin layers of clothing that separated them.

Her sigh shuddered through the exquisite tension and she sank back into the soft bedding, contentment replacing the moment of fear. His intimate touch and her pulsing anticipation were almost enough.

"More?" he teased.

"Oh, yes, more."

Gracie released her lock on his waist and trailed her feet down the length of his legs, luxuriating in the feel of skin on skin.

Stephan slid a palm up her shorts, cupping the bare skin of her butt while teasing the edge of her panties with his thumb.

She moaned.

"If you want more," he said, sliding down her body to press a kiss into her navel, "then you need to be wearing less."

Gracie whimpered at the loss of intimate contact. "Yes, more," she managed. "More and less."

Though she urged him on, Stephan took his time. The touch of his fingers against her flesh as he slipped the button on her waist band free was too slow. The rasp of her zipper sliding open seemed to go on forever.

Even the slick press of his tongue to each exposed millimeter of flesh wasn't enough to ease the torment. It only filled her mind with images of other places he could bury his tongue, and lips, and teeth. And other ways in which they could join.

"You're going too slowly," she complained.

"You're telling me how to do my job." He paused, his fingers resting on her still clad hips. "I'd be happy to stop and listen to your detailed instructions. I won't make another move until you're sure I understand everything. I could even get up and take notes, if you like."

"No, I—"

"Or I could do it my way." He eased her clothing down the barest fraction of an inch then hesitated.

"Your ship," Gracie panted. "Your rules."

"*Aaya.* You learn quickly, *Er'hona-mei.*" He slowly swept the shorts over her hips, his hands and mouth replacing the cloth as he kissed each exposed area. "My ship. My rules. But everything designed for your pleasure."

Dimly she realized their conversation had drifted into a broken mixture of his language and hers, words of endearment and desire bantering back and forth between the two and forming a new love language all their own. Merging, just as they were merging.

His kiss found the moist crevice nestled at the juncture of her thighs and Gracie sucked in a breath. The images she'd imagined moments ago sprang to life in a whirl of sensation that was fire, ice, electricity, and something more.

Desire. Enchantment.

And longing.

Because as soon as his lips awakened the storm of pleasure, they moved on, leaving her wanting more. A nibble on her thigh. A caress on her calf. A kiss pressed into the arch of her foot. Each touch left her throbbing and whimpering, longing for his mouth to return to finish what he'd begun yet wanting the full body caress to go on forever.

He'd all but disappeared at the foot of the bed, sinking to his knees as he continued to work magic on her skin with his touch and his kisses.

Gracie squirmed with pleasure, feeling the force of it consume her one sensuous stroke at a time. When he paused, she gulped for breath and lay still, bound in the net of fire and ice that he'd wrapped her in. When she blinked to clear her vision, she saw his shirt fly through the air. She struggled to remove her own.

"Leave it." Stephan's voice was unfamiliar, rough and commanding. "I have plans for it later." He rose to his feet, towering over her from the foot of the bed, the tender lover transforming into the image of the god he'd once claimed to be.

Eros. Desire personified.

Naked, chiseled, and perfect.

And she was vulnerable. Enthralled. Caught between passion and inexperience. A willing prisoner bound for a destination she'd only read about.

Her gaze skimmed down the firm muscles of his chest to the flat, taut planes of his stomach. And lower still—

Her heart thudded, each stroke distinct and almost painful. Her blood pulsed, thick. Her breathing, heavy with effort. Everything, from the wash of cool air on her puckered nipples to the tingle where his nips and kisses had marked her legs, seemed both sharper and yet more muted—like the sounds and sights of her underwater paradise.

Everything except her center—the prickling pulse in the aching spot between her legs and the deep throb in her belly begged Stephan to return.

And he did return. His kisses were more carnal this time, the nips sharper, the desire he awakened in her more intense. The laughter was gone, replaced by a fierceness that thrilled her.

He grabbed her hips, rough rather than tender, and raised them high, lowering his mouth to her untouched flesh as if she were a feast—or a sacrifice—laid out for his pleasure.

His hold was firm, inescapable and demanding, but when he took her, his kiss was a fiery caress. He sucked spasms of pleasure from her in hungry gulps.

He consumed her, but with slow, thorough licks, savoring each motion, prolonging it. Turning her pleasure storm into something of tropical intensity. Each expert flick of his tongue sent lightning coursing through the very eye of her personal hurricane.

She screamed.

Then whimpered.

Even begged. "Please. More. Please."

His slick mouth was replaced by a gentle nudge of soft latex covered skin and hard desire. It wasn't what she begged for, but exactly what she needed.

"Look at me, Gracie." His voice was ragged, both commanding and imploring. He eased into her, stretching her flesh with the same exquisite care and slowness he'd used to remove her clothing. "Open your eyes and look at me."

She did. The sunlight and shadows glinting off the empty sea that stretched beyond their windows played across his face. It shuttered his smile, shadowed his eyes—hinting at danger before shifting again to reveal the softness and laughter carved into his expression.

Fantasy and myth merged with reality as he slid forward, bit by tight bit, marking the depth of his entrance with kisses along her torso.

Her navel. Her ribs. The valley between her breasts. The hollow of her throat.

"Mine," he declared fiercely, rushing forward even as she bucked against him and arched her back, exposing her throat and breasts to him without a single defense left to shield her.

He lifted her hips higher, forcing her to arch into complete submission before he twisted the shirt around her arms, pinning her helpless and open to his invasion. He took what she offered, devouring her flesh, marking it with nips and kisses and even tiny scratches as he raked his nails lightly across her sensitized skin.

And in the taking, he slid out, returning with more force, opening her tightness wider with each thrust. Commanding the force of the whirlwind sensations, like Neptune shaking the depths of the sea, he moved, sending both lightning and a pelting, stinging rain of desire rushing over her from the point of contact. From the slick slide of flesh within flesh to the frenzied friction of flesh upon sensitive flesh, he drenched her in pleasure.

Gracie screamed and collapsed in his hold, shaking from the force of her release, barely aware of his own shuddering orgasm. As the throbbing ebbed, her muscles squeezed his still hard erection. He rolled onto his back, sprawling her naked across his chest and ran a hand down her body. Without breaking their intimate connection, he stripped away the bonds of her shirt and stroked lower until his hand cupped her butt. Then he slipped one long finger between them to caress her swollen nub.

She jerked, the next shaft of pleasure as intense as it was unexpected. Her muscles clenched harder around his penis even as his fingers coaxed more spasms of pleasure from her.

"More, Gracie," he murmured, "much, much more."

She screamed a second time, and a third, and still her body pulsed to his touch as she surrendered to his demands.

And as the sunlight and shadow glinted off the empty sea to stretch across their naked bodies, reality faded into fantasy and myth, and Gracie surrendered to the man who held her, a willing captive on a journey beyond anything she'd ever imagined.

Stephan nestled Gracie beneath the covers, careful to move her as little as possible. Each movement caused her to whimper in her sleep, tiny little cries that worried him. Slender red lines dotted with larger abrasions marred her pale golden skin.

He'd meant to tease her into a passionate explosion, showing her dozens of ways her body could writhe with pleasure. But he hadn't meant to hurt her. The stiffness with which she moved in her sleep reminded him that he'd been too rough with her, badly underestimating her experience.

He'd known from the way she hesitated at his door that she wasn't sexually experienced. Her awkward starts and stops even had him wondering if she'd been a virgin, odd as that sounded for a woman of her age.

True, he hadn't pushed her into this, she'd come to him by her own choice. He'd tried to take things slowly, preparing her and letting her set the pace.

At least in the beginning.

He hadn't continued that way. The red marks on her body burned with glaring accusations. He should have known that her newly roused passion outpaced her stamina.

She'd needed a gentle, careful hand, but he'd let passion rule over sense. Even after he'd sated his own pleasure, he forced more from her. He'd pushed her into climax after climax simply for the satisfaction of watching her beautiful face shatter in ecstasy. He hadn't stopped until she collapsed in exhaustion.

Gracie whimpered again, only settling back into sleep when he moved closer and let her snuggle into his body. So much for his recriminations. She still sought him out.

He ran the back of his knuckles along the smooth curve of her breast, and she sighed in contentment. He nudged the spot between her legs with his thigh and she murmured a slight protest. The verdict was in. Inexperience caused her discomfort, but she trusted him in spite of it.

If only he could drift off into a healing sleep too. But he was wide awake, his unrepentant body urging him to take her again in her sleep. He could awaken her in more ways than one. Unfortunately, the thought of waking with Gracie's warmth clamped tightly around him had him hard and aching within seconds.

He gritted his teeth in frustration. One day she might find pleasure in a personal wake up call, but not today. Not after the hours they'd just shared.

Guilt nudged him with sharp fingers. He was the experienced partner. He was responsible for more than just her pleasure. The passion he'd given her and the surrender he'd demanded formed a bond between them. One he'd forged with full knowledge of the consequences. He intended to stay by her side, faithful in every way for as long as she'd have him.

With the bond came obligations. He was responsible for her well-being. He'd forgotten that in the heat of their passion last night. No matter how much she tempted him this morning, he wouldn't forget again.

In time, he could give her everything she wanted, but that was the key. Time. Patience. For both of them. So he fought the frustration and pulled her close, determined to put her needs above his own.

"More," she muttered. The soft Melesian word slipped easily from her sleeping lips.

Being responsible was going to be the hardest thing he'd ever done. Still, Stephan smiled to himself. She no longer feared and fought the language. Maybe there was hope that she would one day embrace his country as willingly as she'd embraced him last night. If she could only come to that.

"More," she uttered again.

"Later," he whispered against her hair as he gathered her closer. "Much, much later."

Chapter 24

Sunlight teased Gracie through her half-closed eyes. She clamped them shut against the intrusions and focused instead on the warm, hard body that pillowed her head. She moved slightly, not wanting to wake him, and winced at the tenderness she felt.

Memories of their lovemaking surged in her mind and, for a moment, it felt as if he was still buried within her. Her body pulsed slightly at the memory of his invasion. She'd never felt so physically vulnerable—at someone else's mercy—in her life. Yet she'd also never felt more powerful, knowing that she unleashed the ferocity within him. And that she could control it with a single word.

"*Er'hono-mei*," she whispered, liking the way the endearment felt on her tongue.

He stirred. "Good morning, beautiful one." The words were blurred and roughened from sleep, all the more endearing because they lacked his usual smoothness.

Gracie ran a hand along his chest, enjoying the play of his muscles as they twitched beneath her fingers. "What a," she paused, not finding the words to describe her feelings in either language, "night."

"Do you mean that in a good way, or a bad way?" Humor wove its way through the sleepiness.

"Definitely a good way. Indescribably good. Literally."

"So our incomparable lovemaking leaves you speechless. I'm flattered."

Our lovemaking. Gracie hugged the words to herself. *Ours*. "Actually, you were the one to leave me speechless. You and the aphrodisiac laced dinner we shared."

"Speaking of that, there's something I forgot to share with you." He sat up in bed and moved against the headboard.

Gracie scrunched her pillow beneath her head and gazed up at him, taking in the faint growth of whiskers and his tousled, slightly wild hair. Even in the early morning light, he looked perfect to her eyes.

Stephan uncovered the small platter from the night before and plucked something from it to offer her. "Sugared rose petals," he said brushing the grainy yet soft tidbit across her lips. "A favorite delicacy for lovers."

She took it, letting the sweetness melt on her tongue. The slight tang of the rose followed. "I like it." She struggled to sit beside him, ignoring the twinges of discomfort that accompanied the movement.

Stephan's eyes darkened as he fed her another rose petal. "It's all right, *hona-mei*. These are for you. I won't indulge in any more rumored aphrodisiacs this morning."

At his words, her doubts rushed back. He may have said their lovemaking was incomparable, but why did he shy away from indulging again? He'd called her beautiful this morning, but not desirable. Was her inexperience a turn off to someone as worldly as Stephan?

Gracie pushed away the next treat he offered.

"No more?"

"I—" She shook her head, not trusting her voice. "I don't think I should indulge, either," she managed.

"Gracie? Gracie, look at me." He brushed her jaw gently, encouraging her to turn back to him. She'd steeled herself to resist force, but she couldn't resist temptation. Still, looking at him in this situation was the harder than she could have imagined.

"Gracie, sweetheart, I don't need aphrodisiacs to make me want you. Not last night and not this morning. But I think that maybe you need some time to adjust. It's been a long time for you, hasn't it? Or perhaps this was the first time."

The hint of a question in his voice had her nodding. Heat crept into her cheeks.

He wrapped an arm around her. "First times are like champagne, Gracie. Better sipped than gulped. The aftereffects are less painful that way. I should have warned you, in both cases. I seem to have introduced you into too many forms of indulgence this weekend."

"And I thought you were such a good teacher."

"Next time, I'll teach you to savor the moments. And, I promise, you'll wake up wanting more."

"I already want more."

"In that case, let me teach you about the pleasures of anticipation."

He tilted her head for a kiss that was a mere touch of lip to lip before deepening it to hint at greater intimacy. Each subsequent move was slow, deliberate and an end in itself. When she pressed for more passion, he pulled away, giving her tender exploration instead. At last when he lifted his head, she felt an odd mixture of contentment tinged with disappointment.

"That," he said, "should last you at least until tonight."

"Why should I wait?"

"Making up for lost time, Gracie? There's no rush, you know."

He kissed her again, this time brushing his hand down her body in a languid caress. When he cupped the apex of her thighs, she sucked in a breath and moved, surprised that she still felt tender, despite her rising desire.

Almost immediately, he shifted his caress to her hip and worked his way up her body. "Anticipation," he whispered as he nibbled her ear. "Remember?"

"*Aaya*," she murmured.

"Good. I promise I'll make it worth the wait." He moved away, swinging his legs over the side of the bed to sit. He rested his head in his hands for a long time before speaking again. "Besides, you should give your body time to adjust."

"*Hono-mei*?" She touched his shoulder, feeling the tense muscles bunch beneath her fingers.

"It's like diving," he began, his tone growing more matter of fact with each word. "If you rush back to the surface after a deep dive, your body can't handle the change of conditions. We both dove deeper than we've ever been before. I— You— We need time to adjust," he added almost to himself.

Stephan stood and faced her, a tiny frown creasing his forehead. "Trust me on this, okay?"

His hesitancy tore at her, leaving her unsettled. Was it gallantry that made him walk away? Or something else? Gracie struggled, not sure whether to feel rejected, or chastised, or cherished.

At the threshold to the bathroom, he turned to her, his smile less sure than she'd ever seen it. "I'm headed for the shower. You're welcome to join me." Then he disappeared.

Gracie dug her wrinkled shirt from beneath the covers and shrugged into it. After last night, it shouldn't have mattered, but she wanted the cover. This morning wasn't what she'd expected.

Not that she really knew what to expect. She hadn't planned for hearts and flowers and happily ever after this morning. Still, she'd hoped for more than this on-again, off-again reaction from Stephan. His words said one thing and his actions another.

She walked to the window and gazed into the emptiness beyond. *One times nine is nine. Two times nine is eighteen. Three times nine is twenty-seven. Four times…* She rattled through the calculations as she paced between the window and the rumpled bed. *Thirteen times thirteen is… Disaster.*

If their lovemaking had been incredible for him, why was he putting her off? Or was he? She didn't know anymore. *Thirteen times thirteen is one hundred and sixty-nine doubts battering her into an emotional morass.* There wasn't a formula to explain it.

Gracie headed to his bathroom. The sound of running water guided her through the nautilus shell spiral, tiled in blue and green sea-inspired colors. The calm colors didn't soothe her. The scattered, whimsical fish-painted tiles didn't make her smile. The sight of Stephan, naked and drenched in the spray of the multiple shower heads that lined the tiled walls, didn't make her doubts go away.

He turned. "So you did decide to join me."

"That depends." Gracie looked at him through the curtain of steam. "Are you inviting me for a shower, or something more?"

"*Er'hona-mei,* your desire is flattering, but have I not told you several times that I think you should pace yourself?" Impatience sharpened his voice. "This is frustrating for me too."

"Then why? What's wrong?" Gracie hated the need that colored her words, but once the doubts surfaced, she couldn't control them. She'd known their worlds were too different. They couldn't have forever together. But she'd hoped for more than a single night. "Have I done something wrong?"

He paced to the main water stream, ducked his head under and gave the knob a sharp twist. The steam in the shower dissipated, turning to cool mist. Tepid water lapped at Gracie's bare feet. Lukewarm. Just like his reactions to her.

After a minute, Stephan stepped out of the cold stream, his desire still rampant despite the chill. Sluicing the water from his hair, he turned back to her. When he spoke, both his face and voice were calm, almost diplomatic. "Last night was wonderful. You were incredible. But I didn't expect—" He took a deep breath, and she realized the calmness was an illusion. "I knew you were shy. I just didn't realize how inexperienced you were until, until sometime after it was too late."

"You're telling me you regret sleeping with me because I was a virgin?"

"No. I don't regret anything. But, that is, most women— It's as if you were waiting on purpose. For something special. What if I destroyed that for you?"

"Maybe you were the something special."

"Even so, I feel—"

"Don't." Gracie reached inside for the cold logic that had seen her through so many hurts in the past. Hiding the quiver in her voice behind the same matter-of-fact tone he'd used earlier, she forced the next words out. Truth or lie, they were the words one was supposed to use in this situation—or so she hoped.

"Please don't say you feel guilty. Or responsible. Or any of those things. I don't expect anything from you. I'm a modern woman. You know, no strings attached."

Rather than relaxing, his features hardened. He paced the tiled expanse, muscles tensing beneath his gleaming wet skin. "So now I've gone from being something special to being disposable? That's not how it works in my world, Gracie."

"And which world would that be, Stephan? The island paradise designed to lure lovers? Or the world of the royal family that is so unreachable, it actually rears its brides from birth for their future position?"

"You, of all people, know better than that."

"Do I? Just because my sister broke your traditions doesn't mean they don't exist. Tell me this, Stephan. Would you have been surprised to discover Sophia was a virgin? Or did you expect that from her?"

"That's different."

"Exactly my point. The rules are different for people in your world."

"In my world, a night like we shared means something. Your ideas about a one-night stand are as off base as your images of cosseted virgin brides."

Gracie's stomach knotted. His words had gone from frustrated to angry and they pounded against her overloaded emotions.

A picture of Sophia blandly accepting her role as spare bride to the next available prince burned in Gracie's memory, a stark reminder that Stephan's words and the traditions of his government were at odds. He was bound to those traditions, as surely as she was excluded from them. In spite of last night.

"Gracie, listen to me." Stephan's voice lost its edge as he looked at her through the cool mist. "You were innocent by choice, and that's what this is all about. You. Your choices. And the consequences of those choices."

"I can handle the consequences on my own."

"That's where you're wrong. We both have to deal with them. I invited you into my bed. And you came of your own free will."

"Then I guess I made the wrong choice, didn't I?"

Stephan paused, the hand that was poised to push his hair out of his eyes frozen in place. Tension radiated from him, buffeting her in hot waves. His slack jaw and flat, emotionless gaze frightened her. "You can't mean that."

She didn't know anymore. She only knew that if she stayed any longer, she'd dissolve into a blubbering heap on the floor of his shower. Gracie stepped back. "Good—" she sucked in a shuddering breath. "Good-bye."

She fled from the shower.

"Don't expect me to follow you. I have bigger problems to fix."

His parting words—and the lack of emotion behind them—cut deep. Gracie gathered her belongings and asked Petros to take her back to the mainland in the dinghy. As she watched the yacht recede from sight, she cursed herself for falling for a man who saw her as nothing more than a problem to fix. Why couldn't she love a—

"*Laddos*," she whispered, the word lost in the sound of the motor. Love. She was in love with him. In love with a man she could never have. And there wasn't a thing she could do about it.

Thirteen times thirteen equals a broken heart.

Chapter 25

Stephan slammed his hand against the unforgiving tiles. What did she mean, throwing his heritage into his face like that? He thought she'd been able to see through all the complications of his life and appreciate him as a man. She'd seemed appreciative enough last night.

But that was the problem. He'd allowed his attraction to her to overwhelm his sense of propriety. She'd seen him as a man, all right. Just not the kind of man he wanted to be.

How was Gracie to know that by inviting her to his yacht, to his bed, that he was inviting her into his life? How was she to know that his tender words weren't casual endearments but something more?

He slammed his hand into the shower wall again. Damn it! She should know. She should at least suspect. They'd spent weeks together. He wasn't some stranger she picked up in a bar. If she'd known anything at all about him—even the overly exaggerated media fabrications, for god's sake—she'd have known he wasn't a man for casual relationships.

Despite her claims of wanting nothing from him, he knew she wasn't causal about relationships either. So what had just happened? How had they gone from him trying to tell her how much he valued her to them arguing about musty traditions?

And Sophia. She couldn't have chosen a better weapon against him if she'd tried. Of course, Sophia was different from Gracie. Gracie saw the world and dealt with it on her own terms. Sophia, in contrast, had lived isolated and sheltered by her power-hungry guardians for as long as he could remember. She was the remnant of tradition that always came back to haunt him.

Damn the scheming Duke de Lyons for his political ambitions. Even from the island prison where Constantine had exiled him, de Lyons still created mischief.

After he left Sophia defenseless and miserable, it was no wonder she'd run away. But her upbringing hadn't prepared her for life outside of the protection of the royal court.

The simplest solution of all was the one he couldn't quite stomach. He should marry her once she returned to Melesia, thus forging another bond between the D'Malia and the de Lyons families. It would buy peace for another generation. Stabilize the government. Free his brother to institute reforms.

And it would kill him.

He loved Sophia like a little sister, nothing more. She deserved better than a life controlled by scheming relatives or dominated by cold political necessity.

But before he could figure out a way to make things better for all of them, Stephan had to find her. It was his duty. If he failed, the scandal would haunt the monarchy for decades.

It was just that Gracie made him forget everything but her.

The stricken look in her eyes this morning would live in his memory forever. How could he sacrifice her needs to focus on the needs of his country? And yet how could he ignore his duty for the sake of his heart?

He turned off the cold spray and dried himself, putting on his mask of diplomatic amiability along with his clothes. He regretted his thoughtless parting words to Gracie. He'd intended to tell her about his upcoming schedule and the difficulties of meeting her next week, but not that way. Not like an arrogant, imperialistic bastard.

But guilt alone wouldn't set things right. He had to find her and explain himself. He hadn't lied. He did face a week of problems—starting with the American, Dr. Joyner, and his proposals involving Melesian resources.

Continuing with ramping up his failed search for Sophia. And now, more important than everything, finding Gracie and apologizing for the muddled way he'd handled her feelings. Convincing her that he wanted more than a night of pleasure from her.

It wouldn't be easy, he realized as he emerged onto the deck of the yacht. The distant sound of the motorboat told him before he needed to ask anyone.

Gracie was gone.

Marta pounced on her almost as soon as Gracie entered the dorm. She burst through the connecting bathroom, spewing questions.

"Gracie Smith, how could you keep something like that from me? We're supposed to be best friends. How did you meet? How long have you been seeing each other behind my back? I want details."

Gracie took a deep breath and faced her friend. "I'm a little tired right now, can I tell you later?" She pulled her sunglasses off and tossed them on the desk.

"No, it can't wait. I want detail—" Marta broke off and looked at her. "They can wait. What's wrong? You look terrible."

"We had our first fight. Our first real one, anyway. I left and he—"

She was engulfed in a warm hug before she could begin to explain. A short while later they sat, curled side by side on her bed, chatting over a cup of tea and American Fantasy Fudge chocolates stolen from the supply she used to decorate the pillows of royal guests. Gracie poured out the highlights of the past days, starting with her flight from the club and ending with her flight from the yacht.

"It looks like I'm always running away from trouble, doesn't it?"

"You're running from something, but it isn't trouble. You've been bombarded with a lot of emotional stuff this weekend, Gracie. Anyone would be overwhelmed. And that's if the *hono* were a normal guy."

Gracie sniffed then summoned a smile. "Do me a favor. Don't call your brothers to carry out your threats to him just yet. Despite everything, I'd hate to see Stephan damaged."

"I'll keep them in check until he at least has a chance to apologize. Besides, I have a feeling you're not the only one who's dealing with emotional fall-out today. He was really worried about you when you left the club the other night, Gracie."

"I know."

"I've lived in this country all my life, and I've seen the royal family as much as anyone. More, since I've been assigned to work on Royal Island. But I've never seen him look like that. He's always been charming but distant. That night he looked like, well, I don't know how to describe it. It was like peeling away a mask. He looked real."

"Yeah." Gracie sat up and put her cup on the floor. She stared at it, chewing the inside of her lip in indecision. "He is real, Marta. Listen, there's a bunch more stuff I have to tell you. But it has to remain between us."

"Okay. But start with how you two met. I'm dying to know."

"Here goes." Gracie nodded and turned to her friend. "We met almost two years ago, at my sister's wedding."

Gracie told Marta the truth about everything—her relationship with Jill, her fear of the media, her reasons for using an alias, and her growing relationship with Stephan. She glossed over her childhood and skirted the damning details about her bargain with Sophia. Still, it felt good to unburden herself to someone she trusted.

Marta listened, looking slightly stunned, but taking it all in with only a few interruptions for questions. When Gracie finished, Marta turned to her.

"Bradley, huh? That's quite a story. But I admit, it makes sense when I think about it. I don't blame you for wanting to hide from it. I'd be a lot worse if I were living in the shadow of Queen Jillian."

"I've lived in Jill's shadow all my life. Mom used to call her *the pretty one* and me *the smart one*. Maybe that's why I have so much trouble learning your language. It's the one subject I have trouble with and the one subject Jill excels at. Deep down, I guess I'm reinforcing the differences between us. Unlike my sister, I can't learn languages and I've spent my life proving to the world I'm not pretty."

"Gracie, don't be ridiculous. Just listen to yourself."

"Please, this isn't about how I look or dress. That doesn't matter to me."

"I don't mean look at yourself." Marta paced the short expanse of the room and turned to her, hands on hips. "I mean *listen* to yourself. You don't even realize that you've been speaking in Melesian for almost this whole conversation, do you? You know more than you think. You just never put it all together before. Professor Mikolas is going to be surprised."

Marta was right. Somewhere in the last days, Gracie had stopped worrying about whether her words were right or wrong and just started speaking. The knowledge gave her a surge of confidence. And an idea.

"Marta, don't let her—or anyone—know. I'll explain later because I might need your help." Gracie rummaged through her drawers and headed to the shower, mind racing.

Stephan's no English edict had not only broken through her resistance to the language, but it also gave her a secret weapon to help gather information for Constantine. "Right now, I need a shower and some sleep. Then I need time to think."

Chapter 26

A day later Gracie knocked on a guest room door, steeling herself for the tedium of the next hours. She'd been assigned to act as Mrs. Joyner's personal tour guide and assistant. Playing up to wealthy executives and their wives had never been her strong suit.

"It's a pleasure to meet you," Mrs. Joyner said after Gracie introduced herself. "You speak beautiful English, by the way. The young woman who makes up my room has a very strong accent. She's hard to understand."

"I'm from the U.S., studying at the Royal Academy." Gracie led the way from the guest rooms and headed toward the grand salon of the palace.

"Oh, I see. So what made you decide to study here? Let me guess." The older woman gave her a broad wink. "I'm sure you were as fascinated by the recent royal wedding as everyone. Wasn't it romantic? A beautiful American taming the heart of a powerful monarch. It's the stuff of fairy tales. Life doesn't get more romantic than that."

"Actually, I wanted to study here because the marine biology program is one of the best in the world. Many of the pools and aquariums on Royal Island contain specimens you won't see anywhere else. I could schedule a tour of the national aquarium for later in your visit, if you'd like. The country is home to a number of unique species."

"I'm sure it is. But the fish aren't the only unique species here. Doesn't the king have a very eligible, and handsome younger brother? Surely, he is at least as intriguing as the fish. If I were twenty years younger and single, I'd be studying here too. Tell me a little about him. Gossip. Girl talk. We can chat while you show me around the island."

"You must be referring to Prince Stephan." Gracie swallowed her irritation at another person treating Stephan as if he was nothing more than a cartoon character walking around Melesia for their amusement. She led Mrs. Joyner into the Grand Hall where the floor-to-ceiling aquarium dominated the landscape. "I understand that your husband recently participated in Prince Stephan's Energy and Industry Summit."

"Yes. Dr. Joyner found the prince and his ideas intriguing. In fact, that's why we've returned. My husband thinks there are opportunities here for a man of his skills and the prince's vision. You'll be seeing a lot more of us in the future.

"But let's not waste our time together dealing with weighty business matters. They can't be as intriguing as royal gossip. Have you worked in the palace for long? You must know lots of juicy secrets."

"I'm afraid not." Gracie kept her tone professional and polite, but the image of Stephan as she'd left him haunted her. She'd been wrong to run out the way she had.

"Miss Smith?" Mrs. Joyner snapped her back to the present. "Remembering some juicy secrets after all?"

"I'm sorry," Gracie said, suppressing her irritation at Mrs. Joyner's fascination with gossip. "I was daydreaming."

"I'm sure I can guess the subject of your thoughts." Mrs. Joyner gave her another wink. "I'll have a chance to do some daydreaming of my own tomorrow. Prince Stephan has asked us to join him on his yacht for a tour of Neptune Island. I've heard it's his private retreat, restricted to all but a few privileged visitors. I'm sure he has some exciting secrets hidden there."

"Actually, Neptune Island is restricted because of its expansive, ancient coral formations. Our national aquarium has an entire wing dedicated to the Neptune's Crown Reef."

"I was never much for museums and such. But the chance to see the island from the prince's yacht is too tempting to pass up. Neptune Island has a reputation as one of the last untouched places on earth. Dr. Joyner thinks it would be an ideal site to produce his new line of bottled water."

She made a sweeping gesture with her hands as if unfurling an advertising banner. "'*Neptune Island Bottled Water: The Drink of the Gods. The purest water from the most pristine location on Earth.*' I think it's quite catchy. It would be an instant best seller. My husband's company will provide the equipment, chemistry, and expertise. Melesia only needs to provide the land for the plant, the water to purify, and that yummy, romantic image."

"You want to build a manufacturing plant on Neptune Island?" Gracie swallowed a surge of anger at the thought of building anything on Neptune Island.

Stephan's role was to protect Melesia's natural resources, not exploit them. Why would he even discuss such a proposal with the Joyners? She tried to picture Stephan agreeing to the scheme Mrs. Joyner described, but she couldn't. Were the Joyners simply trying to steamroll him into something? Could they?

"It's a profitable opportunity for both of us. I'm sure the men will discuss it further tomorrow. Speaking of which, I'll see more than enough fish and things while I'm on the prince's yacht. What I'd like to do today is to shop. Doesn't the queen have a private shopping gallery in the palace?"

Gracie nodded, not trusting her voice. Fuming over Stephan's dealings with the odious couple, she led the way to the palace rotunda where boutiques supplied by local merchants and designers kept a selection of goods primarily for the royal family and their honored guests. Or, in the case of Mrs. Joyner, their wealthy guests.

As Mrs. Joyner shopped, Gracie hovered in the background, fighting the queasiness that threatened whenever she thought of the couple invading what had become her private space with Stephan. The images of him relaxing on the reef wouldn't reconcile with the image of him entertaining a proposal by the money hungry Joyners. She needed to speak with him privately.

She slipped a schedule out of her apron pocket and consulted it. The Joyners planned to stay through the week. Which meant she wouldn't have time alone with Stephan for days.

The queasiness in her gut turned into a knot as she replayed their last minutes together. Who had pushed whom away? And why? Everything she'd wanted to say had come out garbled and wrong. Had it been that way for him too? They'd parted barely a day ago, yet it felt like years.

She'd reached for the phone a dozen times since yesterday, but each time she put it away, aware that a phone call was the coward's way out. And she'd silenced it for class and work, only realizing in the last hour that Stephan had been busy juggling the Joyners along with the rest of his official duties.

Voices along the corridor caught her attention. "Believe me, Your Highness, if I know my wife, she'd rather be shopping than going on a tour of the grounds. She's shopped her way through more tourist sights than just about anyone."

The jovial voice grew louder as he continued the one-sided conversation. "Of course, if *you* invited her on a personal tour, I'm sure she'd join you. She's fascinated with your family. Has a scrapbook bulging with photos. That's why I am so pleased that we'll be working together. Assuming you get your brother to buy into the idea. But that's just a matter of time. Just a matter of time."

"I have agreed to consider your ideas, Dr. Joyner. That is all." The implacable tone in his voice reassured Gracie that, while he might handle the couple diplomatically, he would definitely not agree to their business plan. Relief softened the tension in her body.

"I appreciate your caution, son, I mean, Your Highness. But it could boost your economy enormously and your people would benefit. Take some time to think about it and we can talk more tomorrow."

As they entered the rotunda, Gracie twisted, trying to look around Dr. Joyner's bulk, but she couldn't see Stephan's face.

"Oh, there's my wife now. I'll just go fill her in on our plans."

Dr. Joyner walked away, leaving Stephan by the fountain that stood in the center of the rotunda. Even from a distance, Gracie could feel the tension in his stance. He reached into his pocket and brought out a fisted hand.

Gracie left her post, quietly crossing the distance as she watched him pop several antacid tablets. His profile remained as rigid as the marble of the fountain. With a flick of his thumb, he worked another tablet loose from the roll.

She stopped him by laying her hand atop his fist. "You're not responsible for everyone and everything," she said softly. "Give yourself a break, Stephan, you don't have to be perfect all the time."

He looked at her, his eyes bleak and tired. But he also nodded, as if agreeing. "I—"

"I'm sorry about yesterday," she said before he could finish his thought. "I shouldn't have left that way."

"I wasn't trying to push you away. I was glad you chose to be with me. I still am. And I didn't mean what I said when you left."

Gracie rubbed his knuckles with her thumb, feeling some of the tension seep out of him. The look in his eyes softened. She pitched her voice at a whisper, "We both said and did things we didn't mean. Besides, I think the Joyners *are* a bit of a problem. Their plans for Neptune Island are horrifying. I refuse to believe you'd even consider them."

"*Aaya*, their ideas *are* horrid. And they are a problem." A hint of a smile curved along his lips as he took her hand in his. "I will never let them destroy something as special as our reef. The place where we began to trust one another."

Our reef. The words conjured memories of their time together, making her heart overflow with happiness and something more.

A delighted cry and the burst of a flash photo broke the moment. "Oh look, William! The prince and my student guide. It's positively romantic." Mrs. Joyner shot another photo.

"Looks like it's back to work, *hona-mei*," Stephan murmured as he raised her hand for a courtly kiss. "Until later."

"Much too much later," she whispered. She felt him press the roll of antacids into her palm, and she took it, instinctively knowing he didn't want Dr. and Mrs. Joyner to see his weakness. "Thank you, Your Highness," she said aloud in English as she dipped a quick curtsey and backed a step away.

The look in his eyes as he turned back to his guests told her everything would be all right.

Chapter 27

racie toyed with the half-eaten roll of antacids, lost in thought, as she curled up on the couch in the queen's salon.

"He never used to need those, but now he's rarely without them," Jill said.

"How did you know they weren't mine?"

"Probably because you've been fiddling with them for half an hour, but you haven't eaten any. What's up, sweetie?"

"We, um, spent a night together." Gracie flicked her sister a glance, but Jill's features didn't change. "And please don't tell me I shouldn't have."

"That's not my call to make. I used to urge you to wait for the right person, but only you can tell who that is."

"I thought I knew. But then the next morning we had a fight. It was stupid, when I think back on it. But my thoughts were so tangled up that it seemed like I couldn't stop myself from saying and doing all the wrong things. It was almost like I wanted to push him away after the wonderful night we'd had. How dumb is that?"

She felt a surge of annoyance when Jill laughed. "It's not funny."

"No, but the secret I'm about to share with you is." Jill settled back into the cushions, a dreamy smile on her face. "But first, you're not stupid, and you're not unusual. You're also not the only one to pick a fight after making love. I think all lovers fight.

"It's a natural reaction to feeling so vulnerable and in love that you don't know what to do. Especially the first time." Her face darkened for a moment, but the look was fleeting. "And the first time after a long time."

Gracie twirled the roll of antacids between her fingers, addressing her next words to them. "Stephan said something similar. Not about fighting. But about knowing it was a first for me. He said first times are like champagne, better sipped than gulped."

"He's a very caring and perceptive man. But I don't necessarily agree with him. Constantine and I didn't spend much time sipping, if you get my meaning. He was passionate and almost—"

"Domineering?" Gracie looked up.

"Exactly." Jill regarded her with a shrewd eye. "You too?"

Gracie nodded. "He was gentle, at first. Then… it was unlike anything I'd ever experienced. He wasn't cruel or distant, but it was as if he changed into—into something unstoppable. And, to be honest, I didn't want to stop him."

"The brothers sound a lot alike. It's part of what Queen Helena calls the D'Malia charm. They're considerate and loving but passionate beyond belief. It takes a strong woman to handle them. If it's any comfort, I think you're up to the task."

She took Jill's hand and squeezed, grateful for the support. "I only wish I hadn't argued with him. When I left, he was just standing there, in the shower, looking like I'd slapped him."

"Did you?"

Gracie was horrified. "Of course not. I wouldn't think of hurting him that way."

"You're a kinder woman than I was. Only a few people know this, but in our first fight, I threw everything within reach at Constantine. To this day, he claims I married him only to escape capital punishment for assaulting the future king."

"You didn't!" Gracie didn't try to hold in the laughter that bubbled up inside.

"I did. Shoes, books, pottery. You name it. I didn't stop until he'd wrestled me to the bed and pinned me down." She sobered. "Loving a D'Malia man isn't easy, Gracie. I won't pretend otherwise. But I promise you, they are worth the trouble."

"Do you think it could be love?" Gracie glanced at the antacids clutched in her hand and admitted the truth of what she was feeling. But Stephan?

"Honey, if I know the two of you, it couldn't be anything else."

A comfortable silence wrapped itself around Gracie. When she glanced at Jill again, a wave of emotion—longing, love, and regret in equal measures—washed over her. She touched her sister's hand. "Jill?"

"Hmm?"

"I missed this." At Jill's puzzled frown, Gracie continued. "Us. Talking. Sharing. I—I'm so, so sorry that I…" She couldn't form the words.

Jill slid closer, letting go of Gracie's hand and wrapping an arm around her instead. "Shh. It's okay. Everything is okay."

Gracie leaned into Jill's embrace, sorting through her words. "I—that is—" She took a breath and tried again. "Daddy always said I could count on you. No matter what. That you'd always be there for me."

"I am. And I will always be."

"But I didn't deserve you." Gracie raised her head to look in her sister's eyes. "I pushed you away because I didn't deserve you. Not after how I behaved." She launched into the story she'd shared with Stephan, pouring out her feelings of guilt and remorse as Jill's expression went from confused, to concerned, to shocked.

"Gracie. Honey. It wasn't your fault." Jill tightened her hug and rocked Gracie in her arms. Eventually she spoke. "For years, I blamed myself. For his death. For the distance between you and me. For all of it."

"You didn't—"

"I called him to pick me up from a party. A wild, drunken party," she said, explaining to Gracie details they had never before shared. "So you see, it was as much my fault as it was yours."

Gracie stilled, looking at the situation through her sister's eyes. "How horrible for you." She wrapped her arms around Jill, returning the hug and trying to send a message of love and forgiveness. Minutes passed in silence.

"I think we should blame the deer that ran in front of the car. And the rain," Gracie said at last, giving Jill one final squeeze. "Anything but ourselves and each other."

Her sister laughed, a sound half mirth and half sob. "We probably should." When Jill pulled away, Gracie stared at her sister through a haze of moisture.

"What was the last thing you remember about him?" Jill wiped her eyes dry and waited.

"The night before—" She swallowed painfully. "He told me I was beautiful, and that he loved me." Warmth surged through Gracie as the words came back to her. "I'd buried that memory. Thank you. What about you?"

"I remember seeing disappointment in his eyes."

"Oh, Jill." Gracie cupped her sister's cheek. "He was always proud of you. He told me I should always try to be as loving and kind as you were." Jill's eyes shimmered in front of Gracie's face, but whether from her tears or Jill's she didn't know.

"Thank you," Jill whispered, folding Gracie's hands in her own and squeezing. "For the memory, and for being here now."

A brief tap at the door interrupted Jill and Gracie as they talked about memories of their father and their childhood. When Alia walked in, hands filled with papers, Gracie was momentarily startled by the sight of her supervisor. Then she remembered Alia had taken on responsibility for the student workers at Jill's request.

It was another person who kept her secrets just so Gracie could try to step out of Jill's shadow. Looking at her sister now, she realized she no longer wanted to push her family away any more than she wanted to push Stephan away.

"I've brought you the afternoon newspapers, madam," Alia said as she placed the papers on the table in front of the couch.

"Oh, my. They must be bad if you're being formal with me." Jill picked up a thin tabloid from the top of the stack. "I'd be really worried if you were calling me *Your Majesty*."

"Old habits die hard."

"Alia was my first friend in Melesia," Jill explained. "She introduced me to all of the royal protocol. I used to practice for hours with her, in front of a mirror, until I was comfortable with the proper way to receive visitors, the way to address the various nobles and a thousand other things. She started calling me by my new titles—even before my official engagement and marriage—to help me get used to it."

"And now look at you. You are so natural you could have been born to the position." Alia smiled and sat in a nearby chair. "Sometimes even I forget we were friends first."

"Don't you dare. It's easy to collect companions when you're queen. It's much harder to find friends." Jill unfolded the news sheet. "How are things in the world of gossip today, Alia? Do we need to plan any intervention strategies?"

"It's not too bad, really. A couple of unflattering photos, side-by-side, along with a comment wondering if you're really pregnant. Some speculations on whether or not the king is happy about it. That sort of stuff. Nothing damaging. Thank goodness that Mack the Pen character doesn't work for the *Weekly World Stir* anymore. Things could have been a lot worse."

"Who's Mack the Pen?" Gracie took another paper from the stack and scanned the headlines and photos. She cringed at the tawdry implications they made about Jill. "And why aren't you bothered by this junk?"

"My friends," Jill squeezed Gracie's hand briefly, "and my family, remind me of who I really am. Plus Constantine and Stephan and all the royal family have dealt with this their entire lives. They know all the strategies to avoid or minimize damage."

"And Mack the Pen?"

Alia answered while Jill turned to another paper. "He's a tabloid journalist who used to use the byline *All the truth—and a little bit more.* He specialized in covering the royal family. While he never actually lied, he was a master at presenting the truth in as scintillating a manner as possible."

"I have to admit, I used to read his work when I was living in Chicago. It seemed like harmless fun back then. It's different being on the other side of the coin." Jill abandoned the paper. "He seems to have quit the business shortly after our wedding."

"Good thing for you. And for Gracie too." She addressed her next words to Gracie. "If he'd have been angling for a story, it wouldn't have taken him long to figure out who you were.

He would have taken dozens of photos until he found just the right one. Say one of you at work, kneeling to polish a table leg or reaching to plug in a lamp.

"Then he would have run it next to a photo of Jill at a formal affair with a headline like this. "Queen's Sister Forced to Cower in Near Poverty While the Queen Enjoys Lavish Banquets." He would have been scrupulous about describing the student worker program all the while making it seem like you were begging for your education. As his tag line says, his words would have been *All the truth* but the implications would have been *a little bit more.*"

Gracie sucked in a breath and clutched the antacids in her fist. No wonder Stephan was always so careful with his public image. No wonder the royal family created layers of insulation between themselves and the outside world.

"It's a little harder to learn to handle the tabloids than it is to learn the proper forms of protocol. It does get easier with time. Since Mack the Pen left, most of the tabloids are too outrageous for anyone to believe." Jill handed Gracie a headline proclaiming "Queen's Baby Fathered by Aliens" and laughed. "In a few days, something much more interesting will crop up."

Alia stood. "I'd better leave now. I promised the cook I'd give her my mother's recipe for ginger butter cookies."

"You're a lifesaver. Those cookies are the only things that seem to calm my morning sickness."

"She sent you another packet." Alia reached into her apron pocket and passed the cookies to Jill. "And I almost forgot. This came for you."

Jill accepted the cookies and an envelope, thanking Alia. When they were alone again, Jill opened the letter and read it.

"It's from Mom. She's hoping we can both come home for Thanksgiving. What do you think, Gracie? Can the Queen of

Melesia and her undercover sister escape long enough to take a road trip to Ohio?"

Gracie suddenly longed to see the rest of her family. After years of being a loner, all her defenses had come crumbling down, thanks to one man. Now, thanks to him, she had her sister back. And she wasn't going to pass up the chance to mend fences with the rest of the family.

"Let's do it," she whispered, giving Jill a fierce hug. "Let's go home."

Chapter 28

racie fidgeted in the small, stuffy office while Professor Mikolas glared at her like the tropical sun at noon. "I can't say I'm surprised at your request for tutoring, Miss Smith. I wish I could find some satisfaction in your desire to finally take our language and culture seriously.

"Unfortunately, I've seen many students in your position. You're just a little ahead of most of your peers. They typically don't realize the importance of passing the language and the protocol classes until well into their final semester at the academy."

"Yes, ma'am." Gracie tried to keep the dislike out of her voice by thinking of her sister. She hoped by getting closer to the professor she would understand her better. And perhaps Professor Mikolas would let something slip that might help Gracie determine if her political leanings were irritating but harmless or something darker.

She clenched her hands more tightly in her lap. If they were something darker, the king would need to know, even if her methods would make him angry.

When the phone rang, Gracie kept eyes on her fisted hands as Professor Mikolas excused herself. True to Gracie's expectations, the professor spoke freely in Melesian, unaware that

Gracie understood more than she let on. She caught snippets of the conversation.

"…foreign student." The professor glanced at Gracie and smiled, the gesture a contrast to the condescending tone of her words. Gracie forced herself to return the smile. "As for the foreign bride… too great. He will only put her aside for treason or… If the baby is not his, then… But she is difficult to discredit."

Gracie listened to the conversation, frustrated by her lack of understanding. Too many important words were beyond her grasp. But she was sure the foreign bride was her sister, mentally noting the points she would relay to Constantine and Jill as soon as she left this meeting. She was so intent on deciphering and memorizing the words that she only caught the reference to "Sophia" at the last moment.

What about Sophia? Her mind raced, and she itched to get somewhere private to send a text message to her friend. What did this woman want with her? They were, she knew, distant cousins, but she'd never thought they were close. Would Sophia understand? Would she consider coming home if doing so would help her country? Or was she part of the threat to Jill?

"Time to stop daydreaming, Miss Smith." The professor's voice snapped her back to the stuffy room. "In reviewing your progress, I see you grasp the basics of our grammar and can do reasonably well with the written word. I'm going to give you some extra assignments to reinforce this, but I think it best if you come to my office regularly for private tutoring sessions. In other words, you need to learn to speak."

"Yes, ma'am." Gracie repeated.

"You need to speak and practice our language," the professor repeated in Melesian. Gracie kept her face still, not showing she understood. Professor Mikolas repeated the words, louder and more forcefully.

By the third repetition, Gracie reacted. "*Aaya*, Professor."

"Good." She switched to English and handed Gracie a typewritten sheet. "Now that you understand, you will report to my office during these times. We will spend our time together practicing simple conversations and drilling you on your forms of address for the royal family.

"Our goal is twofold. To get you passably able to speak the language, and to make sure you don't embarrass me during your presentation to the royal family. That is all I expect, and it will be enough to give you a passing grade in both classes. Understood?"

Gracie nodded and took the sheet. With a crisp nod, the professor dismissed her, and she left the room, grateful to be heading away from the oppressive confines of the office.

She hurried to her dorm room and pulled out her cell phone, impatiently tapping her fingers against the window ledge as she waited for the international connection.

When Sophia answered, Gracie listened with half a heart as her friend gushed about her new job and the man in her life. It was what she'd wanted for Sophia, but now she wasn't sure she'd done the right thing by helping her hide.

"I'm glad you're doing well." Gracie huddled by the dorm window, trying to sound happy despite the worries that gnawed at her. Instead, she mentally recited the formula for calculating the volume of a cone while Sophia babbled on. "Listen, I'm sorry to interrupt, but I think there might be trouble here."

"There isn't trouble." Sophia's once cultured voice held a hint of an American accent. "And even if there is, what can I do about it?"

"You have a duty to your country. Besides, you're part of the trouble. I overheard Dorinda Mikolas say something about you and—"

"Grace, you're imagining plots where there aren't any. Constantine stopped all of that. What you heard was probably nothing more than Dorinda grumbling about how they failed to marry me off. She likes to complain about that bloodline purity crap. Trust me, my being there would just make matters worse."

"Crap? When did you start using words like *crap*?"

Sophia laughed. "About the same time you started using phrases like 'a duty to your country.' Look, I've got to go. I have a date."

"Are you sure?"

"About my date? Very sure. Mike's a great guy. I'm also sure that there's nothing for you to worry about. Melesia can withstand anything Dorinda can dish out. And believe me, as much as I love it here, I'd be home on the next flight if I thought you were in trouble. You've given me a great gift, Grace. If I can return the favor, I will."

"You already have, in a way. I've started seeing—"

"Hey, sorry to cut you off, but Mike's here. I'll talk to you later. I promise."

Gracie stared at the silent phone and recited the formulae for calculating the volume of a tetrahedron, a bipyramid and a hexagonal cylinder. It was just as gratifying as trying to explain her emotional state to the self-centered Sophia.

Once she'd calmed, she caught the ferry to Royal Island, ready to report what she'd overheard to Jill and Constantine, and to do whatever it took to help her family.

Stephan smiled politely at Dr. Joyner as he wrapped up their current negotiations. He longed for the privacy of his palace suite where he could deal with his pounding head and burning stomach.

Or better yet, the suite on his yacht where he could drown his pains in Gracie's arms and give her the proper, prolonged apology she deserved. A week of stolen phone conversations and chance meetings in the hallways wasn't nearly enough.

"I must say, Your Highness, I had my heart set on Neptune Island, but working on some of the other nearby islands could be a reasonable compromise."

"The integrity and respect you've shown for our wishes are a strong point in favor of working with you. I am pleased that you were willing to compromise."

"Remember, bottled water for export isn't the only issue at stake. To keep up with your tourism growth, you'll need more pure water for potable, recreational, and power generation needs. But after our week together, I feel like I'm preaching to the choir. You've got a keen, scientific mind."

"It's my secret weapon." Stephan smiled at him. "You needn't worry that you're dealing with a mere political figurehead when we talk about scientific matters."

"I'm grateful for that. But let's keep it between us. It might destroy my wife's romantic illusions about you."

Stephan laughed as he shook Dr. Joyner's hand. "It was a pleasure working with you. I will review your proposals and make my recommendations soon. Until then, feel free to contact me if the need arises. Have a pleasant journey home."

"One last thing, Your Highness." Dr. Joyner shuffled his feet a little as he continued. "If you wouldn't mind, Annie will be down soon…"

"I would be delighted to give Mrs. Joyner a suitably *romantic* farewell."

Several hours later, Stephan stretched out on the deck of his yacht, relaxing in the afternoon sun. The slap of waves at the sides of the ship and the clean salt smell soothed away much of his tension. Only Gracie was missing, and the distant sound of the motorboat indicated that she would be there soon.

He gave her a hand up the minute she climbed onto the dive platform. "I'm glad you could make it. I know it's not our usual meeting time, but I didn't want to wait to see you."

"I'd have been here sooner, except Professor Mikolas insisted on giving me extra protocol lessons. She's been drilling me on the proper forms of address for hours."

The way her nose wrinkled in annoyance had him biting back a grin. He schooled his features into an impassive mask and tried for a serious tone instead. "So, quiz time. What is the proper form of address for," he watched her brow pucker in concentration, "the lonely *hono* who's been waiting to see you in private for almost a week?"

Gracie giggled—actually giggled—in a carefree and spontaneous burst of joy that wound its way around his heart. "I know that one!" She threw her arms around his neck and kissed him, the laughter still bubbling from her lips until the moment they touched his.

He locked his arms around her and picked her up, twirling her around in slow circles while the kiss went on and on. The softness of her lips, the crush of her breasts against his chest and the perfect way her backside fit in his arms had him ready to rip her clothes off.

Yet when he pulled his lips from hers and slid her down his body to her feet, he realized the physical excitement was only part of what he'd missed from her.

There was so much more. "Oh, gods, Gracie, I missed you. This week was interminable. Have I told you yet how sorry I am for the way we parted?"

"Only every time we've talked this week. Besides, I was at fault too. Jill says that all lovers fight."

He groaned even as he pulled her tighter. "Please tell me you haven't shared all of our secrets with your sister."

The movement of her head against his chest could have been either a yes or a no, but it didn't really matter. Not as long as he was holding her.

"Just be thankful I'm the calm sister. At least I don't throw things in a fight."

"I don't want to know what you're talking about. But I do think you should practice that greeting again. Maybe even drill it for hours. One can't be too careful with protocol, you know."

He was rewarded with another giggle. Gracie slid her arms from his neck to his waist and leaned back to look him in the eyes. "If I practice too much, I may greet you that way at the official Presentation Tea."

"Thanks for the warning. I'll be sure to bring my body-guards."

Her eyes danced with mischief even though her lips collapsed into a pout. "Would you really have them keep me away from you?"

"Of course not. I'll need them to pick Dorinda Mikolas off the floor and resuscitate her. She'd likely collapse from shock."

The thought of the spinsterish professor put a damper on his rising passion. It was just as well. He needed to control himself with Gracie tonight, not let his wild side run free. He pushed her an arm's length away.

"Let's go somewhere private. The library. We can chart our course for tomorrow and plan the dive."

"And you can fill me in on Dr. Joyner and the bottled water fiasco."

"Dr. Joyner wasn't the problem. Mrs. Joyner was. I swear that woman must feel naked without her camera." He wrapped an arm around Gracie's shoulders, just for the sake of feeling her close to him. "Once, I discovered her taking photos of the library, including my computer and my desk. I'm not sure but I think she pocketed some paper clips for souvenirs. She even tried to follow me into my suite. She was like a shark."

"*Shakak.*"

"*Naaya. Maco. Ma'.* Big. *Ma-ma'shakak.* Huge shark."

She repeated the words, rolling the prefix around on her tongue as if tasting it. Mimicking the cadence and pulse of his words yet adding her own subtle accent to it.

He loved the sound of his language on her lips. Loved that even after a week apart she slipped into his language on board the ship as easily as she slipped into his arms. Stephan steered her past the library and toward his suite instead.

"Never mind the charts. Just tell me where you want to go."

She paused at his door, leaned back against it and faced him. "I think you already know where I want to go."

"Yes. But what about the dive?"

"Let's dive deep again. Now. And worry about the charts tomorrow."

More than her words invited him. Her just-licked lips glistened, and she moved slightly, twisting so the subtle jut of her breasts beckoning to him.

His groin tightened in response. Then his whole body sprang to attention, each muscle poised to take advantage of what she offered. But his mind, and his heart, rebelled.

He pushed aside the animal instincts to claim his mate and focused instead on her soft green eyes. Her words and body screamed seduction, but her eyes whispered uncertainty.

Stephan fisted his hands around the door frame, white knuckled, choking his own passions into submission. Stilling them until they whispered back. Then he bent to touch his lips to hers, seducing with the lightest of caresses.

"It won't be like diving tonight, Gracie," he murmured as he kissed the line of her jaw and nibbled his way to her ear. He loosened his grip slightly and drew in a deep breath. "Tonight, it will be a long, slow swim in a moonlit bay."

"I like the sound of that." Her voice was already raspy, slightly unsteady.

"Did you ever swim naked, Gracie? Ever feel the waves against your bare skin?" He kissed his way down her neck, stopping to tease the spot where neck met shoulder with his tongue.

"No, I—ooh." The long soft hiss of her breath wafted past his ear.

"Let me show you how it's done." He shifted one hand to her waist, not quite sure he had enough control to touch her but risking it anyway. The hem of her shirt brushed his knuckles as he worked his way beneath it to stroke the soft, warm flesh.

Her breath hitched, and he felt the force of it under his palm. He skimmed his hand along her ribs, curving into the slight dip where they met her spine before inching his way down to the tempting curve of her butt.

With the other hand, he cradled her head and tilted it till her lips were aligned with his own again. He took his time with the kiss, slowly deepening it from the mere press of lips, to the mingling of breath, to fleeting touches of tongues.

"Oh, I..." Garbled sighs replaced any words she might have tried to say.

Stephan curled the fingers gently into her curves and Gracie melted against him, her softness cradling every hard angle and ridge of his greedy body.

His body urged him to bury himself in her hard and fast, to make up for the lost hours when they'd been apart. But giving in to the craving would only leave him hungry for something that haste couldn't satisfy.

He needed more than sex. More than release from the throbbing want in his groin. He needed to make love to her. And receive her love in return.

So he savored the torture of having her close. Relished the pre-orgasmic burn and tingle of having her rub against him, soft and willing. And he opened the door to the suite.

"I want to make love to you."

"*Aaya*, I want that too." A spark of confidence replaced the uncertainty in her eyes.

He took her inside, closing and locking the door before leading her to the windows overlooking an ocean bathed in the golden glow of the low hanging sun.

"I want to see you in the light, then watch the sunset paint your naked body in the colors of passion." He slowly peeled the shirt from her.

"I want to make love to you in the sunset." He tossed her bra aside and planted a kiss in the center of her back.

"And the twilight." He eased her shorts and panties down until they slithered in a heap at her feet. She stepped out of them, her bare feet soundless on the teakwood floor.

Stephan shed his own shirt and embraced her from behind, naked front to exposed back. "I want to worship your body by moonlight, find comfort in your arms in the dark night, and wake you with kisses at dawn. Will you let me do that?"

"Your words are like poetry." She arched against him, and he hissed in a breath as her naked backside rubbed against the thin barrier of his shorts. *Control*, he reminded himself. But his throbbing penis bucked against her with a mind of its own.

"Your body is my muse," he said in a harsh whisper. He looked over her shoulder at her pale breasts. His own hand was golden against her pale skin when he cupped her. "You inspire me."

She wiggled closer, seemingly unmindful of the havoc her moves wreaked on his control.

Stephan brushed his fingers against the flower petal softness of her nipples until they hardened beneath his touch. His
mouth watered for a taste of her as he watched her breasts
pucker in response to him.

The sun dipped lower, and he knew it was time.

"Let me see you." He shucked his own clothing and moved
until she filled his view, bathed in the last golden light of the
day.

Her hair shone like a crown of light, falling around her
shoulders. Her body shimmered in pearlescent curves. Even
the triangle of hair at her thighs glowed, golden and untouchable.

Then the light shifted and the Madonna-like perfection disappeared in the flaming oranges and reds of the sunset. No
longer virginal, she burned like Aphrodite—temptation personified—offering him release and pleasure untold for the
mere cost of his soul.

He spread his arms, half in invitation, half in supplication
and stepped close enough to feel the heat from her body, not
daring to touch her lest the illusion shatter. "I'm yours to do
with as you will."

Her features remained cloaked in the pulsing colors of the
dying sun, her expression as undecipherable as Aphrodite herself. She licked her lips. "What woman deserves a prince?"

"What mere prince deserves a goddess?"

The words hung in the air, another offering from a wor-
shipping mortal.

She closed the distance between them and rose on tiptoe to
claim his lips. His heart pounded. Fierce, raging desire for control warred with some ancient Greek imperative to yield to the
goddess.

He gave her what she wanted and offered a tiny bit more,
silently pleading for her to accept. With each offering, she grew
bolder, taking more. Demanding more.

She rubbed against him, her breasts teasing him with their nearness. The slick slide of her cleft along his swollen body made his knees buckle, and he gripped her for support.

"Er'Hona-Er'Thea-Al-Aphrodite." Ancient words of worship poured from him in a voice shaky with need. "Please. Accept what I offer."

Gracie let his words wash over her. She might not understand their full meaning, but the plea in his voice was unmistakable. The last time they met as lovers, she'd been sacrificed to his passions. This time, she sensed, was different. Tonight he'd called her a goddess to his prince. She took the power he offered and savored it.

His body was rigid with control, coiled, yet under her command. She kissed him again, this time gripping his head and boldly thrusting her tongue into his mouth. He responded immediately, giving passion freely at her invitation.

Gracie drank her fill then pushed away, regarding him silently as the purple fingers of the sun's final light mingled with the shadows of night. Boldly she stripped the covers from the bed and piled the pillows high, arranging herself among them in careless invitation while he stood by.

"What else do you have to offer me?" She motioned for him to come to her. "What else do you want to do tonight?"

"I want to kiss you."

"Where? My foot?" She laughed, but when he took her at her word and showered her foot with kisses, the laugh turned throaty. When he licked her instep, it turned to a gasp.

"Now what?" she managed. "My knee?"

He kissed his way up her calf to the knee, repeating the caresses with a slow rhythm.

"My—my thigh?" She could barely breathe as he followed her invitation. The thorough, adoring kisses had her craving more. "What else do you want, mortal?"

"I want to drink your ambrosia, *Er'Hona-Er'Thea-Al-Aphrodite.*"

"Then drink." Gracie fisted the sheets in her hands, fighting to control her rising passion. She sucked in deep gasping breaths as he tormented her. The tingling, rising, building pressure threatened to overwhelm her.

"Stop!"

He paused at her command and looked up, his lips glistening in the darkness.

She guided him beside her with shaking hands, his feet near her head, and urged him to lie still. Her body still pulsed, ready for him as she ran a teasing hand down his torso. Smooth muscle, crisp hair, and more met her touch. She lowered her head to his penis and swirled her tongue across the tip in an experimental lick.

His answering pants had her smiling in the darkness. She nibbled and kissed her way along his length, one hand slipping lower to cup his softer, warmer, more vulnerable flesh. She gave a gentle squeeze.

"Gods! *Er'Hona-Er'Thea,* have mercy."

"But mercy isn't really what you want, is it?" She squeezed again, and his face contorted.

"I want," he panted. "I want—"

"I want you," she whispered. "Inside me. Now. Make love to me in the twilight."

"*Er'Thea.*" He sheathed himself, poised above her and entered, sliding into place with a groan. "Everything I have is yours for the asking."

He stroked her with passion, building the tingling pressure again. Gracie felt her body tighten, tense, and then she let loose, riding the spiral wave until it burst over her, leaving her thrashing and panting in its wake.

As she did, Stephan pressed a kiss to hollow of her throat. Then he reared one last time, his brow furrowed, features stretched to the breaking point—and beyond—before collapsing against her, murmuring words of passion she'd never heard before.

Gracie cradled his damp body, the urge to soothe and nurture him as intense now as her passion had been moments ago. He needed her. It was a ridiculous idea, but somehow true. Since the day in the rotunda when he'd trusted her to guard his secrets, he'd become more than just a friend or lover. He'd become—

She didn't have the words to describe what he was to her. Someone she loved, even if he couldn't love her in return. Someone she wanted to protect, even if he hid his need for her. He might tire of her, but she would never want to be free of him. He was—

Ba'hono-mei.

The word whispered across her consciousness. *Beloved spouse. Soul mate. Heart-of-my-heart* and *love-of-my-life. Chosen destiny.* An endearment he might never return.

The moon rose, bathing the bed in a silvery glow as he slept. A smile curved on his lips, and he nuzzled against her breast in his sleep. Gracie stroked his hair, and he sighed in contentment, the arm that he'd thrown across her belly tightened, pulling her closer.

"*Ba'hono-mei*," she murmured into the darkness. "*Ba'hono-mei.*"

Chapter 29

"**I** want to make love to you in the moonlight," Stephan whispered.

It didn't matter that she couldn't hear him. She would know soon enough. He watched the slow rise and fall of her belly with each breath, entranced by the pale marble perfection of her skin. He propped on his elbow and drank in the sight of her as she slept.

Hours ago, he'd been gripped by a kind of madness, an ancient passion that had shaken his control to its limits simply by demanding that he submit rather than conquer. He'd never given a woman that kind of control before. Never dreamed that it would wring him dry and leave him wanting at the same time.

Now as the moonlight filled his bedroom and his body pulsed with a gentle urge to make love again, he knew he longed for something more. Control didn't fill the need. Nor submission. Nor any brand of fiery passion he'd yet experienced.

What he needed was union. Completeness. Oneness. The unconditional acceptance of soul-to-soul, man-to-woman, equal-to-equal. And only Gracie could give him that. No one else had even tried.

So he stroked a palm along her body, watching her shift and move toward wakefulness as he enjoyed the satiny warmth of her skin. He nuzzled her breast.

"Stephan?" The sleepy mumbled word brought his gaze back to her face.

"Who else?"

Her eyes stayed closed but a smile curved on her lips. "I have dozens of lovers."

"Oh really?" He didn't try to hide his amusement but instead softened his touch on her body until goose bumps broke out on her skin and she giggled with each stroke. "How fortunate for me that I'm at the top of the list."

"For now."

He made his touch firm again, soothing what he'd just awakened and turned his attention to kissing her breast. Her sleepy, half-shy teasing tugged at his heart. "You're beautiful when you laugh, Gracie."

"Not beautiful," she mumbled, her words turning to a sigh as he tugged on her nipple with his teeth.

He smiled against her skin and gave her a minute more of pleasure before releasing her. "How remiss of your other lovers not to mention it."

"I was only teasing."

"So I guessed." He moved over her and slid inside with the ease of a key fitting into a well-oiled lock. "And I hope to keep it that way."

With slow, precise movements he made love to her, delighted when she brought one hand to rest on his butt while the other explored his back. She was trapped in a state of half wakefulness, languid and soft from sleep, but aware and smiling.

When he brought her to her peak, she came with giggles instead of screams. And when he neared his own, he captured her hands, twining his fingers in hers and gave in to the gentle release, knowing that while his body pulsed within her, his heart poured out much, much more.

He pulled her against him and rolled onto their sides wondering at the connection that reached beyond their joined hips all the way to their bound hearts.

This was the connection of the *ba'honii*, the beloved ones. Something he'd seen in others but never known for himself until now. She was more than desirable to him, she was *ba'hona-mei* to him. *Beloved one. Spouse.* In truth, if not yet in law. He held her close wondering if she would understand the significance.

"Stephan?"

"Hmm?"

"Will you get tired of me?"

He laughed, thinking it was more teasing on her part, until the stillness of her body convinced him otherwise. Once awake, her confidence was more brittle than he'd realized. Too insubstantial to understand his soul-searing confessions, without thinking them false declarations of love. So he reached for humor, coaxing her back with the same gentle teasing she'd used on him.

"Let me think. Despite our recent activities, I still haven't taken a good look at that tattoo of yours, so I can't get tired of you until I explore it. Then there's about a dozen other ways to make love that I'd like to try. That takes us well into next week. After that..." he let his musings trail off hoping to entice her.

"But eventually, after that, when I'm not a novelty anymore, what happens?" She toyed with his chest, her fingers tracing small circles with a hesitancy that tore at him.

Stephan wrapped both arms around her and cradled her close. "Gracie, love, it's not going to happen. I'm not going to get tired of you. Not by the middle of next week, or next year, or anytime imaginable. What's got you thinking like that, sweetheart?"

"It's just," she shrugged. "You love my body, but what about my mind? Everyone says that boys don't like smart girls."

"Boys don't like girls at all for at least part of their lives. But they grow into men, Gracie, and their needs are totally different. Besides, what makes you think beauty and brains are mutually exclusive?"

He resisted the urge to pull the covers over them and instead curved a hand around her bottom, drawing her closer. Instinctively he knew her nakedness fed her insecurity even as it increased his chances of getting to the root of the problem.

"Trust me, the minute I start talking like a geek your eyes will glaze over and you'll wonder what you ever saw in me."

"Okay. Talk like a geek. See what happens." He stroked her bottom until she giggled and moved closer. It was a tiny victory.

"I'm serious, Stephan. Petros told me how many tutors you went through before they all gave up on you. And now you're here with a woman whose IQ is almost high enough to qualify for Mensa. Tell me that doesn't make you think twice about me."

"Almost? Gracie, you disappoint me."

"Don't pretend the idea of a brainiac society excites you."

"I consider it more of a social club," he mused. "For thinking people. Besides, IQ tests can be subjective. Have it reevaluated. Or take an admission test for Mensa. There are other ways to get in." He kissed her neck, working his way up to her ear. So she thought he wasn't smart enough to appreciate her?

"Why would I want to do that?"

"Because you're a woman who recites mathematical formulas under her breath when she's nervous. You chant the prime numbers like some people hum the lyrics to songs.

You're probably repeating the value of pi to the sixteenth decimal place right now instead of paying attention to what I'm doing to your ear."

He licked her ear and blew softly into it for emphasis. "Because you're a smart woman, and there's no need to hide it. And because Mensa gives great parties. If you don't join on your own, they may let you come as my guest."

"But you're—" She gasped as he continued the assault on her ear and neck.

"—not smart?" he finished for her between nips and sweeps of his tongue. "For your information, my tutors quit because they ran out of things to challenge me. And my family got so damned tired of my whining about being bored that they threw me into the military corps of engineers when I was fifteen. The military discipline managed to beat some perspective into me, and I came out a better man for it. So don't underestimate me, you brainy, little snob. I promise I'll make you pay if you do."

"I think I already have."

"Then take that." He nipped her earlobe. "And prepare to spend the rest of the night showing me just how sorry you are for misjudging me."

He flipped onto his back and eased her astride him. The moonlight bathed her face as she stared down at him. "So now what?"

"It's simple physics, Gracie. Figure it out." He bucked beneath her and laughed softly as she readjusted. He guided his hands to her hips. "Or let me teach you how it's done."

And they made love in the moonlight.

The next day, Gracie directed him to a cove where the effluent waters from the main island's local power and water plants dumped. They dove as close to the outlet as they could and Gracie measured the temperatures, took salinity samples, and carefully documented the changes in the corals versus the ones they'd seen off Neptune's Crown Reef.

Twice they resurfaced to change tanks and drop off samples for analysis later. Each time, Gracie chatted with him about her findings.

After lunch, Stephan took her ashore to tour the plant. He'd helped with the building expansion and operation years ago during his military time. Even now, the operators and supervisors greeted him warmly, discussing technical issues without qualms.

Gracie took it all in, asking questions of her own and coming up to speed rapidly for one who'd never stepped foot in a power or water plant before.

While Gracie walked through the process with one of the engineers, Stephan stepped aside to chat with the facility supervisor. When the conversation drifted from the specifics of Dr. Joyner's proposals to general topics, he watched Gracie.

Only today did he realize how much of herself she'd been holding back from him. And how deep her fears of rejection had been.

True to her prediction, she did start talking like a geek, but he loved it. Gracie glowed when she discussed ideas, sparked when she analyzed data. She stimulated his mind in a way that few people had over the years.

But it wasn't her mind he was thinking about when he finally led her from the plant and headed back to the yacht. It was the whole package. One that he didn't intend to let slip through his fingers.

"Remember the first day I came on board?" she asked as they shared a light supper and bottle of wine on the deck later.

He smiled at the memory. "You looked more like a condemned prisoner than someone doing advanced research studies. I swear you practically jumped at your own shadow that first day."

"You represented just about everything I thought I hated about your country. Your form of government. Protocol. The life of the idle rich. Privileged classes versus common ones. Everything."

"That's harsh, Gracie."

"On top of it all, despite my beliefs, you still had the power to make me a little weak in the knees. I think I hated that most of all."

Stephan swirled the cabernet in his glass and stared into the ruby depths, seeing Gracie as she'd been that first day. He'd recognized her tension and uncertainty. She telegraphed hesitancy, a slight sense of awe and maybe—maybe—if he stretched his imagination, a hint of fear. All of which had eased during the hours between dawn and dusk.

But he hadn't picked up on hatred. The thought burned in his gut.

"Stephan?" Gracie's touch on his arm roused him from his thoughts. "I was wrong. You taught me that, perhaps without even realizing it. For all my supposed intelligence, I don't know people the way you do, and I misjudged everything in the beginning. Forgive me?"

He covered her hand with his and stroked her knuckles. "If it's any consolation, I wasn't so sure about you in the beginning, either. But I've learned to resist jumping to conclusions, even when it comes to people. I'm glad things worked out the way they did."

"Me too. As I thought back on that day, I realized I feel safe with you now. After all, if my little mistake about underestimating your IQ wasn't enough to make you throw me overboard, I think I can relax."

He faced her, furrowing his brow, but not holding back his grin. "Now that you mention it, that would have been a good reason to dispose of you. But as you were so very good at apologizing, I suppose the time has passed. Still, you would be wise to watch your step."

"Warning noted."

Gracie leaned back and watched the surf, her profile silhouetted against the night sky. Behind them, he knew the lights of the main island would be fading in the distance as the yacht maneuvered into the open ocean for the night. Ahead were only stars, and it was easy to imagine that they were alone in the world.

Stephan took a sip of his wine and relaxed. The sounds of the night ocean and the touch of a breeze soothed him. This was life as it should be. No worries. Only Gracie, the ocean, and the long night ahead.

In other climates, people were preparing for winter. Here on Melesia, his people called this time of year the dark season, because the nights were longer and the daylight hours shorter. A dark season with Gracie sounded perfect. By the end of the season, he'd have her convinced that she need never doubt her appeal.

He had yet to bring the discussion around to his feelings, to the importance of the *ba'honii* and to what it meant for the two of them, but there was time. And Gracie's reaction this morning proved that she needed time.

He studied her profile. She was so silent she might have been counting the stars. Or she might have made it to the 127th digit for pi if she had something on her mind. He took a stab in the dark.

"Constantine tells me that you're planning a visit to your home soon." He took another sip of wine and this time felt the acid burn as it hit his stomach. Instinctively he reached for Gracie's hand and the relief only she seemed to bring.

"Yes. I was just wondering what it will be like to be back in Clarkson County again. It seems like another world. And I seem like another person."

"I like the person you are."

"And I like who I am when I'm with you. But I'm a little nervous with all the cloak and dagger security we have to go through for the trip. I thought we'd just charter a plane and be done with it."

"Like it or not, your sister is an important international figure now. She's had trouble getting used to it, but she's learned to be cautious. With the baby on the way, even more caution is needed."

"That's the part of your world I still have trouble with. The bodyguards. The security. The scrutiny of the press and individuals alike. People like Mrs. Joyner wanting to know intimate details of your life. It's dehumanizing."

"It's the only world I've ever known." Even as he spoke, Stephan weighted her words, balancing the dread in her voice against the realities of his world. A deeper relationship with him guaranteed bodyguards and press scrutiny. He could shield her from some of the unpleasantness, but not all.

Even if he left his country for hers, the status of his birth was as much a part of him as his fingerprints. He couldn't guarantee her anonymity.

There was only one way to do that. To leave her. Take the treasured times they'd shared and let her go.

An icy foreboding gripped his heart as he recounted the times he'd had with Gracie. Every one of them was part of a fantasy. Stolen. Private. Whether she was aware of it or not, each was part of the cloak and dagger mentality she'd just described. If he asked her to stand by him in the glare of publicity, would she? Could she?

Suddenly, he dreaded her trip home. It was every fairy tale he'd ever known turned on its ear. It was Cinderella after the ball realizing that her glass slippers pinched in all the wrong places and that the warmth of her hearth was infinitely preferable to the coldness of the ballroom. Discovering that while a dance was nice, she didn't really want the prince, after all.

The acid burn in his stomach was back and even Gracie couldn't keep it at bay this time. Because he wouldn't ask her to give up her freedom for him. He could only hope that she might come to him of her own free will.

"Don't worry too much about the trip, Gracie. Everything's been arranged so you'll be left more or less in peace once you reach your family home. And I'll be there to help you through the rest of the process."

"You're coming with us?"

"Constantine wants someone from the family to accompany you since he can't be there. He also asked me to do some official work in the States while you're on vacation."

In truth, Stephan was retracing Sophia's last known steps to see if he could discover how—and why—she'd given them all the slip. But holding Gracie's hand in the dark, he already knew why. She was searching for the freedom he would never have. Escaping the ornate cage he'd hoped Gracie could step into.

"So you're off to play diplomat while we eat turkey and pumpkin pie?"

"You could say that. I'll be visiting our consulates to help keep them connected to the homeland. You're welcome to join me if your food holiday loses its luster." But she wouldn't.

"My *Thanksgiving* is going to be wonderful. I have more to be thankful for now than ever before. Because of you."

"On the other hand, my trip will be long, stressful and likely boring. Thanks to you not being with me."

"I'm here now."

He stood and pulled her into his arms. "Then let's make memories while we have the chance."

Ba'hona-mei, he thought as he kissed her and she melted in his embrace. *With you in my arms, all is right in my world.* At least for one more stolen night.

Chapter 30

Gracie tried to relax and think about arriving home, but even the luxury of Melesia One, the royal plane, couldn't take the edge off her nerves. Everything had gone smoothly, with Jill posing for a few official photos while Gracie stood, ignored, with the trimmed down entourage.

But still, something didn't feel right. In the seat beside her, Stephan fidgeted in an uncharacteristic display of nerves. Since boarding, he didn't even try to hide his antacid addiction.

Almost unconsciously, she started muttering to herself. Mathematics. The constants in a world of flux. "Three point one four one five nine…"

"…two six five three five eight nine," Stephan intoned beside her. "What's on your mind, Gracie? The only pie you're supposed to be thinking about is pumpkin."

"Seven nine three two three eight four," she said continuing the string of numbers she'd long ago memorized. "I don't know. Why are you so nervous?"

"Me? I'm not—" He sighed and turned to her, grasping both of her hands in his. "You're right. I am nervous. Gracie, I, uh, I wanted to ask you if…"

Stephan stammering wasn't a good sign. The last time he'd been at a loss for words had been in the middle of a fight. Gracie squeezed his hands, giving him silent reassurance.

"Gracie, I care about you. I wanted to ask you if you would do me a favor."

Her heart did a little flip and landed with a painful thud. She loved him. He cared about her. She'd started, against her better judgement, to imagine spending a life with him. He wanted a favor from her.

So be it. Two fairy tales in a single family was never in the plans, anyway.

"Whatever you want from me, if I can do it, I will." She hoped her pain didn't show in her eyes as she looked at him.

Relief flooded his face. "Thank you." He released her hands and reached into his suit pocket to pull out a small velvet box. "I know this is hard for you, and that you don't like gifts, but I want to give this to you."

Gracie took the box, her hands shaking. The connection between gifts and loss nagged her, filling her mouth with a bitter taste. But she'd promised.

She opened the box. Dangling from the end of a silver chain was an intricately worked replica of a porcupine fish, studded with spikes fully raised. His round filigree body housed a single perfect pearl.

"It's beautiful."

"I commissioned it from the royal silversmiths. It reminded me of our first day together. Of you. How you were always quick to defend yourself. And how you eventually came to trust me. I lo— I want you to have it. No matter what happens."

"I'll cherish it *hono-mei*." *Ba'hono-mei*, she added silently as he fastened the clasp around her neck. His duty might forbid him from saying the words, but she'd caught his slip. It was almost enough.

Too soon after, the plane landed and a flurry of customs officials, security teams, and selected members of the Melesian press descended on them, separating them without the kind of good-bye she longed for.

For better or worse, Gracie was home.

Stephan stared out the windows of the Willis Tower, half listening to the tour guide give his standard speech. Below him the city of Chicago spread out in a maze of activity. Looking to the horizon he could make out boats on the gray waters of Lake Michigan.

The longing for the blue oceans of home hit him with the force of a physical blow. He'd only been away for a day, but since leaving Gracie in Ohio, everything in this cold, restless part of the world grated against him like the sting of fire coral.

With a murmured word about the men's room, he slipped away from his party and easily found an elevator to the ground floor. Before exiting, he took off his suit jacket, rolled up his shirt sleeves and donned sunglasses. Moments later he'd effortlessly blended into a stream of workers headed home for the start of their holiday weekend.

When he reached Chicago's Union Station, only a stone's throw away from the Willis Tower, he called his security team. It had been embarrassingly easy to shake them. How much more so would it be for a woman with a bag that could hold a simple disguise?

He studied the crowded terminal. Trains left at all hours in every direction. By the time it took his team to cover the distance between their location and his, he could be on any one of them, heading anywhere.

Of course, security teams had staked out the Union Station as soon as Sophia's disappearance was known. So wherever she'd gone, she hadn't returned via this route.

Stephan watched commuters surge onto a train as it prepared for departure. The urge to join them, to slip away from the team he'd summoned, drew him to the platform. He'd go west. Somewhere away from this grim city to a place where he could disappear. Then he'd contact Gracie and start a life of freedom with her.

If the urge was this strong for him, how must it have felt for Sophia? Duty bound him to his country, to his purpose, and duty ultimately stopped his steps. But she didn't have a duty or a purpose. Her sole existence had been to marry at her uncle's discretion. No wonder she'd escaped.

"Your Highness," a nervous, plain-clothes security guard stepped up to him, "we didn't expect you to disappear, we were—"

"Precisely my point. It was easy for me to leave because you didn't expect it. No doubt you were prepared for nearly every other opportunity. Let's reconvene at the consulate in one hour to discuss matters. Meanwhile, have your men determine the schedules of every train that leaves this station to any destination."

He headed to the exit, less concerned about the anxious security team than about solving the puzzle in front of him. His private bodyguard hurried to keep up.

Wherever Sophia had gone, she'd left from here. He was sure of it now. He'd overlay the routes of the departing trains with information from the pawn shops where they'd found items suspected of belonging to her.

From there, it was a simple matter of discovering every possible route away from Chicago. Assuming she'd stuck to public transportation, the list would be long, but finite. Then it would only be a matter of eliminating the possibilities one by one until they found her.

But in a secret part of his heart, he didn't want to find her. If she'd discovered something worth having, something as important to her as Gracie was to him, he'd spin the media, control the information, and do everything in his considerable power to give her the chance at love. Even if he couldn't do the same for himself.

"Are the men in black going to hang out in front of our house all week?" Geoff Bradley dropped the living room curtains back in place and stormed into the kitchen. "Don't the members of the Melesian Mafia ever sleep?"

"They're not Mafia, they're Jill's security team," Gracie replied as she scraped pie filling into the shells. "They rotate teams so someone's always on duty."

"Yeah," he grumbled, snagging another sweet roll from a plate on the counter. "They're always there to make my life miserable. My friends won't even come by because the men in black harass them, so I'm stuck here in a house full of girls."

Their mother pinned him with a glare. "Geoffrey, it's Thanksgiving. Your friends are all busy with their families today too. Aren't you at least glad to see your sisters?"

"Jeez, Mom I like Jill and Gracie and all that, but I haven't seen my friends once since they've been here. And I haven't been able to practice my driving, either."

"Your learner's permit won't expire just because you don't drive for a day or two. I'm busy with dinner. Maybe we can go driving tonight." Mrs. Bradley flipped on the oven light switch and checked the turkey through the glass. "Gracie, honey, do you think we should invite the security team in for a bite later? Amber could set a couple of extra places at the table."

"I think Jill's got it covered, Mom. It's thoughtful of you to want to invite them in, but I doubt they'd be comfortable with the idea."

"There's always room for one more at the Bradley table, honey. You know that."

"I do, but they don't see it that way. Jill's their queen. Sitting down with her for an intimate family dinner would be like us dropping in on the president of the United States for coffee. Not comfortable."

"If you're sure."

Gracie hugged her mother, trying to erase the worried look on her face. It was strange, straddling the two worlds. Her mother's sense of hospitality clashed with the security team's sense of duty. And Gracie understood both.

"I'm sure, Mom. But I tell you what, I'll pop upstairs and check with Jill about her catering arrangements for them. Then I'll head to town and confirm everything. Geoff can drive me if he wants. While I'm gone, I'll pick up ingredients for another couple of pies. I'm sure I can convince the security team to accept pie and coffee if you sent it down to them tonight. Okay?"

The look of relief on her mother's face warmed Gracie. Within minutes, she headed upstairs with a carafe of decaf and some toast for Jill, humming to herself.

She set the tray on a bedside table and gently shook her napping sister. "Hey, Your Majesty, time to wake up."

Jill sat up in the bed and looked around the room until she spied Gracie. "Gracie. I thought I got to be just Jill for the weekend."

"Either way, you're still my sister. How are you feeling?"

Jill sat up and accepted the cup of coffee. "I'm better now. I really haven't had a lot morning sickness before, but I think the baby didn't like the flight much."

Gracie indicated the tray. "Mom sent up some stuff that she thought might help settle your stomach. Don't worry, I'll help you dispose of anything that you don't want."

Jill nibbled a piece of toast while Gracie filled her in on the morning's events. "Mom's enjoying every minute of your visit, but she's in caretaker mode. She finally agreed not to invite the security team to dinner when I told her they'd accept some pie and coffee later."

"That was diplomatic of you, little sister. Has anyone I know been giving you lessons on how to handle opposing priorities?" Jill winked at her. "Nice necklace, by the way. I don't remember seeing it before."

"You know exactly where I got this. And you're right, in a way. I think Stephan's rubbing off on me."

"He'd have been proud of the way you handled things today. It sounds like you saw everyone's point of view and came up with a great compromise. You're thinking with your head and your heart." She put the coffee cup and toast down. "Would you mind if I took a closer look at the necklace?"

Gracie unclasped the chain, reluctantly handing it to Jill. She'd only worn it for a little over two days, but already she felt naked without it. Jill turned it over in her hands, examining the little fish from every angle possible, her brow puckered in concentration. Finally she handed it back to Gracie with a smile.

"It's a beautiful piece. Unique. Special, and meaningful. Just like you. And him."

When the familiar weight of the necklace settled in place once more, Gracie turned to leave. At the door, Jill called her.

"*Mi'cochida-ba,*" she said using a Melesian endearment for sister, "remember this. When it comes to Stephan, listen with your heart, not your mind, and you'll never go wrong."

"Watch your speed, Geoff," Gracie warned as they headed down the country road leading to town.

"You're worse than Mom," Geoff grumbled, as he slowed down. "Why do all the women in my life want to pick on me, anyway?"

"It's our job. Besides, is that any way to talk to your favorite sister?"

"You don't know what it's been like around here since you've been gone, G. You were the only one I could ever talk to. Amber and Char are just impossible."

Gracie looked at her little brother. He'd idolized her since the time she'd drawn up plans for a play fort for him using graph paper and scaled down drawings. But now he was on the verge of manhood, a stranger to her in many ways.

"Ever since Jill's wedding, the girls have been dopey-eyed nutcases." Geoff paused while he navigated around a hairpin turn before continuing. "All Amber talks about is how some-prince-or-other paid attention to her at the wedding. She acts like it makes her special or something. And Char does every-thing Amber does."

"How do you feel about it?"

Geoff was silent, clearly wrestling with something while he drove the miles to town. Gracie glanced in the side mirror, grateful that the security team trailing them kept far enough behind not to come to Geoff's notice.

As they pulled into town, he spoke again. "The guys at school are giving me a hard time about it. Asking me when I'm going to wear tights like the other men in the family and stuff like that. Being related to that stupid royal family sucks."

Gracie bit the inside of her cheek to keep from giggling as an image of Stephan in tights popped into her head. Unfortunately, the only way she could get rid of it entirely was to replace it with one of him totally naked. Neither image did her brother any good.

"G?"

Geoff's voice pulled her out of her daydream. "Listen Geoff, I don't know where those guys got their ideas, but I can tell you that all of the kings and princes I know would be as appalled as you at the thought of wearing tights. The only difference is that they could throw people in jail for even suggesting such a thing."

"Cool." Geoff headed for the grocery store. "Do you think they could throw the guys at school into jail, you know, just for a day or two?"

"Only if they were Melesian citizens. Besides, those guys are bugging you because they're jealous. Think about it, Geoff. I'll bet the girls are more interested in you these days."

"Yeah. I do get more girls than the other guys. Even if most of them are dopey like Amber and Char."

"But?" she prompted.

"There is this one girl," Geoff began.

Half an hour later Gracie walked out of the store with two bags of supplies and a new understanding of her little brother. She smiled as Geoff climbed into the car, his lanky frame more relaxed now that he'd found someone to talk to. They headed back to the house.

Halfway home the wail of a siren and the flash of lights stopped them.

"Man. Crap." Geoff pulled to the side of the road.

"I told you to slow down. Looks like you get to learn the hard way."

The officer, a man Gracie remembered from school, winked at her while he gave Geoff a stiff warning. Gracie kept silent and let him do his job.

"Just for the record, Miss Bradley, since you're supervising your brother here, I need to see your driver's license."

Gracie opened her purse then hesitated, wishing she hadn't put off applying for a new ID. "Officer, I think I forgot my license," she lied, mentally crossing her fingers. "I've been attending school abroad, and I just brought my passport when I came home." She passed him the document.

"Well, since I know you and the family, I think this ought to suffice. It's the least I can do for an old friend on Thanksgiving. Especially since I'm letting Geoff here off with just a warning. But be careful. Not everyone who drives along here is sober, if you get my meaning."

Gracie nodded, and they pulled away, heading back to the family and Thanksgiving.

The wind stung her cheeks and Gracie huddled deeper into her mother's coat as she tramped across the stubble that littered the fields. The remains of dead corn stalks crunched underfoot. She scanned the sky. Clouds of gray lint scudded across the equally gray sky.

"Gracie, you've got enough layers on to survive deep winter, and it's just a crisp fall day."

She laughed but didn't stop hugging the coat to herself. "I guess my blood is a little thin after nearly two years in the Caribbean. I'll have to toughen up again once I graduate."

"I don't know," her mother mused. "I was planning on visiting you somewhere warm after you graduate. There aren't a lot of marine biology jobs here in Clarkson County."

"But this is home."

"Home can be anywhere, honey. What we are is family. And that won't change no matter where you live. Just look at Jill. My oldest daughter is queen of an important Caribbean country. But she's still my daughter. Just like you are and always will be."

Gracie smiled at the warmth in her mother's voice. She'd grown up thinking of Jill as her sister, only later realizing that she was, technically, a half-sister. But their mother made no such distinctions between *her* children.

"So you're saying you wouldn't be disappointed if I moved to the Florida coast?"

"Florida, California, even the Caribbean. Wherever you land, you'll do fine." She took Gracie's hand. "There's something else. I've noticed a change in you since you've been back. It's a good change. You seem more confident, happier. One of these days, wherever you are, you're going to find someone and fall in love. When that happens, just remember, we're family, and in our family, there's always room for one more."

"Thanks, Mom."

Gracie hugged her and went inside to pack. She found Jill, sitting on the bed in her old room, a pair of worn, soft blue jeans folded in her lap and a red, crystal-studded stiletto in her hand.

"Those shoes might go better with a ball gown than jeans, don't you think?"

Jill smiled and rubbed a finger along the crystals. "My husband had these packed for me. It's a story that goes back to the night he proposed. I'll tell you sometime, but for now, here's the short version. These are ruby slippers to remind me there's no place like home. It's his way of saying he wants me to come back to him."

Gracie eased onto the bed beside Jill and took the shoe from her. "When did Melesia become home for you?" she asked softly turning the shoe in her hand as if it held some secret meaning.

"Home isn't a place, Gracie. Home is being with the people you love. When you fall in love, home becomes wherever he is. It's something special. Something…" She shrugged. "I don't have a word for it."

"Sure, you do, Jill. It's just not an English word."

Jill took the shoe from her and placed it beside its mate in the suitcase, covering them both with the worn denim. "You've grown perceptive, little sister. And you're right. When you find that one special person and commit to him, when you become *ba'honii*, you'll know the meaning of home."

She zipped the suitcase closed and gave Gracie a squeeze on the shoulder. "Time to change and pack."

"More than that," Gracie said as she drew Jill into a full hug. "Time for both of us to go home."

Chapter 31

Stephan shed his suit jacket, loosened his tie and popped the button on his collar as he headed across the plane's cabin. He sat by Gracie and leaned against the leather seats of Melesia One.

Instinctively, he sought her hand and closed his eyes. "It feels good to relax."

The minute they'd boarded, the churning in his gut had eased. When he saw she still wore his necklace, it disappeared almost entirely. He dared to hope that she'd accept even more from him one day soon.

"You look tired, *Er'hono-mei*. Difficulties?"

"You could say that." He'd never dreaded his diplomatic missions before. He'd looked forward to them. But this time the hours had dragged and his patience had stretched to the point where he'd snapped at his security team more than once.

All because of Gracie.

"For the first time, I looked at my world and saw it through your eyes. There was barely a minute alone. I think I even worried about keeping my image polished while I slept."

She giggled, and he realized he'd missed having her uncensored, honest reactions to him. "Stephan, you're a born diplomat. I'm sure everything was fine. And I can reassure you that you don't snore, or drool, in your sleep."

"Thank the gods. I was worried about the slobber part." He traced the delicate contours of her hand and smiled. "So, tell me about your trip home. Did you have a good time?"

When Gracie remained silent, some of the chill he'd felt in Chicago seeped back into his soul.

"My visit to the family was wonderful," she said at last in a soft, measured voice. "But it wasn't quite what I expected."

"Did the security team bother you that much?" His gut tightened, and the chill turned colder.

"I thought they would, but no. I barely noticed them. The truth is," she hesitated, "I missed the islands. I missed you."

"I was lonely too." He turned her hand over and lightly ran his fingers across her palm, enjoying the feel of her soft skin. Gracie squirmed and giggled.

"Stop that. I'm ticklish there."

"I know. You're ticklish everywhere." He moved from her palm to her wrist with the same light touch.

"Stephan, behave."

He stroked her skin instead and settled more comfortably beside her. The cold fear of losing her receded. "Unfortunately, that's all I'll have time to do in the next weeks. I have a dozen environmental reports to analyze, a handful of publicity events, and I'm organizing some marine life donations to various American locations. There's no time left for fun."

"If it's any consolation, I won't have much time to play, either. I have to study for finals. At least next semester, I can devote ninety eight percent of my time to finishing my advanced research class."

"And the other two percent?"

"Language. And Protocol."

He flinched at the distaste in her voice. "So, you can handle the security teams, but you still hate the language and the protocol."

"Actually, I kind of like the language since I found my private tutor." She pecked him on the cheek. "I'm not quite as resistant to the protocol, either. But I dread spending another semester with Professor Mikolas. Can you make that problem go away?"

A smile tugged at his lips. "I could dig up some unflattering baby photos of her that might help."

Gracie snuggled against him, the warmth of her body chasing away the last of his chill. "Being with you helps," she whispered. "Thank you."

He hugged her closer. "You know I would do anything in my power to help you, Gracie. Anything you would allow me to do, that is," he corrected.

"I know."

She moved against him, and he looked down to see her toying with the necklace he'd given her. He'd instructed the silversmiths to weave the secret design of the royal Melesian court into it. Legend—and tradition—forbade all but the royal family and their intended brides from wearing the design.

He'd bent tradition the way the silversmith had bent the design, working it into something new and meaningful. He doubted the family would notice, but it marked Gracie as his future bride, nonetheless. And when he finally proposed, the symbol would stand as a token of the love he felt long before the words came.

Because the words couldn't come until Gracie was ready to hear them. She'd accepted so much of him already—willingly opening herself to the customs, protocols, and language of his world, despite her initial resistance. Yet so much more would be demanded of her as his princess. He wouldn't force her into what she couldn't give. Not even for the sake of love.

"Gracie, could you ever imagine yourself being seen with me in public?"

"I work on Royal Island. We've already been seen together. The Joyners even have pictures."

"Not that way. Not as a student worker who happens to run into a prince." He hesitated, wondering if he could nudge her just a little further into the role he hoped she'd accept. "As a woman, who chooses to be with me."

"As your date?"

"As what we are. Friends. Lovers. As my *hona*."

She closed her eyes and a flurry of expressions flitted across her features, hinting at her inner turmoil. A puckered brow. Pursed lips. A tiny smile, choked off as her teeth captured her bottom lip. A heavy sigh.

"I'll try," she said finally, opening her eyes and giving him a look filled with both sincerity and confusion. "I want to. It's just that my classes, and my work— You're chancellor of the academy. I'm a student. The gossip... If I graduated first it might be easier."

"The gossip would still be there, Gracie. Now, or six months from now. Speculation and facts are two different things. No one who knows you will doubt your abilities. And there's no reason for you to doubt, either. The rest of the world doesn't matter."

He studied her face as his words sunk in, almost holding his breath until she gave a tiny nod. "Besides, there's more to your alias than just academics, isn't there?"

Another nod, this time accompanied by a small smile.

He'd watched Gracie change over the past weeks. She'd opened to him, to her sister, to her friends, and to a world of possibilities. She'd transformed from a fragile, skittish creature to a more confident woman. A woman who no longer needed to hide. It was a start.

"You don't have to do anything that you don't want, *hona-mei*. I'm not asking for a public declaration of affection. Just a few baby steps."

She gripped his hand and squeezed, her hold on him almost painful. Desperation seeped between their clasped hands, but it didn't show in her eyes when she looked at him.

"I'll try. And if I fail—"

"I promise, I won't let you be hurt."

She let go of his hand and sat straighter, jaw locked in defiance. The image of the prickly porcupine fish that had so intrigued him on their first day together was back. Gracie bristled, opening her spines to protect herself against imagined threats.

"If I fail, I'll try again."

It was all he could hope for.

A little more than a week later, Gracie tried to calm the nervous flutter of butterflies in her stomach. Her hands shook as she smoothed the material of her dress into its elegant folds.

Think of something else, she instructed herself. She closed her eyes and thought about her Advanced Field Research class final. Professor Pontileus had taken her aside afterward to give her letters of recommendation to several prestigious facilities in the United States. He'd assured her that she could have her pick of assignments. Gracie smiled at the memory.

If she trusted herself, and trusted Stephan, she might never leave the islands. But the professor's vote of confidence bolstered her. She'd put the letters away next to the flash drive containing her private photos of Stephan. Whatever else might come, the letters would remind her that respected scholars valued her for more than just her connections.

The chatter of several dozen female students pushed aside her memories, bringing her focus back to her shaking hands and queasy stomach.

Almost the entire week had been dedicated to preparing the Royal Academy students for their meetings with the royal family. The men had been drilled for an intricate, military-style presentation. But the women stood crowded into an overly warm room, awaiting entrance to the hall that would host the Presentation Tea.

She scanned the crowd, relieved to see Marta coming toward her. "Thank God for a friendly face," she whispered as Marta took her place.

"Ladies. Attention please." Professor Mikolas stood at a podium. "Those of you born in Melesia understand the importance of this event. The rest of you have, by now, learned. I am confident that you will all make me proud today. Now, for some last-minute instructions.

"You will be introduced in groups, citizens first, followed by foreign students. Within the groups, you will be introduced in an order determined by your education, skills, and future plans. Those most likely to work within the government will be introduced first, and so on."

"Which means I'll be dead last," Gracie whispered to Marta.

"When you are presented to His Royal Highness, you will use your most formal manners. You will speak only when spoken to. If His Highness wishes to converse with you, you may follow his lead.

"But I stress, keep your interactions polite, brief, and, above all, respectful. Prince Stephan is graciously giving you the chance to meet him. Do not mistake it for an invitation to become friends. Any questions?"

Gracie and Marta edged to the back of the room. "How do you think she'd react if she knew I'd threatened the prince?" Marta asked quietly.

"About as well as she'd react knowing I'd—you know."

"Right. Since you brought it up, why are you so nervous? You have a stronger connection to the royal family than even she does. It's not as if you're meeting for the first time."

"This is different." Gracie smoothed the folds of her dress again, muttering the multiplication tables to herself.

"If you're nervous you could always try the old trick of picturing him in his underwear," Marta said softly.

"Miss Ohanii, I'm sure that would be most inappropriate." Professor Mikolas's voice splashed like icy water over them. "Now stop behaving like a child and join the others. You will be in group number two. Miss Smith, you will be in the last group."

The instructor looked at Gracie's shaking hands. "I am delighted to see you are not in one of your disdainful moods today. Nothing like a bit of nerves to put one in one's place. I will be watching you very closely today, Miss Smith. Inappropriate behavior on your part will have unpleasant consequences. Understood?"

Gracie nodded and moved to take her place at the end of the line. Neither Marta's joking words nor Professor Mikolas's sharp ones helped her nerves. Unfortunately, it was all too easy to picture Stephan naked. And, after he'd made good on his promise to find baby pictures of the professor, she had some uncomfortable images of Dorinda Mikolas in her head too.

Two, three, five, seven, eleven. She bounced between chanting prime numbers, multiplication tables, and pi while the classes filed into the reception hall to await Prince Stephan's arrival.

Faculty milled around the wide hall, all dressed for the official function. A few of her professors flashed her encouraging smiles. Gracie's tension eased as a cool ocean breeze wafted through the open windows. After the stuffiness of the preparation room, she welcomed fresh sea-scented air. It reminded her of simpler times with Stephan. Times when there weren't photographers and formality.

The memory reinforced her resolve. She could do this for him. She could be seen on his arm in public. It was only the Presentation Tea, not a press conference. It was only a baby step. Gracie took a gulp of the sea air. She could do it. She could.

A sound system crackled to life at one end of the room. A small ensemble began to play the national anthem. All eyes turned toward the raised dais along one wall. "Ladies and Gentlemen, Professors and Students, presenting the Chancellor of the Royal Academy, His Royal Highness Prince Stephan Hercules Tantalus D'Malia."

Gracie's knees buckled at the sight of him. The crisp lines of his military uniform accented his long legs, and the high collar emphasized the firm set of his jaw. His insignia and medals of office glinted from their place along a sash trimmed in royal green and gold. He looked regal. Princely.

She couldn't do this.

But the press of the chaperones and the security teams outlining the perimeter of the room didn't leave her an option. She inched forward. Seeing him like this, in his natural state, dressed as exactly what he was—an important leader in an important country—wiped every other image of him from her mind. The naughty, naked memories that had plagued her only moments ago evaporated.

When her turn came, she mounted the steps to the dais on shaking legs.

"Your Highness, may I present Miss Grace Smith, an American biology student at the academy."

Gracie sank into a curtsey and murmured the appropriate response. When he handed her up, she kept her eyes lowered and tried to control her breathing. The slow, tickling slide of his finger along her palm snapped her out of her panic. She looked up, swallowing her giggle, to see a twinkle in his eyes.

"I am delighted to meet you, Miss Smith. How have you enjoyed your studies at the academy?"

"Very well, Your Highness."

"And what is your favorite subject?"

"Language," she blurted, unable to take her eyes from him. "I've found the study of your language very rewarding."

His lips curved in a smile as he raised her hand to kiss it. "I wish you well in your future studies and hope they continue to be rewarding," he said softly in Melesian. As he released her hand, he stroked his thumb along his jaw in their private gesture, reminding her how he hated the forced distance between them. She gave him a smile and left the dais.

Marta caught up with her as soon as she moved away from the prince. "He's a rat," she muttered. "He asked me about my family's security business. Then he mentioned my brothers' interest in lobster fishing and asked if I knew what kind of bait they used."

Gracie laughed, some of her nerves dissipating at the thought of Stephan teasing Marta. "You must admit, he has a great sense of timing for his payback."

"True. It's another point in his favor. But he's still a rat."

Gracie and Marta wandered past the refreshment tables. They joined a knot of fellow students and made small talk. Then, without warning, Gracie's stomach lurched. The students around her stilled.

"Miss Smith, I would be honored if you would walk with me." Gracie turned at Stephan's quiet words. He stood, offering his arm. She'd known he would come to her. She'd promised she wouldn't hide.

His arm felt warm, reassuring, under her hand and Gracie closed her eyes briefly as he led her away. "Breathe, *hona-mei*," he said softly. They walked to the perimeter of the room. "I must apologize. I should have listened to my betters."

"Pardon me?"

"Jill and Constantine warned me that the full-dress uniform and regalia might be startling for you. I'm sorry for not preparing you."

"It was a little overwhelming." The sound of his voice grounded her, even as the sight of him disconcerted her.

"A little? For a minute, I thought you were going to pass out on me. Are you feeling better? Or should I be ready to perform CPR?"

"That won't be necessary, Your Highness," she teased. The sight and sounds of cameras distracted her, and she clutched his arm tighter.

"Don't look at them, Gracie. Look at me."

She listened to his voice and followed his instructions, grasping at them like a drowning swimmer at a lifeline.

"That's it. Now talk to me. Smile. Think about all the wicked things I'd like to be doing with your body if we were alone. Can you guess where I want my hands to be right this moment?"

A flush crept over her body as she thought of all the intimate places he'd touched her in the privacy of his suite. Her own hands itched at the memory of touching him as well. She flashed him a look, trying to convey her gratitude.

As long as she kept her eyes on his face and ignored the royal uniform and regalia, she was fine. As long as she remembered that underneath the formality there was just Stephan, the man she loved, she was more than fine.

"Gracie," he said softly, "I have to leave you to mingle with the other students. Before I go, think about this. While you were busy remembering my hands on your body, you didn't even notice the photographers snapping your picture. If you could block your panic with similar pleasant thoughts in the future, you might find it becomes much easier to deal with."

When Stephan left her, Gracie smiled to herself.

One baby step under her belt.

A thousand more to go.
She could do this.

Chapter 32

racie flipped through her research notes with satisfaction. The preliminary data showed enough differences between the pristine coral at Neptune's Crown Reef and the reef near the industrial areas to support her thesis. The pages of documentation, drawings, photos, and sample analysis results might even merit publication in a research journal once she completed the work.

Another trip to the industrial reef and a more detailed second look at the Neptune's Crown formation might give her enough data to finish. Now that Stephan knew—and accepted—her intellectual side, she could collect the rest of the data she needed.

Thoughts of Stephan filled her mind, pushing the research aside. She looked at the local newspaper article pinned to the bulletin board of her desk. The photo of them strolling together at the Presentation Tea, and the accompanying article, wasn't as bad as she'd feared.

Nothing dreadful had happened. Even Professor Mikolas had complimented her on her decorum. Praise from Dorinda Mikolas was more unsettling than her criticism, but it wasn't dreadful.

And Stephan had sent her a bouquet of island flowers along with a note complimenting her on facing her fears and thanking her for trusting him.

Gracie added a new litany to the list of soothing mathematical sequences that calmed her. *I can do this.* Whenever a wave of panic hit, she repeated it. *I can do this. For Stephan. I can do this.*

She put her notes away and slipped into her uniform, hoping to catch an early ferry to Royal Island. With luck she could see Stephan before she began work today. The moments they'd had together since returning from the States were far too few.

The phone rang as she was pulling on her shoes. She answered absently, unable to identify the caller from the ring tone.

"I thought you were going to stay low and avoid the press, Grace." Sophia's voice was sharp with accusation. "Photos of you and Stephan were all over yesterday's news."

"What?"

"They were picked up by the Associated Press. Most of them are buried in the human-interest sections of the papers, but you need to be more careful."

"It was an official school function. Stephan is Chancellor of the Royal Academy, after all."

"He's also an eligible bachelor prince, and that's news. He's not the kind of person you want to be seen with if you value your anonymity. Or mine."

Gracie sank to the bed and absently picked at the threads of her apron. "Listen, we need to talk about that. It's time for you to come home. You were never supposed to be gone for more than a few days, anyway. Everyone in the family is worried about you, especially Stephan. I've heard he's in charge of finding you."

"All the more reason for you to stay away from him."

"I can't, Sophia. I won't. I—"

"Don't tell me you think you're in love with him. It takes more than a walk at a school function to fall in love. He's not some fairy tale hero that's yours for the taking."

"You're right." Gracie stood, suddenly angry at the dismissal in Sophia's voice. "He's much more than a story book hero. He's a wonderful man. A man I love. And I won't lie to him anymore. I'll give you one hour to call and tell him where you are. Then I'm going to come clean with him. I won't keep your secrets anymore."

"What about your own secrets? Do you really believe a man like Stephan is going to overlook all of the laws you've broken by helping me?"

"You've broken laws too."

"Yes, but I'll claim ignorance. And I'll also be covered by diplomatic immunity. Neither of those things will help you. In Melesia it's a crime to conspire against a member of the nobility. Treason is defined differently than in your country."

"I didn't conspire against anyone. You wanted to disappear."

"A Melesian court may not see it that way."

"But Stephan—"

"You may fancy yourself in love with him, but he'll uphold the law, no matter what the cost. He will always put the needs of his country, and the royal family, above everything and everyone else."

Gracie's hands shook and she fought to keep the phone still. "That's not true. He loves me."

"Has he told you so?"

No. He hadn't told her. *I can do this. I can. Three point one four one five nine…*

"I didn't think so. Don't risk losing everything. Don't tell him."

"But I," Gracie stopped. Her voice wavered, and she couldn't keep the tears at bay.

"He might not want to hurt you," Sophia said more gently, "but he's bound by an oath of duty. All of them are. Even your sister. Just keep my secret for a little while longer, and I'll see that no harm comes to you. Trust me."

"But—"

"Trust me, Grace. Good-bye."

Long after the phone went dead and her hands stopped shaking, Gracie sat, her mind furiously searching for answers. She didn't know the Melesian law or history enough to judge the truth of Sophia's words. But she did know one thing.

She loved Stephan. She couldn't lie to him anymore. And she wouldn't let him set aside his principles for her sake.

Even if it meant exile and a future alone.

Despite the warm Melesian afternoon, Gracie's hands were like ice as she tapped on the door to Stephan's office. An impassive security guard stood to one side, ignoring her after a glance to determine that she was part of the palace staff. Gracie wondered if he'd be the same guard to take her into custody if Sophia's threats were real.

At Stephan's command, she entered the office and closed the door softly behind her. He stood to one side of the room, engrossed in the maze of maps tacked to one wall. When he looked up and saw her, a smile replaced the frown he'd been wearing.

"I didn't expect to see you here at this hour, *hona-mei*." He crossed the distance between them and kissed her. "What's wrong? You're pale. Your hands are freezing. You're not fretting over the newspaper photos, are you?"

She shook her head and let him draw her into an embrace. One that she didn't deserve, but she hugged him anyway, soaking in his warmth and storing up the memory of how his body felt against hers.

"I've got just the thing to take your mind off whatever's bothering you." He pulled her over to the wall of maps and wrapped an arm around her shoulder. "It's a puzzle. I'm sure you know, even though the press doesn't, that Lady Sophia disappeared from our goodwill tour. This is the place where I believe she slipped away from her entourage. These are the possible routes she could have taken." He traced the routes leading from Chicago to various points across the United States.

"I know where she is," Gracie whispered.

"Wow. That's fast, even for you. Where do you think—"

"I did a terrible thing. I didn't mean to, but..." Gracie stopped and squared her shoulders. She wasn't a child anymore. She'd handle her confession like an adult and take the consequences. She looked Stephan in the eye.

"I don't know exactly where she is, but I know how to get in touch with her." She took the phone from her pocket, pushed the redial button and handed it to Stephan.

His face registered surprise, then shock as Sophia answered the phone. His greeting to her, deceptively friendly and soft, warred with the granite expression on his face. He abruptly ended the call, pocketed her phone, then turned to Gracie.

"Explain."

As she told the story from her first meeting with Sophia to their last phone call, Stephan's stoic features melted away. His jaw relaxed, and the cold anger in his eyes was replaced by something else. Confusion, disappointment, and hurt all fought for control of his features.

Gracie watched, each expression tearing at her heart. Surely no court-inflicted punishment could be worse than seeing the look of betrayal that claimed his face.

"I wanted to tell you sooner, but I—"

"You what? You didn't trust me?"

"I'd promised Sophia. It was a mistake to help her, but at the time, I thought I had good reasons. And it happened before I really knew you."

"Granted. But what about later? When you did know me?"

His voice was flat, like a judge issuing a sentence, and she didn't know how to respond. How could she admit that she'd simply forgotten about Sophia when she was with him? Gracie watched him in silence.

"Did you think it would be easier to hurt me after our first kiss? After we made love? When? Or were you just going to watch me flounder through this investigation on my own while you quietly held the key to it all?"

Gracie flinched at the pain that lay just beneath the rising anger in his voice. "I didn't mean to hurt you. I thought I could convince her to come home."

"I don't have time to discuss this." The anger disappeared as quickly as it came, locked behind a calm, almost unemotional voice. His features stilled into an unreadable mask. He turned from her and walked behind the desk then paused, phone halfway to his ear. The look he gave her was as blank and empty as the darkest underwater cave she could imagine.

"I have to send a security team to locate Sophia and quietly bring her home before the political nightmare caused by her disappearance comes to a head. Then I have to meet with the king and the public relations team to determine what potential damage could still occur.

"After that, I'll design a plan to counter and contain said damage and call for a press conference." His voice was cold, matter of fact, and masking pain. If possible, it grew even colder with his next words.

"My duty at this press conference is to assure the world of the innocent intentions of everyone involved. To convince them that this isn't a cocked-up mess brought about by my incompetence. Or, failing that, I have to keep the fall-out from sullying our king and his government. All of which would have been far easier had you trusted me from the beginning."

Gracie stood frozen in place, watching the scene unfold. As Sophia predicted, her transgression had gone from a simple matter of providing a fake ID, to a potential public relations nightmare. Or worse, to a government scandal that could have damaged the country.

And Stephan had gone from a warm and concerned lover to an icy stranger. Someone who locked his emotions behind an impenetrable mask of duty.

Should she stay? Go?

Stephan glanced up from his call, his eyes still empty. "Please. Let me do my job. Someone will inform you of what we need you to do."

She nodded and exited the room, leaving her heart, and her hopes, behind.

Gracie's steps stilled as she approached her dorm room. A team of armed security guards stood in the corridor. More were inside the room. She'd almost convinced herself that they could work through this disaster. God knew she wanted to try. She'd convinced herself that the matter was personal, not political. Until she saw the guards.

In Melesia it's a crime. Treason is defined differently. Sophia's words wouldn't stop repeating in her memory. *Crime. Treason.*

"Gracie, thank goodness you're here. You have to pack. The guards are escorting us back to Royal Island." Marta urged her inside the room.

"Us? What have you done?"

A security guard stepped forward. "Miss Bradley, His Royal Majesty, King Constantine asked that you return to Royal Island immediately. We've been sent to see that you arrive safely. If you could pack your things, our team members will see to it that they are transferred to your new quarters."

"Looks like I'm being put under house arrest," she said to Marta as she quickly packed the essentials. She grabbed her important papers, her computer, and a couple changes of clothing. She asked the guards to bring the rest of her books and belongings later.

Marta slung a small bag over her shoulder joined Gracie as she left the room. "Prince Stephan called and asked me to come with you. He said that you might need a friend." Her words were soft and concerned.

"He called? When?"

"Just before you arrived."

So he hadn't turned completely against her. What had she once said of him? That he was chivalrous even in the throes of anger? A glimmer of hope broke through her darkness as they made their way back to Royal Island.

Chapter 33

*T*wo days later, Gracie looked up from the strewn-about newspapers to the dark stone walls of the windowless room. She'd never been in this part of the palace before, never imagined this underground fortress where the family sat huddled with security and public relations specialists. "This is worse than I thought." A shiver raced down her spine.

"It's our war room," Stephan said from his place near the head of the table. "A secure place to plan our public relations battles. Down here it's easier to keep prying eyes out."

"It looks like a dungeon." Gracie shivered and glanced at Marta who hovered on the fringes of the room. Her face was ashen, and she was quieter than Gracie had ever seen her.

"Yes, it does," Stephan answered, flicking her a glance. A tiny hint of humor gleamed in his eyes. "But it comes complete with coffee, croissants, and room service. Let's all take a short break before we tackle this. Miss Ohanii, please, join us. Like it or not, your friendship with Gracie puts you in the inner circle for this battle."

Stephan motioned the group toward the coffee, maneuvering Marta so that she stood next to Gracie. They fell into groups: Jill and Alia, Gracie with Marta, Stephan and Constantine.

When they reconvened, Constantine spoke first. "I have complete confidence in each of you." He looked at each person around the room, drawing their attention even as he projected his trust. "We've weathered other crises, and we'll get through this one. Stephan has agreed to take the lead in setting our direction, and I fully support him.

"Some of you," he looked at Gracie and Marta, "have never been targeted in the media before. Listen to Stephan's coaching, and, when in doubt, remember that less is more. When you don't know what to say or do, it is always wiser to say and do nothing."

Stephan took over, calmly and analytically reciting each newspaper headline and the main points of the article. Team members recorded his summary on large flip charts which they posted on the stone walls.

Gracie scanned the headlines, her stomach knotting.

"Secret American Plot to Overthrow Melesian Government."

"Sisters Named in Undercover Plot."

"Is It Love, Or A Bid for Control?"

"A Fool for Love: Is the King Fit to Rule?"

"Is Prince Charming in Over His Head?"

"Intended Bride Ousted as American Sister Steps In."

The last featured a photo of Gracie and Sophia, together on the day of the wedding, their striking similarities captured perfectly by the photographer.

Other photos lined the wall. Gracie and Stephan at the Presentation Tea, and in the rotunda where Mrs. Joyner had photographed them. More photos of them, taken separately, but artfully superimposed. Even grainy, poor reproductions of the underwater shots she'd taken of him on their first day together. Innocent photos linked in a damning sequence.

She stared at the underwater photos, wrinkling her brow in concentration, wondering how the press got hold of them.

The other photos were all taken in public. The tea, the rotunda— Mrs. Joyner. In the library on Stephan's yacht. Taking photos of his computer. She curled her fist in anger as the pieces snapped into place.

"The sensationalist tabloid stories are outrageous enough to be ignored." All eyes turned to Stephan as he spoke. "Some of the accusations, however, are being picked up by the mainstream media. At the moment, they are positioned as humorous bits of speculation buried in legitimate stories about Melesia. Our job is to keep them that way."

He looked around the table and everyone nodded. Unexpectedly, he reached out and covered Gracie's hand with his own, giving her a slight squeeze. That bit of warmth gave her courage.

Stephan paced to the poster covered wall. "The recurring theme bears the stamp of traditionalist factions. Though the situation looks bad, it could have been much worse. Most of the articles center on Sophia's disappearance, which could have led to accusations that the monarchy wanted to rid itself of its last de Lyons rival.

"Fortunately for us, no one has picked up on that angle. For now, we claim total knowledge of, and cooperation with, Sophia's disappearance. She's already issued a statement confirming this, which is part of the reason she—and we—are back in the news. But what's more important is that her statement removes any traditionalist accusations that the king and his government were involved in treason or foul play."

Gracie sighed in relief.

"That's the good news," Stephan continued. "Now for the points we need to deal with. The actual reports tie Sophia's disappearance into an alleged plot to unite me romantically with Miss Bradley. That leads to accusations of a destabilizing American influence within Melesia. A takeover by marriage, if you will."

"How do we refute that?" Gracie asked.

"We don't." Stephan smiled at her, offering more warmth despite the unresolved tensions that still hung between them. "We refuse to comment. Our king and queen are experts at supporting one another while ignoring attempts to intrude on their personal life. I'll coach you—and Miss Ohanii—on the techniques you'll need to do the same."

He turned to the rest of the team. "As for Lady Sophia's disappearance, we'll craft a press release describing her extended holiday in America and her wishes for privacy as she visits distant relatives.

"Finally, three days from now, we'll hold a press conference. The official purpose will be to announce Miss Bradley's graduation from the Royal Academy and her intention to stay with her sister to help until the birth of the royal heir.

"The unofficial purpose will be to show a happy family, a united front, and a strong kingdom. With luck, all will blow over and life will return to normal."

With that the team scattered. As the experts worked on their assigned tasks, Gracie knew she'd never be normal again.

"I can't do this anymore," Gracie said, turning away from him. The glittering panic in her eyes had faded to a dull resignation during the long hours of practice. Even moving from the gloomy war room to her airy suite in the palace hadn't restored her completely.

Stephan regretted the grueling hours of mock interviewing he'd forced on her, but he knew he'd regret it more if he let her face the press unprepared.

"Your Highness?" Marta walked from the window back to the sitting area. "Perhaps you should take a break."

"Good idea." He stood and stretched. Thank the gods he'd asked Marta to accompany Gracie to Royal Island. He was too tied in knots to give her as much support as she needed.

Controlling the public reactions to the news demanded his concentration and the wall between him and Gracie seemed almost impossible to breach. "I'll leave you for a while."

"Actually," Marta rushed to the door ahead of him, "I should be the one to leave. I'll check with the kitchens about…something. Maybe I'll bring fresh coffee." She sprinted out the door before he could stop her.

Wise woman.

"Gracie?" He held out a hand and when she took it, he pulled her into his embrace. She huddled against him, frail and forlorn. "I'm sorry about all of this, sweetheart. I wish I could make it go away."

"I brought it on myself." Her voice, heavy with misery, was barely audible.

"No, sweetheart, you didn't." He rocked her and pressed kisses into her hair. "These things happen. They're part of the burden of the royal family. I wish I could protect you from it, but the best I can do is prepare you."

"If I'd told you sooner about Sophia, if I'd trusted you—"

"It hurts that you didn't, but I believe you when you said you tried to fix things on your own. It's that stubborn streak of yours that doesn't want to accept help from anyone. We're going to have to work on controlling that, *hona-mei*."

She looked up at him, her eyes wide and wet. "So I'm still *hona* to you, even after all of this?"

A shock wave slammed into his body at her implications. He tightened his hold on her but strove for a gentle tone as he answered. "Do you think lovers never get angry? Or hurt? Do you think my feelings for you are so inconsequential that they'll disappear overnight? If so, you have a lot to learn."

"Sophia said you'd put country and family over every-thing. That you wouldn't be able to overlook the law. She said I'd committed crimes. Treason."

Gracie shook in his arms as she spoke. *Ba'hona-mei,* he thought silently, *you are family. You just don't know it yet.*

"As it happens, I don't think Melesian law goes into detail about the penalty for supplying a false ID in order to create mischief." He stilled and pulled far enough away to cup her chin and urge her to look at him. "You weren't planning to involve Sophia in smuggling contraband, were you?"

"No." Shock washed over her face.

He smiled and released her chin. "Good. That means it isn't a felony, and it isn't anywhere near treasonous. I think spending most of the day locked in the war room and being forced into a press conference is penalty enough for helping Sophia."

"What about us? About the anger? And the hurt?"

"Time, Gracie. It just takes time to heal." *And we'll have all the time in the world if I get my way.* He kissed her gently, letting her know that things were already mending. "Now, let's get back to the crisis at hand."

But neither of them moved from their embrace until Marta knocked softly at the door and the world intruded once again.

Gracie blinked away the grit from three sleepless nights. She'd finished her Advanced Research Thesis just in time. Circumstances might have forced her into *early* graduation, cutting off six blissful months of study and research, but she refused to accept the ruse without handing in her final project. Too bad she'd never be able to add the research necessary to make it publishable. But at least it was done.

Professor Pontileus had been delighted when he picked it up. He'd also brought more letters of recommendation for her, this time using her real name. For better or worse, she was no longer anonymous.

Gracie stifled a yawn and tried to focus on the last minute instructions Stephan was giving her.

I can do this. She took a seat beside Jill. Her brother-in-law sat on Jill's other side, dressed conservatively and exuding the air of a world leader. Stephan gave Gracie's shoulder a squeeze and moved to stand behind Constantine.

Everything had been choreographed by the public relations team. Gracie's place beside her sister emphasized her role as a concerned family member and a United States citizen who supported Melesian interests.

The distance between her and Stephan downplayed their relationship and potential questions about it. In her head, Gracie knew he'd arranged everything to give her some privacy. But in her heart, she blamed the gap between them on herself.

Just as she blamed herself for the wasted years she'd spent pushing her sister away.

Gracie took a sip of cool water and tried to focus on the hour ahead. Time. Stephan had told her they only needed time to make things right between them. Maybe after today, they'd have the time. She needed to earn his forgiveness and to see trust and love in his eyes again.

But as the members of the press filed in and turned on their lights, cameras, and microphones, her stomach lurched and her mind went blank. This was Stephan's world, and he needed a woman who could hold her own in it, not someone he'd have to shield forever. Suddenly, time didn't seem like enough to fill the gap between them.

If she'd had the chance to take more baby steps, learning to deal with the media in small doses, she might have eventually overcome her fears. But today, instead of baby steps, she'd been thrown into a marathon race. One chance to succeed or fail.

Almost without warning, the interview began. She stammered her way through a rehearsed speech about the academy and her classes and babbled too much about the scientific details of her research.

She breathed a sigh of relief when the interviewers directed their questions to Constantine and Jill. Restlessly, she tapped her fingers on the chair arm while her brain chanted mathematical nonsense. She'd survived her part of the press conference.

"Miss Bradley? What is your opinion? Do you agree?"

"Um," she closed her mouth on the stammer. Think. What was the question? She looked at Jill and Constantine out of the corner of her eye, hoping for a clue. They were looking at each other, loving smiles on their faces. "Yes. Of course, I agree. Wholeheartedly."

Their smiles disappeared and the men frowned at her before quickly smoothing their features into twin masks, devoid of expression. Jill looked ill.

What had she done?

"Just for the record, Miss Bradley, you're saying you agree with the recent accusations that the king has been made into *a fool for love*? That he is unfit to rule because of his love for your sister?"

"Are you implying that there really is an American plot to destabilize the Melesian government?"

"Do you work for the CIA, Miss Bradley? Or an underground splinter group?"

The questions whizzed at her from all sides, each camera and microphone focusing on her every move. Horror clawed at her. "No. I misspoke. I don't think that..."

What had Constantine told her before? *When you don't know what to say or do, it is always wiser to say and do nothing.* She clamped her mouth shut and blinked rapidly.

"For the record, I've decided not to offer Miss Bradley a position as my personal publicist." The king's quip broke the tension in the room, but Gracie could see his smile didn't reach his eyes.

"Seriously, Ladies and Gentlemen of the press," Constantine continued, his voice stemming her panic with its calm, almost soothing resonance, "my wife has been restless lately because of the baby. Her sister has been helping her a great deal during the sleepless nights. I'm afraid the exertion, and the final pressures of her graduation, have taken a toll on Miss Bradley. If you could, as a courtesy, excuse the ladies to get some much-needed rest. Prince Stephan and I would be glad to answer further questions."

He rose and helped Jill and Gracie to their feet, not waiting for the press's response. Gracie glanced at Stephan and flinched. Icy, rigid control radiated from him in waves, quenching her embarrassment like arctic water on molten glass, leaving her sharp and brittle.

Once out of sight in Jill's rooms, she collapsed in her sister's arms. "Oh God. What have I done?"

She broke into sobs, unable to think clearly or to understand Jill's murmured words. Stephan's image was etched into her mind. She'd disappointed him. Again.

She could never be the woman he needed. Never rise above her fears to stand beside him in the spotlight. She'd been a millstone around his neck. One who'd just caused irreparable damage to the people she loved.

"It's okay, Gracie. We'll work this out. It was a misunderstanding, nothing more."

She nodded, taking the easy way out. She didn't believe Jill's optimism, but she didn't have the energy to fight it, either.

Instead, she tried to pull back her wayward emotions and hide them as she'd done for so long.

She swallowed her tears then blinked, squinting through swollen eyes. A flash of red in the corner of the room distracted her. Jill's ruby slippers. *There's no place like home.* She'd once thought that Melesia could be her home, too, because Stephan was there.

It still was, she realized. But she was a liability to it. In order to protect the home she loved, she knew what she had to do. She slipped from Jill's arms.

"I need a couple of aspirin and about a dozen hours of uninterrupted sleep," Gracie said as she headed to the door. "I can't think straight."

"I'll make sure you're not disturbed. Don't worry, things will look better in the morning. Everyone makes mistakes, and our local press is very forgiving."

Gracie nodded, pretending to believe Jill's words. Then she headed through the back corridors to her own rooms. After leaving written messages for Jill and Stephan, she gathered a few things and called for a car. With luck she'd be on a flight out of the country before anyone knew she was gone. For the sake of all she loved, it was time to leave.

Chapter 34

$\mathcal{A}$pollo Mikolas leaned back in his seat of Melesia One, stretched his legs and gave Stephan a sleepy look before closing his eyes. "Tell me again why *I'm* the spokesperson for *your* marine life donation program."

Stephan wasn't fooled. Behind the lazy speech and mannerisms lay a sharp mind and deceptive wit. "You're the new public face of the program because I have other business in the States. While the world is watching you, I'll pay Sophia an unannounced visit. She has something that doesn't belong to her."

Stephan stared out the window of the plane at the empty ocean below. At his urging, Sophia had agreed to a telephone interview which had taken place several weeks ago, putting to rest the rumors about her health and state of mind. But she'd refused to come home. While he respected her newfound privacy, it was time for her to give up Gracie's identity and take back her own.

"And then what?"

Stephan looked up. Apollo was still sprawled across the seat, eyes closed, but Stephan knew his mind was alert.

"I'm going to see Miss Bradley. She's licked her wounds in private for long enough."

"So I'm to play decoy while you go find your girl. Is that it?"

Stephan ignored him. In the weeks since the disastrous press conference, Gracie's image had faded from the press, but not from his mind. She'd fled the islands leaving him a letter saying she wanted to spend Christmas with her family. Alone. Now January was half gone, and she hadn't returned to Melesia, nor had she responded to his phone calls or letters.

He chewed a couple of antacids and ground another slowly to dust in his fist. The last time Gracie had been to the States, she'd come back to him. This time was different. What if she'd decided she didn't want him? What if the silence was her way of saying good-bye?

"No answer? It's not like you to be so undiplomatic, Stephan." Apollo cracked his eyes open. "Would you care for some advice, my friend?"

"I don't need your advice on how to deal with Gracie."

"I beg to differ. This isn't the first time you've lost her. I was at the Paradise Cove club the night she ran out on you." He paused, the lazy silence punctuating his bored observations. "Does she know you love her?"

"Of course, she knows." Stephan straightened, snapping the lapels on his jacket into place and adjusting his cuff links.

"Did you tell her?"

"Not in so many words. She wasn't ready—"

"Then she doesn't know. You may be brilliant, but you don't know women. A woman needs to hear the words. Often."

"That's laughable, coming from a man who discards women as frequently as you do."

"Now I know I'm on target. You've switched from charm mode into attack mode." Apollo sat up, looking him fully in the eye and appearing engaged in the conversation for the first time.

"I know more about love than you give me credit for. You love this woman. I'd bet my family fortune that she loves you too. When you find her, tell her. Forget the champagne and flowers and any other romantic notions lurking in your head. Just get the three words out. Everything else can come later. Believe me. She needs to know. Tell her before it's too late."

The intensity of Apollo's words snapped Stephan out of his sullen, defensive mood. He caught a glimpse of pain in his friend's eyes before Apollo collapsed into his usual nonchalance.

Stephan nodded, disquieted by Apollo's moment of unguarded honesty and his own sour mood. He kicked himself for letting Gracie slip away in a state of distress. His hurt, his anger, his need to control the public image of the monarchy—all of it—had pushed her away when he'd needed to draw her closer.

"Don't worry." Apollo's voice drifted across the cabin, filled with bored indifference once again. "I'll play the charming Melesian nobleman for you. I'll seduce the press, woo the ladies, even stand on my head if it gives you the chance to do what you need to do. I meant what I said. I know a thing or two about love."

Stephan didn't bother to respond. Instead, he checked his watch. Within hours of landing he'd have Gracie's driver's license and be off again in search of her. Time couldn't pass quickly enough.

"Mrs. Bradley barely gave me the time of day." Stephan exploded across the room in his office at the Melesian consulate in Chicago. "Her parting words were *if you love Gracie enough, you'll find her*. What's that supposed to mean?" He grabbed the wall phone by the door and punched in the number of this security team, ready to start an all-out search.

Apollo abandoned his post by the windows and sauntered over to perch on the corner of the desk, an amused smile playing on his lips. "It means you have to stop thinking like a prince who can force her to return. You have to start thinking like Gracie."

"What?" Stephan turned, the phone dangling uselessly in his hand.

"Put yourself in Gracie's shoes. If you love her, you'll know what's important to her. Once you see the world with her eyes, you'll know where to find her."

Stephan replaced the phone without finishing the call and wandered to the windows. A light snow fell from the bleak gray sky, coating the manicured lawns of the consulate.

The last time he'd seen Gracie, she'd walked from the press conference, shock and humiliation etched on her face. It took everything he had to keep his mind on the press so he could help salvage her dignity. All he'd wanted was to hold her in his arms. But, of course, she couldn't have known that.

Apollo came up behind him and laid a hand on his shoulder. "How do you think she felt when she left Melesia?"

"She was embarrassed. Confused. Hurt."

"Of course. Any fool could see that much."

The assessment rankled. He'd put himself in Gracie's position from the beginning. Saving her from the media at the wedding. Protecting her secret identity. Helping her with her research goals. Healing the rifts in her family. Coaxing her out of her shell. It had all been about Gracie, hadn't it?

No, it hadn't. Somewhere along the line it had stopped being entirely about Gracie and started being about them. The couple. The lovers. But in the end, had it become only about him? Stephan shifted uncomfortably, trapped between the weight of his friend's hand and his own guilt.

"Focus on her," Apollo urged. "How does she feel about you? Her future? What does she hope for, and what does she think she has to settle for? And how do you convince her that you belong together?"

"Weren't you the one who said all I needed to do was tell her that I love her?"

"Ah, yes. That's still true. But first you have to find her, don't you?"

Later, alone in the office, Stephan pulled Gracie's cell phone from his pocket. In the turmoil of her last days on Melesia, he'd forgotten to return it to her. He pulled out his own cell phone and pressed the speed dial button. Hers sprang to life, tinkling out the melody of "Under the Sea" and flashing a photo of the porcupine fish she'd taken during their first dive. During the happy times they'd shared.

He cut off the call and the happy memories to focus on finding her. He analyzed and categorized everything he knew about Gracie, like a scientist plotting data. One trend stood out.

Her uncertainty, her fear, paralyzed and isolated her. He'd teased and cajoled her from her self-imposed exile, taught her to trust him, and watched her grow, but at the crucial moment of the press conference, he'd failed her.

Instead of preparing her with mock interviews and stock responses, he should have built her confidence with his love and support.

He replayed the scene in his mind, this time hearing the apprehension in her voice and seeing the foreboding in her eyes. Things he'd missed—or dismissed—before.

I brought it on myself... I'm still hona to you, even after all of this? You'd put country and family over everything. What about us?

He should have addressed the hurt and anger between them, not brushed it off with a joke and good intentions.

Instead of telling her what she needed to hear—that he loved her, no matter what—he'd babbled about his own hurt and given her glib assurances that time would heal the wounds. Then, like a ruthless taskmaster, he'd pushed her back into preparing for the press conference.

No wonder she left feeling that she failed him. No wonder she ran, hoping to hide her broken heart from the world.

What would she turn to when her world fell apart? Suddenly, he knew how to find her. The one thing Gracie had confidence in was her mind. Her science.

A call to Professor Pontileus gave him a short list of places she'd approach for a job. He'd call each one on the pretense of following up with recent academy graduates and their job search.

His first call was to the Chicago Shedd Aquarium. With its extensive research and education programs, Gracie would thrive there.

She'd turned down a position with them.

As he disconnected the call, Stephan glanced out the window at the thickly falling snow and shivered. It wasn't going to be as easy as he'd hoped.

Twenty calls and two hours later, he'd found her.

He smiled at the irony of her choice. When she needed comfort most, Gracie had reached for more than just science.

She'd sought out magic.

And he was just the man who could give it to her.

It was time to rescue his *Ba'hona-mei* and bring her home.

A wave of homesickness washed over Gracie as she stepped back and stared at the spotless aquarium glass. The Melesian exhibit at the Epcot Center's World Showcase featured a miniature version of the palace on Royal Island, complete with the grand entry hall and its vast aquarium. Workers and cast members even dressed in reasonable imitations of the uniform she'd once hated.

She sighed in relief. Her primary job—working with the marine life exhibits—didn't require her to be on stage in the public areas of the exhibit once it opened tomorrow. The palace replica was too real for her comfort. It brought back too many memories.

She wandered through the rooms, eyeing the details. The queen's shopping gallery was almost as immense as the real version, only this one housed boutiques appropriate for tourists. She stared at the fountain, its play of water on stone reminding her of an earlier time with Stephan. She pulled a half-eaten roll of antacids from her pocket and fingered them gently, as if she could still feel the warmth of his hand on the faded wrapper. Funny how such a silly thing could make her heart ache.

Without thinking, she headed to the replica of the ballroom which housed wax figures of the royal family. Alex and Helena, the King and Queen Emeritus, stood to one side. Constantine and Jill took center stage, gleaming in artistic perfection. But Stephan stood alone, dressed in his royal finery, looking off stage at something, or someone, that filled her with regret. He'd once looked at her with love in his eyes. But the glass eyes of the wax figure held no such emotion.

"Gracie, I thought I'd find you here." One of the supervisors in charge of the exhibit came toward her, footsteps echoing on the marble floor. "It's a wonderful display, isn't it? While the little girls are swooning over Prince Charming in the Magic Kingdom, the older ones will be swooning over Prince Stephan."

"His Royal Highness Prince Stephan Hercules Tantalus D'Malia," Gracie replied absently.

"You just graduated from the Royal Academy in Melesia, didn't you? I'd love to hear about it sometime. This afternoon the ambassador from Melesia is dedicating the aquarium in the grand hall and all the marine life his country donated.

"We're going to have real royalty on hand." She checked her clipboard. "His name is Apollo Mikolas, and he's heir to the Marquis of Elonyia. There's to be an evening reception and all of the staff will be invited."

Gracie nodded. Stephan had organized the donations, but he wouldn't be the one present tonight. She turned back to the wax figure, clutching the roll of antacids until her hand ached. It was all she had left of him.

It didn't matter that she chose to save him from herself. She still wanted the impossible. She wanted a fairy godmother to transform her into someone who could handle the pressures of public life. She wanted another chance. But that kind of magic only lasted until she left work each night.

The supervisor demanded her attention again. "Gracie, there's a pageant going on at the Magic Kingdom in front of Cinderella's castle. Some sort of a big promotion. I think they might be filming part of it. Anyway, they need a box of the miniature Melesian flags to pass out to the visitors. Could you run them over? Just pop in backstage and drop these off. Then you can take a few hours to yourself. Everything here is under control."

Gracie took the box of flags and headed away from the exhibit, her mind filled with the sad ending to her personal fairy tale. After arriving at the Magic Kingdom, she slipped through the cast only doors and scooted behind the curtains of the main stage into a flurry of activity.

In a rare relaxation of normal park rules, select members of the press were allowed onto the stage. Gracie shook her head at the unusual situation. Then an aide took the box of flags from Gracie, and she was lost in the crowd.

Three fully dressed Prince Charmings and half a dozen costumed princesses milled about under the watchful eyes of a costume manager and a stage director. Others, costumed as Melesian security guards, stood in front of a curtained-off section of the backstage area.

"I was so in character, I actually answered for him," said one of the princes.

"Me too," answered another. "It isn't easy to tell fantasy from reality today."

A sharp clap startled everyone into silence. "Ladies, line up. We're about to begin." The director hustled a princess—Gracie thought it might have been Sleeping Beauty—to the stage entrance. "Places, everyone. Remember: smile. You're ambassadors from the Magic Kingdom."

Sleeping Beauty disappeared onto the stage and Gracie heard the rumble of applause. She wandered down the line of princesses, heading for the exit, when one of the girls moaned.

"I don't feel well." Cinderella fanned herself furiously. "I need a glass of water. I feel faint."

Gracie was headed toward a water cooler when Cinderella moaned again. She turned back in time to see the girl faint into one of the prince's arms.

The director rushed over. "Oh my god. Come on. Wake up." He shook the limp and unresponsive actress. "Get a medic. And tell the rest of the cast to slow down the procession. I need them to buy me some time."

As Gracie edged away from the scene, the director sprang to his feet and grabbed her. "You. What's your height and weight?"

"I don't see—"

"Height and weight, girl. Now."

Gracie told him.

"Congratulations, miss. You get to be Cinderella for the day. Someone get her into the costume. Skip the makeup and move it. You've got about two minutes."

"What? I'm not qualified to be a walk around character. I work at the—"

"You're here. You fit the costume. And I need a your character onstage in ninety seconds."

A plump, gray haired woman and her assistant hurried Gracie behind a screen, pulling her clothes off then stuffing her into the costume with amazing efficiency.

"All I need you to do is walk on stage and pose for a photo op." The director rattled off a list of instructions. "Nothing to it. Smile. Let the photographers do their job. Get off stage. If you can manage a curtsey, great. If you remember not to turn your back on the audience, even better."

The costumers pinned her hair back and slid a wig onto her head while instructing her to pull on the long white gloves.

"Sixty seconds." The director tossed a pair of clear plastic shoes over the screen.

Gracie stepped into the shoes as a woman tied a ribbon around her neck, stuffing her necklace beneath the wide blue band. "Good enough, dearie. You look wonderful. Now go onstage and make magic."

"The shoes are too big." Gracie took a step forward and nearly tripped.

"Thirty seconds." The director hustled her across the stage. "Just take small steps."

From on stage, Gracie heard the announcer call for Cinderella and she felt the director push her out of the curtain. She smiled at the crowd.

Block your panic with pleasant thoughts. Stephan's advice came back to her, and she thought about the day they'd walked together at the Presentation Tea. That was how Cinderella should walk.

Professional photographers snapped her photo as she glided across the stage, careful not to trip in her too-large shoes. Tourist cameras clicked and little girls squealed. She smiled and waved at them all, keeping her gaze on the children in the audience while she walked toward the figure at the end of the aisle.

Out of the corner of her eye, she saw that he wasn't dressed like the princes backstage. He wore the royal colors of Melesia. At the last minute, she turned to him and froze.

He wasn't just wearing the colors of Royal Melesia. He was Royal Melesia. Stephan stared at her, his eyes registering the same shock that rocked through her. His gaze made her breathing hard and caused the world to swim in front of her eyes.

"Gracie?" he whispered.

"The real Cinderella passed out backstage," she answered before sinking into a full court curtsey. Cheers erupted from the crowd. The official press and photographers edged closer.

Stephan grasped her hand and helped her up, his eyes never leaving hers. Her breath caught, and her heart pounded, not from the crowds or the photographers, but from his nearness. Against all expectation, he was here.

"I—" he paused, his grip on her hand tightening until it was almost painful. "I love you."

She froze, gape mouthed, at hearing the words she'd longed for, yet never believed would come. Was this real? Or some elaborate fantasy? She licked dry lips and forced herself to breathe. "I—"

"Your Highness." The sharp cry from behind Stephan broke the spell and cut off her words. "Your Highness, over here."

Stephan turned, stepping toward the voice.

"This is for hounding Sophia." In sickening slow motion, Gracie saw one of the press photographers swing at him, landing a punch on his jaw. Stephan stumbled back at the unexpected blow, slamming into the iron support for the set.

"Don't touch him." Gracie launched herself at the photographer, not caring that a dozen others recorded her every action. She yanked his camera with one hand while the other landed a loud slap.

The crowd gasped.

Gracie stumbled in her shoes. She stepped out of them, grabbed a pump and swung it toward the retreating photographer. It flew over his head and landed in the crowd. She lunged at him, scratching and clawing. Security swarmed on stage as the curtain crashed down.

She tried to race to Stephan's side, but Magic Kingdom and Melesian security separated them, pulling her away despite her attempts to fight them off. Agonizing minutes later, dazed, disheveled and resigned to her fate, she let them lead her away.

Chapter 35

"I'm so sorry, Your Highness. Nothing like this has ever happened here before. If we hadn't asked you to greet the princesses this would never have happened. We should never have allowed the press on site. But they were carefully screened. I don't know how this happened. I am so sorry." His host paced the small hidden office where they'd taken Stephan after the incident on stage.

Stephan took a deep breath and ignored the throbbing in his head. He accepted a glass of water and a handful of painkillers from his aide and turned to the harried park representative.

"Rest assured, Your Highness, we'll handle everything. The photographer is being held. The girl, of course, will be dismissed."

"No."

"Beg pardon, Your Highness?"

"I have no wish to press charges against the photographer."

"Then we'll escort him off premises immediately."

"Take me to the girl." His jaw throbbed and his head ached, but none of that mattered. He'd seen Gracie and said what he needed to say. Everything else was up to her.

"I assure you, she wasn't one of our regular costumed characters. She was a new hire. She shouldn't have been on stage. I doubt she meant harm, nevertheless, we can't allow her to stay."

"Take me to her. Now." Stephan stood, fighting a wave of dizziness at the motion. He had to see Gracie before this ridiculous situation got even further out of hand. His host took the hint and led him to another room in the hidden areas of the castle.

Stephan brushed past him and entered. A pageant organizer paced the length of the small room as a computer monitor replayed the scene of the fight. Gracie stood to one side, her wig dangling from a gloved hand, her natural hair tangled and wild about her shoulders. She'd never looked more beautiful to him.

"You're a disgrace to the costume. Cinderella does not involve herself in common brawls. She does not launch glass slippers at the crowds." The pageant organizer jabbed a finger at the monitor and fixed Gracie with a glare. Neither appeared to notice Stephan.

"Further, you've destroyed the gown. It's torn, dirty and bloodstained. That will come out of your salary. Assuming that you're still employed at the end of the day. Which remains to be seen. And what is this?" He pointed at Gracie's throat.

Stephan followed his gesture. Gracie still wore the silver necklace he'd given her. Even after the way he'd treated her on Melesia, she still wore the symbol of his love.

"It's against the rules to wear jewelry. And Cinderella most certainly does not wear a necklace."

"However, members of the Royal Melesian court do," Stephan said quietly. All eyes turned to him. He addressed the park personnel but kept his eyes on Gracie. "Surely, you would treat my country's traditions with honor. After all, I am an ambassador from the Kingdom of Melesia to the Magic Kingdom."

The pageant organizer stopped railing at Gracie and stared at Stephan. The executive who'd led him to Gracie pushed his way into the room.

"Gracie, would you care to tell them about the traditions of the necklace?" Stephan nodded at her in encouragement.

"The royal insignia is forbidden to all except members of the Melesian court. Legend holds that the intended brides of the Melesian princes were given a necklace with the royal insignia woven into the design. It was the way the prince recognized his bride in the days when marriages were arranged at birth."

"Even older legends imbue it with a magical power to bring soul mates together, no matter how great the distance between them or the turmoil that might keep them apart. Destined love would always overcome." Stephan smiled at her, ignoring the twinge of pain in his jaw as he did. When he spoke again, his words were in Melesian, intended only for her ears.

"*Er'hona-mei*, I love you. I have loved you for a long time. I was a fool not to tell you sooner. I'm offering you a life filled with security guards, publicity, and all the things you hate, but I can't help myself. There is no one else for me. I love you. Will you marry me? Will you be my wife, my *Ba'hona-mei*? Will you have me?"

The pounding in his head was louder, the throbbing in his jaw sharper, and the dizziness more difficult to ignore, but for this moment, only she mattered. Stephan gripped the door frame and waited for her answer. She didn't move or speak. Then she dropped the wig and took a single step toward him.

"Aaya," she replied in Melesian, her words to him as private as his to her. "I love you too. Enough to brave all the publicity in the world, if you're willing to have a bride who's a public relations nightmare. Take me home, *Ba'hono-mei.*"

With that she walked to him and curled her arm around his waist, supporting him with her own strength. He soaked up her warmth, drawing strength from it and straightening to his full height.

"Gentlemen," he said, turning his attention to the others in the room, "it appears we have nothing further to discuss. Now, my fiancée and I would like a place we can rest. Alone."

Gracie kicked her torn and rumpled costume into the corner and curled on the bed beside Stephan, pulling a thick hotel robe around her. The deeply etched lines at the corners of his eyes and the shadows beneath them eased as he slept. The red marks on his jaw faded, thankfully leaving no bruises.

Before he'd come to rescue her today, she'd watched the replay of events and listened to the pageant director rant what seemed like dozens of times. But the embarrassment and fear that had nearly destroyed her at the press conference in Melesia was strangely absent.

Instead, she only heard Stephan, telling her he loved her. Over and over. When she kept her mind on important things—that he loved her, and she loved him—the trivial things like cameras and microphones and press corps faded into insignificance.

She leaned down and pressed a kiss to his forehead. "I love you, *Ba'hono-mei.*"

"That's worth waking up for." He stirred and gave her a groggy stare. Then his eyes shifted, taking in the room. "Gracie, where are we?"

"I think we're in the Cinderella Suite at the castle."

"Thank the gods. I thought maybe I'd hit my head harder than I realized when I saw the décor."

"They said it was the best room in the resort."

"It is, as long as you're here." He gathered her close. "What happened?"

"You passed out as soon as we were alone in the suite. Your aide came by later with your clothes and told me he'd given you something to help the pain and let you sleep."

"At least it wasn't from Maguire's punch."

"You know the man who attacked you?"

"Mike Maguire. Sophia's husband. Long story," he said before she could ask. "I don't want to go into to it now."

"Neither do I. I'm only interested in you." Gracie ran her hand down his chest, brushing aside his unbuttoned formal coat and feeling his heartbeat beneath the thin shirt he wore. "I was impressed by the way you handled everything today. That bit about my necklace was a flash of inspiration. It was all I could do to keep a straight face when I told them about the traditions."

"There's nothing funny about the legends." He covered her hand with his own, stilling her movements.

"The legends themselves are wonderful. I just can't believe they actually thought my porcupine fish contained the royal insignia."

"It does, Gracie." He snagged the chain with a single finger. "The filigree of the fish's body would form the royal insignia if it were flattened."

Gracie's breath caught as she looked at the charm dangling from between his fingers. "But you gave it to me months ago. Before..."

"I commissioned it long before I gave it to you. Before we danced. Before we made love. I sent the design to the silversmith the moment I knew that I loved you."

"You never told me."

"Would you have believed me if I did?"

"I don't know. It all seemed so unreal to me then."

Stephan laughed. "Much more unreal than being locked in Cinderella's suite with me in full formal regalia and your torn ball gown in the corner."

"And a missing glass slipper lost somewhere in the Magic Kingdom."

"What happened to your shoe? Please tell me I don't have to go looking for it." Stephan groaned. "I'm still recovering from the painkillers my overzealous aide forced on me."

Gracie giggled and snuggled close to him. "I did actually stumble and lose my shoe. But I ruined the effect by throwing it at the man who hit you. It missed him and landed in the audience. Some lucky little girl has a souvenir she'll never forget."

"You're an inspiration to aspiring princesses everywhere, *Ba'hona-mei*. And you inspire me. For as long as I live, I will never forget the sight of you fighting for me."

"I'm sure the press won't forget for a long time, either. But you know what? I don't care. Because you, Prince Stephan Hercules Tantalus D'Malia, are a man worth fighting for."

"If you mean that, then kiss me."

She leaned close, sighing in contentment as their lips touched. "A minute ago, I was worried about having nothing to wear but this bathrobe and that ripped costume," she said between kisses. "I don't mind so much now."

Stephan framed her face with his hands and pushed her far enough away to look in her eyes. "In that case, Gracie, hand me my phone. I want to make sure no one brings you anything to wear. If you're naked, you can't run away from me again."

"I won't run away. You're stuck with me for life, this time."

"Promise?"

"*Aaya, Ba'hono-mei*. For life."

Outside their window fireworks exploded in the night sky and Gracie surrendered to the magic between them.

Epilogue

Stephan scanned the ballroom from his place on the balcony. The graduation ball for the students of the Royal Academy had a new twist this year. In addition to the obligatory gathering of students and faculty, his entire family and most of the Melesian nobles attended. A smattering of international dignitaries, businessmen and Mensa members rounded out the crowd.

Gracie's family mingled comfortably with the eclectic mixture of guests, the situation eased by Gracie herself as she worked the crowd, dancing with professors, fellow students, and nobility with equal ease.

She'd been adamant about attending the student ball, despite their wedding two days earlier. It was her way of celebrating and acknowledging both parts of her life: her union with him and newfound place as Princess of Melesia and her passion for science and education.

He smiled and watched her glide across the ballroom, the blue and silver of her gown swirling about her ankles and giving him an occasional flash of the silver and crystal-studded sandals he'd given her. Her choice of gown reminded him of just how far she'd come from the shattered woman who didn't dare believe in love.

Stephan checked his watch as his brother swung Gracie into a dance. Fifteen minutes until midnight. Ready or not, on the stroke of midnight, he was sweeping her away for a month-long honeymoon aboard his—their—yacht.

He strode into the ballroom and tapped Constantine on the shoulder. "I've waited long enough, brother. It's time I danced with my wife."

As she melted into his arms and they twirled across the dance floor, the musicians segued into a new song. The strains of Gershwin poured over the dance floor.

"Gracie, I'm sorry." He pulled her into a tight embrace, remembering the last time they'd danced to this particular song. "I told them never to play that song."

She looked up at him, her eyes shimmering slightly, but her face glowing. "But I asked them to play "Someone to Watch Over Me" when we danced tonight. You've made all my dreams come true. For as long as we live, I will have you to watch over me. And I will be there to watch over you."

So he danced with her as memories, both bitter and sweet bound them closer together. When the strains of the song died away, the clock began to chime.

And when the clock struck twelve, Gracie and Stephan slipped away.

Counterfeit Commoner

Excerpt

Chapter 1

June, the royal wedding of Constantine Phillippe Ramon D'Malia

Married.

Sophia sank into a brocade covered chair in the empty palace reception room, not caring that she crushed the hand embroidered skirts of her formal gown. Her fiancé, the man she'd planned to marry for her whole life, had finally tied the knot.

With someone else.

Relief surged through her in a giddy rush.

She bounced up and paced the wide room, flicking back a sheer, white curtain here, peeking around an open door there, reassuring herself that no one with a telephoto lens lurked nearby recording her uncontrolled exuberance. The swish and rustle of her skirts echoed off the high arched ceilings and frieze covered walls, accentuating her every step.

Sophia grinned. She could picture her scheming uncle—may he rot in prison—turning purple with rage. She'd slipped from his control. His shattered plans for her held no more menace than a thimbleful of salt in the sea.

She was free—for the first time in her twenty years. No politically obsessed uncle directing every tiny detail of her life. No formidable, distant fiancé looming over her future. No one.

She stopped abruptly, the whisper of her skirts fading into silence. If only she could avoid becoming a dancing marionette in someone else's schemes.

A faint cheer floated through the open French doors on a waft of sea-scented air. The island kingdom of Melesia, with its reputation for romance and fairy tale charm, teemed with visitors celebrating the new royal couple.

Sophia pivoted toward the sound, imagining the happy bride and groom stepping onto the presentation balcony, surrounded by lush island greenery, waving at the adoring crowds. Today everyone—tourists and natives, press and paparazzi—loved them. Tomorrow, who knew?

The people, as fickle as honeybees in a flower field, had buzzed around Sophia and her cousin Helena for years seeking vicarious thrills. But no more.

Now, King Constantine and his bride—formerly Jill Bradley of the United States, now Queen Jillian of Melesia—could deal with the crowds. Sophia was free.

At least until someone posted a blog or started a Facebook page dedicated to poor Lady Sophia de Lyons, the modern princess jilted by her one true love.

What— "bullshit." The word burst out, uncensored and wonderful. She giggled, liking the feel of the forbidden sounds on her tongue. She tried a handful of other swear words, each more tantalizing than the last. No one chastised her for behavior unfitting for a Melesian noble. No one—Sophia stopped at the sound of footsteps in the hall.

She raced back to her seat, smoothed her skirts and donned her mask of indifferent perfection just as the door opened. The bride's sister, Grace, entered, shoes dangling from her fingers with a casual carelessness that Sophia envied. If Sophia mussed her hair and slouched, could she become just another average blonde like Grace?

And if she could, what would it be like to not care how the public viewed you? Not to wonder if today's innocent gesture would turn into tomorrow's front page?

"Someone else seeking refuge from the crowds," she said softly. Sophia suppressed a smile as Grace snapped her head around, startled eyes widening. Grace's grip tightened on the shoes, turning her knuckles white as she edged away, gaze darting to the door. "I envy you," Sophia added quietly.

Grace hesitated, slowly facing Sophia again. "Why? You belong here. I'm just the bride's sister, dressed up and trying not to embarrass her."

"Exactly. Soon the press will forget you. They'll hound me for weeks, prying to see if my wounded heart is mended." Sophia sighed. Grace had been almost invisible since her arrival in Melesia. Sophia wished she knew the trick to being invisible. She wished she knew about life outside the palace walls.

Grace crept closer and perched near the carved arm of the brocade covered sofa, questions dancing in her eyes. "Was your heart really broken? Were you in love with Constantine?"

The blunt, intrusive question shocked Sophia. Until she remembered what freedom felt like. *Bullshit*, she repeated silently, enjoying at her new, blunt, reckless streak. *Bullshit, bullshit, bullshit.*

"Love was never part of the picture for us," she said out loud in her normal, boring voice. She rose and walked to the French doors—in her normal, sedate, *boring* steps—beckoning Grace to follow. "I envy him too. He broke the rules and found love. Alex and Helena are also in love," she said, referring to the ailing King Emeritus who'd recently abdicated in favor of his half-brother. "I'm just the spare bride who's now out of a job."

"I don't understand."

"How could you?" How could anyone who hadn't grown up a pawn to be married off for the sake of her family's political ambitions? She pointed to the new bride and groom. "Look. A royal wedding is a fairy tale come true. If I'd been on the balcony instead of your sister, the fairy tale would have unfolded in exactly the same way. Except the looks in their eyes are real. They love each other. He and I would have been pretending.

"I'm very good at pretending," she continued, voicing feelings she'd not dared to express until now. How easily a small taste of freedom unraveled a lifetime of control. "From the moment I came to live with the Duke de Lyons, he's prepared me to be the spare bride. He fed the press with enough romantic nonsense to fuel the illusion. I played along."

"What do you mean—the spare bride?"

"Royal sons are *the heir and the spare.* Alex was the heir. Helena was raised to be his bride. Constantine was the spare. I was the spare bride. At least that's what the duke planned."

"It must have been awful."

Sophia shrugged. "It makes a great story. *Lady Sophia, Foster Daughter of The Disgraced Duke, Jilted by the Prince Who Broke Her Heart.* The tabloids will adore it."

"If your tabloids are anything like ours, they'll have you engaged to someone else within a week."

She shuddered, recognizing—and hating—the truth in Grace's words. "Of course. When Alex abdicated in favor of Constantine, I suppose Stephan became the next spare. One brother should be as good as another. But I don't wish to be bounced from prince to prince until the public gets its next big romance."

Sophia glanced at Grace. Years of decorous protocol, pounded into her by everyone from her uncle down to the castle cook, warned against speaking openly to this near stranger.

Bullshit.

The rebellious voice won. "I'm tired of being controlled by the papers. And by my family. And even by the king. I want a life of my own."

The American didn't flinch at her shocking words. Sophia envied her all the more. What would it feel like to be so unfettered by propriety?

The glint of sun off a camera lens made Sophia stiffen and move back inside, quickly this time. "Photographers," she explained to the wide-eyed Grace. "Tabloids. We're this week's entertainment."

If she were truly free, she'd march into the offices of the *Weekly World Stir* and give the reporter "Mack the Pen" a piece of her mind. And an imprint of her royal slipper on his backside. Or she'd live incognito right under his nose, invisible but happy, daring him to peel away her disguise. But no Melesian blue blood was that free. Not even the king.

"I see why you envy me," Grace said. "No one cares about the bride's brainy half-sister." Grace chewed her lip. A pensive gleam lit her eyes. "Do you ever want to just disappear?"

"All the time," Sophia replied, wondering if Grace had somehow read her mind. "I've made plans to spend a year abroad with Princess Lydia at her home in Europe. After that, I'll join a Melesian goodwill tour scheduled to visit Europe and the Americas."

It wasn't the escape she wanted, but it was better than nothing. "The press will speculate I'm nursing my broken heart. If I'm lucky, I can stay away until the next heir to the throne is born. When your sister becomes pregnant, I'll have a measure of peace. I will never have the freedom that you do."

"What if you could be someone other than Lady Sophia for a few days?" Grace paused, staring off in the distance. Sophia nearly squirmed with impatience. "Someone like me?"

Sophia stared at her, impossible fantasies swirling in her head, begging for the chance to become real. What if this brainy young American could come up with a better plan than a scripted, goodwill tour where her every move would be choreographed with brutal precision? Sophia would gladly give the de Lyons wealth—now under her sole control—for the chance to walk barefoot in the grass or eat a double scoop of ice cream from a dripping cone or swear in public without censure. She'd trade her designer gowns, Hermes clutches, and ancestral jewels if she could be invisible for a single day.

"You said the goodwill tour is scheduled to visit the Americas eventually," Grace continued. "If you could get away from the entourage while you're in the U.S., I could buy you a few days of freedom."

Sophia's heart slowed, its thud, thud, thud stretching between beats as if it were afraid of drowning out a single word that Grace said. Sophia held her breath. If Grace truly had a plan…

Sophia asked a carefully worded question. Then another. Skillfully she pulled information from Grace and planted suggestions in Grace's head as she'd done so many times in ballrooms and political receptions around the world. Then she listened, hiding a smile of triumph, while Grace created a perfect escape plan for her.

Later that day, Sophia sat in Grace's room staring at the United States driver's license in her hand, the triple-fast pounding of her heart making up for lost time.

She glanced in the mirror. The similarities between them were close enough to be believable. The plan Grace had outlined just might work. She clutched the pages filled with Grace's cramped script, detailing precise instructions for Sophia's escape from the tour and her return home. With nearly a year to refine and modify the specifics, what could go wrong?

For a few glorious, free days, she would become Grace Bradley, free to roam the United States at will. Free to sample all life had to offer.

"Hot damn." Freedom had never tasted so good.

AUTHOR'S NOTE

I hope you enjoyed Gracie and Stephan's story.

Readers often ask how much of my work is inspired by real life, so here are some special insights regarding *Reluctantly Royal*.

First, this story is about more than just Gracie and Stephan finding love with one another. It is also about the love of family and the healing the rift between Gracie and Jill. The journey of the sisters and how they helped one another heal old wounds is very special to me. The age difference between Jill and Gracie is similar to the gap between me and my "big" sister. I drew heavily on personal experiences to create their sub-plot.

No, my sister and I didn't have a falling out and no, she didn't marry a literal prince, but watching the fictional sisters rediscover one another reminded me that one of the joys of growing up transitioning from being "just" sisters to being best friends.

My other favorite aspect of *Reluctantly Royal* is the way Stephan teaches Gracie about his language. As a world traveler, I understand how difficult it is to be in a country where you don't speak the language. Thanks to many kind hosts, generous natives, and others, I've always managed to communicate and enjoy my trips. But in the case of Melesia (pronounced Mel-ee-see-ah) before I could fully explore this topic, I needed to create a language. Using a spreadsheet and my imagination, I created a series of "root" words that could be combined with prefixes and suffixes to make a more fully realized language. (Channeling my inner Tolkien was fun!) I hope you enjoy the result.

- If you would like to learn more about the Kingdom's language, check my website where I will share the Melesian lexicon.
- Also stay tuned to the site because a talented young musician is creating a national anthem for the Kingdom of Melesia! Another is creating a map of the area. When these tidbits are ready, you'll find them on the website!

As always, I appreciate you taking the time to enter my world. I hope you enjoyed the Kingdom of Melesia and its royal family.

While you are waiting for the next installment, can I ask for your help?

Reviews and word-of-mouth are critical for authors when it comes to finding new readers. Please consider leaving a review or even just a rating of the book at Amazon, Barnes & Noble, Good Reads, Book Bub, or wherever you go to find new books. Then tell two friends about the book and ask them to do the same!

Thank you from the bottom of my heart!

ABOUT THE AUTHOR

Photo Credit: RJRICE Photography
http://www.rjricephotography.com/

Kelle Z. Riley, writer, speaker, global traveler, Ph.D. chemist, and safety/martial arts expert has been featured in public forums that range from local Newspapers to National television. In addition to her works of fiction, a personal story was included in "Chicken Soup for the Soul: Living with Alzheimer's and Other Dementias."

Her fiction publications include cozy mysteries and contemporary romance.

In the Undercover Cat Mysteries a cupcake baking scientist turns sleuth—an much more. *The Cupcake Caper, Shaken, Not Purred, The Tiger's Tale,* and *Studying Scarlett the Grey,* as well as free short stories set in the Undercover Cat world are available on Amazon or wherever books are sold.

In the *Riches and Royals* series, modern career women fall for princes-in-disguise, only to discover that *"happily ever after"* isn't guaranteed. Can love turn their cautionary tale into a glittering fairy tale, or will their hearts shatter like glass slippers?

A former Golden Heart Finalist, Kelle resides in Chattanooga, TN. She is the past program chair and popular speaker for the Chattanooga Writer's Guild, a member of Sisters in Crime, Romance Writers' of America and various local chapters. When not writing, she can be found pursuing passions such as being a self-defense instructor, a Master Gardener, and a full time chemist with numerous professional publications and U.S. patents.

To learn more about the Riches & Royals world, as well as Kelle's other works, visit www.kellezriley.net or scan the code below.

Book one of Riches & Royals: Read My Lips
Book two of Riches & Royals: Royally Scandalized
Book three of Riches & Royals: Reluctantly Royal
Book four of Riches & Royals: Counterfeit Commoner

Join Kelle's newsletter list to get announcements for FREE short stories, upcoming releases, deleted scenes, and inside information on how the Kingdom of Melesia was born!

 www.kellezriley.net

 www.facebook.com/kellezriley

 www.twitter.com/kellezriley